A D

Courage

A Daughter's
Courage

RENITA D'SILVA

bookouture

Published by Bookouture
An imprint of StoryFire Ltd.
23 Sussex Road, Ickenham, UB10 8PN
United Kingdom
www.bookouture.com

ISBN: 978-1-78681-178-3
eBook ISBN: 978-1-78681-177-6

For my mother, Perdita Hilda D'Silva,
the kindest, warmest, most generous and wonderful person I
know; my role model and inspiration.

Prologue

The Temple

Happy Dreams

In a scenic corner of India, beside sparkling fields and across from a jungle, near rain-bejewelled coffee plants lined with areca trees and pepper vines, a small temple nestles, slowly going to ruin. It has seen many generations come and go; it is hiding countless secrets deep within its crumbling walls. Woodlice have burrowed into its pillars and anthills adorn its steps and cling to its small veranda. Cobwebs stretch from one end of the temple bell to the other (once gleaming yellow, now tarnished rust; once heralding devotees and massaged by a thousand pious palms, now caressed by silvery skeins of spidery secretions and frantic with the frenzied patter of trapped insects).

Peepal trees have conspired to form a canopy over the temple, hiding it from the world. Warm air, infused with the zesty tang of ripening pepper and the smokiness of coffee, hangs respectfully still around the temple, loath to disturb the sombre peace.

A falling-down cottage is just visible between the columns of deciduous roots gracing the temple courtyard, which are almost as tall as the overgrown trees to which they belong. The disintegrating, moss-steeped walls of the cottage glow orange-gold in the shafts of sunlight occasionally piercing the vibrant green awning of branches, playing hide-and-seek with the ants that scurry around, searching for crumbs. The wall of tumbledown bricks surrounding the temple and the cottage is almost completely covered with velvet moss.

From certain angles, with its foliage-festooned steps leading up to its open cave of a mouth, lush vegetation parting to afford a tantalising glimpse of the deity within, its small shrine draped with vine and creeper garlands, its offerings of rotting leaves and mulchy bark, the temple looks as if it is smiling; a slumbering child experiencing happy dreams.

Chapter 1

Kavya

Verbal Volley

Kavya hears the landline ringing as she puffs up the stairs to the flat – she recognises it as hers from the ringtone. Loud and strident. It will most likely be her mother. (Fitting then, the ringtone.) Everyone else has her mobile number. She considers leaving it, taking her time up the stairs. She's not quite ready to have the conversation she knows she must with her mother. But… what if it's an emergency? What if something's happened?

She sprints up, cursing for the millionth time, the fact that she lives on the fifth floor, cursing Balu, the lift attendant who keeps promising to call the engineer to fix the broken (permanently, it seems) elevator and then sits about smoking and gossiping with the gatekeeper. He pulls a suitably sad face and shrugs his shoulders when Kavya grumbles to him, scratching his head and drawling, languidly, 'Engineer is coming, naa, give him some time. This time of year is very busy for him.'

As Kavya pauses to take a breath – noting that the phone has stopped ringing and feeling stupidly relieved – she thinks back to the several rants she has voiced at the tenants' meetings, trying time and again to rouse the residents against Mr Nandkishore, president of the Tenants' Association, who is in cahoots with the landlord and lets things slide.

What a waste of energy that I could have put to better use!

She has tried talking to the other residents when passing them on the stairs, attempting to make them enraged enough to dislodge Mr Nandkishore. She even tried to bribe them with those divine cream buns from Hazmat Bakery once – the last time she's spending good money on them. They agree with her, but when push comes to shove, side with Mr Nandkishore – who, she has since found out, makes sure they get certain concessions, including leeway when paying the rent. Which is why they are lukewarm towards her righteous anger, lethargic despite the perpetually broken lift, despite having to climb endless flights of stairs.

But this is the absolute limit, she thinks as she shifts her shopping from one hand to another. She cannot remember the last time the lift was working.

'Tell the landlord I have exposed him on that blog that rates rental properties,' she raged the last time she saw Mr Nandkishore.

'Arre, who will listen to your lone dissenting voice when everyone else is happy?' Mr Nandkishore had said with a smirk.

'They're not happy. They keep quiet because you bribe them,' she had spat.

'Move, if you're not happy,' Mr Nandkishore had said, grinning, expertly skirting the issue of the bribes.

But Kavya *likes* her flat. Aside from the fact that it is on the fifth floor, it is perfectly suited to her needs. She likes its central location, likes that it is a two-minute walk away from the train station. Besides, why should she move? It would be accepting defeat; it would be bowing down and giving in.

She has always told herself and anyone who will listen, plus her mother, who won't, that she will live her life on her terms only – not her mother's or Mr Nandkishore's or the landlord's.

But now, after the events of the past few weeks, she's not so sure…

She pauses on the stairs and closes her eyes, trying to chase away the upset that swamps her.

It's over. You've survived. Pick yourself up now and look ahead.

'You are a warrior.' She hears her beloved grandmother's voice in her ear, pictures her eyes twinkling with pride when she says it and is struck by a sudden pang to see her, speak with her, explain her situation. Her grandmother would understand and sympathise. Unlike her mother…

'You were born screaming. Ready for a fight. A tomboy. Hai! What shall I do with you?' Her mother's vociferous tones push away her grandmother's soft, soothing presence inside her head. Her mother, eyes flashing fire, hitting her forehead with her palm. 'You should be a lawyer, the way you argue with me.'

Which is precisely why Kavya *hasn't* become a lawyer. Or a doctor. Or an engineer. Or pursued 'something respectable' – she hears those two words in her mother's voice, spiked with disappointment.

The phone has started up again. She charges up the stairs – as fast as she can, which is not fast at all. Everything, including the gym, has been on hold since she—

Oh God, she cannot think about it, not now when the phone call is most likely her mother. It will require all of her energy just to field her mother's incessant prying once Kavya informs her of her decision.

Out of breath, she fumbles with the key and pushes open the door to her flat.

'Hello,' she pants, her palms hurting from where the shopping bags have dug into the flesh. She looks at the bags, by the door where she unceremoniously plonked them as she came in, and sighs at the spreading puddle underneath them. The eggs? Or the tomatoes that she spent an age selecting, making sure she got the juiciest ones, fancying a salad to chase away the headache that's been rippling through her skull?

Her mood is not improved when she hears her mother's voice yelling, 'Is that you, Kavya?'

She's tempted to yell right back, 'Who else could it be?'

'Kavya?' her mother's voice thunders down the line.

Why does her mother always shout when speaking on the phone?

'Yes, Ma. I'm right here.'

'What's the matter? Why are you huffing and puffing, sounding like you have a herd of elephants chasing you?' Her mother chuckles. 'Speaking of elephants, you'll never believe what…'

Now that Kavya has discerned from her mother's familiar greeting, her tone of voice, that nothing catastrophic has occurred, irritation buds, chafing, overflowing, despite all her resolutions, after every altercation with her mother, to be nice the next time.

'I sound breathless because I *am*! I ran all the way up the stairs, thinking it was an emergency. How many times have I told you not to keep calling unless it's urgent, Ma?'

She hears the petulant whine in her voice and bites her lip. Why does her mother reduce her to a whinging thirteen-year-old every single time? Why does Kavya let her?

'What do you mean "don't keep calling"? If I don't, then I might never get to speak to you, what with your "busy" life.'

How can her mother make a perfectly ordinary word like 'busy' sound so obscene, so worthy of disdain?

'I want to speak to my only daughter at least once a week, thank you very much. I think that constitutes "urgent" in my book…'

Kavya sighs. Her mother is nothing if not tenacious. If she has made up her mind to speak to Kavya, she will, even if it means having to keep ringing on and off all day and into the evening until Kavya gives in and answers the phone.

Kavya closes her eyes and leans against the wall as she catches her breath. She wants to strip down to her underwear and lie down under the fan. She wants to open the fridge, pull out the bottles that survived last night's binge and down them to drown her troubles.

She wants to hide in the folds of her grandma's voluminous sari skirts like she used to as a child when she was wanted by her mother for some infraction or other, breathing in the scent of stale talc, old celebrations and mothballs, comfort and sweat. It was unfortunate that wanting to be with her grandmother meant that she had to also endure her mother's censure emanating off her in chagrin-scented waves; her mother's smell when Kavya was around: disapproval and heartache.

What would you do if you found out the truth, Ma?

She wants to run away from her mother's forceful voice in her ear, back down the stairs, out into the bustle and throb of humanity, and keep walking until she comes to the sea, letting the warm waves lap over her feet and ankles, her thighs, her waist.

'I have elephants on my mind,' her mother says.

Outside, the world moves on, while in her apartment, her supposed haven, Kavya is catapulted back into childhood and young adulthood. No matter how far she goes, she can never outrun her mother's upset, her displeasure in her. And it is only going to get worse when Kavya tells her ma that she has decided this career is not for her – the bland statement hiding a truth her mother must never know as she will never be able to handle it.

Kavya shudders, tempted to put down the phone, but her mother would just ring again. And keep on ringing. Not accepting no for an answer.

Once, in the midst of a raging argument, Kavya had unplugged the phone and her mother had called old Mr Singh next door who, despite being short of hearing, heard Kavya's mother's summons, so insistent was her stubbornness in getting hold of her daughter. How she had Mr Singh's number, Kavya doesn't know. But if there is one thing Kavya has learned, it is not to underestimate her mother when she wants something. This is why it gives Kavya particular pleasure that so far, she has managed to resist her mother's attempts to slot her into a neat little box – to shape Kavya according to *her* ambitions and desires for her.

So far yes, but… She sighs deeply, then pulls herself together. *I might be defeated but I am not giving in. I have no choice but to go back, yes, but it is only a temporary measure until I figure out what to do…*

In the small strip of land generously called 'the garden' five storeys below, the mali is half-heartedly tending to the plants, the hibiscus like open red palms bestowing blessings, the sunny smiles of marigolds. The watchman at the gate waves a car in and manoeuvres another, wanting to leave, into waiting in a corner, while at the same time talking non-stop to Balu the lift attendant, who is smoking perfect rings into the sky as he watches the drama unfold. The man in the waiting car puts his head out of the window and curses at the gatekeeper (Kavya can't hear anything from up here, even with the windows wide open, but she can guess what is being said). The gatekeeper remains unperturbed by the driver's agitation, pausing in his directing to guffaw, bony shoulders shaking with mirth, presumably at something Balu has said.

Outside the gates, by the roadside, a boy skips in the puddles left behind from the morning's rain. Rickshaws honk, cars horn, each trying to edge past the other, none of them giving an inch. Chickens from the slums by the pipeline dance on to the road, making the creeping traffic even slower, the drivers even edgier – the exhaust- and petrol-scented air rent by the cacophony of horns and swearing that is the soundtrack to Mumbai's streets, faint strains of which drift in through the windows of Kavya's flat.

Cows nudge their way through the traffic, the mess of sweaty, shouting drivers and overcooked passengers. The children from the slums sit astride the pipeline inside which some of them sleep at night and, plucking at their raggedy clothes, their matted hair, they chant songs in tune to the honks – Kavya knows this because she has heard them while walking to and from work. She watches their mouths move, their grimy, hunger-ravaged faces alight with smiles as they note the ever-increasing frustration of the stalled drivers.

The paan and chaat stall by the gate to her apartment complex does brisk business. A woman shoves a whole panipuri into her mouth while keeping a phone pressed to her ear. Men stand outside the small shop selling tandoori chicken and egg bhurji, eating and gossiping and holding on to their paper plates as they jump out of the way of cars spraying streams of dirty water as the traffic finally starts moving. Pedestrians check watches, talk into their phones, walk to work, walk away from work.

Work. She doesn't want to think about her (disastrous) acting career, although her mind hovers, dredging up the humiliation.

All she ever wanted was to get away, do something under her own steam, something not mapped out for her. She wanted to break the mould, not lead a boring, conventional life like her parents.

Well, you have definitely done that! a voice in her head chimes.

She thinks of this morning, serving tea and coffee to tourists – something her mother doesn't know about, her working in a café while waiting for her career to take off. Sweaty tourists, wiping their faces and commenting on the heat and talking about the sudden shower and asking her for tea and then no, make it mango juice instead, and leaving her five measly rupees as tip.

'Kavya?' her mother shouts in her ear.

'I'm here, Ma.'

'You'll never guess who I bumped into at the post office…'

Kavya sighs. Here it comes, the first point on her mother's agenda. She imagines a list in her mother's big, bossy handwriting: *1) Make Kavya realise what she is missing out on because of her dog-headed wilfulness; try to spur her on by offering a little competition.*

Her mother is waiting, breathing impatiently down the line, and so Kavya says, 'Who?' Knowing her mother will tell her anyway, whether she wants to hear whatever titbit she is about to offer or not.

'Your high-school classmate, Vidya. Remember her? Short. Bespectacled. Unruly hair. Nowhere near as pretty or as bright as you…'

'Ma—'

'But now, she is a jet-setting software engineer, working at a multinational company in Bangalore. Regularly travels all over the world.'

'Good for her.'

'*And* she's married to a doctor and is pregnant! Glowing. She looks amazing.'

Kavya shuts her eyes tight against the tears that threaten, salty heat in her mouth. She has shed enough tears. *Move on. Look forward.* Her chant, her mantra.

'She's visiting her parents, which is how I bumped into her…' her mother is saying.

'Ma, I don't want to get married. Not quite yet…' Kavya says, wearily. They've had versions of this conversation too many times to count.

'Who said anything about getting married? I was just telling you about your school friend… Although, if you just said the word, there are a few eligible men I've had my eye on who would be perfect for you…'

'Ma—'

'You're not getting any younger. Soon, all the good men will be taken and you will be left with nothing. And after thirty it is much harder to have children, you know. Infertility increases. There's more risk of children being born unhealthy.'

A tear escapes, travelling down her cheek. Kavya furiously rubs it away, her anger at herself transferring to her mother. 'Ma, for the last time, I don't want to get married or have children just yet...'

Unless it's with the right person and I thought... Oh...

'Then when? Is it too much to expect grandchildren from my only daughter before I wither and die?'

If only you knew...

'Ma, I cannot think of marriage or children at the moment. I'm still figuring out what to do with my life!'

A pause. Then, 'I thought this was why you are in Mumbai, so far away from us. Because acting is what you want to do with your life.'

Kavya takes a deep breath. She might as well say it now and be done with it. Although all she's planning to tell her mother is that her acting career is over and she's coming home, she feels horribly unprepared. But then, how *do* you prepare for this, especially with a mother such as hers? 'Ma, I'm glad you called... I was going to call you anyway.'

'Ha! That would be the day! How many times since you moved to Mumbai have you voluntarily called home, tell me?' And then, her voice lowering a notch, worry beading through it, 'Why? What's happened? Are you okay?'

'I'm fine.' *I'm not.*

As if her mother has read her mind, she asks, 'Have you been ill?'

Oh Ma, I have. Desperately... Only not in the way you think. 'No, but...'

'Do you have enough money?'

Kavya is ambushed by the annoyance that flares so quickly where her mother is concerned. Now she's started to tell her, she just wants to get it over with. 'Ma, can you let me finish—'

'Ah, there she goes, blaming me again! To think of all we have done for you...'

'Oh God, not again with the emotional blackmail—'

'What emotional blackmail? I'm just stating the truth...'

Her mother sounds suitably hurt. Kavya pictures her all-too-familiar pout and sighs again. She seems to constantly vacillate between guilt and frustration when talking to her mother. After taking another deep breath she says, in a placatory voice, 'Look, you don't need to persuade me—'

'As if I can persuade you to do anything! When I call, why do you assume that I want you to do something? Can't I just call to chat to my daughter?' Her mother's voice rises to a falsetto.

Ha! Her mother calls with one goal only: to convince Kavya to 'give up your madness and come home' – her words, delivered in an uncompromising voice, as if stating an inviolable fact, at some point during every conversation, which only makes Kavya more determined to stay right where she is.

'Anyway, what don't I need to persuade you about?' Her mother's voice keen now, all pretence of hurt brushed off.

'I... I was thinking...' Oh God, this is excruciating. 'I've come to the conclusion that acting is not the right career for me.' She says it defiantly, her voice too loud.

Silence.

Kavya has achieved the impossible and managed to render her mother speechless for more than a minute.

'Ma?' She leans against the wall and closes her eyes as she waits for the verbal volley her mother is preparing to lob.

'You...' Her mother sounds unsure at first, then, all in a rush: 'This is what we've been telling you all this while! You would have known this sooner if you weren't so obstinate, if you had listened to us.'

'That's right, Ma, rub it in, why don't you?' Her voice trembles and she despises herself for this show of weakness.

'Kavya,' her mother's voice soft, her empathy hurting more than her nagging, the tears Kavya has tried to hold back running freely down her cheeks. 'It's a tough industry to break into—'

'You think I don't know that?' Kavya's tone is sharp to hide her upset. 'Why do you think I'm giving up?' She hates saying this. *Hates* it. She who mulishly never gives up even when it is the only option (as her mother likes to remind her time and again; not meaning it as a compliment either).

She wants to shout the truth, tell her mother that she *did* break into the seemingly impenetrable world of Bollywood, that she was well on her way to making a success of this career she had chosen for herself, until she made one bad decision and it all crumbled around her...

'You could have saved yourself time and heartbreak if—' her mother begins, and then stops as if realising she has said too much again. It must take all of her considerable willpower to not finish that sentence and Kavya feels a sudden rush of affection for her. 'Anyway, what's done is done.' Her mother's voice is brisk. 'So you're definitely packing up and coming home?'

Kavya looks around the flat – her home for the last few years, the place that has witnessed her cloud-tasting highs and bone-crushing lows, and, recently, her hurt, her anguish and her heartbreak. She looks out of the window at her own little slice of the city she has come to love, vast and busy and alive. She thinks of the decision she's arrived at, finally, a decision that has loomed over her, that she has agonised over and postponed – to give up, go home, although every instinct screams for her to stay and fight.

But...

There's no way she can win this. Nagesh is too powerful, knows too many people.

The audition two nights ago was the last straw. The director, a friend of Nagesh's with whom they had dined many times, had taken one look at her, a lip-curling sneer that said it all, and called, 'Next!'

It had taken all of her strength not to yell at him and make a scene – it would only serve to make her look deranged. Instead she had kept her head up high as she walked away, the long line of wannabe actresses staring at her and whispering among themselves. She knew that by the time she was on the metro home, everyone in that line would know her story. A cautionary tale for all of them.

But then she had heard so many such tales herself when she was starting out and they hadn't stopped her…

The industry, the well-oiled machine that is Bollywood, has closed up around Nagesh, shutting her out, and that is that.

She shuts her eyes, takes a deep breath. 'Yes. I am coming home.'

'Good.' Her mother's voice sounds satisfied, as if she has orchestrated all of this herself. 'You've seen sense at last and it couldn't have come at a better time. Your ajji needs you.'

'Ajji, why? Has something happened to her?' A sliver of panic threading up her spine. Ajji. Kavya's ally, her cheerleader and staunchest supporter.

'She's fine. But you know all the hoo-ha that's been happening over in Doddanahalli?'

'Doddanahalli? Where's…' Then, as the memory of coffee plants stretching into the distance nudges her, 'That village we stay at on the way to Da's…'

'Yes, that very one.'

'What hoo-ha?'

'The elephant rampage.'

'What? Did you just say *elephant*—?'

'Never mind listening to me. Haven't you been watching the news?'

'Doddanahalli has made the national news?' A tiny village, no more than a cluster of shops flanking the road.

'Yes! Where have you been?'

Getting drunk, trying to forget myself. The thought of saying it aloud and hearing the shock in her mother's voice makes her smile.

'Are you very upset about having to leave there, Kukki?' her mother asks, her voice gentle.

Hearing her childhood nickname and the tenderness in her mother's voice brings a lump to Kavya's throat.

'I'm fine, Ma,' she mumbles, although she definitely isn't, for she feels an urge to reach down the telephone line to her mother and bury her face and her woes in her shoulder, like she used to do at family functions when she was very little, taking comfort from playing with strands of her mother's hair, the smell of coconut oil and security. Her mother would hold her tight, knowing Kavya was tired of meeting all the numerous aunts and uncles and that her cheeks hurt from where they had pinched them, all those fleshy, sweaty aunts sporting leering orange mouths dripping like vampires (she eventually discovered that it was just paan – harmless – but that was much later) and uncles who smelt sour and did not smile at all.

When did that change? When did Kavya stop being the little girl who could look up at her mother in a certain way and her mother would know exactly what she wanted, read her mind and offer the solace she needed?

As Kavya grew up and became independent ('I'm not Kukki, my name is Kavya. K. A. V. Y. A!'), first refusing to wear the clothes, the salwars and ghagras that her mother chose for her, and then refusing to go to the functions altogether, and the endless arguments started, her father hiding behind his newspaper, her grandmother the gentle arbitrator, perhaps it was then…

'Are you sure?' her mother's voice still tender and uncharacteristically soft. Ironically, even though she is softer and thus harder to hear, it makes Kavya feel as if her mother is closer, right beside her, almost.

'Yes, Ma,' she says and realises with some surprise that her voice sounds almost as tender as her mother's. 'Now tell me what's happened—'

Her mother doesn't need much urging. 'You know the coffee plantation resort on the outskirts of Doddanahalli where we stay overnight?'

Kavya pictures the sprawling hotel that was the plantation owner's residence during colonial rule, with spacious rooms looking out on to manicured lawns and the coffee estate beyond. They always stop there on the way to and from her father's ancestral home in Coorg. She loves to walk among the tall coffee plants, the plump, lush beans turning from green to red, some yellow, the taste of burgeoning life with the bitter undertone of ripening coffee. 'Yes.'

'You know there's a jungle surrounding it?'

'How can I not? You always warn me not to go into the jungle when I set out on my walk.'

'With good reason, as it happens. One morning last week, a wild elephant got separated from its herd, and went on a rampage, right across the plantation. It was finally caught and reunited with its herd – not before it caused significant damage, though. And then the men cataloguing the destruction saw something gleaming in the foliage across the road from the plantation. You know, where the jungle encroaches onto the fields. We drive by there.'

Kavya can picture it. Driving out of the plantation gates and joining the road, the jungle on one side, giving way to fields on the other. 'Yes. What was gleaming?'

'You'll never guess!' Her mother can't keep the thrill from her voice.

'Tell me then.' Her excitement, throbbing down the line, is contagious.

Her mother does love to narrate a tale. She makes a production of telling a story. No wonder, then, that Kavya chose acting over the more sedate professions like engineering and medicine that her mother was pushing her towards – she takes after her.

Kavya had put forward this argument when announcing her wish to move to Mumbai and try her hand at acting, but of course it didn't wash.

Her mother had been devastated. She had also been scandalised. 'Acting! That's for flighty girls! How will we get you married?'

She had ranted and threatened to disown Kavya and, when that didn't work, begged and pleaded. When that didn't work either, Kavya's mother had used the biggest weapon in her arsenal, one that hadn't failed her yet: emotional blackmail. She had gone on a hunger strike. For a woman who loved food and feeding, it was the ultimate sacrifice.

She had sat on the floor in the front room, refusing to eat, hitting her head and sobbing to everyone who visited – and of course everyone had turned up to watch the spectre of Laxmi being driven to fasting by her wayward daughter.

But Kavya was just as tenacious and she had not budged, not this time. The fast lasted for four days.

Kavya's father took to visiting his friend Chandra after work to avoid the stalemate between his wife and daughter. 'Plus, for the first time since I married your mother, there was no food in the house,' he confided to Kavya later. 'And – please don't tell your mother this – Chandra's wife is the best cook in town. She felt sorry for me; she kept plying me with home-made snacks. This way I could at least have a full stomach before I returned to the war zone that was our house at the time.'

On the fifth day, Ajji had intervened. 'Laxmi, eat. No point starving yourself when Kavya is set on what she wants to do.'

And, with Kavya's mother's defences weakened by hunger, Kavya had got her way.

'Your ajji spoils you,' her mother had shouted through a mouth full to bursting with laddoos. 'Go on then, ruin your future. Only don't come crying to us when it is too late.' Her chin wobbling perilously, even as she stuffed her mouth with cashew barfi.

Ajji had patted her daughter's back. 'Everyone needs to find their way, Laxmi. You know that.'

Kavya's mother had said nothing (she who always had to have the last word and never ran out of things to say), instead silently picking up some syrupy tubes of jalebi and turning away from both her mother and her daughter.

Ajji. If she was here now, she would open her arms and fold Kavya into them: 'Don't worry, child. It will all work out, time will heal all wounds. You'll be fine.' She would spout platitudes but somehow, coming from her, they would feel fresh and true.

'The gleaming object…' her mother is saying, '…was a gold bangle glinting in the sun, clinging to a pile of bones from a child's body, splayed across a mound of disintegrating bricks – which led to a temple, of all things.'

'No!' Kavya sees in her head a child's small bones, smooth and shiny white, glistening among the verdant green like teeth in an alien's head. The gold bangle an anomaly. Bricks slippery with moss leading up to a secret temple, hidden from the world. She shivers.

'Yes.'

'But… This happened in Doddanahalli. How has it made the national news?' Even as she asks the question, Kavya knows. She sees eager bodies pressing upon the temple, intruding into this space that has lain secret for… Decades? Centuries? The hot, sweet smell of perspiration and fresh gossip. Awed whispers growing, becoming rumbles, spreading outwards. And amidst it all, bones lying uncovered. Small, forlorn. A tiny bangle circling a creamy wristbone. Shouting a story that nobody knows but everyone wants to claim, to narrate.

'Wait for it… After that, there was no hiding the temple from the world. Rumours abounded – they are still doing so. Tales flying that this temple too hides a treasure trove within its foundations like the Sri Padmanabhaswamy temple in Trivandrum. A sanyasi wants to take up residence at the temple under the peepal trees, which he says must be left alone, as they've been guarding the temple and are holy. A priest has arrived, ready to start doing pujas, as soon as the temple site and the temple itself is cleared of the vegetation that has encroached upon it. There's a long line of people eager to worship…'

Kavya pictures the scene: the calm of the jungle, populated by birdsong and monkey-chatter, inundated by people, hordes of them, chasing away the birds and upsetting the monkeys. The temple ambushed by men eager to claim it back from the wilderness. Rumours of gold bringing venerating devotees faster than the time it takes for scandal to smear a pristine reputation.

'And now, a man has come forward claiming that the temple belonged to his ancestor, who was the landlord of Doddanahalli…'

'The whole village?'

'Yes, that's how it used to be, one person owning all the land and leasing it out as he saw fit. Anyway, this man is claiming to be the landlord's great-grandson or something like that. He's saying that his family own the temple and the land surrounding it, that his family's wealth is hidden in the temple vault. Protestors are grouped outside the temple, claiming that the land belongs to everyone as there is a temple on it, so how can it be private?

Some want to dig up the vault – if there is one, others want to leave it alone as it belongs to the deity. There's talk of miracles and secrets. Muslims are claiming that the land the temple is housed on is the resting place of one of their holy elders. Hindus have gone up in arms against this, both the ones who want to dig up the vault and the ones who don't, uniting against the Muslims. People are coming from everywhere to claim the temple and the treasure.'

Her mother pauses to take a breath and Kavya sees her chance. 'Ma, how is this connected…?'

Outside she sees a child run across the road, almost falling under a bus. His mother lunges after him, catching him just in time. She lets out the breath she has been holding.

'When they finally managed to clear the vegetation enough to get inside the temple, they found that the main deity was Goddess Yellamma.' Her mother pauses suggestively, Kavya's cue, she guesses, to ask a question.

'Goddess Yellamma?'

'You know. The patron of the devadasis.'

'Devadasis?' she asks, seemingly her mother's echo.

Beside the road the slum children, mud-stained faces, brown, scrawny bodies, chase away the crows that have dared settle on their pipeline, the birds startling in a tizzy of agitation, black wings against slate sky.

'Girls dedicated to the goddess and prostituted in her name.'

'I know what a devadasi is, Ma.'

'Stories of devadasis who were dedicated to Yellamma in this temple have emerged. The practice is illegal now, of course, but it still takes place and some of these devadasis have started flocking to the temple to worship Yellamma. Women's rights activists are also getting involved, informing devadasis of their rights. It's a circus up there.'

Kavya's mind snags on the role of prostitute that was supposed to be hers, the lead in a Bollywood rehash of *Pretty Woman*. Shooting was all set to start when she decided to tell Nagesh, and then…

She blinks the hurt away.

'The deity is now polished. The cobwebs are cleaned from the bell, the anthills are anointed with garlands and fed with milk, just in case they house the snake gods who guard treasure. Men are still working on cutting back the vegetation around the temple and the cottage – they discovered a cottage too, by the way, beside the temple – steering clear of the holy peepal trees,' her mother is saying.

'How do you know so much about all this anyway, since the temple is in Doddanahalli? It's nowhere near us.' But, once again, even as she asks, Kavya knows the answer. If something is of interest to her mother – and for some reason this temple is – she will not rest until she has found out everything about it. Take, for example, her research into eligible men for Kavya, even though Kavya has stated a million times that she is not yet ready to marry.

'I am coming to that,' her mother says. 'The temple is small in itself, but because of the accounts of miracles and gold, it has come under discussion and dispute. There's talk that the lands surrounding it, including the cottage, belonged to a devadasi.'

One thing about her mother: she will talk and talk, expecting hardly anything in return. It is a small blessing.

'The newspapers have had a field day, reporting that the temple is privately owned by a devadasi who hasn't come forward yet.' Her mother's voice laced with excitement – and something else Kavya can't quite place.

'Is it?'

'Aha…' her mother says and Kavya waits for the big reveal.

It is clear that her mother has been building up to something all this time. This was to be the main item on her mother's agenda,

Kavya supposes, but Kavya had distracted her by announcing that she was coming home.

She pictures her hometown, the honeyed sun gleaming on gold-tinged green fields, rows of black crows on telephone lines, coconut trees angling towards the water of the river, where boatmen languidly wield oars made from fronds or sift sand from the sandbank in the middle of the river while they sing songs about lost love and heartbreak, haunting and vaguely familiar, their ebony bodies shiny with sweat, sinewy arms flexing.

Home... Her mother's cooking, sweet-smelling air fanning her from the banana fronds outside her window, her father smiling at her over the top of his glasses, her ajji's wrinkled grin and welcoming arms...

Warm though the image is, the prospect of going home smacks of defeat. She will be regressing back in time to the teenager who couldn't wait to get away from her mother's nagging and her high-handed 'I know what's best for you' decrees.

Kavya's always wanted to be someone in her own right. And much as she tries not to be affected by her mother's evoking of her classmates' successes, now, in light of her disappointment, they sting.

She had imagined returning on a wave of success, being feted and adored and admired. She had pictured her mother saying, 'You were right, I was wrong. I'm so proud of you.'

And it would have happened too if it hadn't been for—

Her eyes water, hot tears welling. She tries to push them away and concentrates on listening to her mother.

'The government is now involved, trying to determine if the temple is public or private. Everyone wants the land, and they're all at cross purposes with each other.'

Kavya muses on how the scent of gold can wash a whole population's eyes with its glimmering promise, turn them greedy and grasping, willing to believe anything at all.

'And the temple sits serene, as it has done over the years, and presides complacently over the commotion.'

Despite her upset, Kavya grins. 'When did you get so poetic, Ma?'

'I am quoting one of the journalists – the last line from the opinion piece in the *Hindu*.' Kavya can hear her mother's smile and suddenly she wants to be there in person to see her flash one of the sudden, glorious beams that transform her face.

'So, we need to go to Doddanahalli,' her mother says, abruptly switching track.

'Why?'

'Oh, didn't I tell you?'

'You know perfectly well you didn't. Tell me what?'

'The deeds to the land surrounding the temple, the cottage discovered beside the temple and even the temple itself…'

'Yes?'

'Your ajji has them.'

Chapter 2
Gowri

Why?

Goddess Yellamma,
    Why?
    Why me?

Chapter 3

Lucy

Summer and Innocence

'What do you mean, you're engaged? We've just come out. We've barely had time to have fun yet.' Lucy clutches the hand of her best friend, Ann, as if by holding on to her she can quash what she has heard, her voice fervent with outrage.

They are sitting side by side in the love seat in the rose arbour at Fairoak, Lucy's home. This is where, over the years, they have imparted secrets and shared confidences and made promises, where they have concocted grandiose plans for their future, giggly with happiness as they revel in friendship and summer and innocence.

And now, Ann has declared that she is to be married to the first man who has paid court to her and Lucy just cannot believe it. 'But Ann, you barely know Edward,' she sputters.

'He's the one for me, Luce.' Ann's plain face glows with conviction and, sitting there framed against the crimson roses, her face more radiant than the flowers around her, Lucy's childhood friend looks beautiful.

Perhaps Edward *is* right for her, Lucy thinks, casting her mind back to try and conjure up the face of the man who had danced with Ann last night. But she cannot remember, busy as she was, dancing with one admirer after another, drunk on the attention and compliments she was receiving, men jousting with each other to attend to her.

'But Ann, what about the plans that we made, to travel the world, go on adventures, experience life that is more than just this?' Lucy waves her hand around to encompass the honey-speckled green lawns stretching out around them, the orangery behind them, the neat rows of flower beds and, beyond that, the house rising wide and tall and elegant.

'*You* made those plans, Luce, not me,' Ann says in that gentle voice of hers.

Yes, it's true, Lucy thinks, breathing in the perfume of roses and sun-warmed meadows, flowers nodding and bees gossiping in the saccharine breeze, the glorious dappled caramel-gold of an English summer.

'I'll travel the world in search of adventure,' Lucy has declared, sitting right here, many a time. 'I want to *be* someone, *do* something.'

And although she always assumed Ann agreed with her, she knew – she has always known – that what Ann really wants, all Ann has *ever* wanted even from the time they were very little, is a good man to love and care for her and a big family with him.

But now, despite noting Ann's happiness, Lucy can't help the disappointment that spills inside her, her mouth tasting bitter with it – in all her plans for her future, she has always envisioned Ann, her faithful friend, accompanying her. Without Ann to validate her every decision, she would be lost.

'We've hardly been to any parties. How can you be so sure? Don't you want to wait, go to a few more balls, see if someone else, someone better, comes along?'

'Lucy,' Ann's voice is mildly reproaching, 'Edward is the man I want to marry.'

'You've fallen in love?' Lucy is awed.

'Yes. That's what I've been trying to tell you all this while.'
She smiles.

Lucy looks at Ann, her best friend since childhood; she knows
her inside out, knows all of her deepest secrets and fears. Her face
is beaming, her expression content, and for the first time in their
lives, Lucy feels envious of her. How can Ann know with such
certainty that Edward is the man for her? Will she ever feel like this?

'How does it feel? How did you know?' she asks of her friend.

'He smiled at me, took my hand and I knew then. And when
I met his gaze, I knew that he did too.'

Where are the fireworks, the rainbows, the ardent declarations,
the grand overtures? Lucy has imagined love to be thunderclaps
and sparklers, her heart – her whole body – arrested, taken captive
by passion. Her world changed irrevocably, altered and remade
in a fantastic way. It would be earth-shattering, all-changing. It
would be a festival, an orchestra, a symphony, a celebration…

'But Ann, did you feel a thrill when he touched you? What
was it *like*?'

'I recognised something in him. Like I had been waiting for
him all my life and there he was.'

Lucy throws her arms around her friend. 'I never thought of
you as poetic, Ann, but you are speaking poetry now.'

Ann grins. She has never looked more beautiful, Lucy thinks.

Lucy closes her eyes and throws her face up to the sun, knowing
then, as she sits there with her best friend on their favourite bench,
that nothing is going to be the same again.

Ann will get married and move away.

And she, Lucy, will go to the balls and the masquerades, the
hunts and the tea parties, missing having Ann at her side. She
will dance and she will charm the women and flirt with the men.
But will she ever find the love she is looking for? *Her* version of

love, magnificent and all-consuming, as opposed to Ann's sedate, demure version?

She opens her eyes and her gaze is captured by someone in the distance, walking towards them.

A broad-shouldered, muscular man, hefting what looks like an apple tree. The new gardener, she realises, the man who has replaced old George.

His skin gleams in the sun; beads of sweat have collected on his face. He catches Lucy's eye, tips his hat and smiles, the beads of sweat dislodged as his face creases pleasingly.

A thrill travels from the base of Lucy's spine right up to her chest, and something in her heart tips over as she smiles back.

Chapter 4

Gowri

How It Begins

Goddess Yellamma,

You are a goddess and your job is to look after the world, not cater to the whims and fancies of every person in it. I know this. You cannot answer everyone's prayer, for it is impossible, even for a goddess, to satisfy everyone. But what you do, what you ask of the girls you choose to serve you, how do you live with that, Goddess? The only explanation I can think of is that you don't really know or understand what goes on in your name.

So, let me tell you.

This is how it begins.

Picture a poor but happy household in a small village in Karnataka. A farmer, his wife, their two girls and precious young boy.

But their little hut is beset by illness and grief and desperation. For the adored, longed-for son who makes their family complete is very ill. Dying.

He lies on a mattress in a corner of the dusty windowless room of the cottage, which is swilling with distress and fear and the sickly heat emanating from the small body on the floor.

No number of cool, wet cloths, lovingly placed by his mother on his forehead, will bring his temperature down. The air in the room is thick with the angst of the mother; it blisters with the delirious mumblings of the little boy, the despairing hopelessness of the father and the anxious boredom (and guilt for being bored) of the two young girls, who don't know what to do in the face of their parents' torment. They want to make things better but cannot. They want to go to school but don't know if they should – it feels blasphemous to be doing ordinary things while their little brother is grievously ill.

But the girls love school, especially the older one. For the older girl, school is the one place where the world makes sense. There is a teacher there called Vandana Ma'am who encourages her and pushes her to realise her full potential. And the girl enjoys this; she loves a challenge.

Sometimes secretly she wishes that this teacher was her mother instead of her real mother. Then she feels guilty and tries to make up to her mother for thinking these thoughts by being extra dutiful, doing more than her fair share of chores. The girl hates being absent from school but she also feels bad for wanting to do things she loves, like studying and learning new things from Vandana Ma'am, when her beloved brother is so ill. Her legs ache from sitting beside his sickbed, watching him struggle to breathe.

She wants everything back to normal: to be outside, skipping through the fields towards school, her hands clutching the slate on to which she writes with chalk her sums and her learning before transferring it into her mind, her legs sinking into the mud, birds singing, her sister beside her, her mother washing her brother (healthy and his old mischievous self) by the mango tree, even as he tries to escape, the dog dancing at their feet.

But instead she keeps vigil, along with the rest of the family, afraid that something bad will happen to her brother, praying and hoping for him to be returned to them, while outside, the sun shines down on another scorcher of a day and cows moo and the dog whines and chickens cluck as they peck at the charred earth.

The girl sits there and questions pop into her head:

1) Would her parents be this sad if it was she who was ill?
2) Why when girls are born is there melancholy and much hitting of foreheads, while boys are heralded with joy?
3) Why are boys considered better than girls? Who decrees this?
4) Why is school not seen as important for the children of the village, and especially for the girls?

The girl once made a mistake of pondering the last question aloud in the presence of her mother, back when her brother was well and she was chopping onions while her mother rolled dough into chapathis.

'Because you're going to get married and why do you need book knowledge for that?' her mother huffed.

'I want to be a teacher,' the girl said, thinking of Vandana Ma'am, her role model.

Her mother hit her forehead then, her eyes going dark and small and hard, like custard-apple seeds. 'Don't you be getting ideas into your head! Teaching is not for the likes of you. As it is we only send you and your sister to that school because that teacher... I forget her name...'

'Vandana Ma'am,' the girl said with reverence.

Her mother didn't notice. She was busy placing the rolled-out chapathis on the fire. 'Yes. She visited every house in the village when that girls' school was starting up and gave all of us a long lecture on how important it was for girls to be educated. In the end I promised to send you just to get her to leave!'

Vandana Ma'am rose even higher in the girl's estimation when she heard this.

'In any case, that school is free, funded by the missionaries,' her mother added, 'otherwise you wouldn't be going. You'll stop when we find a groom for you.'

As she waits for her brother to get better, the girl allows her mind to ponder:

5) Why do girls like her have to learn to cook and keep house from the moment they are born? Why do they have to get married and produce children and do as their men say? Why can't they work instead, be teachers, like Vandana Ma'am?

6) Why do women have to give dowry to the men and not the other way round?

7) Why does the girl's father have to work all day and night sometimes, slog through drought and monsoons, on land that isn't even his? It belongs to the landlord, who visits every so often and shouts at her father and doesn't seem to work hard, if at all.

8) Why are they poor while the landlord is rich?

9) Why do her brother and father get to eat first – the best parts of the fish when there is fish – and she, her sister and mother have to eat the leftovers?

The girl likes school because things are ordered there. For example, if a question is posed, an answer is given as well. When the girl is a teacher like Vandana Ma'am (and she will be, despite her mother's discouragement), she will follow in Vandana Ma'am's footsteps and encourage girls to study and she will treat them the same as boys. She will try to answer her students' every question instead of telling them to forget questions and concentrate on learning to cook and keep house.

She will.

This girl, Goddess, is me.
I am Gowri. I am fourteen years old.
And these were my dreams.
Were.

So anyway, back to my little scene.

The boy lies on the ailment-soaked mattress, fighting for his life. The father has asked the landlord for a loan and used it to get the doctor from town to pay a visit, but the medicine is not helping.

The boy is slipping further into unconsciousness, further away from his parents and sisters. The dreams the parents had pinned on the boy – how he would one day buy a farm of his own so he wouldn't be dependent on the landlord like his father, working all hours, on land that he can never own, for very little return – are fading away.

The priest comes to the house and does a puja. But even the gods don't seem to be in a benevolent mood and the boy lies unresponsive, barely breathing.

In desperation, the father decides that he had better do something constructive. He cannot stay in the small windowless room populated by his wife's helpless grief, his son's laboured breaths, any longer.

He goes to the field, lying neglected since his son's illness, and he starts to till the land. Across the road separating the fields from the jungle, monkeys scamper and birds fly off from the tops of trees. Nothing has changed and yet, for him, time has stood still these past few days, hope fading away with every one of his son's fevered, agonised breaths.

The buffaloes greet him like an old friend, gently butting him with their horns. He urges them along, churning the earth as he feels his whole being churned, displacing clumps of baked reddish-grey soil. As he works the land as he has done every single day since he was a boy of fifteen and took over from his father, he feels his anxiety ease briefly. At least here the buffaloes and the earth do his bidding. There is order, a meaning to what he does. If he urges the buffaloes, they obey and neat furrows are wrought on the land, to be filled later by paddy saplings.

Later. Will that include his son?

Please, gods. Please.

He prays as he works, sweat pooling on his eyebrows, his neck, running down his face and back.

He looks beyond the brown earth, the dusty haze, the hot sun shimmering in the horizon, towards the hut where his wife and daughters are huddled beside his beloved only son's unresponsive body.

Please, gods, save my son.

And then a chink. A clunk. The buffaloes are pushed off their stride, the plough shaft snagging on something and almost tipping over. He manages to right it at the last second.

The buffaloes grind to a halt, swishing their tails, turning to look at him, baffled brown gazes.

He digs in the upturned earth, trying to find what it was that tripped up the plough. He digs, the sun beating down on his head, unremitting, like the fever that has taken his boy hostage.

Please, gods.

And then, buried in the mud, something solid. Winking gold in the auburn, powdery dust.

He digs with renewed vigour, and his hands close around an unwieldy object. After a couple of tries, he pulls it out.

A statue. Of a goddess.

He has been praying to the gods when all the while this goddess was waiting, patiently, in his land (borrowed from the landlord).

Majestic. Smiling beatifically at him. Promising the world.

Leaving the buffaloes there, he runs, cradling the statue in his sweaty arms.

He runs barefoot across the fields, past the stream and up the hill to the hut.

He charges into the sickroom, disrupting the fumes of worry and illness, the heavy air weighted down by hopelessness and the hot, waning breath of his only son, startling his wife, who drops the cold cloth she was about to lay, for the umpteenth time, on her son's forehead, the cloth that would boil up in a couple of minutes, exuding steamy fumes and a mildew scent.

The two girls look up in surprise at their gasping, out-of-breath father, cradling something in his arms as if it were precious.

It is mud-covered and yet, golden glints shimmer through.

The older girl sighs with relief. At last, a break in the monotony. Something is happening.

She is instantly guilty for feeling so when her brother is so ill.

She does not guess that this is going to change the course of her life. If she had then she would have run away, right then, in a bid to outrun her wretched destiny.

Or would she? Perhaps not. For in her absence, her younger sister would have endured her fate. And she would not wish it on anybody.

I wouldn't, Goddess.

Not even on you.

Anyway, back to my scenario.

'Vasanthi,' the farmer – my father – says to his wife and there is something in his voice, a skein of hope, that makes my ma look up eagerly. 'I found this statue of the goddess in our field.'

Ma bows low in front of your image, her head touching the ground in reverence. 'A sign,' she whispers.

'Yes.' Da's voice is layered with hope.

'Get the priest. I will wash and clean the goddess.'

By the time Da returns with the priest and the landlord (for the statue has been discovered on his land, after all), Ma has washed you, Goddess, and adorned you with garlands made from flowers she had us pick hastily from the courtyard and sew into wreaths. She's washed herself for the first time in days and made us wash too, and don our best clothes – the only ones we have that are not torn. She has oiled our hair and hers, combing ours into neat plaits and hers into a bun.

And all the while our brother sleeps, his breath laboured, with you keeping watch, Goddess.

The priest intones mantras and we close our eyes and fold our hands in veneration. The sickroom is now a prayer room and feels too small and cramped to accommodate so many people. But it is the only room in the house besides the kitchen, it is the room where we eat, sleep, and live, and it has to make do.

'This is the goddess Yellamma,' the priest declares, when he has finished chanting.

He turns around and his gaze flits between my sister and myself.

It lingers on me.

The landlord's more insidious gaze follows his and when it fixes on me too, I shudder. I feel dirty, despite having just had a wash.

'A temple must be built for the goddess on the land where she was found,' the priest pronounces. 'And the goddess requires a dedicated devotee, someone who will serve her and worship her.' His gaze finds mine, holds. 'You will do.'

I stare at him, uncomprehending, unaware of the silence that has descended like a hawk on an unsuspecting mouse, conscious only of the thudding of my heart.

'Wha… What do you mean?' my mother says, finally.

'Your son will live. But in return, your daughter must be given to the goddess.'

'I will build a temple on the field where the deity was discovered,' the landlord says, his voice reverberating in the silence, echoing in my stunned heart.

My sister's hand finds mine. I hold it, tight, finding succour in her small fingers intertwined with mine.

'Your daughter will become a devadasi.'

A devadasi…

My mind flinches away from the word, my head reeling from what I have heard. How did this come about?

Until this moment, I knew where my life was heading: I wanted to study, to become a teacher. My only concern was talking my ma and da round to my way of thinking. I was determined to convince them that I did not want to get married early, plead with them to let me learn instead of marry.

But now…

'I will build a cottage for her on the land beside the temple, so she can live there,' the landlord is saying, nodding in my direction.

Me, living away from my parents, my beloved siblings. Living alone in a cottage and serving you, Goddess – a statue.

'How old is she?'

'Nearly fourteen,' my mother whispers.

'And she is… not a girl any more?'

I blush as I infer what exactly the priest is asking.

My mother looks at my father, her gaze as dumbfounded as mine, as she says, 'No, she's… she's not a child, no.'

'Then it's settled.' The priest nods. 'The temple must be built as soon as possible. We will have a puja on the day of the full moon and dedicate Gowri here to Goddess Yellamma.'

I find my voice. 'No, Ma, I—'

My mother looks away, towards her son. My brother.

'Your son will get better,' the priest insists.

My mother covers her mouth with her sari pallu. She rubs the tears from her eyes. She looks at me and when she does, I know: she has made up her mind.

My father, standing beside the landlord, runs a hand across his eyes and nods once.

The priest stands. So does the landlord.

I sit where I am, feeling weightless as I look at my brother, his small body, his chest moving up and down, and wonder why I have to be sacrificed to save him.

So, Goddess, my brother is better and here I am. In a windowless cottage across the road from the jungle, missing my home, my family, my life as it was.

All it takes is the dislodging of some earth for a life to change. The Christians dislodge earth and bury a body. My father dislodged earth, found you and buried me, the girl I was. Exchanging my freedom and my life for my brother's.

This was your plan?

To sacrifice me to save my brother?

How is this fair?

The landlord has claimed me for himself, declaring that it is my duty to please the men who serve you, Goddess, and since you were found on his land, I am to serve him.

Did you know that this goes on in your name, Goddess?

The landlord paid for me, of course. My parents are well provided for. My father now owns a piece of land. A small piece, but his own land nonetheless. The dream he did not dare envision for himself, the dream he wished upon his only son, he has achieved, in your name, Goddess Yellamma. He works for himself now.

This is how fortune turns. A clump of freed earth. A buried statue uncovered. A girl's dreams buried in its place while her father's dreams are realised.

A small sacrifice, perhaps, in the large scale of things. But this is *my* life, Goddess. A life I have to lead that I did not choose, that I would not choose even for my foes.

Growing up, like all little girls, I dreamed of marriage – after I had become a teacher, of course, ever the pragmatist that I was – and I had great hopes for my first night as a wife. I didn't know all the details, but I did know that there would be love involved.

I never expected this.

A cottage on the outskirts of the village, at the edge of the jungle and beside a temple dedicated to a statue I am contracted to serve for the rest of my life. A man older than my father. A married man with three daughters, one of them my age. A man who looks at me in a way that makes me feel unclean. Who treats me like the possession that I am.

There is no love, there will never be. Not for me. Not now.

'You are blessed, chosen by the goddess herself,' the landlord said to me when he came to me in the cottage, that first time.

I tried very hard not to flinch away from his words, his touch, his breath smelling of fish and lust.

'My properties have yielded the best profit in years since the goddess was discovered on *my* land and I built the temple for her, which I am kindly allowing the villagers to worship at. You, as the goddess's chosen one, bring good luck and I will share you only with the men I see fit. You will not go with men of your own accord. You will do as I say. You are mine. And the goddess's. Remember that.'

How can I serve you by serving a man who is not my husband, who will never be? A man who is planning on sharing me with other men?

What gives him the right? You do? How?

Why me?

I feel dirty all the time, no matter how much I scrub my body, how many times I wash the landlord off my skin.

I accept that I will not become a teacher, although a secret part of me still holds out hope.

I accept that I might have to live out the rest of my life here, my days spent worshipping you, my nights pandering to the landlord and his chosen friends.

But…

I will not be broken.

I will not.

Chapter 5

Lucy

A Witch

Lucy hides in the maze, the twigs of the hedge digging into her shoulders. She shivers, throwing her arms around herself, thinking, *I should have brought a shawl along.* But she didn't know she would be here in the maze, hiding from her Aunt Ingrid's foul attentions. Aunt Ingrid, who smells of mothballs and nostalgia, who clasps Lucy's arm in a pincer grip so it is red and sore of an evening and monopolises her, making her dance to her bidding as if she is doing Lucy a huge favour by doing so: 'Here, hold this for me. Here, will you carry this up the stairs. No, stay with me, child, I want you, not the maid.' Lucy is fed up of having to listen to Aunt Ingrid's unending observations about ancient and long-dead ancestors and life in Dorset.

It is only about five in the evening and yet the air is cold, bringing the chilly foreboding of winter, tasting crisp, of yellowing leaves and dying summer, that orange, ripe-marrow scent.

I am bored, Lucy thinks for the millionth time since Ann got married and left her to visiting aunts and fellow debutantes who titter and giggle at Lucy's every word, not contributing a whit to the conversation and not listening either. *I am bored, bored, bored.*

Nothing is the same without Ann. Even the balls and the masquerades that Lucy had so looked forward to attending. She is never without men paying her attention and asking her to dance. But the endless revelries – and even those are dwindling now that the season is at an end – aren't the same without having Ann to discuss them with afterwards.

She can write to Ann of course, and she does. But Ann is a married lady now and mistress of her home in Brighton, and by the time her replies to Lucy's letters arrive, Lucy has forgotten what Ann is commenting on.

Not for the first time she wishes she had siblings with whom to talk, share the day's events. Ann was the closest she had to a sister. Ann knows her inside out – her fears, her hopes, her secrets.

'Looooceeee…' she hears Aunt Ingrid call from the house, her voice, musical and terrifying, floating down to where her niece is hiding.

She loathes Aunt Ingrid. She is fed up with her life; she is ready for an adventure. An exciting escapade to break the tedium of her days is what she wants.

Lucy knows she is expected to do what Ann has done: find someone suitable from among the host of men who pay court to her at the balls she attends, marry him and keep house and produce children.

But Lucy doesn't want to tread the path chalked out for her. She doesn't want to follow the crowd.

She wants more, so much more.

She wants the world.

The day is drawing to a close, shadows settling between the hedges of the maze, a darker emerald contrasting with the lush green of the path. It must be later than she thought.

She will leave now – she can make her way out of the maze with her eyes closed – and try to slip into the house through the servants' entrance (Aunt Ingrid would not be seen dead in the servants' wing), pinching one or two of Cook's divine jam tarts on the way.

She shuts her eyes and walks briskly, laughing to herself and talking to Ann in her head: 'Ann, I bet you can't do this, walk blind out of the maze!'

She rounds the corner and comes to an abrupt stop. She's bumped into a solid wall. The smell of perspiration and sun and apples and smoke. A *human* wall?

She pulls back, sways on her feet to gain balance, opens her eyes.

A man stands before her, wielding secateurs. Bearded, sweaty face, twinkling eyes.

'So sorry, Miss.' His voice is deep and masculine, liquid chocolate. The new gardener. Well, newish. Old George, whom he replaced, has been gone almost six months now.

But Lucy is not sorry. She quite liked the sensation of being pressed against his firm chest.

'Oh, it's my fault, I'm sure,' she says.

'If you'll pardon me saying so, Miss, you *were* walking with your eyes closed.' He smiles, his face creasing in ridged grooves.

She laughs.

'Lucy?' she hears from just outside the maze.

Aunt Ingrid.

She squats down, although she knows Aunt Ingrid can't see her, pressing herself against the hedge. 'Shhh,' she says to the man, a finger pressed to her lips.

He stays quiet while Aunt Ingrid circles the exterior of the maze, calling for Lucy, muttering, 'I'm sure I just heard her.'

'She's back at the house,' he whispers after a while, his voice wry.

Lucy stands up straight and pats down her dress, feeling pleased with herself. This was a good hiding place. She knew Aunt Ingrid wouldn't attempt to come into the maze, afraid she'd never find her way out – and she'd be right too, Lucy thinks wickedly, smiling to herself at the image of her aunt trapped in the maze for days and days, her constant chatter quieted at last.

'You've tired of your visitor, have you?' he asks.

Lucy stands on tiptoes and peers up at the house. Aunt Ingrid is standing near the steps leading down to the herb garden, scanning the grounds for a sign of Lucy.

'Oh, she's so boring. *Life* is so boring. Nothing to look forward to. Nothing to do, except for a card party tomorrow to which I will have to accompany Aunt Ingrid. I am tired of card parties.' Her voice rises in a whine and she realises that she sounds like a peevish child.

He raises an eyebrow at her but doesn't say anything, going back to his pruning while whistling a tune.

She can't prove it but she has a feeling he is mocking her. It annoys her immensely. She wants to wipe that sardonic grin off his face.

'I want an adventure. I'm tired of doing the same old thing every day.'

Again he refrains from comment but she knows from the set of his face that he is not impressed. She doesn't know why she wants his approval, only that she does.

She is not used to anyone not agreeing with her, even when she is wrong. Everyone *always* goes along with her.

'Don't you ever get bored?'

'No, plenty to do,' he says.

'Have you always wanted to be a gardener?'

He shrugs. 'Needs must.' And then, 'I like plants. Growing things.'

'I like plants too,' she says.

He smiles. 'Perhaps the adventure you're seeking is to be a gardener for a day.'

'I like that,' Lucy says. 'Where will you be tomorrow?'

That gets his attention. He stops pruning to look at her. 'I was joking, Miss.'

'I want to escape Aunt Ingrid. If I spend one more minute in her company, I will scream. She leaves the day after tomorrow. But until then, I need to be out of her sight. Where will you be, tomorrow?'

'Miss, I don't think—'

'*I* do.' Her voice sharp.

'I'll be in the orangery in the morning.'

'Good. I'll see you there. What's your name?'

'Robert, Miss.'

'See you tomorrow, Robert.'

She gathers up her skirts and runs out of the maze and up to the house, hoping to slip up the back stairs and into her room before Aunt Ingrid catches her...

'Ah, there you are! I've been looking all over for you,' Aunt Ingrid says, materialising in front of her as if from thin air.

She is a witch, Lucy decides, sighing resignedly, but the thought of spending time with the gardener tomorrow and giving Aunt Ingrid the slip – her adventure – makes her feel able to endure the long evening ahead of her.

Chapter 6

Gowri

The Pain of One Instant

Goddess Yellamma,

It's been a month since I wrote to you – four endless weeks spent waiting, longing. For acknowledgment, release from this prison. For *something*. Anything other than this.

To think that I resented the vigil I kept at my brother's bedside, bemoaning the wasted time that I could have spent at school. At least then I had hope – the hope that some time in the future, I would go back to school.

But that was before you were found, Goddess.

And now…

Now I only have you.

Goddess, in the weeks since my last letter, which I left hidden under your likeness at the temple, you have given no indication of heeding my pleas. You have not responded to my entreaties. You have not given me a sign that you have heard me.

I am still here. Waiting for you to intervene on my behalf.

Have you not heard enough? Do you want to know more?

I will tell you, Goddess. I will enlighten you as to what young girls experience when they are dedicated to you. I am sure you don't know the whole story, for if you did, wouldn't you stop this?

I save some of the money I receive from the landlord (for the upkeep of the cottage, groceries, etc. – necessary, but I feel ashamed taking it), giving the rest to my parents. They have moved out of the hut now, to a bigger house in the village. My brother is thriving. When I visit my family – of which I am no longer a part – I urge my sister to study, to become the teacher *I* wanted to be. She, like me, has an aptitude for learning.

I give some of the money I have saved to my sister and, when my parents are out of hearing, ask her to get books for me from Vandana Ma'am, the teacher who inspired me. She had come to visit me at home when she found out what was to happen to me, and had held me wordlessly as I cried.

'You can't do this to her,' she said to my parents. 'She's one of the brightest students I have ever had. She has an amazing future ahead of her.'

'The goddess has spoken,' Da said while Ma wrung her hands and held her son close to her.

'The goddess is a statue. Mute. A piece of metal that someone discarded.'

Ma shut my brother's ears with the palms of her hands and glared at Vandana Ma'am in speechless shock.

'Aiyyo, don't say that. Don't use blasphemy in this house where a miracle has occurred, thanks to the goddess. My son was at his deathbed and now he is well. Is this what you teach our children at your school? Disrespect? If so, I will stop sending my younger daughter there!' Da yelled, his eyes radiating sparks, it seemed.

Vandana Ma'am's grip on me tightened while my sister cowered in the corner.

'No, please don't.' It sounded as if Vandana Ma'am was squeezing the words out through gritted teeth. 'Your younger daughter is very good at her studies too.'

'No use learning when she is going to get married.'

'Please. Your older daughter's life is going in a different direction. At least send your younger daughter to school until she gets married.'

Da nodded and walked to the door to indicate that she should leave.

'Run away,' she had whispered in my ear, as she was going. 'I will help you.'

The marigold bushes nodded in the breeze and for a brief moment I entertained the dazzling idea of escaping from my fate, with the backing of this woman, who in my wishful fantasies I had cast as my parent. *Why wasn't I born to you, Vandana Ma'am?*

Then I heard my brother's voice from inside the house – my brother who couldn't speak or even breathe properly until you were found and I was promised to you, Goddess.

'I can't. If I do so, my brother will die.'

'Rubbish.'

But I couldn't take the chance, not when my parents were setting so much store by me, not when it had been decreed by you, Goddess, not when, since the day you had been found, my brother had been getting steadily better.

The day after I ask my sister to buy some books for me from my favourite teacher, I receive my first visitor at the cottage. First visitor other than the landlord, that is, but he is the owner – of the cottage and of me – and so not really a visitor at all.

Vandana Ma'am, the woman I look up to and admire, comes to see me.

'You shouldn't be here. I am…' I can't complete the sentence, can't call myself a devadasi, although that is what I am.

I cannot get over the fact that my teacher is here. Even my parents and siblings have not been to visit. They have been to the temple, but not to my cottage. I suppose they do not want to acknowledge what happens here. Nevertheless, I keep the cottage tidy; arrange my few possessions neatly, just in case they might visit one day.

'Rubbish.' Vandana Ma'am scrutinises me, her sharp eyes missing nothing. 'How are you?'

'I'm okay.'

'Really?'

How to put into words the loneliness of the long, fearful nights, when I flinch from the sounds of the night: an owl hooting, a roar, the calls of nocturnal animals, the noises of the forest, the screaming of the wind, the rustling of the trees? When I picture menace slinking in the jungle, big cats prowling in the shadows, a hungry lion's soft padded toes making their way towards me, when I imagine its teeth sinking into my flesh and think that might be preferable, the pain of one instant, to spending the rest of my days like this, alone except for the occasional visits from the landlord.

How to say how much I miss the sounds I did not even register when I was living at home: the snores of my father, the soft sighs of my sister on one side of me, my brother's dream mumblings on my other side, my mother's sputtering exhalations. The air populated by the slumber-tipped reveries of my family.

How to tell her that I miss being a sibling – teaching my brother to write, to count, tickling him until he rolls around in the mud giggling, unable to stop; playing hopscotch with my sister, plaiting each other's hair, taking turns drawing water from the well and arguing about whose turn it is to chop the vegetables and peel the garlic.

How to say I miss being a daughter, the way my father's eyes softened when he looked at me. Now he doesn't look at me, but at a spot above my head, as if he cannot meet my eye and see the knowledge hidden there, of what he has done and what I have to do as a result.

And my mother, her work-roughened hands, her interminable sighs, the way she stretched when she was tired, the way her lips thinned when she disapproved of something, the way she would pat my head when she was pleased with something I had done. How she too will not meet my eye now. How her lips disappear when I visit and the neighbours collect to stare and whisper to each other, how she does not know how to treat me any more. How I wish she would shout at me, nag at me to come and help her, not look at me like a guest who needs to be pandered to, to overcompensate for what has happened to me, what they have done. Roll the mat out for me to sit on. Give me a tumbler of water.

'I don't want to be a guest,' I want to shout. 'I just want to be me. Your daughter who frustrates you with her desire to study and not get married, who is always writing on her slate or working out sums in her head when she should be helping you out.

'Don't smile at me in that fake way, your eyes not meeting mine. Tell me to get a move on. Don't bring me food, ask me to cook. Go on, Ma, be a mother to me, not a stranger.'

How to tell Vandana Ma'am about my brother – the only one who is himself with me. Unchanged.

Every time I visit he throws his arms around me. 'Akka,' he says, *sister*, asking me to hug him, carry him up high and wheel him around like I used to do. 'I miss you, Akka.' Pressing his small body against mine.

I want to hold him and I want to hit him. I want to hurt him, snub him. I cannot be myself with him for all the anger, the misdirected rage that I feel about having had to exchange my life for his.

How to tell Vandana Ma'am, or anyone, of the long days when, after I have swept the temple and the courtyard and the cottage, after I have adorned you with flower garlands and rose-scented incense, after I have given food to the priest, I sit on the washing stone and look at the chickens pecking away at the dirt, at the birds and monkeys in the jungle beyond, and wish I was them. Carefree.

The other day when there was a storm and thunder rattled and lightning danced and rain lashed at the cottage, I wanted to be with *someone*, even you, Goddess. I thought of running into the temple, but the priest sleeps there and I knew that if the landlord got word of it, he would be livid – even though the priest is old. The landlord gets so angry when he thinks I have looked at someone the wrong way, which is every time there is a puja and other men are present.

'You belong to the goddess and, by extension, to me. You do as I say,' he repeats often, a dangerous glint in his eye.

I wish I could go back to the untroubled days before. Before I was rubbed with turmeric, washed with neem water, decked in a gold and vermilion sari and dedicated to you, when I did not have this knowledge of what happens between a man and a woman, the knowledge of how being with a man, looking at a man, can be misconstrued.

The landlord never stays the night. After he's had his way with me, he rolls over and goes to sleep for an hour, sometimes two. The snores escaping his open mouth make the hairs poking out of his nose jiggle. I want to wash myself but I wait until he wakes up and leaves. Sometimes he will wake up ravenous and want something to eat. Other times, he'll reach for me again.

After he has left, I ride out the hours of night, waiting for dawn to brush a rosy swathe across the walls and seep brightness and light into the cottage, washing away the shadowy monsters and the scent of fear.

For what have I to be afraid of really, when the worst has already happened?

I can't say all this, so I don't say anything at all.

But somehow Vandana Ma'am understands.

'Run away,' she whispers, repeating what she has said before.

'I… I can't. My family – I have to give money to them. They have moved to a bigger house… My da, he is so happy that he owns land now, but he needs money to buy crops, make a go of it…' I don't tell her that I have considered running away myself, many times since she suggested it last. But I am afraid to do so. Afraid of what the landlord might do. Afraid of spurning you, Goddess, of your wrath. If I ran away and my brother died, as a result, I would never forgive myself.

'But you, child… It's not fair what is being done to you,' Vandana Ma'am says.

'I'm okay,' I lie.

'Here.' She presses books into my hands, her eyes wet. 'Read these and when you have finished, send word through your sister and I will bring more.'

'Thank you,' I say.

'It's nothing.'

She is still crying when she leaves.

I watch her, dry-eyed.

I am all cried out.

I cried and pleaded with my father, with my mother and with you too, Goddess.

It achieved nothing.

And so, I will not cry.

I will stay strong.
I will create new dreams.
I will not break.

Goddess, now you know what goes on in your name, *everything* that goes on in your name.

Are you okay with it?

If so, how can you be when you are a woman yourself?

Chapter 7

Lucy

Not a Game

'I love him, Ann,' Lucy says, pacing up and down the carpet in Ann's bedroom. 'What is so wrong with that?'

She is visiting Ann in Brighton. She's been here a week and already she is missing Robert dreadfully. She had been looking forward to seeing Ann, but now that she is here, she is torn. It is wonderful being with Ann and yet it is not the same. Not any more. Ann is a married woman now; there are demands on her time. She cannot sit all day giggling and chattering with Lucy like she used to. She has changed, become more mature. She doesn't find the same things funny that she did before marriage. She is transforming before Lucy's eyes, becoming one of those stuffy matrons, becoming like Lucy's mother. Lucy feels uncharitable thinking this, but it is the truth.

When Lucy realised that she had fallen in love with Robert, she had written to Ann. Ann had always, all her life, been the recipient of her secrets, the person she went to first when she had something important to share.

Lucy had assumed Ann would be pleased for her, happy that she had found love. When Ann's reply arrived, she had grabbed it from the tray and run away to the library, curling up in her favourite armchair and looking out on to the garden, hoping for a glimpse of Robert, even though she knew he would be in the glasshouse.

She had opened Ann's letter eagerly.

She read it once, then again, her whole being pulsing with anger. 'Don't rush into things,' Ann cautioned. 'Use your head, not your heart, my friend,' she urged. 'Are you sure this is not because you are lonely, Lucy? Come for a visit, stay with me for a while?'

Lucy was tempted to fling the letter away and only the thought that Mother and Father might find it stopped her. She wanted to tear it into little pieces and throw it into the fireplace; watch as the glowing embers rendered those hurtful words to ash.

Instead, she tucked it into her bodice and went in search of Robert.

He was in the glasshouse packing seeds into earth, his long fingers tenderly manipulating the soil.

'She has no right to lecture me,' Lucy had raged. 'She fell in love as soon as she set eyes on Edward. She followed her heart, not her head, and now she is a smug, married woman. Why is her love acceptable while mine is not?' She paused for breath. 'She is belittling my passion, setting too much store by her own importance in my life. Does she think a visit to her will make me forget you?'

Robert finished what he was doing, washed his hands and grinned at her. 'You look…' he said, pulling her into his arms, '…so beautiful when you are angry.'

'I am so cross with Ann…'

'She cares for you,' he whispered in her ear and she was distracted by his scent of fresh earth and hard work. 'She doesn't want you to lose your head to a mere gardener.'

'But this…' Lucy said, breathless, as his lips brushed hers. The intoxicating aroma of burgeoning vegetation and first love. The taste of man – musk and salt. '…is what I want.'

While she was getting ready for bed, she found the letter crumpled among her clothes and carelessly tossed it into the pile of Ann's other letters without reading it again.

A few days later, while she was still fuming, another missive arrived from Ann. *I am so sorry, my dear, if my last letter was a bit harsh. I didn't mean to distress you. I said those things only because I love you and don't want you to get hurt. If you truly care for him, I will stand by you, of course. But do come and visit, Lucy. I miss you so.*

Ann had always been able to read Lucy's mind; she knew Lucy was upset. Lucy had replied to that letter, poured her heart out.

And now she is here, with Ann and wanting to be with Robert again. She misses his strong arms. The mischievous glint in his eyes. His smell of hard slog and raw masculinity, so unlike the well-bred fops Mother and Father foist on her, all of them interchangeable, the same words coming from different mouths, their fake compliments, their phoney delight in her every observation.

Robert… He is thrillingly different. So strong and virile and yet so gentle with his plants and with her. Regaling her with tales of home, his mother and five sisters. His life so very different from hers. When she is with him, she is never bored.

Ann takes a deep breath and Lucy knows what is coming.

'Are you certain,' Ann says, throwing her arms around Lucy and looking deeply into her eyes, 'that you are not doing this just because you've been lonely?'

'Oh, Ann!' Lucy explodes. 'You've asked me this every day I have been here.'

'Humour me.' Her friend's face is soft and in that moment, Lucy sees the old Ann, the two of them snuggling in the love seat in Fairoak, dearest friends, closer than sisters, surrounded by the heady scent of roses and secrets.

'I admit now, it was a shock when you left. I was bereft suddenly, I had no other friends. I had had no need for anyone else when I had you. I suppose I never expected you to marry first – I thought we'd do that together too, like we had done everything else. Even our birthdays are so close – only two weeks apart – and we always celebrated them together!'

'Oh, my darling,' Ann says, pulling Lucy closer into her embrace.

Lucy will never tell Ann this – there are some things that need to be kept even from best friends – but if she is being completely honest, she had expected herself to fall in love first. She had always assumed it would be her instructing Ann on what love was like. Her love would be glorious and perfect and Ann would be the one on the sidelines, the one trying to find love like Lucy's, not the other way round.

After all, Lucy has always been the one all the men flock to, the one who stands out. The one who turns heads and breaks hearts.

'I confess to some jealousy towards Edward when you got engaged to him and then married him within the space of a few weeks. All our lives up until then I had had first claim on you.' Lucy knows that if it had been the other way round, she wouldn't have given a second thought to how Ann was feeling. She would have expected Ann to be happy for her and to accept being knocked to second place in Lucy's affections without any qualms. But Ann... Ann was different. She had made sure Lucy didn't feel left out; she had included her in every detail of her wedding preparations.

'Are you sure, Lucy, that you are not with Robert for the thrill of it? That you are not confusing the novelty and illicitness of it with love?' Ann is saying.

Lucy feels a flash of anger. She bites her lower lip to stub it out. She doesn't want to fight with Ann, not again. They always seem to fall out when Lucy talks about Robert and yet, she can't stop talking about him, thinking about him...

Yes, she admits to herself in her head, she *is* enamoured by the thrill of it all. The clandestine meetings. Keeping what they feel for each other secret from Mother and Father, from the other servants. Hiding the knowledge of it in her heart when she is dancing with the men who make a beeline for her. It seems to add to her beauty – more than one man has commented on her reserve, her mysterious smile: 'As if you know something we are not party to.'

'Yes, perhaps the thrill is part of it,' Lucy admits now. 'But it is so much more than that.'

'Is he... he might have designs on you and leave you in...' Ann says, anxiously fingering the locket Edward gave her on their wedding day that she is never without.

'Oh, Ann! I know you care for me, and that is why you are saying these hurtful things, but believe me, Robert is not like that at all. When you come back to Fairoak for a visit and meet him, you will see for yourself. In fact, Robert was against it at the start. He had his reservations. He did not pursue me, Ann. *I* pursued *him*.'

'It appealed to your sense of adventure, your desire to do something different,' Ann says. She knows Lucy so well.

Lucy thinks of the debutantes who flock around her at the parties they are all expected to attend. She knows they are as jaded by the rites and rituals of polite society, the eligible, insipid men, as she is. She also knows that all of them fantasise about falling in love with *real* men with muscles firm from doing *real* work, but they wouldn't dare do anything about it. But *she* has.

Lucy colours and she sees Ann take note.

'Lucy, my darling friend, this is not a game. Be careful.'

Ann has always been the sensible one, with Lucy leading the two of them into all sorts of capers. But Lucy has also been adept at getting them out of fixes; she has always been able to inveigle her way out of a sticky situation.

As if she has read Lucy's mind, Ann says, 'You won't be able to charm your way out of this one. Luce, you're playing with lives here. His, your parents' and your own.'

Oh Lord, when did Ann become so correct, so tedious? If this is what marriage does, leaching the sense of fun and adventure out of one, then Lucy does not want to get married.

'Are you sure you're doing this for the right reasons?'

'I love him!' Lucy snaps. It is hard not to lose her temper with Ann when she persists in saying the same thing, over and over.

'If word gets out, you will have to marry him. Are you ready for that? Your father might disown you. You might have to live in disgrace.' Ann's gaze is probing.

If Lucy hesitates, it is only for a moment. 'Of course,' she says, secure in the understanding that she is Father and Mother's cossetted only child and until now, they have never denied her anything. Anything at all. 'I would. But Father would never do so.'

Chapter 8

Gowri

To Be Ordinary Again

Goddess Yellamma,

I celebrate my sixteenth birthday – I cannot believe it's been two years since I was dedicated to you – with Vandana Ma'am, the best possible present. She doesn't know that it's my birthday, but by a stroke of fortune, it coincides with the day of her visit. A good omen if ever there was one and I need them in my life, Goddess.

Vandana Ma'am is the only one who visits me. The only person who does not treat me like a pariah.

She brings me books and she questions me on the books I have read. She is teaching me English – one of the first books she brought me is a Kannada to English dictionary.

I can read and write in English passably now.

'But not good enough,' Vandana Ma'am says. 'You need to be fluent, in reading, writing and speech, for when you leave here and have to stand on your own two feet.'

I love it when she says that: *for when you leave here*. I repeat the words softly to myself after she has left and during the nights when I am feeling down.

Vandana Ma'am has high hopes for me, hopes that I dare not entertain for myself. She insists I speak to her only in English. She makes me repeat sentences until I am assured and flawless. She is a hard taskmaster, quizzing me, pushing me, treating me like one of her students. It is the greatest gift she can give me.

'Thank you,' I said to her the second time she visited, while she was quizzing me on the books she had given me and making sure I had understood every word.

Like her previous visit, this one too was a welcome surprise. Nevertheless, I felt I had to say, 'I can collect the books from my sister. You don't have to come here, I know what the villagers say about me.'

She cupped my face in her palm then, and the tears I had been holding in check for what felt like aeons threatened to flow as a result of this simple human contact that expected nothing of me. Given freely, with love.

My parents do not touch me, not any more. They are flush with the money I give them, although they do not want to know how I earn it. They look away, from me, from what I represent, from the fissure in our family, from it all.

When I visited last, Da said, fiddling with his vest, 'Ah… I've found someone to till the land we own, so we're not tied to the village any more.'

'You *are* tied to the village,' I wanted to yell. '*I* am here. Your daughter.'

Instead, I kept quiet, waiting.

'We – we're thinking of moving to Bangalore. More prospects there. For the children and for us…'

'What about me?' I wanted to scream. '*I'm* your child too.'

'Don't go,' I wanted to cry. 'I'll be all alone, completely at the mercy of the landlord.' Instead, I looked down at my lemon-yellow sari – such a beautiful colour, so unsullied and innocent, like I will never be.

'That's good,' I said.

My brother came and clung to me. 'You come too,' he sobbed.

I gently disentangled his arms. Turned away from my family.

My family. No longer mine, really.

Especially now they are moving away, putting distance between me and themselves.

I am glad for my sister; and for the brother who loves me but whom I cannot love wholly any more, for every time I look at him I see what I sacrificed in order for him to live. I suppose this is why my parents cannot look at me too, for when they see me they feel torn and upset, their love tempered by guilt and shame and embarrassment.

We cannot go back, any of us, to how we once were.

On the way out, I held my sister close. 'Study hard,' I said. 'Become a teacher. Be somebody in your own right.' *Unlike me.*

My sister nodded, her huge eyes, so like mine, bright with tears.

'I will miss you, Akka,' she said, even as my brother launched himself at my knees and bawled himself hoarse.

'Write to me,' I told her.

And then I walked away from my family. My eyes stinging, but dry. My throat hoarse with the words I wanted to say but was keeping inside. My head covered by my pallu but held up high, facing the villagers who had collected, as usual, to gawp at me, the devadasi. They don't know what to make of me and so they treat me with a mixture of awe and disdain. I looked at each of them in turn. The men stopped leering and glanced up at the sky or down at the ground and the women gathered their children close as if who I was were catching.

I did not go straight back to my empty cottage, void of noise, of life. Instead, I took a detour, into the jungle. I walked a few paces into it, touching each tree, feeling around the bark until I found what I was looking for in the fourth tree from the road: a hole in the trunk and tucked into it, a rope. I pulled it out, recalling the time Da had sprung a surprise on my sister and me.

* * *

Our little brother was being born and our cottage was full of women, coaxing my mother on, urging her into giving birth.

One of them was drawing water from the well, another lighting kindling, yet another setting a big pot to boil. A couple chopped vegetables, while others cooked. One of them sponged my mother's forehead, another held her hand. My mother screamed and all of them, these women who had taken over our home, screamed louder, 'Come on, push. Harder. That's it. Push.'

The mood was festive, like a celebration, and yet there was my mother, prone in their midst, clearly in great pain.

My sister started to cry and Da, who looked very pale, said to the two of us, 'Come with me.'

He took us across the road from his field, into the jungle, where we had been warned many times never to go.

My sister looked at me, her eyes wide with fear, lower lip wobbling dangerously, and even though I was older, I felt close to tears myself.

'Are you coming or not?' Da called.

With him leading the way with his long, confident strides, I felt able to shrug off my dread. 'Come,' I said, holding my sister's hand, pulling her along.

Da had stopped at this very tree, groped around in the trunk and, as if by magic, pulled out a rope.

My sister's eyes became even wider, but her lower lip had stopped wobbling. She clapped her hands in delight. A bird flew off from the top of the tree as if in response and she laughed.

Da had looked at us, beaming. 'Ta da!' he said and the rope became a ladder.

This time, I joined my sister in clapping and more birds flew up from the trees as our delighted laughter echoed off the giant branches.

'Who is going up first?' Da asked.

'Going up?'

'Of course! Who wants to see heaven?'

That was one of the most magical days of my life. We climbed and we climbed, higher and higher, until, all of a sudden, we came to the top of the tree and there was a house made of branches! We sat there, the three of us, looking at the world spread out below us – feeling like you and your compatriots, Goddess, like birds, like magical beings. Dappled sunlight fell upon us like a blessing. Da regaled us with stories of sages and holy men, of witches and wise women. He tickled us until we fell about laughing, there among the treetops, the peaty smell of excitement and adventure, the heady taste of heaven and enchantment, the emerald caress of branches, the silken hug of the sweet-tasting breeze, the warm feeling of being loved.

When we climbed back down and made our way home, after Da had extracted a vow from us never to come to the jungle on our own as it was a dangerous place for little children, it was to merriment and revelries. Ma was no longer crying but smiling, although she looked exhausted. She held a small, swaddled bundle in her arms.

'You have a son,' the women declared and my father grinned, lifting my sister with one arm and me with the other and swinging us around and around until we choked on our laughter and begged him to stop.

That day, when I came back from visiting my family, after they told me they were moving to the city, I stood in the forest, with its soft rustling and squeaking sounds, its green fertile aroma of burgeoning life and its flavour of menace and latent danger, fingering the rope in my hand, debating whether to go up to the treehouse.

In the end, I tucked the rope back inside the hole, tucking away my memory of that wonderful, charmed day with it. I wiped my eyes with my sari pallu and made my solitary way back to my soulless cottage.

Since I have become a devadasi, many other daughters from poor families have been dedicated to you, Goddess. Men have claimed them and set them up in cottages around the village. It seems the landlord has also claimed a couple of new young girls, although he still visits me every so often and keeps tabs on me always.

'You are the one the goddess chose, which is why you are the only devadasi living next to the temple, the only one allowed to serve and adorn the goddess on a daily basis. You are the most blessed, the prettiest of them all,' he says and I wish I could tear away this beauty I am cursed with.

I am tempted to maim my face, scar it with hot oil. Only the thought of what could happen if I was no longer able to serve you, Goddess, what the landlord might decide to do instead, stops me. I know that I am to serve you for life – my life in exchange for my brother's.

The landlord does not like me to consort with the other devadasis; in fact with anyone at all other than him and the men he shares me with. He wants to be aware of my whereabouts at all times – he knows I go into the village on market day to buy produce for the week and that I visit my family every Sunday. He likes to remind me that he has ways of checking up on me even when he is not around, to make sure I am not doing anything untoward, anything not sanctioned by him.

'I don't know what goes on behind those pretty eyes of yours, Gowri,' the landlord says often, in that wily tone of voice I have grown to dread. 'But know this. If anything happens to you, there's always your sister.'

I chase all thoughts from my head, throwing away the horror I feel at the thought of the landlord's hands on my sister, smiling sweetly at him and saying, docilely, 'Nothing is going to happen to me.'

I will endure anything if it means my sister is untouched. Free to pursue the dreams we weaved together when we plaited each other's hair under the mango trees, back when we were innocent and untouched by fate and promises and exchanges and you, Goddess. Back when we were poor but happy and life was simple and free. Back when I belonged and I was loved.

This is why, when Vandana Ma'am cupped my chin in her palm when she visited that second time, I said she didn't have to, for I knew if she was associated with me, she would, like me, be the subject of gossip and speculation, her reputation sullied by scandal.

'Child,' Vandana Ma'am said and my throat felt salty with the effort of holding back my tears.

I couldn't recall the last time anyone had called me child. That term of endearment, bringing to mind purity and carefree happiness, was no longer applicable to me. And yet it felt wonderful. For a brief moment I could forget who I was and bask in it.

'I gave up marriage and children for the sake of my career; my parents still haven't forgiven me for it. I did not care about what people would say or think then and I'm not going to start now – if they find out I am coming here, that is, for I have no intention of telling anyone.'

I nodded, too choked to speak.

'You, Gowri, you're a girl after my own heart and what's happening to you...' Her eyes overflowed. 'I want to help in any way

I can. You will not run away and I can see why. The landlord is not an easy enemy to have but if you ever change your mind, I'm here for you.'

'I know,' I said.

'I don't want money for the books I bring you. No more paying me via your sister, understand?'

'But—'

'You're like a daughter to me, Gowri. The daughter I never had.'

I cried then, and she held me. I cried for the first time since I had vowed not to, when I had realised how futile tears were.

I cried tears of awe, of wonder.

Here, of all places, I had found an ally.

I had thought that love was denied me and yet here was this woman, whom I admired and who inspired me, giving of hers freely.

Since then Vandana Ma'am and I have worked together on my studies. The landlord is unaware of this, of course, my one rebellion.

Vandana Ma'am is very discreet and keeps her visits secret from everyone. She comes on a Saturday afternoon, at a time when the priest is having his siesta.

'I loathe gossip,' she has said, her voice dripping disgust. 'I have been the subject of it and I know how it feels. What I do with my spare time, whom I visit, is nobody's business but my own.'

I have told no one about her visits, not even my sister. She has not asked me why I stopped buying books from Vandana Ma'am, and I have not volunteered information.

On the days that Vandana Ma'am is due to visit, I finish my chores, the adornment of you, Goddess, the sweeping of the temple grounds, the mopping of the temple, the wiping of the bell, the feeding of the priest, as quickly as I can. Then I cook. I make vegetable cutlets and mint and coconut chutney. I make tomato rice and lentils with spinach. I prepare kheer, sprinkling it with the plump raisins that I have been saving all week. The cat who turned up one day, bedraggled and scrawny, purrs and rubs against my legs, wanting scraps. The chickens peck at the doorway, wary of the cat, not daring to come inside.

I hum as I cook, looking forward to seeing Vandana Ma'am. We will talk about books and she will grill me and test me and scold me for not learning properly, for making silly mistakes. She will give me more work and new assignments and then she will produce her treat: storybooks. Different stories from different worlds. Written in English.

'To broaden your horizons and also to improve your English,' she will say, dangling the books in front of me while I try to look at the covers.

I love these novels, the ability they have to transport me to exotic realms so apart from mine, where women have a choice, where they are strong and follow their minds, choose their fate, make their fortune.

I hide the books she brings me – the storybooks as well as the textbooks – among my saris and undergarments. The landlord never looks in there. Keeping this secret from him makes the long, lonely days and nights bearable. It makes me feel that I am not that helpless after all, that I have a small say in my own destiny.

In the long hours after the landlord has had his way with me, eaten and slept and finally left to go home, climbing in – I imagine – beside his wife, smelling of me, and I cannot sleep (for I am still afraid of the night, the proximity to the forest, the danger lurking there), I read. And it is magic – I forget the yearning for my family, the ache in my soul; I forget myself. I am an adventuress, an explorer, intrepid and unafraid. I am not beholden to anyone, I am in charge of my own life.

I read in the light of the flickering lamp, the smell of oil and the taste of unattainable dreams, until the navy shadows fade to grey, creamy pink dawn licking the edges, and the cat comes up and rubs at my legs and the chickens start pecking at the door and the priest rings the temple bell – his way of telling me he is awake.

I stow the book away; wash the landlord from my body. Even though I already do so when he leaves, I still don't feel clean, so I always wash again. Then I make ginger and cardamom tea and upma with peas and coconut shavings, and take it to the temple for the priest.

Vandana Ma'am holds out hope that one day I will rebel, that I will run away, like she wants me to; that I will escape you, Goddess.

She wants me to take my matriculation exam.

'I'm going to apply for you along with my other students. I'll get the question papers here and supervise you while you take the tests. It won't be cheating – you will be doing the tests properly, under exam conditions, with a teacher present, only not at school. I'll send them away to be marked, along with the other students' papers.' She smiles fondly at me. 'You will get such high marks that colleges will court you. And the landlord will have to let you go.'

A dream that I too entertain, briefly, as she puts it to me, carried away on the wings of her optimism. But I know, in my heart, that it will not happen. I cannot let it. For the landlord will take my sister.

'She is growing up nicely,' he has said, those nights when I am tired of pretending and show my reluctance to do what he wants. 'She is turning into quite the beauty.'

I know that even when my family move away to the city, the landlord will hunt them down. He will find my sister and ask her to replace me to honour the pact with you, Goddess. And my parents will meekly go along with it, just as they did with me.

I recoil at the thought of the slimy hands and grasping bodies of him and others like him anywhere near my sister. I will willingly sacrifice myself, the secret hopes that I have begun to nurture again, thanks to Vandana Ma'am, many times over if it means my sister is safe.

In the dark of night when sleep evades me, and I have read and reread the books Vandana Ma'am has given me, I dream.

I dream that I am home again, sleeping in the bosom of my family, that little hut on top of the hill, overlooking the fields and the gushing stream, where we all shared one room, where we slept, ate and lived and were happy.

In my dream, I dress myself and my sister. We wash our faces, plait each other's hair and we walk to school, waving goodbye to my mother. My brother sits on her hip and gurgles happily. He bursts into tears when he realises that we are leaving him behind and our mother distracts him with a hibiscus flower plucked from the bush, a fresh guava, the dog splashing in the bucket of water by the well under the tamarind tree where we washed our breakfast things.

I wake from these dreams and I am bereft, my face spattered with tears, the pillow wet with them. I walk through my silent cottage, dense with loneliness, loud and heavy with all that is missing: laughter and companionship and joy and innocence and love; reverberating with whispering ghosts of the different lives I could have led, the soft yellow slivers of remembered memories of happier times mocking me, the anklets the landlord has given me and insists I wear chiming a cheery tune, laughing at my misery, my solitary existence, the mistress of the landlord and his cronies, the slave of you, Goddess.

During the somnolent sun-baked afternoons after my chores are done, I sit on the washing stone and listen to the monkeys chattering in the trees, watch them picking lice from one another's fur, see the baby monkeys clinging tight to their mothers as they jump from branch to branch, and I envy them the company of their fellows. I am so jealous. Of the gossiping monkeys and the screeching parrots and even my chickens!

This is what I yearn for, Goddess:

To be ordinary again, and not someone branded with the label of devadasi.

To be part of my family once more.

To go to school, amass knowledge.

To never run out of books to read.

To become a teacher like Vandana Ma'am.

To get married. To a farmer, perhaps. One whose hands are scarred with honest labour. One who, when he touches me, does so with love.

To have a family. A small house among the fields, filled with children, love, laughter.

An uncomplicated life. Like my parents' before my brother fell ill. One I took for granted that I would have. One I will never have now.

Even if I did manage to leave, would I be able to shrug off my status as devadasi all that easily?

I am not a virgin. No man in his right mind will marry me even if the landlord relinquishes his claim on me.

And even if, by some miracle, the landlord lets me go, *you* won't, Goddess. For won't something bad happen to me, to my family, if I break my pact with you?

I know through advancing my learning that some people – Vandana Ma'am among them – condemn what I believe as mere superstition. And yet... How did my da find you just when he needed you? How did my brother get better?

I believe in you, Goddess. How can I not?

And the more I advance my studies, keeping it secret from the landlord and my family and the villagers and the priest (I am not foolish enough to believe it is secret from *you*), the more I worry that something will happen. That you will assert your power over me, show me who's boss, who's running this show.

Am I right, Goddess?

Will you?

Chapter 9

Lucy

Inane Pleasantries

The room where the recital is to take place, which Mother has insisted Lucy attend along with her, is oppressive – packed with bodies decked out in finery. Ladies corseted into tight-fitting gowns in the latest fashions, men in their evening best. The smell of rosewater and anticipation, the polite murmur of elite society exchanging inane pleasantries while waiting for the evening to begin.

Once, not too long ago, Lucy would have revelled in all of this, while pretending to be bored by it. She would have been the centre of attention, the one in the midst of the group of young ladies collected in a corner of the room discreetly eyeing the men from beneath their eyelashes. She would have made them laugh, her clever conversation rendering them spellbound and envious, while attracting the regard of every man in the room.

Now, she stands beside Mother, desultorily waving her fan over her hot cheeks, where she can feel the rouge her mother insisted she wear collecting in clumps. She still commands the attention of all the bachelors – and even some of the more daring married men – but whereas once it pleased her, now she couldn't care less.

After everything she has been through, she feels dead inside, her spirited self so stifled that she doesn't have the energy to resist her parents. It is easiest to go along with them and their plans for her. After all, isn't this what she has, ultimately, chosen for herself?

She thought she was different, but when it comes right down to it, she isn't at all so. In fact, she is more conventional and far more foolish than the other giggling debutantes whom she once looked down upon. At least they are shrewd enough to acknowledge what they have and to embrace it. Unlike her.

Lucy had thought she was fed up of all this, the trappings of high society, that she wanted rid of it. But when it came right down to it, this was what she chose. And for this, she had to… *Oh, oh, oh…*

She wants to hide away in a quiet corner and sob. She wants to keen and shout at herself for being such a dreadful fool. She wants to—

'Smile.' Mother nudges her. 'We don't want Lady Howell thinking the entertainment she has put on isn't good enough for you.'

Obligingly, Lucy lifts the corners of her lips upwards. Two men across the room smile at her in return. She turns away from them towards her mother, who is making small talk with a rotund, heavily perspiring woman in a bright yellow gown that does no favours to her florid complexion.

A sudden hush descends on the room and Mother pauses mid-conversation, trying to discern the reason for it. Lucy looks up too, curiosity briefly getting the better of the apathy that seems to be her default stance lately.

'Ah, there he is,' Mother says, satisfaction threading her voice as she nods discreetly towards the doorway.

A man is poised there, speaking with their hostess. He is tall and good-looking in a conventional way. Lucy wonders if he is aware of the retinue of gazes trained on him – how can he not be? And yet he carries on as if he isn't, his gaze fixed firmly on Lady Howell's face, and Lucy likes him for it. Does he know that he is responsible for the silence that has descended on the room, that he is the hope of every mother of every debutante in this room, while being the dream of the debutantes themselves – barring her?

He is a catch, Mother has explained to Lucy, because this late in the season most of the other eligible men are taken. Lucy herself has been 'indisposed' for most of the season – at least this is what her mother has told all the curious and gossipy matrons, although that has been not enough to satisfy them, of course. They have caught the whiff of scandal and they will not rest until they unearth the story behind Lucy's conspicuous absence from society at the height of the season. Which is where this man comes in…

'James Bell, Plantation Owner and Eligible Bachelor,' Mother whispers, her breath hot in Lucy's ear, flavoured with eagerness and bergamot.

Lucy hates the way Mother emphasises every word, as if conferring a royal blessing. Everyone has heard of the plantation owner who is in London looking for a wife, and Mother and Father have decided that wife will be Lucy.

'Determined though Lady Drew and her coven of gossips are to get to the bottom of your supposed "ailment", Lucy, even they will lose interest when you marry that plantation owner and move to India.' Her mother has reiterated this at least twice a day since she heard about James Bell's arrival in London.

'I know what I must do, Mother. There's no need to state his credentials in quite that way,' Lucy hisses now, under her breath so that the girls waiting beside her and whose eyes are fixed on the newcomer do not hear.

'There is every need,' her mother snaps back in the same hushed whisper, shaking her head so vehemently that her elaborate hairdo grazes Lucy's cheek, 'if only to show you what you can have if you set your mind to it. You are by far the most beautiful debutante in this room. Work your charms.'

'I will not,' Lucy wants to say, stamping her foot as she used to do as a child. 'Especially not when you speak to me in this hateful way.'

But her mother has every reason to speak to her like this, and Lucy understands that she has no option but to win over this James Bell. After what she has done, what has happened, this is the best opportunity available to her – to marry this man, with his plantation in India, far enough away so any errant rumours won't touch him, or her.

He walks into the room, his bearing straight-backed and regal, and Lucy feels rather than sees her mother preen in approval next to her. His cool blue gaze drifts over every woman in the room and when it settles on hers, she smiles bashfully at him.

When his face lights up in appreciation, she looks away, at her mother, who nods discreetly once.

And Lucy damps down the ache in her heart that flares and throbs and sets about winning this man who, in the light of everything that has happened, will have to do.

Chapter 10

Sue

An Ordinary Day

When Sue's life shattered, it didn't do so with a bang. Not the first time, and definitely not the second. It crept up on her, surprised her out of the blue, on an ordinary day.

It was an ordinary day when she came home from school and found her mother crumpled and still at the bottom of the stairs.

It was an ordinary day when she received the phone call about Tony. An ordinary day that preceded extraordinary news, so that every single day after was nowhere near ordinary.

And today is another such day.

Sue stands in the bathroom and rests her cheek against the window.

Birds sing in the garden, the sun shines. But there are clouds lurking, of course. As they always do, ready to rain shadows upon smiling faces enjoying the warm weather, bring grey gloom on sunshiny complexions, wet dry eyes with raindrop tears.

Tony is dead.

And Sue has just found out, standing alone in the bathroom of the house they bought together, with myriad dreams for its future, *their* future, that she is pregnant.

Three weeks since she got the news that stalled her life. And now, a new life on the way.

Soft golden warmth from the spring sun caresses her cheek, pressed against the dirty glass of the window, and Sue recalls that last evening before Tony left for the Middle East, how they had held each other all night, whispering assurances and love-filled declarations, making plans for when he would be back, reiterating endearments that would last them the months apart.

She did not know then that they would have to last her for ever.

She did not know then that a mere fortnight later, she would get a phone call, a male voice, gruff with distress, explaining that there had been an accident. A roadside bomb. Two casualties. One of them Tony.

She knew of course when she married him that there would always be a risk she might lose him like this, too soon. But she dared hope that he might be spared. He was young, he was hers. Her mother had already been taken from her too young. Surely God, or karma – she didn't believe in either – dictated that Tony be spared?

He had crushed her to him, caressed her cheeks, kissing the tears he found there, whispered, 'Write to me. I'll be back sooner than you know.'

A wink. Another kiss.

And then he was gone.

And now... Something of him.

She strokes her stomach.

They had dreamed of having children. A big family. Both of them were only children and had wanted to give their kids the sibling companionship they themselves had been denied.

They had moved into this house, with its two and a half bedrooms, with the money earned from selling Sue's grandmother's house, for just this eventuality.

'One more year, sweetheart, then I'll quit the army. I don't want to be away from home when we start a family. I'll do that garden design and landscaping course I've had my eye on and start my own business. And once it takes off, you can give up journalism and write that book you've always wanted to, while also being the best mum in the world,' Tony had whispered to her that night – his last with her.

Had he thought of her as he was blown up? Of the family they never got to have? Of his unfinished dreams, of the life that was being cut short? Did he know he was going to die? Was he in pain?

That first week she wouldn't accept he was gone. She spent long days and nights pacing the empty house, each room brimming with memories of him: his twinkling eyes, the way he had surprised her in the kitchen that time with a hug and a bunch of flowers from the garden, the laughter in his voice, the dimple in his left cheek that showed up only when he smiled and when he frowned, deep in thought. She couldn't sleep and when her weary eyes closed of their own accord, she saw the jeep blowing up, throwing him into the air, his startled face open in an 'O', calling to her, his desperate eyes, the plea in them. She had written enough articles about the forces abroad – in fact she had written one about accidents in the field – so her imagination supplied everything in vivid detail. The dry powdery dust turning soggy and rust-coloured, blotted by sluggish pools of blood. The children of war, with their naked eyes and concave hungry bodies, gathering to watch. The overturned jeep. The open, bloodshot eyes staring into space.

Please, let him have died instantly, she prayed. *Let him not have known.*

The second week she spent trashing the house, turning it upside down for traces of him. Anything would do. Anything at all.

She found a button from his shirt, and wore it on a string around her neck. The tie he had been looking for, wedged behind the wardrobe. That box of stuff she had lugged there when her grandmother's house sold that she had never got round to sorting – behind the dresser in the study (which they had decided would be the nursery when they started a family). A photo of her that had slipped from Tony's wallet, and that he had spent a whole afternoon hunting for, under the sofa cushion. She was laughing, her head thrown back. So innocent and joyous and young. She had no idea what was coming, none at all.

She searched for something of Tony to cherish, to keep. Some physical evidence of him.

And now she has it. Growing inside of her.

But…

All her life, she has been sure of one thing: that when she starts a family, she will do so with a man who loves her. Unlike her mother, who never knew who Sue's father was.

She wanted a family *with* Tony. How can she do this without him, the love of her life?

Sue waited a long time to find love and when she found it with Tony, it was glorious, perfect. She should have known nothing so wonderful could last for ever. Why didn't she – always so cautious, such a worrier – see this coming?

Not for the first time she wishes her mother was here, or her grandmother even, so she can share with them, talk to them.

Her grandmother, Elizabeth, the high-flying archaeologist whom Sue barely saw in the few years she lived with her before she went off to university… The odd time that her grandmother was in the country, she was giving lectures, attending conferences and being courted by various committees and organisations. Elizabeth was as different from Sue as it was possible to be – absolutely fearless and unafraid to speak her mind. She had been unfazed by the scandal she caused when her daughter, Sue's mother, was born and in fact, according to her daughter, she had courted the infamy, worn it like a badge of honour. The whole time Sue had been living under Elizabeth's roof, she had been in awe of this woman to whom she was related and yet didn't know at all.

Sue's mother, on the other hand...

When her mother was not abusing her body, when she was not out of it on alcohol and who knows what else, she was good company. They had had some good times, Sue and her mum, before she went and died on her.

Now, she wants to talk to her mother or grandmother about Tony, to bring him alive in that way, the vital, vibrant person that he was.

It was with Tony that she was finally able to discuss her mother, express all those feelings she hadn't been able to share before, with anyone. The emotions she'd kept hidden, presenting a calm, reserved front while inside she was in turmoil as she was passed from one foster carer to the next, until her grandmother returned from Egypt and said that of course she would take her. Sue had tried to refuse the counselling that the social workers had offered and when she was made to go, had sat sullen, not talking or scribbling on the sheets of paper they gently placed before her. What did these women know about her life? How could they console her? They could not replace her mother, they could not bring her back.

But with Tony, ensconced in his arms, feeling loved and secure, she found she could finally air her grievances, her love and her sorrow regarding the only parent she had known. It had felt so liberating, so cathartic, to finally allow all the conflicted feelings she harboured for her mother to see the light.

'I am so angry with her. For dying. But not only that – for leaving me long before that. For losing herself in alcohol. For having me and then abandoning me.'

He had held her, his eyes liquid with love and concern.

'She was hurting, you see. She felt she had been unwanted by *her* mother – that she was a hindrance in her mother's life, that her mother preferred her career over her. She was okay while Uncle Mark was alive but she went off the rails completely when he died…'

'Uncle Mark?'

'It's a long story.'

'I want to hear it.'

'Well, my mother was dark-skinned, dark hair and eyes, dusky complexion. My grandmother was pale and blue-eyed, and my grandfather, Sean, was a strapping Irishman, red hair and green eyes – so I'm told, I never met him. He left my grandmother when my mother was born, convinced Elizabeth had cheated on him with Uncle Mark. It caused quite the scandal.'

'I can imagine. So this Uncle Mark was dark-skinned then?'

'Yes. He was Indian. A friend of the family – he had accompanied my great-grandmother back when she returned from India…'

'Your great-grandmother had been in India?'

'My great-grandfather had owned a coffee plantation in India – my grandmother was born there. Apparently Uncle Mark was the only one who could console my grandmother, Elizabeth, when she was upset. They had a very close bond and he was the one who walked her down the aisle at her wedding. It caused quite a stir. But then gossip never fazed Elizabeth, she always maintained Mark was like a brother to her.'

'Was he? Or was she cheating on her husband with him?'

'It seems she laughed when her husband accused her of cheating on him with Mark, insisting that she and Mark were just good friends, never lovers. By all accounts, Sean was a possessive man and was consumed by jealousy and suspicion, unable to even look at my mother, who Elizabeth maintained was his daughter. Elizabeth wanted to be trusted by her husband rather than accused of infidelity, and so, instead of trying to placate him, she let him believe what he wanted. When Sean said he was leaving, Elizabeth said "Fine," and that was that. And to make matters worse, after Sean left her, she asked Mark to move in with her and her daughter.'

'Oh wow! She seems a remarkable woman!'

'She was, but not a great mother.'

'No.'

'Anyway, Mark stepped into the breach created by Sean leaving and Elizabeth travelling all over the world because of her career, and my mum said he was both mother and father to her. Mum wanted Mark to have been her dad. She hoped he was, but she could never get Elizabeth to acknowledge it. Elizabeth maintained that she hadn't cheated on Sean, right up until she died of a heart attack during my second year at uni.'

'Hmmm… Strange.'

'My mother always said that her only parent was Mark. She went to pieces when he died. Completely and spectacularly off the rails. Cut off all ties with her mother and before long, she was pregnant with me.'

'Oh, Sue…'

'This is why I don't drink. After I saw what it did to my mum – the unrecognisable person she turned into when she'd had a few – I hated alcohol, I blamed it. And then when it killed her…'

She shuddered and Tony had held her tighter, gently rubbing her back, his arms, his presence, a balm.

'Although it was me looking after Mum from the very beginning, we had some good times. She loved me, I know this. My grandmother did too, in her way. But then they died.'

Tony had held her as she cried, he had kissed her, comforted her. He had loved her.

She says his name out loud in the hushed stillness of the bathroom. The air shifts briefly, dust motes swirling. It is no match for the vitality that he exuded, the person he was, the way he transformed everyone around him.

She was a different, brighter, lighter person when she was with him. He made her relax, come out of herself. He taught her to be impulsive, to live in the moment. With him, she cast her anxious, worrying self aside. With him, she was a more vivid, less apprehensive version of herself, a girl who could be happy without being fearful.

'You are a mass of contradictions,' he had said in the early days of their relationship. 'You write these hard-hitting articles about war and hurt and the horrible things people do to one another and yet you are afraid of the littlest things. How does this work? How do *you* work? I plan to find out, I want to know you inside out.' All the while holding her so close she could hear two hearts beating, unable to distinguish which beat was whose heart.

'Journalism fascinates me. I have so many questions about my own family and no one to ask. My mother didn't know anything – not even who my father was. And when my grandmother was alive, I couldn't pin her down long enough to ask her anything personal. And anyway, we did not have that kind of relationship. She provided for me materially – I never wanted for anything – but she was never *there*, always either away or just leaving. When

I emailed to tell her I had secured a place at Nottingham Uni to study journalism, she wrote back immediately. "Good for you, Sue," she wrote. "You and I are alike in this way – both of us looking to the past for answers, piecing together lives and histories from clues left behind, the debris of lives lived. You'll be looking in the recent past while I hunt in the distant past. What impelled you to study journalism?" I replied with a question of my own, one of the few I had dared to ask her. It was easier via email. Face to face I wouldn't have dared – I'd have been cowed by her boundless energy, her sharp intellect.'

'What did you ask her?' Tony said.

'I turned the question back on her. "What compelled you to pursue archaeology?" She replied, and I have read it so many times that I know it by heart: "Ha! My own question back at me! You'll make a good journalist! I chose archaeology because I have felt all my life as if something is missing from it. I don't know why I feel this, but I do. And digging through the past, sifting for answers, getting clues as to how our ancestors lived, goes some way to easing that part of me that feels incomplete." And then, at the very end, a couple of sentences that I will always treasure. "Wishing you all the very best with your studies. I am proud of you, Sue." That email is the only personal thing I have of this woman who I admired and looked up to. I've saved it and when I'm down, I read it again and again.' She paused, swallowed. 'Although Elizabeth burrowed for answers in the past, she wasn't a hoarder. In fact, quite the opposite. Her house was like a museum, all archaeological artefacts and valuable antiques, but no photographs, letters or anything personal. The only photos she saved are the ones I found in the attic when I was selling the house and I've brought those with me. My own past is a mystery. I don't know who my father is – my mother maintained she was seeing a few people at the time of my conception. I don't know who my grandfather is, if it is Sean, Mark or someone else.

Hence journalism. Rooting about and finding answers, making sense of something, writing about it – I feel...'

She couldn't put into words what she wanted to say. That while writing articles, she could be someone else, the bland, unbiased person whose name appeared on the byline and not the nervous girl she actually was before Tony, undone, some days, by something as small and necessary and inevitable as opening the door to her house – flashbacks to walking in that day, calling out to her mother and clocking the stillness, the sour-sweet smell overlaid with an iron tang, then seeing her mother...

'When I write about the atrocities happening in the world, I realise how lucky I am, how insignificant my own personal tragedy is in the grand scheme of things.'

'What happened to you, it was huge, Sue. Finding your mother like that when you were barely fifteen, having to look after her all your life before then, cope with her depression and her alcohol abuse. Going to live with your grandmother, practically a stranger, who was never there and left you to fend for yourself... I admire you for what you have made of your life. You are amazing.'

Nobody had said this to her before; nobody had looked at her quite this way. Tony made her feel special. He lifted her – ordinary Sue – far above the ordinary.

She had met him when interviewing soldiers about their experiences. And instead of answering her questions, he had asked his own: 'What are you hiding within the depths of those beautiful eyes?'

He had seen inside her, to her grief and her loneliness and her vulnerability. He had listened to her and ferreted out everything about her.

He had *known* her, the only person in the world to do so.

On their third date, he took her to the beach. It was a cold, squally day, gulls squealing and whirling and trying to steal their chips. The wind whipping her hair across her face, into her mouth. The oily tang of vinegar and salt and deep-fried batter.

Two boys messed about in the freezing water, shouting instructions to their parents, who were trying to build a sandcastle to their detailed and elaborate specifications.

'Making you work for your dinner, are they?' Tony laughed as he and Sue walked past.

The dad had winked at Tony, waving a plastic spade, saying: 'This will be you in a few years.'

Sue had laughed.

But Tony... He turned to Sue and the next minute he was on his knees on the sand, pebbles digging into his legs, waves lapping at their feet.

'Marry me,' he said.

The parents stopped digging the moat around the sandcastle, and even the two little boys stopped splashing each other and arguing about whether they wanted shells or pebbles on the sandcastle turrets and turned to watch.

'We hardly know each other,' she had said, even though her heart was saying yes.

'I know I love you,' he had said. 'I know I don't want to live another day without you.'

'Yes,' she said, just as a huge wave came and splashed them both and she did not even notice or care and he kissed her, salt and ice and foamy spray, and the family cheered, sandcastle forgotten.

'I will protect you and make sure you are never hurt again,' he had whispered in her ear then, as the tide advanced and they were surrounded by water, their jeans soaked, the waves buffeting them, and it was as if they were floating and yet she had never felt more moored in her life.

'I will not abandon you,' he had promised.

And yet, a few weeks after their wedding, he went away as she had known he would. He had to; it was his job.

'I'll come back,' he vowed.

She went to bed with his shirt in her arms. She waited, counting down the moments, her writing frenzied and passionate while she longed for him to come home.

And he did come home that time. And the time after. He kept on coming home, keeping the promise he had made to her, and so she stopped guarding her heart, fearing the worst. She became hopeful, she who should have known better than anybody else that hope is a shallow friend, a good-time fellow. She who should have known that you can come home from school one day and find your mother dead, your life turned upside down.

Subconsciously, she'd thought that by losing him for a few months at a time, she was paying her dues to the universe or karma or the great person up there, that this was insurance against losing him for ever. Her reasoning had been flawed through and through, she sees that now. He could be taken at any time, and he would be. In just a few short years.

Not enough time. Not nearly enough.

She can't cope.

How will she give this child what it needs? She has no family, no support network, no friends.

When her mother was alive, she couldn't bring anyone home, never knowing what state she would be in – not that she had any friends or the time to make them. Sue was bullied for her dirty clothes, her bedraggled appearance. She would always run straight home from school, in order to look after her mother.

After her mother's death, the same children who had bullied her tried to reach out to her, the girl who found her mother dead when she came home from school. But she hated her notoriety and she didn't want friends who wanted to be with her so they could pick the bones of her mother and her relationship with her.

'Is it true that she was drunk?' they would whisper as she walked past and she ignored them, set herself apart, kept her head down, worked.

She was glad when her grandmother said she could take her in and she had to move school.

In the new school, she kept herself to herself, not wanting to have to explain who she was, her past. And after a while it became hard to make friends, to talk normally with people, to be like the other giggly girls, who went out for drinks, hung out with boys.

Her job had suited her. Deadlines, working from home… It was perfect. Even when she had to interview people she could lob questions from behind a professional veneer, jot down answers, write sympathetic and yet forthright articles.

It was relationships, simple friendships, affection that she couldn't do. Or so she thought.

Tony taught her different.

She had thought a husband and children were not for her, although she secretly wanted both. Tony showed her it was possible; he taught her to love.

And now he is gone. And she is undone. Lost. Untethered. Drifting. Falling apart.

Pregnant.

Is it right to bring a child into the world when she is so unmoored by grief that sometimes she cannot even dress herself?

A butterfly, the yellow of unfurling spring buds, alights on the windowsill just where Sue's head is resting, on the other side of the pane, soft wings fluttering like a child's heartbeat.

He used to call her his butterfly.

She hears Tony's voice, vibrant and alive in her ear. 'You are the strongest woman I know. You will get through this like you have everything else, my love. My beautiful butterfly.'

As if it has delivered its message, the butterfly flaps its gossamer wings – the glorious gold of miracles – and flies away.

Chapter 11

Lucy

Warning Glint

The ballroom is crowded – sweaty, heated bodies, the smell of vanilla and bergamot, enjoyment and anticipation, the low hum of chatter and the eager susurration of gossip, flirty ladies and matchmaking matrons, the tingle of music, the tapping of shoes and the rustle of gowns.

Lucy dances with James and allows her gaze to drift over the throng.

Mother is at the far end, exchanging tips and confidences with other mothers, all engaged in the all-consuming task of arranging a good match for their daughters in such a way so as to appear that it was all their daughters' choice.

Every so often she catches Lucy's eye and smiles, a warning glint in her gaze.

'He hasn't left your side since he first set eyes on you at that recital. He's made sure to attend every social event that you've been at,' Mother had said the previous evening at supper.

She did not need to qualify the 'he' with a name. They all knew who she was talking about.

'You are a catch and he knows it. Not only the most beautiful debutante but also the one with the most dowry, a fortune to your name that will chase away any lingering smear of scandal.'

There had been talk and speculation when Lucy had missed out on most of the season – which still upset her mother no end – although the details of what she had done never became public, thanks to her mother's gargantuan efforts at limiting the damage Lucy had wrought on all of them.

It was only as her mother spoke that it occurred to Lucy, with a start, that just as she had heard of James long before she met him, he must have heard of her. Just as she was interested in him only because of what he could offer her – the chance to start anew in a place far away from here, untainted by disgrace – so perhaps he was interested in her only for what she could offer him: her family pedigree and a hefty fortune. Perhaps he had made a beeline for her the first time he saw her that day at the recital because he recognised her from what he'd heard of her, not because of her beauty.

'He'll most likely propose tomorrow at the ball.' Mother had set down her cutlery, jutting out her chin in that way she had when she expected to be challenged. 'And you will say yes.'

Father had paused in his perusal of the tumbler of brandy he was nursing, and looked at Lucy over the top of his glasses.

A pregnant pause as they both waited for Lucy to respond. She had stared at her plate, the tendrils of soggy pastry, the congealing gravy, the soiled knife glinting silvery brown.

'Lucy?'

She had cleared her throat. 'I should tell him—'

'You will do no such thing,' Mother had said, her voice rising. 'You have brought disgrace upon us and upon yourself, which, thankfully, we have managed to keep under wraps so far.'

'But surely, if I am to marry James—'

'There are secrets in every marriage,' Mother had said, swirling the liquid in her glass, not looking at her or at Father. 'And this is one secret you will have to keep if you are to stay married – or, indeed, get married at all.'

'But Mother—'

'He is from a good family and the owner of a plantation. You will marry him and be a good and dutiful wife to him.'

Father picked up his tumbler and downed his brandy.

And that was that. End of discussion.

Lucy wrote to her friend that evening. *You'll not recognise the person I have become, Ann. The girl I used to be, that brash, devil-may-care, confident, cossetted girl, the apple of her parents' eye, is no more. That girl would have rebelled, created a scene. Instead I sit here, meek and accepting of Mother and Father's decrees – for there is truth in them. After what I have done, what I've subjected all of us to, this is the least I can do.*

Ann, I tell myself I am doing it for them, but in truth, I am doing it for me too. Even if Mother and Father had urged me to be open with James, to confess what I have done, I don't think I could. I'm too mortified, too upset to bring it up.

Now, dancing in James's arms, being the recipient of his solicitous attention, Lucy feels shame burning inside. He deserves to know that she is not who he thinks she is, that beneath the beautiful exterior she is but a shell. He deserves to know the whole truth.

But she will not tell him.

Not too long ago she was a selfish girl, spoilt and immature, aware of her own charm and with a long line of admirers to reinforce it for her, which is what had got her into the mess she is in now. And the woman she has become in that wilful girl's place, a woman who lies, keeps secrets, hides truths – Lucy doesn't much like her either.

But, she thinks, as she meets her mother's cautioning gaze, what choice does she have? If she is to have a life at all, then she has to do this.

'Would you like a drink?' James asks when the dance comes to an end.

'Shall we step outside for a bit?' she says, wanting to escape her mother's piercing eyes, wanting to be rid of the unspoken messages she has been sending her, if only for a short while.

'It's cold.'

'I don't mind.'

They stand on the balcony and look out at the dark garden, full of shadows. The trees broody silhouettes, the sky a moody grey, not a star in sight.

The wind that strokes her face is chilly, carrying a hint of ice and the taste of night: frosted blue. Snatches of music and laughter waft from indoors.

James clears his throat.

Ah, she thinks, *here it comes.* She is grateful they are alone, that her mother is not watching this tableau, although she has, in part, orchestrated it.

'Marrying James will go some way towards righting the wrong you've done us and especially yourself,' Mother had said that afternoon as they were getting ready to come here.

But what about the wrong I am doing by marrying him without being completely honest? Lucy had thought, but she had enough sense not to say it out loud.

Lucy's very first impression of James had been that he was a quiet man, content to be silent rather than rush to fill a pause. It was restful after everything that had happened in her life, and subsequent meetings – during which he had, time and again, paid court only to her, leaving her in no doubt of his intentions – had confirmed that first impression, ironed it into fact.

'Lucy,' James says, 'will you do me the honour of becoming my wife?'

She is aware of cold air on her hot face, the press of scorching tears behind icy lids. She knows what she must say. And yet, the word catches, sticking in the salty lump in her throat, leaving a navy, bitter tang.

A face rises before her eyes, beloved, longed for. With great effort of will, she pushes it away.

Ann comes to mind instead, her plain face beautiful as she spoke of love – 'I knew when I saw him that he was the man I would marry.' Ann, happily married, still glowing.

I always thought it would be you, Ann, who would have to settle for a loveless marriage of convenience. How selfish I was, how spoilt and inconsiderate and arrogant! I thought I would have fun with my long line of suitors, pit them against one another, lead them along, and then drop them when I found my one true love.

I didn't know then that love doesn't choose or discriminate, that love has no barriers, that it can happen in an instant and humble you, level you out, that it is glorious and exultant, and that it can rip your heart to shreds, that it can hurt worse than anything you have ever experienced.

'Lucy?'

For a brief moment Lucy's earlier feisty spirit, which has been largely squeezed out of her by everything that has happened, makes an appearance and she wants to refuse just to thwart Mother and Father, who so badly want this.

She looks up at this man, quiet and correct and proper – her parents' idea of a perfect match – so different from—

No, don't go there.

He is waiting. If she is going to tell him the truth about herself, it should be now.

She knows this rigid, stiff man who wears his propriety like armour will not marry her if he knows the truth about her.

She can't do this to her parents, who adored her, cossetted her, denied her nothing, who have been beaten by what she has done, devastated and wrung out and upset.

She has wounded them enough.

And she can't do it to herself. Especially after what she has sacrificed, the horrible things she has done, to arrive at this point.

Hasn't she done it all for this?

Her parents want the best for her and what this man is offering is the best choice she has in the circumstances…

'Yes,' she says, pushing the word out through a tongue that is engorged and swollen and reluctant to do her bidding.

He bends down to kiss her and when his lips touch hers, she shuts her eyes tight against the tears that threaten to spill, the taste of another man's kiss in her mouth.

Chapter 12

Gowri

Two Kinds of Women

Goddess,

After months of preparation, the matriculation exams are almost upon us.

'You're ready,' Vandana Ma'am tells me, every time she visits. 'You'll do very well in the exams and we'll get you out of here.' She smiles fondly at me. There is a gleam in her eyes – it has taken me a long time to understand, and even longer to acknowledge, that it is pride. She is proud of *me*.

'Why are you surprised?' she asks, cupping my face in her palms as only she does, something I never take for granted, no matter how many times she does it, as it is an expression of her love, with nothing expected of me in return. A love so precious and rare, even more so as it is freely, selflessly given. 'Gowri, don't sell yourself short. Don't let this place get you down. Don't let it eat away at your self-esteem and self-worth. Don't let it destroy who you are inside.' She says, her voice fierce. 'Promise me.'

'I promise,' I whisper.

'We will get you out of here.'

I wish I shared her conviction, her unwavering belief. I shudder as a sudden picture of the landlord's hands on my sister's slender, beautiful, untouched body comes to mind.

'Gowri!' Vandana Ma'am says, eyes flashing. 'Don't you dare stop believing in—' Her words are swallowed by a long painful gasp. She bends over, gripping her stomach.

I clasp her, terrified. 'What is it?'

She waves my concern away, mouthing something although no words come. She is in desperate pain, I can see, from the wildness in her eyes, her huge pupils, even as she tries on a smile that ends in a grimace.

I sit her down, and wipe her wan face with my sari pallu, my heart thudding against my ribcage.

Please, I pray.

I am not sure whom I am speaking to. I don't know if I am calling upon you, Goddess. From the time I was dedicated to you, although I have danced for you and served you and the priest in lieu of you, although I have cleaned the temple and adorned you with flowers, although I believe in you, I haven't prayed to you, not really. I haven't been able to.

But now... Now I wish I could pray to you, Goddess, like everyone else seems to.

I want Vandana Ma'am. I *need* her. She is the only good thing in my life at the moment.

I love her.

I fill a tumbler with the water I keep in the earthen pot so it is cool in the summer and feed it to her. She sips it, slowly, between painful gasps.

I loathe seeing her like this. It terrifies me.

I have noticed that she is more and more tired every time she visits me. The short walk from the village to my cottage seems to wipe her out. I have tried ignoring it, blaming it on my watchful, cautious imagination concocting problems. But now how I wish it *was* just my imagination...

I pull out the mat and ask her to lie down. I lay cool cloths on her forehead as her noisy breathing settles and she eases, slowly, into sleep, the cat coming up to her and lying beside her, effortlessly offering comfort.

I wish I could do the same. Show my love for this woman, claim her, as the cat does with casual abandon.

But I can't – I don't have the right. She gives me some time each week, but she is not mine.

I sit beside her as the afternoon fades to evening, as the shadows get longer, the sun travelling languidly over the horizon, leaving honey-coloured, sweaty trails in its wake.

I do none of my usual chores. As the shadows deepen, the panic of losing her is replaced by the dread of the landlord arriving and finding her. He never tells me when he is going to turn up. He likes to surprise me – it's his way of checking up on me.

I haven't cooked for him. He likes to eat after he's been with me, usually expecting me to have prepared a meal for him although he did not inform me he was going to visit.

I stand up, hide my books away. I quickly cobble together some semolina pudding, adding raisins and sugar syrup. It is quick and easy to make and he loves it. I grate carrots and make halwa. When the halwa is cooling, I sense movement behind me.

'Smells wonderful, what is it?'

'Carrot halwa. Would you like some?'

'What is the time, child?'

'Late.'

'I'd better get going then.' Her eyes, ringed with tiredness and soft with sleep, meeting mine. The knowledge in them tinted with sadness and liquid with love for me. Vandana Ma'am, *my* Vandana Ma'am. She is the only one who will meet my eyes, acknowledging what goes on and sympathising with me. The colour has returned to her cheeks. She rolls up the mat, sets it aside. 'My parents will be worried.'

Please don't leave me, I think, even though I know the landlord's arrival is imminent. It has been so very nice to have her stay into the evening, even though it has been tempered by my fear and worry for her, even though she has been ill. I briefly entertain a fantasy where she stays with me and I care for her, she teaching me in the mornings, us pottering about in the afternoons. But… there is the landlord. There is my status as a devadasi. There are her old and ailing parents.

'You've put the books away?' she asks, knowing without my ever having told her that I am keeping her and my studies a secret from the landlord.

'Yes.'

I pack some carrot halwa and semolina pudding into a tiffin box for her.

'Has it been happening long?' I ask casually as I pack, my face turned away from hers, busying myself with the food as if it is nothing at all, as if we are having a conversation about the weather, the possibility of rain.

'I… I've been experiencing some pain in my stomach, yes.'

Some pain… She's the master of understatement.

'Have you seen the doctor?'

'N… Not really. I thought it would go away.'

How can this smart, fiercely intelligent woman be so naïve in this regard?

What I saw her endure today is no ordinary pain, it is not going to go away.

I sigh around the lump that has been sitting in my throat all afternoon, the terror that has bloomed in my stomach, mirroring the pain in hers. I turn to her, press the tiffin box into her hands. 'Please,' I say, looking into her eyes, shadowed with exhaustion. 'You have to see a doctor.'

She hesitates. 'I…'

She's afraid of what she will find; I am too.

'You need to get this checked out.' I want to offer to go with her, but I can't do her this simple courtesy, this woman who has done so much for me. I wish, for the umpteenth time, that things were different, simpler. That I could show my affection for this woman without who I am getting in the way. Return, in a small way, the countless favours she has done for me.

Outside the shadows are edging closer. The sky has gone from dark pink to the grey of a sickly complexion. In the jungle, the nocturnal animals stir and the birds call as they fly home for the evening, fan-shaped shadows, the trees having morphed into waving silhouettes.

She pulls me in for a hug. 'Thank you for today.' She smells of stale sweat and fear.

'Please get it checked,' I repeat.

She nods without quite meeting my eyes. Then, clutching the tiffin box to her, she slips away into the gathering darkness and I stand at the doorway and watch as her slight figure recedes down the path, the red mud now dusky black, and is swallowed up by the shadows.

Afterwards, I tidy the house, quickly sweeping away all traces of Vandana Ma'am. I wear the sari that the landlord recently got for me, his current favourite, and on my face a big smile, hoping to distract the landlord from any suggestion of an alien presence that I might have missed but he will pick up on, and I wait.

Goddess, since I became a devadasi I have learned that there are two kinds of women: one like my mother – passive, meek, allowing fate to walk slipshod over them, sacrificing their daughters in the name of religion and closing their eyes to what is really happening to them. And one (this type, very few and far between) like Vandana Ma'am: brave, feisty, believing and fighting for what is right.

Which kind are you?

I am inclined to think the first kind as it is because of you that I am here in the first place. But I hope that you are like Vandana Ma'am, really, that you are biding your time and will one day (soon) rescue me from my fate, now that you know what really goes on in your name.

After I wrote my first few letters to you, I slipped them underneath your shrine while decking you with flower garlands, and I waited for you to save me. To release me from my bind to you.

I took the letters back, tucking them into my sari skirt, when there was a puja in your name and you had to be washed in milk. I could not risk someone else finding them.

I kept the letters with me and I hoped.

I waited for you to act.

I waited for two years, until, on my sixteenth birthday, I wrote to you to remind you that I'm still here. Still waiting.

And now, after what happened to Vandana Ma'am, after seeing the vulnerable side to this strong woman, I am scared. Terrified for her and for me.

And so I am writing to you again, Goddess, hoping you'll act now.

Am I crazy to wish that you are the second type of woman, Goddess, the one who fights for what is right?

Show me I'm not, Goddess, go on.

Chapter 13

Lucy

A New Life

When she returns to the ballroom on James's arm, her mother is watching, her eyes anxious. In that instant, seeing the furrows on her mother's forehead that her rouge cannot hide, the lines that Lucy's actions have wrought evident upon her mother's apprehensive visage, every pang of consternation Lucy has been feeling eases, along with the fluster of indecision in her stomach. The conviction burning inside of her – that she is compounding her mistakes by marrying a man she does not love and to whom she has lied through omission – is doused, at least for the moment, and she smiles at her mother.

When her mother smiles back, a genuine smile at last, Lucy feels a rush of tenderness towards her, realising that their roles have been reversed, that she is now protecting and reassuring her mother instead of the other way round. She understands that this is how it is going to be from now on, that this is what it means to be an adult – making compromises to shelter and nurture the people you love. *A bit late now to start sheltering and nurturing, isn't it*, Lucy's conscience pipes up, *when you have overturned their lives and those of others? Whatever you do now to patch things up isn't enough. It will never be enough…*

* * *

After that, events occur at alarming speed – the selecting of designs and stitching of gowns for the wedding and the reception after, the shopping for a wedding trousseau, deciding upon the menu; all the small and big details involved in the planning and execution of a wedding. And before she knows it, Lucy is a married woman.

Mrs Bell.

In the eyes of everyone around her, she has made a good match, as befitting the only daughter of parents who are reputable pillars of society.

But… she has paid such a high price for this. Done things she never imagined she would. Found out things about herself and what she is capable of that she would rather not have known…

As she smiles at the assembled guests and poses beside her husband – her *husband*! – she is aware of admiring and envious gazes and her parents' relieved approbation. Despite everything that has happened, she has landed on her feet, married to a respectable man and soon to begin a new life in India.

India – a place she has never imagined she would visit, despite her assertions to Ann, growing up, that she would travel the world.

India – far enough away perhaps to put what happened behind her and to begin again as best she can. She quashes the voice inside her head that yells: *If you think you can put what happened behind you, you are a fool. But then, you are that anyway, otherwise you wouldn't be here.*

India – so very far away from her loved ones. Ann. Her parents: Father, who had once loved Lucy so fiercely and had just as fiercely renounced her when everything imploded. Mother, who had insisted that she— *Oh…*

She can't bear to think about it.

Just as much as Mother and Father had loved her once, now they want Lucy gone. She had hoped Father would be upset that she would have to go far away, but he seemed to agree with Mother when she said, 'It is for the best that you'll be moving to India. No chance of anyone dredging up anything untoward…'

Chapter 14

Gowri

The One Good Thing

Goddess Yellamma,

It is that time of year – the festival to celebrate you. The landlord has arranged for a grand puja, to which he has invited the whole village. I am to dance at it, alongside the other devadasis.

'I don't want to attend, Gowri, see you and the others being gawped at. But my parents are very religious, as you know, and don't want to miss the puja,' Vandana Ma'am says when she comes for her usual weekly visit. She looks after her parents, they live with her. She tends to them and puts up with their vocal disapproval at what, she has told me, they see as her failings: her never having married and given them a son-in-law and grandchildren.

She hasn't mentioned the episode she suffered and neither have I. I understand that she wants to put it behind her, pretend nothing happened.

But... I know it's not nothing. I can see it in the way she holds herself, the way she moves. She is in constant pain, and she is finding it harder to camouflage it. The formidable Vandana Ma'am is shrinking before my eyes. Becoming a shadow of herself.

'It's this relentless, unseasonal heat,' she murmurs when she gasps mid-lesson and has to sit down and gather breath. 'It tires me out.'

I nod, reading the plea in her eyes and going along with the fiction.

But when I am saying goodbye, I'm unable to stop myself. 'Go to the doctor. Please.'

I need you.

'I will,' she reassures me, not meeting my gaze. 'But now, the important thing is getting you to do your very best in the exams in April. So, revise hard – we need to get you out of here, Gowri.'

We. My heart expands as ever when she says that word.

The important thing is getting you healthy again. Your hopes sustain me, Vandana Ma'am. Please get better.

She must note the entreaty in my eyes for she says, 'Let's make a deal. You learn those equations and formulae for next week and I will see the doctor.'

I smile, but I am terrified. What will the doctor say?

I stand by the washing stone and I wave until she disappears round the bend. The late afternoon sky is cloudless and resplendent. The mud road beside the cottage exudes a heavy, baked smell. Her steps are measured, as heavy as my heart, which is telling me something is very wrong.

Goddess, I don't pray to you, although I clean your shrine and adorn you with fresh flowers, although I sweep the temple that houses you and feed the priest who worships you.

Should I pray to you? Prostrate myself before your smiling face and sing your praises like the other devadasis do? Is that what you want?

But from what I can see their lives are not any better. They too are used by men in your name, while their families prosper from the money they make. They drag little children in their wake, conceived from fathers who will never claim them, little girls who are destined, when the time comes, for the same fate as their mothers.

Whatever the case, Goddess, I am praying to you now for I am desperate.

Please don't take Vandana Ma'am from me.

She is the one good thing in my life.

Please.

On the day of the puja, I keep a smile fixed on my face and wear the sari the landlord has gifted me, decking myself in the neem leaf necklace, the gold and saffron bangles he has insisted that I wear.

And then, in front of you, Goddess, and the assembled villagers, leering men and their wives, faces covered by sari pallus from behind which they judge me, I dance, along with the other devadasis, as the priest performs the puja, breathing in the bhajan-steeped aroma of incense, my mouth bitter with the taste of mortification. We devadasis dance and the landlord sits right in front, with his wife and his daughters, while his mistresses, decked out in the clothes he has bought for them, perform for him.

As we come to the end of the dance, I see Vandana Ma'am at the back of the crowd, one arm around each of her frail parents. Of the three she looks the most washed-out and pale, as if she is the one who needs bolstering, not them.

She holds my gaze and lifts her head up and pushes her shoulders back. And I do the same, holding my head up high as I dance, trying to let go of the shame that no matter how many times I do this never quite leaves me.

You have nothing to be ashamed of. You have had no say in what happened to you. If anyone should be ashamed, it should be the landlord and your parents, is what she is transmitting via her gaze, I know.

It is a mantra she has chanted countless times. *And in any case, you won't be doing this for much longer, Gowri.*

I clock the exact moment when she faints. Her face loses what little colour it has and she sways like a sapling in a storm-bolstered squall and collapses in a crumpled heap, like a sari dropping off a tired body after a long day. I lose my step, tripping up the girls next to me as around Vandana Ma'am people scream and shout instructions: 'Get water!' 'A wet cloth!' and her mother wails while her father looks set to faint himself.

I want to run to her, tend to her, nurse her back into good health.

But I can't.

Colour rises up the landlord's neck as he turns around to see what all the commotion is about.

I look at you, heavily garlanded and smiling beatifically.

Why are you doing this? Is it because she is helping me to escape? Are you that vengeful, Goddess? That possessive?

Please.

My family have moved to the city, I have as good as lost them.

I can't lose Vandana Ma'am. I cannot.

Please, Goddess.

Then I hear her voice, feeble but strident, carrying over the crowd's panic. 'I'm fine, help me up. Why all this fuss?'

Weak with relief, I dance. I dance with vigour and without shame – I dance like I never have before.

The puja is over finally, and in the crush of people coming towards you, Goddess, to lay their prayers and offerings at your feet and partake of the prasadam laddoos, I lose sight of Vandana Ma'am.

I want to go to the cottage, shut the door on the world and do my revision, the only way I can think of to honour Vandana

Ma'am. What I really wish to do is care for her, attend to her, but since I cannot, I will study. All those hours she has invested in teaching me must not be in vain. I will do very well in the exams, so that her belief in me is realised. She wants me to escape and I will – for her, and also for me.

But the landlord says, 'Wait,' and once the temple and courtyard have emptied of devotees, Vandana Ma'am and her parents among them, he pushes aside the stone that conceals the trapdoor to the basement and goes down to the temple vault.

Nobody, besides the landlord, has been down there, not even the priest. Only the landlord has the key to the vault, which he wears on a chain around his neck.

'I keep all my most precious valuables in the vault,' he has boasted to me. 'Nobody dares steal from the goddess.'

Today, on the day of your festival, he is thanking you with gifts of gold and money for visiting good fortune upon him, as he has done at every puja since you were found, Goddess.

His wife and daughters wait as well, toes scuffing the dirt outside the temple steps, not looking at me. The sky is the colour of embarrassment, the air tight with unsaid words, held in accusations, hurt and upset. Across the road, monkeys chatter from among the trees, ready to pounce on any prasadam left untended, eyeing the landlord's wife and daughters, the glittering gold on display.

The landlord's daughters whisper among themselves, casting sidelong glances at me, their bangles jingling as they push their hair, dislodged by the wind, zesty green and fresh, behind their ears.

The older daughter catches my eye, her gaze disdainful, haughty, making me feel like an ant that dares cross her path. I suppose she is justified. And yet, I will not be made to feel as if I am in the wrong, when it is her father who is.

I stare at her, making my gaze just as contemptuous, until she looks away. She is the same age as me, and I scrutinise her carefully, even after she looks away. She is taller than me and is wearing a bright green sari that does nothing for her dusky complexion. Her skin is pockmarked, her eyes a bit too close together.

'I am searching for a groom for her, but no matter how much dowry I offer, no one is willing to come forward. Not as pretty as you, see,' the landlord, drunk on cashew feni, has opined, while reclining on the bed he bought for me, for us.

When he is not there, I sleep on a mat on the floor, loath to lie on sheets that recall the landlord, no matter how many times I wash them.

He comes out of the vault looking smug and satisfied. 'That's the goddess taken care of. After this she will be showering me with more blessings. I might even get you married,' he says, nodding towards his eldest daughter.

She blushes and looks down at the ground, where she has scratched a trail; her shiny sandals now a dirty red, polished toes sporting an additional coat of dust.

Despite everything, I feel sorry for her.

'I'll see you tomorrow,' the landlord calls to me, as he ushers his wife and daughters into the waiting car, the chauffeur hiding his smirk behind a deferential bow as he opens the door for his employer and his entourage.

Relieved to be given this reprieve, I close the door to my cottage, change out of my finery and settle down with my books.

Goddess, until now I have not really believed it possible to escape who I am, this bind I am in.

I have allowed Vandana Ma'am to dream for me and when she dangles the likelihood of colleges offering scholarships if I do well in the exams – paying me to do what I love, can you imagine! – a small part of my brain has been carried away while the bigger, saner part has detailed all the reasons why I cannot entertain that possibility.

But now I go through all my objections rationally. The one big reason holding me back is the landlord and what he will do to my sister, whether he would ask for her to be dedicated to you and tied to him as recompense for losing me. But what if when I left here, (*when I left here!*) I took my sister with me? I don't know how it would work, *if* it would work, but it is a plan.

And the second reason: You, Goddess.

This objection I don't know how to counter as I don't know you.

I sometimes think, as I place sweet-smelling incense sticks by you and adorn you with flower wreaths that I have weaved, that you didn't want any of this, that you didn't ask for it – that this is men interpreting what you want in order to satisfy their lustful desires.

Hence my letters.

These letters are my prayer to you and my plea.

Are you there, Goddess? Are you reading this? Are you listening to me?

I am afraid to dismiss you like Vandana Ma'am does.

I will be honest with you here, Goddess, as I have been all along during the course of our conversations – or, rather, my one-sided correspondence with you. The rational part of me, the scholar, does not quite believe in you, even as I write letters to you. But the other, frightened and lonely, lost-child part of who I am is afraid not to. On balance, I would rather go with the part of me that believes you do exist, rather than spurning you and being proved wrong.

I am promised to you for life. If I don't keep that promise, if I seek a different life, will you mind? Or will you turn your wrath on me? You have determined the course of my life. You saved my brother but stood by while I was sold to the landlord in your name.

Do you love me or loathe me?

Are you an ally or an enemy?

You are a woman. You were a mother once, I gather.

And yet, I cannot read you. I don't know what you are capable of.

And this terrifies me, even as I dare to hope.

Chapter 15

Kavya

No Stranger to Controversy

Kavya puts the phone down after the stressful conversation with her mother, feeling relieved and undone.

She looks around her small flat, this space that has been hers and only hers all these years, representing the independence she has fought so hard to achieve.

She is going back home, with nothing to show for all the time she's spent here.

All it took was one mistake, one false move, listening to the impractical, destructive, siren call of her heart over the sensible directive of her mind, for her world to come crashing down.

It's not all bad. Look at the positives – no more working at the café for one.

The café…

It was there that she first met Nagesh. The whole reason for working at that particular café was because it was rumoured that top Bollywood directors and producers frequented it. All the waiters and waitresses on the café's books were aspiring actors and screenwriters.

Kavya had been in Mumbai two years, taking acting classes and attending every audition religiously, and had garnered all of two roles, both as a non-speaking extra, one of which did not even make the final cut, when she found out about the café.

She had been queueing up for another audition (4.00 p.m. sharp, the director had said and she had been queueing since two and was maybe the hundred and fiftieth in line; it was now 6.00 p.m. and no sign of the director yet, although the queue had quadrupled in size) when she overheard the conversation – two men behind her nattering to pass the time – that would change her life.

'Arre, this industry is not for the likes of us. You need to know the right people to get somewhere in this business. The only thing that works, gets speaking roles, is recommendations.'

'So why are you here then?'

'What else to do, bhai? I don't know anyone who can put in a word for me. I tried getting work at that café, Sunrise, over on Marine Drive. You know all the directors go there, don't you?'

'Is that so?'

'Ah, don't look so hopeful! It is harder to get work there than it is to find gold in the sand or indeed, to land speaking roles by auditioning like this.'

Kavya had walked away from the audition queue right then, the line inching forward to fill her place – she had heard enough. But she soon discovered that the man she overheard had been right – Sunrise was one of the most sought-after cafés to work at in Mumbai. It took Kavya another year to finally start working there (the girl she replaced having obtained a role in a TV serial – through connections made at the café). Kavya got the job through the recommendation of a friend (after she had bribed her every day for a month with treats from Hazmat Bakery) of a friend (whose friendship she cultivated for this very reason).

Kavya had been at Sunrise a couple of months when Nagesh walked in.

'I hope he sits at one of my tables,' Shailaja, aspiring actress and co-worker, had whispered, nudging Kavya. 'He's one of the best directors in Bollywood. All the movies he directs become hits.'

Kavya had looked askance at the small, unassuming man, bespectacled and grey-haired, his clothes slightly crumpled, an air of absent-mindedness about him, and wondered if Shailaja was pulling her leg.

'I'm not, ask anyone,' she insisted, as if anticipating Kavya's disbelief.

As it happened, Nagesh sat at one of the tables assigned to Kavya, and Shailaja huffed in disappointment.

Nagesh had barely glanced at the menu, pulling out his phone and proceeding to read something on it as soon as he sat down. Kavya had walked over and waited for a minute or two, but he was completely absorbed in what he was reading, his concentration absolute. She inched closer to him, peered over his shoulder.

'It's a script idea about a boy adopted from the slums by a couple in America, who discovers that he is, in fact, the illegitimate son of a prince,' Nagesh said, holding out his phone to her, and Kavya jumped, her face aflame at being caught out. 'What do you think? Good idea?'

He had looked up at her, genuinely courting her opinion, and, pinned by his intelligent, intense gaze, she faltered for a moment or two before recovering, finding her voice. 'I think it might work, yes. Everyone loves a good rags-to-riches story.'

He had smiled, his face creasing, dimples dancing in his cheeks, and she revised her opinion of him. He wasn't unassuming at all; he was handsome in a man-next-door kind of way.

'That's what I thought.' He'd looked at her keenly, that forceful gaze. 'Am I right in assuming you are a wannabe actress?'

'Yes.' Was this it? Could it be?

'So… would you like to audition for the role of the lead's girlfriend? You have the look I am after.'

She had nodded – coolly, she hoped, trying to keep her eagerness from showing on her face.

'Come to NJ Studios tomorrow at four. Ask for me. Here…' He had handed her his card.

She had walked back, speechless, and Shailaja had looked only slightly miffed before throwing her arms around her. 'You've made it, you lucky girl! Can I come too?'

Kavya bites her tongue, tastes the coppery tang of blood.

Her life has not gone the way she planned.

This was not what she envisioned for herself when she fought with her parents and moved to Mumbai to pursue a career in acting. She had blithely assumed that, by the time she was twenty-five, she would a) have a starring role in a film and b) have found the love of her life. Instead, she is almost twenty-eight and bankrupt, barely eking out a living by working shifts at the café, and thirty – the number she has always associated with security, with knowing exactly where one is headed, and with success – seems just around the corner.

Soon she will be back home, scrounging off her parents, her dream of gracing the big screen put to bed, trying to tune out her mother's incessant nagging while she decides what to do with her life. She is grateful her parents and Ajji haven't visited her here (they don't like Mumbai, declare it too noisy and crowded for them) so they don't know about her dire financial situation and her even direr personal one…

* * *

She went for the audition. Like a magic mantra she invoked Nagesh's name and was allowed to skip the queue, to the consternation of all the other wannabes.

She did not get the part of the hero's girl but she did get one of the smaller – speaking – roles, a career jump in the right direction. And to top it all, Nagesh asked her to stay behind, and after the audition he took her to an exclusive club, where she met some of the top names in Bollywood. She drank cocktails, each of which cost more than a month's worth of rent, and by the end of that intoxicating evening, she fancied herself in love.

Kavya can feel a headache coming on. She switches on the television, needing a respite from her thoughts, channel surfing until she comes to the news. She waits, wondering if there will be anything about the temple, the deeds to which her mum claims her ajji has.

Her patience is finally rewarded by the newscaster announcing, 'And the controversy surrounding the newly discovered temple at Doddanahalli, a hitherto unremarkable village in Karnataka, continues, with devotees campaigning to be allowed in to worship and others protesting against it as the temple deity is the Goddess Yellamma, who is no stranger to controversy herself. Every year, young girls are dedicated to the service of this goddess, despite the practice being illegal as these girls end up becoming prostitutes. It remains to be determined whether the temple is private or public and, most importantly, who owns the land housing the temple and the little cottage next to it – one of the more intriguing claims being that it belongs to a devadasi. Devadasis have been congregating from all over Karnataka to worship at the temple, several claiming that the land belongs to them. We will now hand you over to our reporter at Doddanahalli.'

The camera zooms in on Doddanahalli and Kavya blinks, for it is almost unrecognisable as the sleepy village they drive past on the way to the coffee plantation resort hotel. The hotel itself and the plantation, Kavya knows, had belonged to an Englishman back during the British Raj. There are photos of him and his wife, she recalls, in the dining hall and on the veranda of the resort hotel. A handsome couple. There are also plenty of photographs of local people from the times of the Raj adorning the walls.

Now, as the camera pans over the village and into its outskirts to where the temple was found, Kavya sees that it is overrun with people. The jungle abutting the coffee plantation, so beautiful and lush, is brimming with protestors and worshippers; it is hard to tell one from the other. The devadasis, however, are distinctive – dressed in colourful saris, hands adorned with bangles, painted faces, haunted kohl-lined eyes. A group of women with determined expressions and boards stating, 'Abolish Prostitution in the Name of Religion' stand beside them.

A small, pale man is speaking into the camera. 'This land belonged to my great-grandfather. He was the landlord of this village. He built the temple for our family to worship in. It belongs to our family.'

'So, how do you explain the devadasis who are said to have been dedicated here to Goddess Yellamma?'

The camera zooms in on the devadasis, who seem to be conferring among themselves. The group of ladies holding the 'Abolish Prostitution' banner move forward, led by a stern-faced woman, who asks, 'Did your great-grandfather participate in this despicable practice?'

The pale man ignores her, facing the reporter, saying heatedly, 'My great-grandfather must have allowed the villagers to worship at the temple, but it was on *his* land. I do know he buried a lot of treasure somewhere on his land – treasure that was never found.'

Silence spreads through the gathered crowd like waves pushing outward from a stone rippling a still pond.

'We grew up hearing tales of our ancestors' treasure that our great-grandfather buried somewhere on the property. When we were little we used to take turns searching for it,' the pale man says.

'You didn't find it?'

'No. It was an impossible task as he owned almost the entire village. But now it makes absolute sense. Of course he placed it in the goddess's custody. Buried it in the temple vault.'

'What do you make of the bones found by the temple steps?'

The man goes even paler, sweat pooling on his face. 'I… I don't know about that.'

'So, do you have the deeds to this land then?'

'Um… No. But it is ours.' Said with a conviction it is obvious the man doesn't feel.

'How do you know?'

'Well, we have records stating which of the ancestral lands were sold – I have been going through them since this temple came to light. The land on which the temple stands is not among them. So, if we didn't sell it, we must still own it. You see, my great-grandfather owned all the land around here. When he died, his daughters – he had three daughters, no sons – who were married and had settled in Bangalore and Mumbai, or Bombay as it was then, did not want to come back, so they sold the land, little by little. Not all of it. We still own some of the fields around here. And this temple obviously.'

'Obviously?'

'Well, if my great-grandfather built the temple for his family to worship in, he wouldn't have sold it to anyone, would he? What I'm trying to say is that since we owned all the land around the temple and beyond except for the coffee plantation, it goes to show that this temple belongs to us.'

'Do you think it might belong to the coffee plantation?'

'No. Their land is the land abutting the road on the other side, beside the jungle. Everything on this side is ours. So that must include the temple.'

It seems to Kavya that the pale man is trying to convince himself he owns the temple by repeating the fact every chance he gets.

'Do you know if this cottage belonged to him too?'

'Must have done.'

'But where are the deeds then?'

'My sisters are searching for them. They will turn up. Or perhaps they are buried in the vault, along with the treasure.'

They aren't, Kavya thinks, feeling a frisson of excitement. *My grandmother has them for some reason. My ajji!*

Although even as she thinks it, she can't quite believe it. It is hard to comprehend how her sweet, gentle ajji could be connected to all of this.

'Surely, Ma, there must be some mistake?' she had exclaimed when she finally understood what her mother was saying over the telephone, after a couple of minutes of stunned silence.

'Your father thinks the deeds hold up, that they are genuine. The deeds are for the cottage and the land it sits on, but from the dimensions of the land, it appears to include the temple as well.' Kavya's father, a former bank manager, now retired, has read enough documents to know a false one and if he had given it his stamp of approval, then…

'But Ma, how…?' Incredulity and scepticism colouring Kavya's voice.

'Come home and see for yourself. We will explain everything then.'

Chapter 16

Lucy

An Attempt at an Apology

Her wedding night.

As soon as they are alone, James says, 'Lucy…' His voice so grave that her hands still where they have been worrying the upholstery of her chair. *What am I about to hear?*

And again she thinks: *I have my reasons to be here, with you, my husband, practically a stranger. What are your reasons for marrying me? Am I about to find out?*

James's face is grim, forbidding. He is such a rigid, closed man. Very unlike Robert, who was so at ease with himself—

Don't bring Robert here, into your marriage with James.

But how can she not? He is all she can think of, he haunts her every moment.

You forfeited the right when— She silences the voice in her head. *Not now.*

'I did not want to tell you this morning. At the church…'

'*There are secrets in every marriage.*' Her mother's voice taking over from her hectoring conscience in her head.

Is she about to hear James's secrets?

I don't want to know. If you tell me yours, does that mean I have to tell you mine? Will you still want me when you know the truth about me? I wouldn't, in your place.

'There's been some trouble at the plantation and… My foreman
– he can't manage alone. He wants me back there. I received the
telegram this morning.'

Is that all? Her whole body sags with relief. No unburdening
of secrets, at least not quite yet.

'I will have to travel to India as soon as possible.' He takes a
deep breath. 'I am so sorry, I wanted to leave with you, but now…'
His curt voice an attempt at an apology.

She has been given a respite. She married James because she
had to, because it was expected of her. But she did not realise
how much she was dreading what would come after until just
now, when she found herself alone with her husband, Mother's
words echoing in her ears: 'Whatever you do, *don't* tell him. It
will destroy your marriage.'

While courting, there was always a posse of well-meaning
matrons, debutantes and her mother around them, and their
conversation had meandered along the same few, oft-repeated
lines deemed acceptable by society.

What will we talk about when it's just the two of us? she had
worried. *Will he see through me to what I have done, what I am
capable of? How will I hide my true self from him? Especially when
being intimate with him, when— Oh…*

But now, a breather—

'Lucy?'

She strokes the velvet back of her chair. 'When do you depart?'

'I am trying to book a passage on the SS *Rajputana*, which
sails in a week.'

She nods, trying not to let her relief show.

He flashes her a brief smile, his eyes distant, his mind, she
understands, on his plantation on the other end of the world and
what needs to be done there. A place she'll be travelling to soon,
to join him. A place she cannot envision, spanning a distance she

cannot fathom. She will be removed from everything familiar; living with a near stranger.

You deserve it.

'Do you like being a plantation owner?' she asks.

'It is hard work. There have been some problems, still ongoing.'

Trouble at the plantation. Money troubles? Is this why James came to England – in search of a rich wife to bail out his plantation? Mother and Father, indeed everyone in polite society, had assumed James, as sole heir to his uncle's plantation, was a man of means. But perhaps, as in Lucy's own case, things with him are not as they seem. Did he marry her for her money? Does it make a difference? *She* hasn't married for love, why should he be any different?

'My uncle made it look so easy when he was running it,' James is saying. 'But… I have good men working for me.' Then, 'I will get everything ready for when you arrive. I hope you like India. It takes a bit of getting used to, but once you do, it's amazing.' Something resembling passion colours his voice.

He steps forward and perches on the arm of her chair. He smells of lemons and something spicy.

His image rises before her eyes. His musky scent of hard work and green vegetation and fertile earth. The way his arms…

She tries to push the image away, the ache for Robert, but it lingers.

James puts his arms around her. She cannot help it; she flinches as he leans in to kiss her.

'What is the matter?' He pulls back.

You are not him. She shudders. 'I…'

'I'm sorry.' He is stiff, his face expressionless as he stands up, moves away from her.

'No. I – It's… I just… I'm not ready.' *I will never be ready.*

'I understand.' He clearly doesn't. How can he? How can anyone? He nods tersely. 'Goodnight.'

She wraps her arms around herself and stares at the door that has closed behind her husband. *Come back, James, let's start again.*

She sits in the chair all night, waiting, dozing on and off, dreaming of suntanned skin, capable hands pruning the hedges of a maze bathed in the golden haze of an October evening, a bearded face creasing pleasantly into smiling grooves.

He does not come.

James is polite to her all week. But that is all.

He does not rush into conversation and does not expect Lucy to either, which is a relief. He answers the questions that she asks, but does not pressure her into volunteering information she doesn't want to. He is unworried when she lapses into silence.

Lucy cannot help wondering why he is so uncurious about his new bride. Is this how he is in general? Or is he angry with her for what happened on their wedding night and this is his way of punishing her? Does he hold grudges? Will he be like this when she joins him in India?

Perhaps he is just not interested in her. Perhaps he doesn't care enough to want to know everything about her. Is he keeping something from her? Has he, like her, married for his own reasons, seeing her, as she does him, as an escape route, a means to an end?

He does not come into her bedroom again. Though relieved, she is also worried: has she ruined her marriage even before it has begun?

Who has she married? What is going on? What is he hiding? Does he know what *she* is hiding? Should she tell him?

None of her questions are answered and a week later, he leaves.

Lucy is left torn, worried but also feeling a grateful sense of release. Married and yet in limbo.

All that she did, the terrible choices she made, the hurt she wrought, was for this?

Chapter 17
Gowri

Once Upon a Time

Goddess Yellamma,

I have always been on the fence about you.

For how could you, a woman, condone what happens in your name?

Hence my letters to you. Begging you, pleading with you to act.

In a corner of my heart I hoped that if you did exist, you didn't really know what happened in your name. I thought as a woman and a mother you would be kind.

Now I know.

She's dead. My Vandana Ma'am, my one ally.

I do not go to her cremation. I cannot, in her death, acknowledge what we kept so carefully hidden while she was alive. I cannot show the world, and especially the landlord, what she meant to me.

And so, I have a little service for her at home. I picture her cremation. The little circle of mourners standing around the funeral pyre. Her parents, hunched and old, mourning the loss of the daughter they despaired over, for never having married, for not reproducing, for bringing disgrace upon them.

The daughter who, in the end, was the one who looked after them.

'They had hoped my brother would,' Vandana Ma'am told me, one of the last times she visited, when the stark truth of what was going to happen to her was written in her face, in her fading body, the hollows etched into fragile skin. She was getting frailer by the day, the constant pain she was in (she could no longer disguise it from me, however hard she tried) shining out of her eyes. 'But my brother… When he married, his wife and children took over and he distanced himself from my parents, moving to the city. Good job they had me, eh, although they will never acknowledge that they are now glad I did not marry and leave them too. They still go on about my refusal to marry, can you believe it? They call it a *wasted* life, just because I didn't tie myself to a man. Ha!' Sighing, her voice merely a whisper – she was constantly tired then, and even speaking for too long fatigued her. Despite this, she came to see me, walking discreetly to and from my house. I knew I should ask her not to come, but I couldn't. I understood she didn't have long and selfishly, I wanted whatever time she could spare for me.

'Mind you, I am leaving my parents for ever soon,' she said when she had gathered her breath – it was the first time she had openly admitted that she was dying. 'But I have made provision for them. I have hired a nurse to look after them and a maid who will stay in the house. My brother has agreed to pay for both, but I made him promise me to do so only when he is satisfied they have been doing a sterling job. This means he *has* to visit my parents every week to check on the nurse and the maid. So, two birds with one stone – now, what does that saying mean, Gowri?' Her eyes twinkled as she quizzed me, not missing an opportunity to educate me, despite the exhaustion in them from battling the disease. Even towards the end she was insistent on us speaking with each other only in English.

How I miss her!

My sister sent word when she passed away. She knew I had liked Vandana Ma'am when I was at school, but not how close we had become, how much she had come to mean to me in recent years, what she had been doing for me.

'Your favourite teacher has died,' my sister's note said. 'I am sorry, Gowri.' I knew she meant it too. I touched her words, and imagined I was touching her. Patting the soft skin of her cheek. My sister. She used to be so proud of me, once upon a time.

I pictured her in her room in their house in the city (where I have never been and am not invited either), writing the note to me.

*I have a room of my own! I sit by the window to study and when I need a break, I watch passers-by on the street: Sahibs and memsahibs bedecked in regal finery, driving past in carriages and trolleys and cars even posher than the landlord's new one,*she had written in her first letter from the city. *I go to a school run by nuns. They speak English so beautifully, each word like a polished pebble. I am learning to speak just like them. I am one of their best students, not bad at all for a native, they say. Missionaries come in and tell us about Jesus. He is a good god, he does not punish. Instead, if you do something wrong, it seems he dies for you and then comes back to life!*

I read and reread that letter, her excitement, her joy to be in the city, jumping off the page. I was pleased for her. If I felt a tiny worm of jealousy uncurl in my stomach, I quashed it immediately. At least one of us deserved to be happy and I was glad she was.

* * *

I sit where I used to when Vandana Ma'am visited and I talk to her, pretending she's there beside me – in English, like she wanted me to.

'I miss you,' I say. 'I wish you were here.'

She did go to the doctor as she promised me she would.

When she came to visit me two days after the puja, where she had fainted, she said, 'I kept my side of the promise and went to see the doctor. Did you learn all those formulae by heart?' She seemed jaunty. Did this mean it was not as bad as I thought? She looked tired, wrung out. Did this mean it *was* bad news?

'Yes,' I said.

'Well, let's see then. What's the formula for kinetic energy?'

I answered all of her questions, my body tense, my nerves taut, as I waited for her to finish.

Finally, I couldn't wait any longer. 'Please, just tell me.'

'Everything is fine. Just old age creeping up on me. Blood pressure is a little high, that's all. I just need to rest more and eat the right food. No more bingeing on sweets, like I have been doing.' She looked right into my eyes as she lied.

And the fool that I was, I allowed myself to believe her because I wanted to, because I could not countenance the alternative, although deep down I knew she was lying, and I also knew that she wouldn't be lying if it wasn't bad.

'Now, can we concentrate on your studies, please? We have less than eight weeks and I want to see you blaze your way out of here. I'm not going anywhere and nothing is going to happen to me until then.'

Another lie that I believed – and this one, I think she did too.

She *wanted* to be there for me and if she could have controlled her body and her illness in any way at all, bought just a little more time, until I had sat the exams, she would have.

But she couldn't.

She was up against you, Goddess, and where she went wrong, where she lost, was a) by aligning herself with me and b) by steadfastly refusing to believe in your existence.

She thought book knowledge would win over faith, science would triumph over religion. And towards the end, I allowed myself to be swayed by her arguments too.

You proved us both wrong.

She underestimated you by refusing to acknowledge you and I – I who should have known better, I underestimated you too, choosing to attribute to you characteristics you have never displayed: kindness and empathy.

I will not do so again, I have your measure now.

I should have recognised your authority – you chose me, just like the landlord declares. You orchestrated this by being found in my father's field, by healing my brother.

And yet, I did not see how commanding you were. I was blind. *So* blind.

You have decided I am to serve you for life – that it is my destiny – and you wouldn't allow Vandana Ma'am, a mere mortal, to come in the way. You waited until the month of the exams that were to be my escape route, and then you took Vandana Ma'am away from me in the most final way, to show me exactly what you are capable of.

I kept asking you for a sign.

When Vandana Ma'am was taken ill here in the cottage, that was my first sign from you and I didn't see it. I should have stopped then, begged her to stay away. Perhaps then she would still be alive.

Goddess, you see, I still believed then that you were benevolent, kind. That you didn't know what went on in your name. I thought you were on my side and so I was looking for another type of sign. The fool that I was, I hoped you would *heal* Vandana Ma'am.

If I had not given my sister money that fateful day and asked her to get books for me from Vandana Ma'am, if Vandana Ma'am had never come here, if I had recognised the signs you sent me and asked her to stay away, she would still be alive.

I know this.

I cannot escape you, I see that now.

Too late, I acknowledge your power, Goddess.

Everything good wanes.

And I am left with you.

Always you.

Towards the end, when she knew she didn't have long, Vandana Ma'am extracted a vow from me.

'Stop worrying about the landlord's wrath, the goddess's ire. Go to Bangalore or Bombay. You are fluent in English. You can get a job, you can survive.' She pressed money into my hands, a *lot* of money, much more than the pittance the landlord gives me every month for my household needs. He has reduced my allowance drastically, giving me just enough to get by. He worries, I suppose, that I will use it to run away.

'You're not as docile as the other devadasis,' he says often. 'I can't read what's behind your eyes. You're not grateful. I can't trust you, not completely, Gowri.'

No matter how meek I try to appear, I suppose I cannot keep my true nature hidden from him.

I wish I had one of those bland, plain faces that look submissive and accepting.

I know that my spirit would be broken by now if I didn't have Vandana Ma'am. But her books, her constant messages of encouragement, her belief in me have meant that I have channelled my inner strength and, most importantly perhaps, that I do not blame myself for the situation I am in.

But I *do* blame myself for what happened to her.

'Please, child. You have to get away. You are worth so much more than this,' Vandana Ma'am said, waving a hand around the cottage one of the last times she visited. She knew as I did that her dream, of getting me to pass my matriculation, might not be realised. She was too ill to teach at the school, and thus she could not implement her plan of bringing the exam papers to the cottage for me to take the examination. She did not want to give up – she had come up with another plan: writing to the nuns at a convent-run school in Bangalore, asking if they would allow me to sit the exam alongside their students.

But I knew this wouldn't happen; there wasn't enough time. She was small and frail by then, the disease having eaten her away from the inside, hunched double with pain, looking so much older than her fifty years. She forgot things easily, even sentences she had just uttered. Which day it was.

And yet, she did not forget me. She came to see me, religiously, every week until one day, two weeks before the exams that I was prepared for but would not take, she didn't.

And I knew.

That last time, when she pressed into my hands the money she had brought with her, I tried not to cry, but with her, as always, when she showed me such unconditional love, I could not stop my tears.

'Promise me you'll leave here,' she said, her voice breathless. She had walked here, despite being so very ill, so she would not compromise our secret by letting others in on our arrangement, thus getting me into trouble with the landlord. My Vandana Ma'am.

So I promised.

I did not tell her then that I couldn't leave you, Goddess. That I was in no doubt now as to your might. That if I did plan to leave you again, you might take someone else I loved – my parents, my brother, my sister.

I let her have this.

She smiled, her face glowing, and for a brief while the old, spirited Vandana Ma'am shone through, and I was grateful I hadn't told her.

I did not want to take the money but she looked so offended, so hurt when I hesitated, that I did. I have kept it hidden away, along with the books she gave me. It is my talisman, the evidence of how much she loved me, how much she cared. I will use it to keep my promise to her – if ever I feel able to.

I have a remembrance service for her at home.

'I love you, Vandana Ma'am.' I whisper the words I couldn't say when she was alive into the empty space that used to reverberate with her caring, kind presence.

You promised me you would leave here, Gowri, she whispers in my head.

Briefly, despite knowing better, I entertain the thought.

I could go to my family. But my parents, would they accept me – they who cannot look me in the eye? And what of my sister?

There is a peril, I understand, in loving people. It makes me vulnerable, open to hurt. It gives the landlord and you, Goddess, ammunition. You can hurt me through them.

All the time Vandana Ma'am was alive, I worried that the landlord would find out about her, put a stop to it. I never even considered the possibility that it was *you* I should worry about more.

Goddess, I accept that I cannot run away quite yet. I am not tough enough to snub you, to withstand harm coming to someone else that I love. But I *will* keep my promise to Vandana Ma'am. I will wait for the day you no longer wield this power over me, Goddess.

And it will come.

I will school myself not to love, not to care for anyone else. I will teach myself to be strong, to weather anything else you throw at me.

I have endured three years here. I have survived losing my innocence and my childhood. I have learned the meaning of many words since I have been dedicated to you, Goddess. Loneliness. Violation. Shame. Ostracism. Rape. Bitterness. Rage. Hatred. I have experienced these words, lived them.

I will survive this too – losing the woman who was like a mother to me, who believed in me.

Thanks to her, I have found love and friendship and exquisite moments of starburst happiness.

You own me, Goddess.

But Vandana Ma'am, she… she *loved* me.

I will not be broken.

This much I owe to Vandana Ma'am and to myself.

Chapter 18

Lucy

Inviting Vista

Lucy writes letters home to while away long hours on the ship, to stave off the loneliness that grips her, in between bouts of apprehension and homesickness. She writes to the gentle rhythm, the swell and tuck of waves. Gulls circle, birds call and the bluish green, foam-capped water ripples with flashes of silver as flying fish skitter the surface. A baby cries and its ayah shushes it, singing to it in a strange tongue.

Her missives to Mother and Father are determinedly cheery, full of interesting things she is learning, the ship already feeling a world away from home. She writes, *'Ayah' is nursemaid, in the unfamiliar English, peppered with Indian words, which they all seem to speak here and which I will be speaking soon too, no doubt. The servants are all called 'Boys' even if they are grey-haired and hunch-backed!*

This is how it will be from now on, she thinks. Her relationship with her parents reduced to superficialities, with Lucy never daring to say what she really feels, what she really thinks, afraid of upsetting them more than she already has by the impulsive actions of her past.

It is hot and sweat trickles down her back, plastering her skirts to her body. She feels as if she is melting away, her insides slowly turning to mush, both from the humid heat and from worry.

To Ann, she pours out her heart.

Ann, there are no secrets between us, there never have been. You know the best of me and the very worst. You have been party to my dreams, my hopes, and you've been there to pick up the pieces when they scattered in a crumpled heap around me.

I recall us giggling together in our secret hideaway among the rose bushes, wondering what marriage entailed and speculating about how babies were made. Now you know and I do too. With the right person, it can be beautiful. You have found that with Edward. I did too for a while with Robert. Will I find it again with James? I hope so, although I do not deserve it.

'I will travel the world in search of adventure. I don't need a man, unlike you, Ann,' I used to say, so carelessly condescending, when we sat in the rose arbour and mapped out our lives, the future a glinting, inviting vista spread out before us, waiting to be conquered. I was insufferable then, wasn't I? And yet you put up with me, in your usual good-natured way.

I never appreciated what I had: a privileged, indulged upbringing, love freely given. Freedom and as much independence as a woman is allowed, and given Father's affection for me back then, before I disappointed him, perhaps more than a woman is allowed.

I did not appreciate my home, the comfort and ease of it, the beauty and luxury that I took for granted.

'I want to go places, to the ends of the world,' I would declare.

And here I am.

Each night after supper, Lucy stands on deck and looks out into the horizon. It is noisy and hot, despite being evening, but every so often there's a cooling breeze, carrying the salt and fish smell of the sea, mingling with the meaty aroma of salt pork and syrupy yellow custard from supper. The water is dark, surges and hums, crowned with froth tinged blue by evening, the splash and glint of fish scales and in the distance the twinkling lights of passing ships. Up above her, a canopy of stars, sparkling merrily, stretching from here to England. The sight of them is strangely soothing. They connect her to everyone she loves. Father and Mother, Ann and even— No, she will not go there.

In the months since James left, Lucy has received a few letters and a telegram from him – all businesslike, describing the plantation, sending details of the journey. 'I'll be there to receive you at the harbour.'

No 'I miss you'. No 'I love you'.

She has recalled their every encounter, replayed it in her mind. He never once said, 'I love you.' Not when he proposed, not on their wedding night. (Their disaster of a wedding night… Oh…) Not when he had to leave.

To be fair, she hasn't said those words to him either. She cannot tell him things she does not yet mean, she cannot be dishonest in this way. As it is, she has been deceitful enough, keeping what she is, what she did, from him.

So does his reticence mean that he is reserved? Or that he is like her, unable to say things he doesn't mean? Is he also keeping secrets from her? Then again, why is she torturing herself by thinking this way? It is done. She is here, on her way to him; she has to make the best of it.

You don't deserve the opportunity to start again, make the best of it, the waves chastise.

She closes her eyes, feels the zesty twilight breeze, tasting of salt and remorse, on her face. Somewhere someone laughs, a carefree, happy sound. The waves swish and buckle and burble and heave. In the distance dusk gently kisses the horizon, wrapping it in a rosy caress, a shawl of twilight the shade of romance, the blush on a maiden's cheek.

Do you think you can run away, the ocean chides her, *from what you did?*

She will go inside. She will dance and smile and eat and make conversation with the other wives. She will listen to them as they advise her on how to address the servants, how to put them in their place. She will watch them with their ayahs and their children, their husbands, and she will take note of their expressions: joy, love, excitement, bashfulness and in some cases, glazed boredom.

She had hoped for so much. She had wanted love. She proudly declared to Ann that she would not marry for anything less. And yet here she is, on board a ship sailing towards India and a man she does not love, to whom she is wed.

Around her, the delighted giggles of children as the deck is sprayed with water. They slip and slide on the wet floor, their small feet dancing, nimble, their laughter ringing in her ears like an accusation.

On Sunday mornings there is a service in the ship's ballroom, which is transformed into a church, with one of the priests on board presiding. Lucy looks at all the bent heads, the closed eyes, the hopes and pleas and petitions swirling in this swaying room, buffeted by water, the priest calling them to prayer above the sound of the waves.

She wonders how God has time to answer every single one. Perhaps He picks and chooses, depending on His mood, based on which entreaty takes His fancy.

Lucy has always been unsure about God. Disbelieving. She did not thank Him every day, like Mother had coached her to, back in the days when Mother used to supervise the nanny dressing Lucy in her Sunday best and they would take the carriage together to church, the nights when she would come to tuck Lucy in, smelling of roses and excitement and a tang of something vinegary, before leaving with Father for a ball.

When Mother lost her other babies, her belief in God only became stronger. Lucy is struck by a sudden pang of longing for her mother, recalling the way she would bow her head and say grace before every meal, her severe features softening as she closed her eyes and communed with God.

'He will listen to you if you turn to Him, no matter how big a sinner you are,' Mother liked to say.

Are you sure, Mother? Why would He answer my prayers after what I have done?

But despite her doubts, now, with her fellow travellers in the ship's ballroom masquerading as a church, floating on the high seas, Lucy prays. For she is scared. Nervous about the future. She can't begin to imagine what awaits her in India, but surely it will be better than what has transpired these past few months…

This man whom she has married as a means of escape – what she recalls of him most is what he is not. He is *not* charming. He is *not* garrulous. He is *not* the man she loves.

And yet, he is her future. She *will* remember this.

She will not look back, only forward. She will learn to love James.

Chapter 19

Gowri

Ribbons of Fabric

Goddess,

I don't quite know why I am still writing to you. Habit, I suppose.

Or, more likely, loneliness.

For, whether I want it to be so or not, at the end of the day, you are the only constant in my life.

You. And the landlord.

And I definitely don't want to write to him…

'Finally found a groom for my eldest daughter,' the landlord tells me one evening. 'He is from one of the best families in Bangalore. Wedding is fixed for this coming Friday. I will combine the celebration with the goddess's festival and have a huge puja and reception. I will invite all the landowners and dignitaries in the kingdom of Mysore, including my cousin, the Maharaja.' The landlord puffs out visibly when he utters the last sentence. It is meant as a boast and as a threat. *My cousin the Maharaja.* 'You must take care to look your very best, Gowri. Who knows, I might even choose to give you as a gift to the Maharaja himself.' Winking suggestively at me.

I think of the puja last year, when Vandana Ma'am was alive, along with the hope that I would escape your clutches, Goddess.

I think of how she had held my gaze, urging me to shed any shame I might feel, imparting her belief in me, despite her failing strength. *You have done nothing wrong, Gowri. Hold your head up high and face the world. You will be leaving soon anyway.*

You left instead, Vandana Ma'am.

The next morning, after my chores are done, I sit under the peepal tree, on the washing stone, as is my wont. Overhead, the sun beats down, relentless. Chickens peck about my feet.

Since Vandana Ma'am has been gone, my days have slipped into pallid whorls. When she was alive, I had her visits to look forward to, prepare for. I had my revision to keep me occupied. I was buoyed by her faith in me, her hope for me.

Now, I seem consumed by a desultory darkness, even on the sunniest of days. I try to coax myself out of it by reading and rereading Vandana Ma'am's books every night and attempting to channel her voice, her presence by day. I want to keep the promise I made to her, summon up the energy to stand up to you, Goddess, but I have lost the motivation. Without Vandana Ma'am, there are no new books. There is no one to nag me, believe in me, love me, care for me. There is nothing to aim for. There is no hope.

If she saw you now, she would be disappointed in you, I chide myself. And yet, I cannot rouse myself from this blackness that has engulfed me, this hopeless lethargy.

I am weary. *So* weary.

I have discovered that there is no loneliness quite like the loneliness you experience when you have had the pleasure of company, when you have enjoyed the warmth of kindness and the vivacity of conversation and are now bereft of them, to have touched love and lost it again. Emptiness, the loud clamour of silence, keeps me awake at night, the awareness of what is missing, the echo of what might have been, resounding in my ears as the walls pitch forward to envelop me in a hollow hug.

I go through the motions, do my chores, feed the priest, the chickens, the cat, dust your shrine and adorn it with fragrant garlands I have fashioned from the flowers in my garden. I sweep the temple and the courtyard, I wash the clothes, I eat when my stomach cramps with hunger.

The days stretch before me, stripped of colour, each one the same. Some nights the landlord visits. Others he barters me off to one of his friends. I close my eyes then and channel my imagination, pretending I am one of the heroines in the novels Vandana Ma'am gifted me, feisty and devil-may-care, living in lands where girls are not sacrificed to goddesses and sold to men, where they have a choice, a say in their future.

Over by the temple, men set up marquees for the landlord's puja, which the King might attend.

Laughter and banter as they heave poles and drape a stripy turmeric-and-vermilion awning over it. Others hoist bunting, triangular flaps the colours of watermelon, hibiscus and bougainvillea fluttering in the syrupy breeze.

The priest sits by the bell. He is too old, really, to be in charge of the temple, but it suits the landlord's suspicious nature to have him stay on – this way, the landlord does not have to worry about anything untoward going on between the priest and myself. I am the landlord's possession and he treats me as such – he will give me to the men he chooses, happy to share me if it is at his instigation, but he will not stand for me doing anything without his permission, even looking at anyone in what he deems the 'wrong' way. I don't know how he would react if he found out how much Vandana Ma'am was helping me and I am glad he hasn't and hopefully never will.

The men work around the priest, calling to him, and he smiles vaguely in their direction. He is swathed in gloom too, but of a different kind – he has been slowly going blind.

'I can see colour,' he informed me. 'Just a wash of colour with no delineating features. Nothing aligning to form shapes. Like going into a sari shop and being presented by ream upon ream of cloth in different shades.'

I close my eyes and picture ribbons of fabric. Green and brown and gold and orange, red and yellow and blue and white.

But when I open my eyes, there is only blackness.

We dance to a packed, seething crowd, the other devadasis and I. The King does not make an appearance but the temple and its grounds are teeming with the landlord's strutting, self-important contemporaries. Smirking men assess us while their wives stand by, looking down at us with scorn from their superior position as married women; never mind that their husbands are cheating on them with us. I want to tell them that we are the same, really – wives, mistresses, all dancing to the whims of males, tied to them.

I dance and take advantage of the landlord's distraction, his attention to familial duties meaning he cannot keep a policing eye on me; my gaze sweeps over the crowd. I look at the little girls, some watching shyly from behind their mothers' skirts, others smiling boldly agog up at us, yet others bored and fidgety, and I want to issue warnings. 'Beware,' I want to say, 'your security, your place in the world is but ephemeral. You can lose it at any time. A priest declares that you need to please the goddess and you are no longer your own person but Yellamma's – everyone's.'

And then my gaze snags, explodes into light. Startling. Blinding. There is a flash and a loud whirr. People stop watching us dance, distracted. They turn, whispering and pointing, a murmur surging through the crowd.

I dance and watch, surreptitiously now, in case the landlord has noticed. The offending item is lowered, and my curious gaze meets a bright blue one. White skin. Hair and beard as yellow as the landlord's teeth.

I realise then, Goddess, that I know this man. Or rather, I know *of* him. The new plantation owner – the only white sahib for miles around. There was talk at the market, which gathers every Wednesday, when his uncle, the previous owner of the plantation, died.

'This one is green around the gills,' I overheard at the market. 'Don't know if he'll be able to manage all the warring factions at the plantation.'

'The landlord is causing discord at the plantation as usual, whispering in impressionable ears and rousting the plantation workers against each other. The older sahib was wise to the landlord's tricks and managed to keep his men united and under control. Not sure about this one…' This from two women inspecting tomatoes beside me, their voices slick and juicy with paan and speculation.

'The landlord will be up to more of his tricks now – he wants to be the top man in the village and with the old sahib as contender, he could never quite achieve it…'

'But this man – so young. Doesn't wield the same authority as his uncle and his men know it…'

'I heard from one of the servants up at the young sahib's house that his brother was supposed to take over the plantation – he was the one who was to come here, but he died in the war.'

'Perhaps that's why he's so morose. He needs a wife, someone to care for him…'

The women spat noisily, right beside the mound of tomatoes, ridding their mouths of betel juice, attracting a buzz of flies.

'And I heard that...' The rest of what they were going to say was swallowed by a rustle, a flap, a manic screech. A chicken had landed, squawking, in between me and the gossiping women, wings flustering, its feet splatting among squashed tomatoes and paan dregs, rotting onions and eggshells. It was followed by the man from the chicken stall, yelling obscenities at it and brandishing a scythe. The man swooped on the chicken, gathering it in his arms, along with rotten vegetables, split tomatoes and dirt.

'Hey, before you go, pay for the tomatoes you and your bird destroyed,' the tomato vendor yelled.

'I will not! Those tomatoes were already crushed,' the man holding the chicken yelled back, the bird shrieking and struggling in his arms.

A heated argument ensued, a crowd collecting and everyone taking sides, and there was no more gossip about the new owner of the plantation, that day at any rate.

After we have finished dancing, everyone comes up to you, Goddess, to offer their prayers, their gifts of flowers and fruit, milk and sweets. The aroma of incense and perspiration and exhaustion and impending dusk.

Lamps flicker. Shadows stir.

And then, in the midst of all of this, a fresh clean smell. Ginger and lime and smoke and kindling. The crowd parts and he is there, suddenly, in front of us.

The young sahib. The new plantation owner.

He carries himself stiffly, with grave import.

'Excuse me,' he says in Kannada. He speaks slowly, as if finding his way around the language.

Close up, his eyes are an extraordinary blue: the aquamarine of the river by my grandmother's house, which I once crossed in a boat when I was a child; the exact shade of the centre of the whirlpool. I had thought we would all die. I had prayed for deliverance then, while clutching my sister to me.

Now, too, I feel like I am falling, that same thrilling sensation of the boat tipping. Of being caught in a whirlpool.

He holds up the machine that made the flash earlier. 'Can I take a picture of all of you?'

I must have nodded, or perhaps one of the others did, for he lifts the machine up and again there is a whirring sound and an almighty flash. I blink and then the landlord is standing there, legs planted firmly apart.

'What on earth are you doing?' the landlord shouts in English. I can just about understand but beside and around me, most faces screw up in incomprehension.

'Just taking a photo, that's all.' The sahib lifts up his hands, taking a step back from the fuming landlord, the machine dangling from a strap around his neck.

'I did not give you permission to do so, Mr Bell.'

His smile disappears, his lips thin and yet, he still looks wholesome. Wonderfully real in contrast to the landlord, who is a sweaty, angry caricature. 'I did not know I needed permission from you.'

'You've only just taken over the running of the plantation after your uncle's demise, I know. But you need to learn our ways.'

His blue eyes flash orange sparks. He says, his voice curt, like stones banging against a window, 'I'm sorry.'

'And if you're so interested in the devadasis, then here…' The landlord looks at us and his gaze finds mine, holds, a calculating grin taking over his face.

Oh, I think.

He whips his hand out and encircles my wrist, pulling me forward. 'You can have Gowri, just for tonight, as a magnanimous gift from me. She's very special, is Gowri, and not only because she is the most beautiful. She is chosen by the goddess herself.'

The man looks shocked, his face going pale as the mist that hangs over the forest at dawn. 'I – I don't…'

'Do you mean to say you refuse the gift I am so kindly offering you, Mr Bell?'

Around us the throng swells with rustling whispers, the thrum of intrigue.

The man looks at me and clears his throat. 'Doesn't the woman have a choice?'

'What exactly are you implying, Mr Bell?' The landlord's voice is silky smooth and dangerous. 'I've had some dealings with your uncle, not all of them friendly, but when he died, I decided to put that behind me and get off to a fresh start with you. Hence your invitation to this puja. And although you've already crossed a line by taking photos of the devadasis, I am prepared to overlook it and give one of them as a gift and you…' The landlord breaks off, shaking his head, seemingly unable to come up with words strong enough to express his vexation.

I see the young sahib swallow, his Adam's apple bobbing nervously in his throat. In that moment he looks impossibly naïve, especially in comparison to the landlord's cutting anger.

'Thank you, Mr Wodeyar, but I cannot accept.' His voice tight and dry.

The landlord's gaze hardens. 'Your loss, Mr Bell.'

'That's as may be.' The man nods, a brusque incline of his head. 'Thanks for inviting me, it has been enlightening. Shame your cousin the King couldn't make it – I would have liked to meet him.'

The landlord goes purple and the crowd takes a step backward, the gossip-flavoured whispers stilling on their lips. Silence spreads with the parting crowd as Mr Bell turns and walks away.

I inhale, sharply, in fear and admiration. This man is not only naïve but also foolish to stand up to the landlord like this.

Vandana Ma'am would have liked him. The thought arrives, strident and sudden in my head.

'What are you staring at? Go and pray to the goddess or leave,' an apoplectic landlord roars at the crowd.

All that evening and later that night, as I stumble along the pebble-littered path, barely illuminated by the shadow-dappled yellow light angling from the lamps lit at the temple, to my cottage, I think of Mr Bell, marvelling at his courage.

The next morning, as I sit on the washing stone after taking breakfast up to the priest, I realise that something has changed within me. I am no longer despondent, as I have been since Vandana Ma'am passed. The darkness that I have been engulfed in seems to have lifted, ever so slightly. Why?

A face rises before my eyes: yellow beard, yellow hair and startling blue eyes that flash anger and turn hard like stones washed clear by the sea.

The air that teases my hair from its bun and brushes my face is cool, smelling of incense and prasadam laddoos and a brand new day, the sky the pink of a blushing bride. The forest gleams emerald gold. The temple courtyard is littered with scraps of multicoloured bunting and drooping flower garlands. I will be sweeping those up later, after the men have come to remove the marquees they put up just the day before yesterday.

The new plantation owner. He is the only one to my knowledge who has dared stand up to the landlord, regardless of the consequences. And watching him do so has ignited in me something that I have lost since Vandana Ma'am died: hope. The assurance that one day I too can be free – of the landlord and of you, Goddess.

Mr Bell has a lot to lose – in the absence of family, the plantation is his home and his livelihood – and yet he stuck to his principles, daring to go against the landlord. Perhaps I can too.

In order to keep the promise I made to Vandana Ma'am, I need to be like this man, with his machine which captures images in a burst of light and his foolish bravado.

For the first time in a long while I am able to look forward into a future where I might be relieved of my bind to you, Goddess. For the first time since Vandana Ma'am's death, I am able to entertain the possibility that perhaps, one day, not far from this day, I *will* be free.

Chapter 20

Sue

Random Times of Day

The knock on the door is tentative, as if the person on the outside hasn't quite made up their mind if they want to come in.

Sue considers leaving it, allowing whoever it is to get bored and move on. She is slumped on the sofa she and Tony picked out together, shattered after another sleepless night and a particularly vicious bout of morning sickness that, stubbornly, does not limit itself to the morning and strikes at different, random times of day.

Another knock, firmer this time.

Go away, she thinks. But she stands up and goes to the door. It might be something to do with Tony. Something they forgot to tell her. *He's alive, it was a mistake.*

Stop this, she remonstrates with herself, flinging the door open with more vehemence than necessary, surprising the woman on the other side, who has her hand raised to knock again.

A slight woman. Middle-aged. Dyed blonde hair, wide eyes behind square glasses frames, pert nose, painted lips.

'Sue Bantam?'

Sue closes her eyes at the sound of her name. Memories rush ᵗ Tony, when she interviewed him, dashing in his uniform, t his hand, saying, 'Tony Bantam. And you must be Sue everyone has been talking about.'

Signing her name for the first time after the wedding, her hands trembling with joy, Tony asking, 'What's the matter?' in a concerned voice and she, unable to reply, unable to keep in the rush of emotion she felt at seeing it written down: Mrs Sue Bantam.

'Um... are you okay?' The woman's voice, high-pitched with concern, pierces her reminiscences, bringing her back into the colourless present.

She opens her eyes, pushes her shoulders back. 'Yes... Yes, I am.'

'I'm Margaret Soames. Sorry to barge in like this, unannounced, but my son Paul and Tony went to school together... For a time they were inseparable, the best of friends, getting up to all sorts.' The woman smiles, her gaze wistful. 'He's in Australia now, my Paul, but when he heard, he wanted me to give you this.' She holds out a bouquet of freesias, pink lilies and roses. The syrupy fragrance induces nausea and makes Sue want to gag.

'He was always a risk-taker, Tony. And yet, so loving and loyal too. My Paul was bullied something terrible at school, you see, but then Tony joined, popular Tony, everyone's favourite, and he took Paul under his wing. After that, Paul blossomed. My boy, so terrified of going to school, so cowed, transformed before my eyes, thanks to your husband.'

My husband.

Sue has wanted to talk to someone about Tony, and here's this stranger standing on her doorstep and spinning to life with her stories the vibrant, vivid person her husband was.

'Come in,' she says to the woman, overcome by a sudden impulse so unlike her cautious self. 'Please.'

She settles the woman – Margaret – in her living room – untidy, she sees now, looking at it through the other woman's eyes. She pulls back curtains that haven't been touched in three weeks, the room sombre in grief, overflowing with cards and dotted with wilting bouquets that she cannot bear to throw away. She switches on the television to bring some life to the silent room, and opens the window to allow fresh air in to dilute the scent of decaying flowers and cloying sympathy that hangs over the room like a shroud.

'Tea?' she asks.

'Yes, please. White with one sugar.'

Sue busies herself in the kitchen, using the last of the milk – she really must go shopping – and trying to calm her nerves as she spies on the visitor through the gap in the door hinge. *What was I thinking, allowing a complete stranger into the house? This is so not me. Grief has turned my mind.*

'I'm sorry, I've run out of biscuits,' Sue says as she sets the tea down in front of Margaret.

'Please don't worry, I've just had my lunch,' the woman says, taking a sip of the tea. Then, 'I'm sorry for your loss.'

I'm tired of these platitudes, Sue thinks wearily. *They have no use except to make the person saying them feel better. They will not bring Tony back.*

Outwardly she nods and waits for Margaret to finish her tea and leave, regretting inviting her in. She has never been one for small talk and she cannot think where to begin now.

The television is tuned to the news channel and the newsreader's expressionless monotone spills into the silence. 'Scientists have found a new species of...'

'I used to collect Tony and my Paul from school every Thursday and he would stay at ours for tea. His ma used to work late on Thursdays and she was ever so grateful. I assured her that it was no trouble at all. Although it was a tragedy, both his parents passing within months of each other, at least they were spared this...' Margaret sets her cup down and looks at Sue. 'He was a lovely boy, ever so polite. And always praising my cooking, thanking me for it, finishing everything on his plate. It was a pleasure to see him with my Paul, encouraging him, bringing him out of himself.'

Sue swallows, overcome. She manages a nod. *He was like that with me too.*

'Dozens killed in an explosion...' the newscaster announces into the silence, and Sue flinches, hunting for the remote to turn the blasted TV off.

As if I want to hear about more bloodshed, more horror.

By the time she locates the remote, Margaret is standing up. 'I really should be going.'

Sue sets down the remote down. 'Thank you so much for... for everything.'

But Margaret is riveted by something on the television. 'That's the story about the elephant rampage and the discovery of a temple in India.'

'An elephant rampage?' Sue can't quite keep the dismay from her voice as she too turns to look at the screen.

'Don't worry, nobody got hurt, although some bones were discovered. A child's, they say.'

Sue is even more horrified. 'A child's bones?' Her hands go protectively around her stomach, almost without thinking.

'They've been buried for years, they think. They're still trying to determine whose they are.'

'Oh.'

'I... I'm sorry. You...'

Sue waits, realising, with a jolt of surprise that she likes this small birdlike woman with her soft, bumbling voice, the way her eyes grow wide as she says something, her flustered way of speaking. Margaret is about the age Sue's mother would have been, had she lived. Sue recognises something in this woman. She reminds Sue of a version of herself, the anxious, eager-to-please woman she was before she met Tony.

Now, Sue doesn't know who she is, which version, if any. She is lost, blundering down the many pathways of grief. She is numb, encased in a layer of disbelieving sorrow that seems to act like a shell, so she feels removed from everything. Even the baby – Tony's baby… Although she knows she has to make decisions, that she doesn't have much time, she cannot quite bring herself to act just yet. So she paces the house, she procrastinates; she thinks of Tony, she waits for something to happen.

And now, despite Sue's reservations after impulsively inviting her in, here's this woman providing some distraction in the form of new memories of Tony to add to her collection, a brief respite from the fug of grief and lassitude that envelops her.

'I'd better get going. You take care now,' Margaret says, touching Sue lightly on her shoulder.

Sue closes the door, exhausted by even this smallest of human interactions. *I really should start going out, mixing with people*, she thinks, and in the next breath, *but what's the point?*

The baby.

The baby is the point.

The television is still blaring noise into the room – something about how children are spending too much time indoors. She picks up the remote and silences it.

A child's bones, Margaret had said.

A temple in India. An elephant rampage.

Even grieving and undecided as to what to do about the baby growing inside of her, Sue is curious, her journalistic instincts aroused for the first time since that devastating phone call informing her of Tony's accident.

She goes to the study, fetches her laptop and turns it on.

Chapter 21
Gowri

Sari Scarf

Goddess,

I dream that I am consumed by fire. Orange flames eating me, charring my body to a crisp, flesh falling off me in brittle, scorched flakes. I am hot, sweltering, my throat parched, my soul clamouring for escape from my burning, ruined body.

I wake gasping for air, raging with thirst. The stale air in my windowless cottage is clammy, slick with the fiery vapour from my blazing dream.

I go to the earthen pot where I store water – it is empty. I sigh, recalling waking up in the night and drinking the last of it. This means I will have to draw water from the well.

I open the door to a humid morning, the air hot and muggy and aching for the monsoon, which is weeks late arriving now. Farmers frequent the temple with offerings to you, Goddess, but the rain they plead for in return doesn't come. They are desperate, for the landlord only pays them if the land he leases to them produces crops from which he can make a healthy profit; he will not tolerate excuses, even genuine ones like the weather (crucial for a good harvest) not cooperating. And so they pray to you, Goddess. The temple has never seen so many visitors. Your shrine is inundated with flowers and food. But you too, like the landlord, do not yield easily. You are not the best at answering prayers and pleas. You like your subjects to grovel and even then you will not bend. I know that better than anyone.

The signs of drought are everywhere. The vegetables and other wares at the market are dwindling, pallid and past their best. It has been a long, harsh summer and it shows no signs of easing. Everyone wears long faces, tired and parched and worried. We all look at the sky at regular intervals, willing a cloud to mar the sunny, bright perfection of it. The grass is yellow, overcooked; the land dry and cracked. When, we are thinking, will this relentless fiery baking end? When will the earth be born again by the reviving baptism of rain, heralding fresh green shoots and new life?

I smell smoke when I open the door. At first I think it is the dregs of my dream slipping over into morning, taking reality hostage.

The mud road beside the cottage exudes an acrid, charred odour, dust rising in a mauve-tinged yellow cloud, spiked with indigo. The trees in the jungle wait expectantly, branches arched as if in supplication to the sky, begging for rain.

The chickens peck at my feet and the cat rubs itself around my ankles. The priest sits on the temple veranda and squints in the general direction of the cottage. He has been waking earlier every day – he says he can't sleep well at night due to the heat. I understand. These, my dependants – the nearly blind priest, the chickens and the cat – want sustenance but I am thirsty, so desperately thirsty.

The well, thankfully, is not yet dry but it is getting close. The pail scrapes the bottom of the well – I have to let out all the rope – and the water I draw up is mostly sludge. I sigh – I will have to sieve this and then boil it before I can drink it.

'Is that you, Gowri?' the priest calls.

'Yes. I'll have your breakfast ready in ten minutes.'

'Can you smell the smoke?'

Ah, so it isn't just me imagining my dream into life.

'There's a fire somewhere close. Hope it doesn't blow this way.' The priest sounds worried.

'There's no wind to blow it,' I say. 'Don't worry.'

But I note the swirls of ash colouring the air the dusky blue of a cloudy sky and I know that the fire is nearby. Not for the first time I am grateful for the sturdiness of my cottage – built with bricks for the landlord's convenience as he would be spending time here, and not mud like the villagers' huts – what with its proximity to the jungle, the threat of wild animals, like that time when there was talk of an elephant stampede in the next village.

All morning, the navy auburn scent of smoke lingers, becoming stronger as the day wears on – another bright day, not a hint of cloud in the sky. Later, after I have delivered the priest's breakfast and settled him for his siesta – he now dozes in the morning as well as after lunch – and am washing his plate under the peepal tree, I see balloons of smoke, wafting above the yellow green of the forest. Thick ashen swells of doom. Are they billowing closer?

'Hello?' A young, plaintive voice.

I jump, dropping the sari I was hanging out to dry on the line that stretches from the mango tree to the peepal. I am startled because nobody visits the temple at this time of day when the sun – especially the potent, drought-inducing ball it has recently morphed into – is approaching its zenith, and they certainly don't come for me.

The boy who called for me bends down, catching the sari expertly before it lands in the dust, and it drapes around his face and shoulders.

I cannot help it; I laugh at the sight of him, swathed in a maroon and magenta sari scarf. He is all bony arms and legs, huge eyes in a thin face, looking pleadingly at me as I lift the sari off him and hang it on the line. I would put his age at about twelve.

Noting the worry in his eyes, I swallow the last of my laughter, wipe the smile from my face and ask, 'What's the matter then?'

'Sahib…' It is only then, as he gasps for breath, that I realise he is panting. He must have run all the way here. But from where?

'He fainted.' Pointing across the road and into the forest, in the direction of the curling tornado of orange-edged smoke.

'He was in the fire?' I ask as I tuck my sari pallu into my waist and prepare to follow him. I'm not sure who his sahib is, but this boy obviously needs my help.

'He tried to stop the fire. All morning he has been working to put it out. Now finally it's out and we were making our way home via the shortcut when he fainted. We should have taken one of the cars but he used them all to take those hurt to the clinic in town.'

'Wait a minute. Where was this fire?'

We are crashing into the forest now, the smell of burning stronger here, tinged with the dying green of thirsting plants. I open my mouth and taste ash and flames.

'The plantation,' the boy says. 'Thankfully it didn't spread to the coffee plants. But it destroyed the storage sheds – luckily they were empty – and some plantation workers' cottages. Sahib thinks – no, he is sure that the landlord started it.'

'Oh.' We come to a clearing in the forest and there he is, the golden-haired blue-eyed young Mr Bell who stood up to the landlord, lying prone and spent on a bed of yellow leaves and fissured earth, the ground dry and powdery and hot to the touch. A mangy dog stands guard over him, all patchy fur and scrawny legs.

The landlord has had his revenge, as he always does – getting back at this man for daring to defy him. He bided his time, waiting for the drought to be at its worst, and then started the fire, knowing that there wouldn't be water to douse it, not caring who was hurt in the process.

In contrast, this man fought to put it out and made sure his cars were used to transport his people to the clinic in town so that he has fainted from exertion and heat – and burns, judging from the blisters blooming on the exposed skin of his hands.

Mr Bell's eyes open as the boy and I are carrying him to the cottage, the dog loping after us. It is a slow and arduous process, as he is heavy and also because we hold him gingerly, so as not to further bruise his burnt and suppurating skin.

His blue gaze meets mine, startled and uncomprehending for a minute before relaxing in a soft smile. 'Kitty,' he whispers and his eyes flutter closed again.

The timbre of his voice, so tender, at such odds with what I have seen of this man so far… Who is this Kitty, I wonder.

The chickens scatter, squawking, as we approach the cottage, and the cat watches the dog warily from the rim of the well.

We carry him inside, the dog waiting obediently at the door, and lay him down on the cool floor of the cottage. I try not to think of what the landlord will do if he gets word that I am entertaining the man who defied him here, in this cottage that he built for me and him. I wonder how to rouse this man, how to minister to him, as it occurs to me that the boy expects me to know this.

Thankfully, just as I am deliberating over what to do next, Mr Bell opens his eyes again and this time the dreamy look is gone, replaced by sharp alertness.

He looks around, tries to sit up when he realises he is lying down. 'Wh… where am I?' he asks in English.

'Please, Sahib, you need to lie down, you are ill,' the boy says to him in Kannada.

I get a tumbler of water and set it beside Mr Bell. The boy lifts the tumbler to the man's lips. Mr Bell sits up, ignoring the boy's protests. He looks spent, fatigue etched into the lines on his face, his face and hands scorched and smoke-stained.

'Thank you, but I am fine,' he says to the boy, taking the tumbler from him and drinking the water in great gulps until there is not a drop left.

'Would you like some more?' I ask.

'No, thank you.' His eyes meet mine and this time recognition dawns. 'You are the dancer…' Then, his gaze taking in the two rooms that make up the cottage, 'You live here?'

I blush and am angry with myself for doing so. I will *not* be ashamed. 'Yes,' I say, my gaze unwavering.

'Thank you for bringing me here, tending to me. And for the water.' His voice brisk as he stands up, lurching ever so slightly before he rights himself. 'Come,' he says to the boy. 'We need to get back.'

He nods to me once and then walks out of the cottage, ducking in the doorway, the dog and boy following.

I watch them long after they are gone, the air fiery blue and tasting of ash.

Chapter 22

Lucy

Even the Sky

The morning the ship is to dock in Madras Harbour, there is great excitement on board. Stewards cleaning the decks, people piling on to it, whites and natives, separated by the ropes that divide first class from second and third, everyone angling for a glimpse of this land they are moving towards. The slimy green flavour of anticipation – and vomit, as children retch, the thrill too much for them. Toddlers jump in their ayahs' arms, pointing to shore.

The land that looms is reddish orange, hazy with a film of grit. As they get close to shore, Lucy's nostrils are assaulted by a potpourri of spices so strong it makes her sneeze.

'I missed this so much, the scent of home,' Miss Daly, who is returning after years at boarding school, says from beside her, breathing in deeply.

Lucy smiles politely at Miss Daly and turns her attention to the sight in front of her. Cloudy yellow water dotted with small boats; the harbour spilling with colourful people clad in all sorts; barely clothed native children weaving in and out of the horde carrying baskets and begging bowls and naked babies; people waiting to welcome the passengers off the ship; the unrelenting cloudless white sky shot through with scorching yellow sun; the trees: exotic palms with their woody brown fruit, arching towards the water; crows and seagulls cawing and screeching and swooping low; small squat tiled buildings – like home and yet so different, mud-coloured, tinged with green; whinnying horse-drawn carts and men in turbans and in suits and women in dresses and in patterned cloth and jalopies and buggies and trolleys and noise carrying over the muddy waves, overpowering aromas and clouds of ochre dust.

A different country, at the other end of the world.

As the ship gets closer, people line up along the shore – gentlemen in suits, women holding parasols – grin and wave. They look like exotic grey-winged birds among the vibrant natives – the men with their gleaming bodies, some naked except for a strip of cloth shaped like a skirt covering their loins. The native women, in contrast, are draped gracefully in crimson and sapphire, peach and emerald cloth that glimmers in the harsh sun, covering them completely, even their heads. They avert their eyes from everyone while the men stare, their gazes frank and curious and assessing.

Hawkers clamber on to the ship as it docks, persuading women into buying small white ropes of sweet-smelling flowers, garish toys that children beg to have, along with bright yellow, greasy orange and lurid red sweets.

In the water some of the natives bathe, dunking into the waves and out again, bodies shimmering, ebony hair plastered to their skulls. Women squat beside rocks jutting into the sea, and, right in the midst of all that busyness, wash clothes, blue soap-sudsy water mixing with the murky beige froth.

An amalgam of tongues, the spill of languages competing with the call of the birds. A miscellany of smells. Vendors weaving through the crowds selling rainbow-hued bracelets and sweet-meats and trinkets. Snatches of unfamiliar dialect, voices raised in question, in greeting. Laughter. Grunts and heaves as cases are dragged ashore. Dense, pressing heat, trickling in droplets down Lucy's face, her back.

Lucy's mouth is thick with the taste of adrenalin and fear, anxiety and hope. What does this country, with its myriad people, the rise and swell of melodic but incomprehensible speech, mysterious customs, unusual sounds and scents, have in store for her? Even the sky here is different – wider somehow, with scarcely a cloud. So hot and white that it makes Lucy's clothes cling to her in a sweaty embrace. She is struck by a sudden qualm as she scans the crowds of people. Will she recognise him?

Of course you will, stop being so melodramatic. The chiding voice in Lucy's head sounds very much like Mother and she is consumed by a pang of homesickness.

She quashes it, focusing instead on trying to recall James's face. Even now, after everything that has happened, the features seared behind her eyes are different from the ones owned by the man she has married. The features she is searching for, the features she traces in her dreams, they are not here.

Here a man waits for her, a man with whom she has vowed to share the rest of her life. A man who is a naïve, accepting fool for trusting Lucy, for refusing to see beyond her comely face to her hidden depths, the havoc she wreaks on those she loves and also on herself. Lucy is grateful for his blinkered vision, for his blind trust. And if he is a fool then so is she, for hoping for something different, something better, despite knowing that she doesn't deserve it.

And then, she does see him. His gaze meets Lucy's and he smiles and lifts his hat to her.

Lucy turns around then, and, like some of the children drunk on excitement and exotic sweetmeats, she is violently sick. For the first time since she set foot on the ship, as she is about to leave, she retches and retches until there is nothing left in her body, until all the hope and love and dreams she once nurtured have been regurgitated, until her past is no more and only her future awaits. With this stranger, her husband, in this new country, busy and noisy and hot and dusty and alien, that she must now call home.

Chapter 23

Gowri

Human Spite

Goddess,

The air smells scorched for a few weeks after the fire at the plantation. The smoke residue hangs above the forest, a brooding blue cloud of human spite, standing in lieu of the rain clouds that the farmers desperately plead with you for and which you are withholding. You are so much like the landlord, Goddess, both of you thriving on the power that you wield, revelling in others' helplessness.

The market that meets the Wednesday after the fire is alive with rumour.

'It was the landlord,' I hear. 'He sent his thugs down to start it.'

'The sahib and his workers were able to stop the fire before it spread to the plants, causing too much damage.'

'If the landlord wanted to destroy the plants, he would have done just that – the fire would have spread quickly and been devastating, especially now, when the vegetation is this dry. Instead he got his men to start it in the empty sheds. I think he just meant to give the sahib a scare, show what he is capable of.'

'Watch out!' I am shoved from behind as a man barrels through, pushing a handcart filled to the brim with dry chillies, their pungent potency making me sneeze. The sun beats down, ruthless. My clothes stick to my body, slimy with sweat.

I walk up to the vegetable vendor couple – the only ones in the village who are civil to me, who don't leer at me, like the men, and sneer, like the women. They have a daughter my age who is married and lives in the city, too far to visit often.

'You remind us of her,' they say fondly each week when they see me.

They give me the choicest vegetables and, I suspect, charge less than they should. They are kind to me, the only people other than Vandana Ma'am to see *me* and not the devadasi.

'No good vegetables today,' they sigh now, wiping their dripping brows, their moist faces. The produce in front of them is a sorry mishmash of wilting greens, yellowing leaves.

'Hai, what to do if this continues,' the wife laments, fanning her face with the pallu of her marigold-hued sari. 'All the wells dry. People fighting for water…'

'On top of that, the wild animals have been coming to the villages in search of water. Did you hear of the leopard in Bannihalli who made off with two goats after killing several?' the man says, as he sifts through his pitiful stock to find something he can give me.

'You make sure you are safe, girl, the door locked at all times, seeing as you live next to the forest,' the woman tells me.

'Stop, thief!' someone shouts beside me and a couple of men follow a skeletal boy who is nimbly ducking through the throng, clutching a bruised banana to his chest – perhaps his sustenance for the day.

Escape, I urge the boy in my head.

He does, the men coming back empty-handed and dejected, and I am relieved for him.

'Did you hear about the fire?' the vegetable vendor asks as he hands me the best of his sad pile of produce.

'She lives almost right next to it, of course she heard and most likely saw it as well,' his wife says, nudging him. 'Thank goodness it didn't spread to your cottage.'

An argument starts up behind us, men shouting at each other at the tops of their voices. The drought is fraying tempers as people become more desperate, their throats perpetually parched, their livelihoods at stake.

'That landlord wanted to get back at the sahib,' the vegetable vendor yells, in order to be heard above the argument, which is attracting a huge crowd. 'But what the fire has done is rally the men around their new boss. They weren't sure of the young sahib at first but now, what with him fighting the fire alongside the men, and making sure they were taken to the clinic in town, given medical care...'

Two points to Mr Bell and none to the landlord, I think. A brave man, this Mr Bell, unafraid to stand up for what he thinks is right.

You need to be like him, I hear Vandana Ma'am's voice in my head. *Leave, girl, when you can. Regardless of the consequences.*

The consequences...

My sister... She has embarked on her pre-university course and plans to become a teacher, like I wanted to. I am thrilled that at least one of us is on track to realise the dreams we shared when we were growing up. My parents are looking for grooms for her, she writes.

If I went away, I couldn't take her with me as I had planned to, to save her from the landlord. I would be uprooting her life. But if I didn't take her with me and if the landlord claimed her... She is older than I was when I was dedicated to you. She has tasted life, touched the possibilities that were just distant dreams for me. No – I can't even bear to entertain the likelihood of my sister with the landlord.

And then of course, there is you, Goddess, what happened the last time I planned to leave you...

I cannot leave yet, I have too much to lose. But I will. Mr Bell and his rebellion have inspired me, returning to me the hope I lost when I lost Vandana Ma'am.

'The young sahib's promised to pay the wages and medical bills of those injured while they recover, even though they can't work. He's pledged to build new cottages for those whose homes were destroyed, so their families are not destitute. He's a funny one, morose as anything but generous where his men are concerned,' the vegetable vendor's wife says, refusing the money I hold out to her.

'Please take it,' I say.

After a bit of back and forth, they take the money and I gather the paltry bag of vegetables and push my way out of the mob – people and animals; crows, barking dogs and the stray cow – all egging the arguing men on for a physical fight.

As I am walking out of the market, I spy the boy who was with Mr Bell, his decrepit canine companion at his side, heading towards the commotion that is taking place behind me.

He smiles when he sees me.

'How is your sahib then?' I ask, keeping my voice low, so nobody hears and reports back to the landlord. Although there is not much danger of this as almost everyone is watching the quarrel, which, from the oohs and aahs I can hear, seems to have developed into a full-blown fight.

The dog bounds up to me and starts licking the dry earth off my feet. I rub the patchy fur behind his ears and he gives a low contented growl.

Crows swoop on rotting vegetables, the pungent odour of fish and decay permeating the air; thirst an arid gasp at the back of everyone's throat.

'Sahib is tired. He refuses to rest, always at the plantation,' the boy says. He has a high-pitched musical voice, an eager, honest face.

'How are his burns?' I ask.

'Not healing fast enough.'

'Come to the cottage tomorrow afternoon. I will give you a poultice to apply to your sahib's burns.'

'What time tomorrow afternoon?' he asks.

'Right after lunch.' Nobody will see him then, as everyone will be sleeping off their midday meal, including the priest, who will be napping inside the temple. Even the forest is still at that time of day, slumbering in the languorous noon heat. Nevertheless, I add, 'Make sure no one sees you. I don't want the landlord getting word that someone in Mr Bell's employ was visiting me.'

He nods, his eyes shrewd. He might be young but he understands everything, I can tell. He is fiercely loyal to his sahib. And he likes me, I can tell that too – he will not betray me. He grins then and melts into the crowd spurring on the fight, the dog beside him.

I walk back to the cottage in the sweltering heat, taking a detour into the forest to collect the medicinal leaves that grow in the mulch beneath the fallen logs in the beds of giant trees – these also yellowing in the famine. I take the leaves home and grind them into a poultice, recalling my mother doing the same and applying it to our sore bodies when we were ill. I shrug away, as soon as it ambushes me, the ache of homesickness for a home that is no longer mine and of which I am no longer a part. I have only just got over the depression that had engulfed me since Vandana Ma'am's death and I am not about to submit to it again.

This is my life for now and I will make the best of it until I can figure out a way to get out of it. I will not give you the satisfaction of having defeated me, Goddess.

I will not.

Chapter 24

Kavya

No Going Back

Kavya packs up her life in Mumbai with the determination that has always characterised her. She has made up her mind, informed her mother of her decision, quit her job at the café. There is no going back now.

She is back at the starting point, only much older and, as yet, completely clueless as to what to do next. ('You don't know what to do next? I'll tell you. Get married and have children,' her mother yells in her head. Kavya pushes her mother's voice away. God knows it will not be this easy once she is home.) She is penniless. Zero savings. Nothing to show for her few years of pursuing her supposed dream.

But at least she tried. At least she saw where this acting lark would lead. And yes, to all appearances and purposes she has been unsuccessful in the career she chose for herself, and she has to maintain that lie in order for her mother not to get at the truth, but *she* knows she hasn't failed. Not at acting. She was – she *is* – a damn good actor; even Nagesh would agree. All those years quarrelling with her mother have helped, of course, and she will be putting her skills to good use when she is back home again, standing up to and lying to her.

The reason she is at this juncture, now, is because she made the wrong life choices. She became a cliché – the younger woman falling for the suave, successful, older man. She was stunned and blindsided by love...

It didn't take Kavya long to find out Nagesh was married but by then she couldn't stop seeing him. She was besotted, utterly charmed.

'You are beautiful,' he said. 'You drive me crazy.'

'I will leave my wife,' he promised. 'I want *you*,' he declared.

Like a fool, she believed him.

She knew, of course, that all married men said these things to their mistresses but she was different, *they* were different. Their love was the real thing.

Kavya drifts quietly around the small flat, gently placing her scripts, the writing that is her escape and which has been her salvation recently, into her bag. After her starry-eyed hopes collapsed around her, she took to writing every night, putting into words the ideas brewing in her head as she brewed coffee for customers – she had not quit her job at the café when it happened; why should she? If Nagesh dared come in, she had a few questions for him. He never did, of course – the coward.

She cast the customers who addressed her breasts instead of her face as victims in murder mysteries, where she killed them off as soon and as violently as she possibly could. In this way she had been spending her days recently, her imagination taking over, providing a different reality, rescuing her from upset and depression.

During nights when her dreams teased her with tantalising glimpses of what might have been, she would eschew sleep, and, to the music of cockroaches scuttling around the kitchen surfaces, she would sit by the open window and write. Noises would drift from outside, cars, arguments, the sound subdued yet also weirdly amplified by the night. Five storeys below, in his little hut by the entrance, the gatekeeper smoked, the glow of his beedi a pinprick in the smoky blue wall of night that was punctuated here and there by the red and yellow lights of passing cars, bicycles, rickshaws, the odd bus, everyone going home. The soft saffron glow of streetlamps lighting up hawkers: the kebab cart, the panipuri seller yawning as he wrapped up for the evening. Kavya watched and she wondered how many people were like her, loath or unable to sleep, in this great city. She would breathe in the reverie-soaked, diesel-scented, spicy air and she would write.

When she wrote, she was able to put her upset about what had happened and her anxiety about her future on hold for a brief while.

That first speaking role Nagesh secured for Kavya was just the start. He quickly discovered that Kavya was good at acting – more than good, in fact. Soon she was landing bigger roles, her talent speaking for her. Those were heady days, when she could do nothing wrong. She had more work than she could handle and she was in love.

'You are my shining star, my lucky charm,' Nagesh told her and she believed him.

And then she was cast in her first lead role in the big-budget Bollywood remake of *Pretty Woman* that Nagesh was directing. Shooting was all set to start when she discovered she was pregnant. She thought Nagesh would be pleased. How naïve she was for daring to think her love story would be different!

Nagesh had been promising to leave his wife for months. Although he took Kavya to clubs and restaurants, he was very discreet and made sure they entered and left at different times, taking care not to be photographed or linked romantically with her.

'Pooja is very possessive and it takes little to set her off. I want to divorce her but she will refuse if she knows there is another woman involved, just to make my life difficult,' Nagesh told her when Kavya moaned about the fact that they had to be so secretive.

'Get rid of it,' Nagesh said when Kavya told him about the baby, as casually as if he was asking her to alter her pose during a scene they were shooting.

She had blinked, stared at him to see if he was joking.

He wasn't. 'Your acting career is just taking off, you cannot afford to have a child,' he told her.

You' cannot afford to have a child. Not 'we'.

'I have never wanted children. If I did, I would have had some by now,' he added. And then, seeing her face, 'Come now, we have a good thing going.'

'I want to keep this baby,' she had said, caressing her stomach.

'Well then, sweetheart, I have no choice but to look for another leading lady.' His eyes stony, voice hard. 'As far as I am concerned, the child is not mine. If I hear any rumours connecting me to it, you'll be sorry.' And the parting shot, '*We* are over.'

Utter devastation was an understatement. All Kavya wanted to do was stay in her flat and bawl. But she had summoned all of her willpower and attended the shoot she had scheduled with another director the next day, only to find that her role had been given to someone else.

Again and again over the following days she went to shoots only to find that she had been summarily replaced, until she was back to being the nobody she had been before Nagesh.

At least I have the baby. Her child gave her the strength to keep going when all she wanted was to crawl into bed and not get up, to mourn her lost love and her dashed hopes, her crushed dream. And then, twelve weeks into her pregnancy, she was climbing the stairs after another shift at the café when she felt a twinge in her stomach, which, by the time she reached her flat, had become a raging cramp. That evening she lost her baby.

Her eyes sting but she blinks the tears away, stuffing her bag with clothes and jewellery and the paraphernalia of the life she has built here, her entire adult life, a testimony to her standing up to her parents, her independence.

Look at the positives. No more broken lift, no more serving coffee to demanding tourists.

Hurt, loss and sorrow lodge like a cramp in her stomach, alongside the emptiness that fills it in place of her baby. Her child, her secret. She loved it so much; she always will.

She does not know what she is going to do next. She *does* know that her mother will nag her relentlessly and try to fix her up with the eligible bachelors she is even now lining up, of this Kavya is sure.

But, she thinks as she zips up her bag and lies on the bed and stares up at the cracked ceiling, dusty with cobwebs, the bumpy, paint-bubbled, shadow-stippled contours of which she has traced those long nights when she cannot sleep, *I will be okay. I'll make sure of it.*

Chapter 25

Gowri

An Offering

Goddess,

A few days after I hand the poultice over to the boy, he is back.

I am washing clothes – mine and the priest's – trying to use as little water as possible. Most of the villagers' wells have dried out and they have to walk three miles to the next village, or five miles into town, for water, and carry it back in the sweltering heat, trying not to spill a precious drop. Some of the village women have asked if they can borrow water from the well here to slake their children's thirst – the first time they have graced me with a civil word. They come to worship at the temple armed with pails, their hopeful faces falling, habitual gaunt expressions returning, as they look at the wet sludge that stands in for water that I tip from the well into their pails.

The first I know of the boy's arrival is when the chickens scatter and the cat hisses and spits from its perch on the rim of the well. The dog bounds up to me and dances around my legs, licking my feet in frenzied affection.

'The sahib said your poultice is magic!' the boy says, grinning, as I turn to him, wiping my hands on my sari skirt. 'He asks if you can make some more for the workers – they have come home from the hospital but their wounds are taking a while to heal. He has given me this to give you.'

He hands out a roll of money, his mouth wide in a smile, most teeth missing, the few remaining ones yellow and crusted.

'I don't want the money. Come tomorrow for the poultice.'

'But the sahib said—'

'I don't want the money,' I repeat, wiping my streaming face with my pallu, staring up at the sky. *When will this end?*

The next afternoon, I am sitting in the shade of the peepal tree, fanning my face with the pallu of my sari, when the boy and dog materialise in the simmering haze of swirling dust rising from the road. I swear, Goddess, the cat actually sighs when it sees the dog, its stance defeated. If it was human, it would also roll its eyes, I imagine, disgusted at the company I have taken to keeping.

'What?' I say, going up to it and stroking its fur. 'I don't exactly have many friends to pick and choose from! And the dog loves me.'

As if on cue, the dog comes bounding up to me, pawing at my sari skirt, mouth wide open and drooling. The cat sidles away, offended, as I squat on the dry and burning yellow grass at the base of the well and throw my arms around his neck.

'Who were you talking to just now?' the boy asks, looking curiously around.

I blush, glad that my face is hidden in the dog's dirty, patchy fur. 'Nobody.'

'I swear I heard you speak.' He shrugs. 'Anyway, the sahib says he will only take the poultice if he can pay you.'

'I don't want money.'

'He said to ask what you want then, in return for the poultice.'

And that is when it comes to me, Goddess, my chance to do something towards honouring the promise I made Vandana Ma'am.

'Could you ask him to lend me some books?' I say, fetching him the poultice. 'English books,' I add. If anyone will have some books to give me, it will be Mr Bell.

I am pleased with my plan. This way, I can better my knowledge and my English, or at the very least maintain the standard Vandana Ma'am expected of me. And then when I do finally escape your clutches, Goddess, I will not be at a disadvantage.

I know, I know, I am a fool to reveal my masterplan to you. But eh, Goddess, don't you see everything anyway? Don't you know it all?

I am no longer the naïve girl I was. I know now exactly who I am dealing with, Goddess. I know *you*.

'Books?' the boy asks, scrunching up his face.

'English books,' I repeat. 'Don't you forget! And I am trusting you to be discreet. I don't want you repeating a word of this to anybody except your sahib.'

The boy curls his lip, affronted. 'What do you take me for?'

The next day is the fieriest yet. The air is still, shimmering with heat. The chickens lie on the ground, lethargic, and the cat snoozes in the shade of the peepal tree. The sky is wide and glaring white, not a speck of cloud in sight. The forest is unusually quiet.

I see the dog first, appearing from the eddying screen of dust shrouding the road.

I wait for the boy but instead I am caught by surprise when I see Mr Bell emerge. Yellow hair, blue eyes. Disconcertingly out of place here.

Flustered, I brush my sari down to rid it of dust, pat my hair in place.

He nods when he sees me.

I look at his hands; they are healing nicely.

He catches me watching. 'Thank you for the poultice. It really is helping me and my men.'

I nod, open my mouth, but no words come. *What is the matter with me?*

He holds out several books. 'Books, like you requested. I brought them myself – I wanted to check this was really what you wanted. You can read English?'

'Yes.' Finally my mouth works, dropping out the word like an offering.

He nods again. His face is grim, forbiddingly closed, and yet… He has honoured my request, brought me the books himself.

A shadow falls across the cracked, flaking dirt, staining it the dark brown of ripe tamarind. I look up at the sky. It was clear a minute ago, but now… Great big clouds are rolling across it. Where on earth did they come from?

'Look, you've brought rain!' I say, joy bursting through my reserve, ousting my shyness at finding this man here, at my cottage, with books for me.

An arc of lightning splits the sky. The dog cowers and from under the peepal tree, the cat mewls.

'Come inside, it's going to rain,' I say, grinning widely, forgetting to worry about the landlord, so happy I could cry. 'The drought is over!'

He smiles, a brief lifting of his lips. It is as beautiful as it is unexpected. 'Good news for the plantation. Thank you for inviting me in, but I need to get back.'

A great crack of thunder. I can smell the eagerness of the earth, the anticipation in the air.

'Here…' He thrusts the books at me. 'A couple of classics and a few childhood favourites. I didn't know what you wanted or liked.'

I flick through the books, unable to stop myself exclaiming, 'I know I'll love these. Thank you *so* much! I've been longing for something new to read.'

When I look up, there is a strange expression on his face. 'You remind me of someone,' he says.

'Kitty?' I ask without thinking, the name falling unruly out of my mouth.

His face shuts down. Only a muscle twitching in his cheek gives him away. 'How do you know about Kitty?' His voice is sharp.

The wind has picked up now and smacks my face, carrying, along with dust, the first hint of coolness and moisture in a long, long while. The trees in the forest sway in welcome expectation.

'You – you said her name that day when you fainted…'

I watch in fascination as his face suffuses with colour.

'Thank you for your help. Hope you enjoy the books.' He turns round and is gone, just as the first glorious drops fall to the ground like blessings.

I stand there, holding the books to my chest, covering them with my sari, tasting the rain on my lips, feeling it consecrate my body, washing away the dust and slaking the thirst that seems to have parched my throat for months, the flavour of rain-washed earth, fragrant and sacred. I watch him walk away and disappear into the forest, swallowed by trees dancing in celebration of this miracle that is the monsoon, the dog by his side, a stiff man with a ramrod-straight back, but hiding a tender secret called Kitty, who seemingly I remind him of.

Chapter 26

Lucy

Pulsing, Riotous Colour

When Lucy is finally able to get off the ship, having rinsed her mouth, powdered her face and dabbed perfume behind her ears and on her wrists, she sends a little prayer heavenwards, to the bleached, unrepentant sky so different from the fog-stained grey canopy so frequent over England. *Please, Lord, let what is to come be better than what has gone before.* Although she knows the Almighty might not be inclined to heed her plea, it calms her nevertheless, this small token of faith.

'Welcome to India.' James smiles, gathering Lucy in an embrace – smoky musk and a hint of lemon – but not lingering. He leaves his arm on her waist as he gently guides her through the crowd of natives and luggage and horses and carriages and trolleys and cars and memsahibs (which is what ladies are called here, she has learned since boarding the ship) and gentlemen and hawkers and street performers and even some cows and dogs. Crows alight for scraps and add to the awful din, the general chaos. A porter follows with Lucy's luggage, balancing it on his head with ease, barefoot on the baked ground, which must be blistering, but he walks nimbly, elegantly weaving through the throng.

Beside Lucy, a bare-chested man, sweat gleaming on his skin, wearing nothing but a colourful turban and a striped loincloth, squats on the dirt and coaxes a haunting tune out of a piece of holey wood shaped like a flute but with a conical end, voluptuous as a curvy woman. From the basket in front of him, something writhes and uncoils, something hooded, its forked tongue flashing, and Lucy recoils, shock bitter in her mouth.

A snake, she understands, although she has never seen this particular one before, not even in picture books, and she decides, swallowing down bile and fear, that she never wants to again.

James leads her away, smiling. 'It's all a bit overwhelming at first, but I daresay it will grow on you.'

Grow on her? Snakes? *Never!*

Beads of perspiration sparkle on James's upper lip, his face glowing reddish gold.

'Are they dangerous?' Lucy asks.

He nods. 'Always take a stick with you when walking in the grounds and on the plantation and keep your eyes peeled. Don't veer off the path if you can help it and never walk in bushes or thickets.'

Lucy feels suddenly light-headed, her throat parched with dread. 'There are snakes on the plantation?'

'Don't worry, one of the servants will come with you and look out for them for you.'

She is aware of sweat pouring down her back and soaking her armpits. Her face powder, she can tell, is collecting in clumps. She closes her eyes and wishes herself away, into the cool, mist-drenched iciness of a winter's morning, or soaking in a bubbly rose-scented bath. *Rose-scented, I wish!*

The air here smells of dirt and sweat and excrement, with a hint of spice. A potent combination that incites a constant urge to sneeze. There are people everywhere, edging past in an infernal hurry. The dusty path is littered with stones and she trips, more than once, grateful for James's arm holding her up.

Something stings her leg and she spies a red creature scurrying across her ankle. She emits a strangled whine.

'Stamp your foot, hard,' James says. 'There, it's gone. Keep walking. If you stand still, they'll climb up your skirts.'

Lucy shivers, despite the sticky heat.

She walks as fast as she can, James guiding her, her overwhelmed gaze alternating between her surroundings and her feet to prevent more red creatures climbing up them – there is a whole army, scampering across the mud, skirting over pebbles; they are everywhere.

'What are they?' she asks.

'Ants.'

'*Ants!* They're monstrous!'

James smiles. 'You'll get used to them.'

How can he think this? What has she done? Why on earth did she listen to her parents and think India was a good place to run away to? What possessed her to come here?

Lucy cannot believe these huge red monsters are related to the tiny black creatures in the scullery at Fairoak. She tamps down a sudden pang for the coolness of the scullery, drinking cold milk to chase down the hot cheesy scones Cook used to make especially for Lucy and Ann, when she visited, as they were their favourite snack.

There is a loud cheer right beside her and she jumps. Two mangy dogs, half their fur missing, are involved in a growling fight and men have gathered to egg them on. Dust swirls in thick red clouds. Native women hoist cloth-covered baskets on their heads, hips swaying in rhythm to their steps. Lucy wonders if their baskets contain snakes too and inches away, sticking close to James.

A cow defecates by the side of the road, tail raised up in a swishy salute, the dung settling with a pungent splatter, a swarm of flies descending.

A vendor fries something next to them, hot oil sizzling. There's a woman squatting beside him, selling ropes of small orange flowers. She thrusts one in front of Lucy's nose and for a moment, she breathes in the sweet, fragrant smell, which is immediately masked by the oily, piquant tang of whatever the man is frying.

'For memsahib,' she says in thick accented English. She grins at Lucy, and Lucy tries not to flinch at the cave of her toothless mouth, her red-stained, dripping gums, the dank odour of something rotting.

'No, thank you.' James smiles politely at her.

She winks at him. 'Pretty wife,' she says, nodding at Lucy.

'Was her mouth bleeding?' Lucy asks when they have moved away from her.

'What? The flower vendor's? Oh no!' He throws back his head and laughs. His laughter is unrestrained – a departure from his usual stiff deportment – and would be infectious, perhaps, in other circumstances. But she is not tempted to laugh along, not when she suspects he is laughing *at* her.

'That woman was eating betel nut,' he says when he has stopped laughing. 'It's like tobacco, very addictive. Many of the women here chew it.'

'Oh.'

'Not much further,' he adds. 'Our hotel is just around the corner. Sorry you had to walk, the driver couldn't get the car any closer to the harbour for the crowds.'

A man hawks mounds of rice and garish orange-coloured sauce emitting a cloying, peppery aroma. Beside him, a woman peddles raw fish that is wilting in the heat. Even though Lucy's stomach is empty, she feels nauseous as she smells the rotting fish.

Another woman sells tomatoes and other produce Lucy does not recognise, in bright colours, but droopy and beset by flies and dust. Mosquitoes buzz, bugs swarm. The heat is stifling; the air rent with languages, sounds that weave and swell and flow, odd and alien and yet strangely musical. Bracelets glint from native women's hands, round grooved circles of vermilion, scarlet, purple and gold. A rainbow of pulsing, riotous colour. The younger women cover their faces demurely, so only their mouths are visible. The older women are more brazen, like the flower vendor, and chat to the men, their bare heads helmeted in grey hair, pulled back in thick, unrelenting buns, crimson globes the size of a thumbnail gracing the centre of their foreheads.

Suddenly there is a loud, stomping noise, the earth vibrating around them. Chanting sounds accompany it, reverberating, surging.

Lucy stops walking, terrified, inching even closer to her husband. 'What's that?'

A long, low sound like a foghorn, but not quite. The earth rumbles and shudders as whatever it is comes closer. The chanting is getting louder. She can hear bells ringing, something rattling.

'Oh, a procession, I think. It must be one of the natives' feast days.'

Procession? Feast days? Not an earthquake?

And then she sees it. Everyone moves away from the road to the edges of the path as a huge grey monster with a long swaying trunk comes down the path. It lifts its long trunk up and down and side to side graciously as if acknowledging the deference of the crush of people who have moved hurriedly to the side of the road, carts pushed aside, luggage set in the mud, the road emptying in a matter of minutes, apart from a squashed tomato or two. It has huge flapping ears and small beady eyes. An elephant.

Lucy inhales, awed, speechless. She has only ever seen one in books. She thinks of Robert then. What he would have made of it? She wishes he was here with her, sharing this miraculous spectacle; that it was his arm around her waist.

How dare you? You have no right, not after what you did.

The elephant lifts its trunk and makes a sound. And Lucy understands that this is the foghorn-like sound she heard before.

It is decked in garlands, its forehead smeared with orange lines. Men dance around it, beside it, carrying a huge statue of a strange being: elephant's head, human torso. The statue is also garlanded and smeared. The men chant and sing, they ring bells and pound tambourines and exotic-looking drums, and the effect is strangely hypnotic. The earth rumbles as the elephant walks past. And for the first time since Lucy set foot in this unfamiliar country, she smiles.

James notices and squeezes her shoulder, beaming. 'Quite a sight, isn't it?' he says, eyes sparkling. But she can only nod as she watches the elephant disappear round the bend, rising above the mass of humans, so elegant and dignified despite the clamour around it.

The hotel is cool and luxurious and opulent, all high ceilings and gold furnishings; palm trees and soft music and attentive porters. Lucy lounges for as long as she possibly can in the bath, rinsing the dirt and dust from her body. Fragrant and fresh, feeling more like herself again, she emerges in a cloud of vanilla-scented steam to find her husband fast asleep on the double bed, encased in net drapes (which, he had explained when they entered the room, were to keep the mosquitoes and flies out), whistling sighs escaping from between his slightly pursed lips. Lucy perches on the edge of the bed and studies him, this man she has married, and once again, all she can see is what he is not.

He is handsome, but his eyes, his nose, his mouth, they are not the ones she has loved.

And yet, he is here, and he is hers.

Gently, she eases on to the bed next to him. He sighs, shifts away from her and is snoring again in two beats. Lucy releases the breath she has been holding and then, pulling the sheets up to her nose, as is her habit, she sinks into the soft, alien bed and, looking at a world distorted and pixelated by the mosquito net, she falls asleep.

'Lucy?' A stranger's voice.

Lucy's eyes fly open.

A man with a shadow of beard, yellow gold, his eyes thick with sleep. She is in a small confined space with him, encased in a net, it seems, the sheets smelling musty and of dreams of a cold, green, rain-plagued country, of a man who is not the one beside her.

She is hot, her body sticky with perspiration. Around them, the world shimmers, demarcated into tiny squares by the mesh curtains swathing the bed, lit with sunshine angling through the tiny gap between heavy brocade drapes.

James. My husband.

'Sorry, I didn't mean to wake you,' he says. 'You were murmuring something and I didn't know if you...'

She feels a stab of fear. 'What did I say?'

'You were calling for Ann.'

She releases the breath she has been holding. *I have to try to exorcise Robert from my mind.*

'I'm sorry I fell asleep last night. It's been all go at the plantation, that and the drive down...' He sounds apologetic.

'How is the plantation, the trouble you were having?'

'All settled down now.' His voice brisk. 'Just very busy.'

My dowry must have helped, she thinks. Then, immediately, *Stop this. You are being uncharitable.*

'Sleep well?' he asks.

She nods, uneasy in his presence, his closeness. His masculine scent. Unwashed skin and woodsmoke mired in something sharp and spicy.

Don't look uncomfortable.

The expression she has schooled her face into must appeal to him, for he leans forward.

Don't flinch.

I am not ready. I am not.

What if, when I am with him, he divines the truth?

He kisses her.

She closes her eyes and, although her head chides her to be faithful to her husband, her heart has its own ideas. It yearns for Robert – a man firmly in Lucy's past, separated not only by time but by a continent too, and yet who insists on intruding into her present.

James pulls away, looking deeply, assessing, into her eyes.

Does he know? Has he guessed?

She forces herself to return his gaze, her eyes stinging, trying not to allow the flush that is creeping up her throat to paint her face the hot crimson of guilt.

'You must be hungry, let's have breakfast.' He pushes away the mosquito net and gets off the bed.

She sags back on the pillow, spent.

What happened? she wonders. *What did I do wrong?*

But she knows, of course. James must have sensed her reluctance, her disquiet, when he kissed her.

For it isn't her husband that she wants but the man she has sacrificed at the altar of her ambitions, her selfishness. The man whom she pursued with single-minded passion because he was her stab at 'adventure'. 'It is not a game,' Ann warned, again and again. But, for the immature, spoilt girl that Lucy was, it was exactly that.

Robert had resisted her advances at first, but when he did love her, it was with all his heart, a love that was pure and honest. He had loved *her*, not her money. He had wanted to marry her when her parents found out and threatened to disown her. But she, cowardly traitor that she was, chose the cushion of respectability, a good name and her parents' approval over his love.

And that was not the worst of it. She then proceeded to lie, telling her parents that Robert had seduced her so that they sacked him without a reference. His face... That expression...

She will never forget it. She will never forgive herself.

When she had to choose between Robert and propriety, comfort, family name, high society (all the things she had pooh-poohed and claimed to tire of, to be stifled by), she chose the latter. And now she is here because she thought this was what she wanted. This is what she gave up Robert for. So why then is she pining for him? Why is she ruining her marriage before it has even properly begun?

You are destroying everything. You have made your decision, now stick to it. This is your life now, James is your husband.

She has lied to James. And she continues to do him a disservice.

Lucy keeps her eyes shut tight against the hot tears that threaten to escape, tasting salt and regret as she gulps them down.

She will not weep, not any more. She will look forward, not back. She will think *James*, not *Robert*.

She will wipe Robert's name from her heart, his features from where they are scored behind her eyelids.

She will make her marriage work. She will be a successful planter's wife and support and complement her husband in every way to make up for all the things she has done wrong, every mistake she has made, every lie she has uttered in the process of arriving at this point.

I will.

Chapter 27

Gowri

The Darkness of Evening

Goddess,

'You are different,' the landlord says when he visits the day after Mr Bell's visit, eyeing me suspiciously.

'What do you mean?' I keep my voice casual as I drain the water from the rice, as I stir the spinach, adding coconut shavings to the pot.

'I've heard that Mr Bell – the plantation owner – has been sniffing about here.'

Be still, I tell my heart. I am glad that over the years I have trained my face to remain expressionless in the presence of the landlord, unruffled, no matter the upset inside. This is one small way in which I rebel against his possession of me. He can have my body – albeit without my consent – but he will *not* read my mind. He doesn't like it, of course. That is why he is overly suspicious of me.

'I haven't seen him around,' I say. My voice is calm as the trees in the jungle, silhouetted dark grey against the darkness of evening. Inside I am roiling, undone, terrified. I think of the books Mr Bell gave me, hidden in my closet beside Vandana Ma'am's books.

'So he hasn't come this way then?' the landlord looks at me, his eyes piercing.

He doesn't know.

I breathe a secret sigh of relief as I heat up the vegetable cutlets I have made and serve them with chutney while meeting the landlord's assessing gaze, which attempts to strip me to the core, with a bland one of my own.

'What are you implying?' I allow a thread of anger to weave through my voice. I sound righteous, miffed.

'Ah, there's no need for drama,' he snaps. 'I get enough of it from my wife. Now, come here.'

I do as he asks, wondering, *What does he suspect?*

Thinking, *Does he believe me?*

The months drop away like stones from rice sieved through a colander, each day much the same as the one before. The landlord, the priest and, once a week, the vegetable vendor couple at the market are the only people I interact with, except for the times I have to dance at pujas in celebration of you, Goddess.

I read and reread the books Mr Bell gave me. I do not see him or the boy, even though I look out for the boy at the market. I miss the boy, and the dog – they were company, however brief.

And then, as the monsoons come to an end, I hear Mr Bell's name mentioned at the market. The market is particularly busy that day; it swells with rumours, it is rife with conjecture.

'The young sahib is leaving for England in search of a wife.'

I recall that dreamy look in his eyes, the tenderness when he called me 'Kitty'. Is he going to England to marry his Kitty?

'About time. He needs someone to care for him, wipe away that long face, that glum expression.'

'I think the glum expression is because of the landlord and the trouble he is still intent on causing at the plantation. The landlord has been up to his old tricks again, getting his minions to whisper in susceptible plantation workers' ears.'

'I thought the fire brought the workers together.'

A moment of speculation as the women I am eavesdropping on chew their paan in comfortable companionship.

'You talking about the plantation? I work there…' A man joins the nattering women.

I edge closer, keeping my back to them and my ears peeled.

The sound of spitting and much rustling as fresh paan is inserted into an eager mouth. 'We were talking about the fire.'

'Ah, the fire…' the man says. 'Although it did not touch the plants, it caused huge damage. Since many of the workers were seriously injured and will not be able to work for months, with the sahib still paying their wages, and constructing new cottages for those whose homes were razed by the fire, he is in a bad way. Hence he is off to England, to find a rich wife.'

'Oh?' The gurgle of keen mouths agape for fresh gossip.

'Why else would he leave now, when he should be trying to get the plantation back on track? To top it all, the foreman quit after the fire – it was all too much for him. Anyway, the sahib has appointed Ganesh, the old sahib's trusted aide, as foreman – a wise move. He will keep the plantation going for the months the sahib is away and also watch out for the landlord causing trouble.'

Is Kitty rich? I wonder. *If she isn't, will Mr Bell marry someone else, sacrifice his love for his plantation?*

I chide myself gently – I have read Vandana Ma'am's story-books too many times to count and my imagination has gone berserk – and walk away from the chin-wagging trio and up to the vegetable vendor couple, debating whether I should buy the okra or the aubergine.

Chapter 28

Lucy

Unfamiliar Sky

Lucy and James breakfast on the balcony of their opulent room, overlooking the city.

James is exactly like he was that week they spent together after their marriage: polite but distant, masking the awkwardness between them with a cloak of reserve.

Waiters attend to them, unobtrusive yet attentive, bringing exotic fruit: mango (juicy yellow, every bite a syrupy explosion in Lucy's mouth), watermelon (a pink ridged fruit dotted with black seeds, every mouthful light and refreshing), pineapple (sharp yellow sugariness), pomegranate (tiny magenta seeds like jewelled buttons on a dress, bursting with a feisty honeyed flavour); baked rice cakes and green sauce that is spicy but sweet, freckled with black seeds that are crunchy and bitter but which work surprisingly well with the sauce. (They are mustard seeds, James informs her – Lucy cannot equate them with the yellow stuff she likes so very much.)

'I'd like us to leave in the next hour – we have a long drive ahead. We'll stay overnight in a town along the way and then carry on. It can be done in one go, but it might be too strenuous for you. I hope that is all right with you?' James asks.

Lucy nods her assent.

He hails one of the waiters. 'Tell Ram to get the car round for twelve, will you?'

'Ram is one of the chauffeurs,' he tells Lucy after the waiter is gone.

'There are many?' she asks, thinking of Jack, the coachman and groom-cum-chauffeur, at home at Fairoak (no, *not* home any longer, she reminds herself).

'You'll find there's double the amount of staff here. It can get overwhelming but I'm hoping you'll like it all the same.'

Why is he so worried? Is the apprehension and anxiety Lucy is feeling so evident on her face? Or is there something he is not telling her, something she should know?

She doesn't realise she has said the last out loud until James startles and a red flush spreads across his face. 'No, I just – I know how different it must all feel for you. Having lived in England all your life, the heat here, the noise… The first impressions can be quite off-putting. But where we live, it's not like that at all, I promise. It's quiet, serene. Not many people around. But there is much involved in running the household, and you'll keep busy. I have arranged a luncheon at home in a few weeks so you can meet the plantation owners near us and their wives, make some friends…'

As he talks Lucy looks up at the unfamiliar sky, the sun a hard ball even at this time of the morning, to centre herself, stem the panic that engulfs her as she realises that this is happening, it is real. She is a coffee planter's wife, mistress of a household.

'As for the luncheon, once you've settled in you can plan the menu. Cook will advise you on what can be served here, what is available and what is not. The heat makes certain dishes inadvisable, of course. And do inform me should you need more staff or anything else for that matter and it will be arranged…' James is saying.

Lucy thinks, with a stab of homesickness, of Mother, who efficiently runs Fairoak, planning menus and answering questions from the staff about what meat to buy, what linen to use, hosting parties and coffee mornings with devastating ease, and looking lovely and unruffled at the same time.

How will I manage in this strange new country with its different rituals and routines and even a strange language – English peppered with so many new and unfamiliar words? What if I make a mistake, get something very wrong?

You'll manage, Lucy's conscience chides. *After all, you've proved to be very good at making mistakes and getting others to pay for them.*

I paid too, she remonstrates with her conscience in her head. *I did.*

'Every one of the staff is quite friendly and eager to please,' James is saying. 'Don't hesitate to come to me if you…'

Lucy thinks of Ann. She was so young when she married, and yet, when Lucy visited her, just a few months into her married life, her staff were already in love with her. Ann won them over, just as she does everyone else. She too manages her household so efficiently. How does she do it?

I wish I had thought to ask Ann for some tips before I left to come here.

She looks at the city spread out below her, a collection of tenements and huts and red brick buildings, and in the distance the port and the sea, everything coated in a film of dust. Teeming with people and carts and carriages, just as busy and noisy as the previous day, if not more so. A crow screeches, a horse neighs, a man yells, a woman begs, a child cries.

It is only eleven in the morning but already devastatingly hot, although James and Lucy are in the shade, sitting under a parasol.

I will be taking a lot of baths in this country, Lucy thinks, aware of her hair curling and sticking to her head in soggy clumps, perspiration making her clothes cling limply to her body. She sees a heavily pregnant woman, a child on either side of her, cross the road below. A man sitting on a cart whips his beasts – buffaloes? A little boy skips among the pebbles, barefoot, barely clad, yet looking content.

Stop worrying, she admonishes herself. *You are agonising about keeping house, something you have been groomed for all your life! So what if it is in a different country? You are no longer the spoilt, indulged only child of doting parents. You have grown from naïve girl into a woman who has tasted sorrow. You can do this, you* will *do this.*

After breakfast, Lucy writes to Ann. Homesick and feeling more than a little dazed, she is upset by the distance that has already crept between herself and her new husband because of her actions, although they've been together barely any time at all. She has an intense urge to talk to someone who *knows* her, and writing a letter to her friend is the only way she is able to come close.

Ann, I always dreamed of travelling to the far ends of the world, of tasting new experiences, sampling adventure. I hadn't factored homesickness into this grand plan. Truth is, Ann, I miss home terribly, I miss you all. I yearn for one familiar face among all these strangers – yes, even including my husband, whom I hope I will slowly get to know.
I don't quite fathom how I feel about India yet. It is different, so very, very different.

I don't know how long this letter will take to reach you and how long I will have to wait for your reply. I laugh now to think of how, when you moved to Brighton with Edward, the two or three days between the sending and receiving of letters were too much for me. I have always been impatient,

as you know. If I fix on something, I want it immediately.
But now… Now I have no recourse but to wait. And wait.
Oh why do we have to be so far away from each other, Ann?

When I used to fantasise about voyaging to the ends of the
world, seeking adventure, I think at the back of my mind I
always assumed you would come too. I did not think of the
why and how. In our fantasies everything is possible, isn't it?

She pauses for a minute, before picking up her pen again, the
end of which she has chewed beyond recognition – a bad habit
that she should surely stop now that she is a respectable married
woman.

Respectable? Ha! her conscience mocks.

Ann, I don't think I ever thanked you, properly, for all you
did – for being there for me during the worst few months of
my life, for not judging me, for accepting what I had done
without a word of blame or admonishment and for loving
me through it all. And, especially, for talking to Edward
and hiring Robert yourself, despite his lack of references, thus
making sure he was not destitute because of my actions. I
will be forever grateful for that, my friend.

I am a married woman now, and should look ahead, not
back. But I must say this: it gives me great solace to know
you are looking out for Robert, Ann. I hope he will be able
to move on from what I did to him and find happiness with
someone who deserves him.

Chapter 29

Gowri

A Mistake

Goddess,

A few months after Mr Bell leaves for England, I hear that he is back. Alone.

'The landlord again, causing mischief at the plantation. Ganesh the foreman couldn't control the warring factions in addition to managing the plantation. It is still reeling from the after-effects of the fire – no storage sheds, see, they were destroyed in the fire, and the new ones not yet built as the sahib insisted on constructing homes for the workers who lost theirs to the fire first. Poor sahib had to come back early, leaving his new bride behind. She will be following on later,' I hear.

So he is married. Is it to his Kitty? I wonder.

'I have never known a sahib to work so hard. He is at the plantation all hours of day and night,' I hear.

'The landlord has a lot to answer for,' I hear.

Like mine, the villagers' sympathy seems to lie with Mr Bell. He has proved himself loyal and kind to his workers and that is enough to sway their opinion in his favour.

* * *

The year ends and a new one begins. My days continue just the same as always. I cook, I clean, I feed my chickens and the cat and the priest. I write to you, Goddess, a habit that has grown on me. I do as the landlord asks. I read, I dream. I survive.

Then summer is upon us, scorching, unrelenting. Everybody is on tenterhooks, hoping, praying this summer will not stretch into the monsoon season like the last. The remembered agony of thirst on dry lips.

You have plenty of visitors, Goddess, bearing gifts and entreaties. And as always, you are unperturbed, unmoving. You have seen it all before. And what's it to do with you, anyway? You have your devotees and your devadasis. Why do you care?

The market that Wednesday is abuzz with news, rippling with gossip, tangy with fear.

'What's the matter? Why is everyone looking so alarmed?' I ask the vendor couple.

'There's a tiger on the prowl, that's what,' the wife says, her voice low and shocked as she picks the juiciest mangoes, the ripest guavas, and sets them aside for me.

'A tiger? Where?' I resist the urge to look around me, behind me.

'It was stealing cattle in the village across the river and the farmer the cattle belonged to tried to stop it.'

'Stop it? How?'

'Apparently he lost his farm after the drought and all he had left were the cattle. So he was foolish and desperate enough to try and tackle the tiger…'

'And what happened?'

'The tiger left the cattle and took him instead.'

I close my eyes, rock on my feet. *Oh, poor, poor man.*

'And now it has acquired a taste for human flesh and has been terrorising the village and neighbouring villages too. Already killed a couple of people. Only a matter of time before it comes here,' the man says, gloomily.

'Make sure to shut yourself inside your cottage – or better still, in the temple, if you hear a noise,' his wife avers as she hands me my bag of vegetables and fruit.

The panic is catching and I walk back thrumming with nerves, alert to every sound, sticking to the edge of the road farthest away from the forest, clocking every shadow, every movement, wondering if, even now, the tiger is waiting, hiding among the vegetation, keeping watch, ready to strike.

That night I dream of sharp claws digging into my skin, drawing blood, a majestic yellow and black striped beast sprawled on top of me, jaws wide open, blood dripping from pointed teeth. I wake up screaming, drenched in sweat, scaring the cat, who shrieks and scrambles off the mat in fright. I am alone in the cottage, the door is locked. I am safe. And yet...

In my dream, Goddess, the tiger opened its mouth to take a bite of my flesh and its face – its face was leering, grinning sadistically. It was the landlord. And it was *you*...

A few days later, Sunday evening, just as I have finished my chores for the day, made sure the priest is fed and in bed, there is an almighty banging at the door to my cottage, which I have made sure to lock and barricade with the stool the landlord sits on when he visits. My hand stills in the process of combing out my hair. I have had my wash and freed my hair from the plait I wear it in during the day, in preparation for bed.

It cannot be the landlord. He has already been, the previous night – he rarely visits two nights in a row, having to divide his time between his wife and the several devadasis he has claimed for himself. And in any case, he saves Sundays for his family.

The banging continues, urgent.

'Who is it?' I call, and I am surprised to hear my voice shaking. That dream, and all the talk of man-eating tigers, has affected me more than I had realised.

'It's Mr Bell, please let me in.'

I am stunned into stillness. *Mr Bell. Here? Now?*

Slowly, I lay down the comb and walk up to the door, removing the stool and pulling back the bolt.

Evening smudges the pink dreaminess of twilight with broad grey brushstrokes. The temple is quiet, the air around it rife with prayer-infused, incense-flavoured shadows. Mr Bell is silhouetted in the doorway, yellow hair standing in relief against the dark, the machine that he had brought to the temple the first time I saw him, the man behind the flash of light, dangling from his neck.

'Quick, shut the door behind you,' he says, entering, and I notice that he is breathless, panting, as if he has run all the way here.

This man is not the stern sahib I have encountered up to now. He appears worried, tense – human.

I bolt the door and stand with my back to it, gazing at him in the flickering half-light cast by the lamp. Why is he here? What would the landlord do if he found out? My heart lurches at the thought.

'I'm sorry to barge in like this,' Mr Bell says, sounding abashed, the desperate urgency of before now gone. He is passably fluent in Kannada, although he speaks it with a crisp accent. 'I... I think I heard the tiger.'

I startle, stumbling away from the door, barricading it once again with the stool.

'You did?' I ask when I am convinced the door is shut tight enough to require a lot of force to open it from the outside. 'Where?

Did it follow you… here?' My voice dips at the last word as panic takes my whole body captive.

'No, no, please don't worry. I wouldn't put you in danger,' he says.

You already have by being here. The landlord… I think. *And how do you know the tiger hasn't followed you?* My ears are alert for any alien sound.

'I – I was taking photographs – the light in the forest is perfect at sundown. Then I heard a roar coming from within the jungle. I slipped away, came here. I… I don't think it saw me. I'm pretty sure it didn't—'

'What if it did? What if it's right outside?' My voice is thick with fear.

The darkness beyond him when I opened the door to him… Was there something slinking in there, biding its time, waiting to pounce?

We stand there for a couple of moments listening. Crickets chatter, an owl hoots somewhere in the darkness. The rustle and slither of nocturnal animals in the undergrowth. Ordinary sounds.

My heartbeat returns, gradually, to normal. 'I don't think the animals would go about their business if there was a tiger on the prowl,' I say softly.

He nods. 'Sorry to have disturbed you, I will go now.'

'Are you going to walk back?'

'Yes.'

'I suggest you wait then, for a while, just in case.'

He hesitates and then shrugs. 'I was foolish. The servants warned me not to go out, or if I did, to take the car. But I… I wanted to walk, to be by myself for a few hours before going back to the plantation—'

He stops talking abruptly, as if realising where he is, and with whom. This is a different side I am seeing to the firm and collected

Mr Bell. The scare with the tiger seems to have shaken him, made him come out of himself.

'Are things okay at the plantation now?' I ask.

He looks at me sharply, his face closing up. I have said the wrong thing, it seems.

'I… I mean, after the fire,' I say.

His features relax and he inclines his head at me. 'Thank you for helping out that day and for your poultice.'

'You have already thanked me, and given me books too.'

'You've read them?'

'Many times.'

He nods. I know he wants to ask me how it is that I can read English – I can see the question blooming in his eyes – but he doesn't.

A roar, long and loud and menacing, from the jungle.

I meet his gaze and for a brief moment I see the dread that I feel reflected in the shimmering blue depths of his eyes before his habitual reserve comes down like a screen.

The silence in the aftermath of that chilling sound is ominous, eerie; a stealthy pause before attack. I picture a stirring outside the cottage, a sleek, striped body stretching as it prepares to swoop, and I shiver. All the vivid monsters conjured by my imagination since I moved here raise their heads and batter the walls of my mind.

'I'm sorry, I didn't think. I just came here as you are nearest…' His eyes bright in the shadowy light.

'The cottage is stronger than it looks.' *I hope it is.* My voice sounds strange, hoarse and too loud, although it is barely above a whisper. My eyes dart to the door, checking to see the stool is in place. 'You are safer here than out there in the wild.' To my surprise a giggle escapes me, and then I am laughing, involuntary chuckles rife with hysteria.

'Look—' Mr Bell begins, but whatever he was going to say is swallowed by another roar. Louder. Nearer.

Oh...

Mr Bell's eyes meet mine, flush with the terror he cannot disguise.

I shudder, throwing my arms around myself. I cannot seem to stop shivering.

'Kitty, it's okay. It's fine...' he says softly, his voice raw and slippery with telltale tremors.

I look up at him, the shock of hearing him call me *Kitty* again quelling my shaking.

His face suffuses with colour as he realises his error. 'I'm sorry, you do look so very like her.'

'Who is she?' I ask.

The mask he routinely wears takes over his face again so it becomes the rigid visage I am used to. 'Someone I used to know,' he says, his voice curt.

From nowhere, I am overcome by rage, sharp and hot, like biting into a chilli. All the emotion I feel, fear at being eaten by the tiger, or if not, discovered by the landlord to be harbouring a man in the cottage, turns to anger at this man. 'That's twice now you've called me Kitty, she's obviously more than just an acquaintance. You have come here, running away from a tiger that might be circling the cottage or feasting on my chickens right this minute. At the very least I deserve an explanation.'

I am breathing very hard when I have finished, my whole body tense.

Outside it is eerily quiet. My ears are peeled for sound but there is none. No roar, no friendly cricket music, no croaking of frogs, no crackle of leaves. Nothing.

'You are right, you do deserve an explanation,' Mr Bell says and I look up at him, worry suspended. 'Kitty...' Her name on his lips is reverent, like a prayer. 'Kitty and I… our mothers were close friends and we grew up together. We – we were in love. She was the one who got me interested in photography; she gave me my very first camera as a present.' He takes a deep breath. 'We were going to get married once I finished my studies. But then…'

So he did not marry her, then? The memsahib who is to join him here soon is not Kitty?

'Her letters to me at boarding school kept me going after the news came that my brother had died in the war. Then later, when my parents succumbed to the consumption, it was Kitty, her letters, that gave me hope, allowed me to look ahead. But then her mother died and her father married a baroness and they decided that I, as a soon-to-be plantation owner, was not good enough – that Kitty deserved better. She wrote to me and we decided to elope, but it was too late. By the time I intervened, she was married.'

I have never heard him speak so much; he sounds defeated. I want to make him feel better. 'Please sit,' I say, indicating the stool barricading the door. 'Would you like something to eat?'

He smiles, a sudden, glorious lifting of his lips, the shadows in his eyes dissipating. His whole face creases into pleasing lines and somehow, despite this, he looks so much younger. I feel, despite my fear of the tiger and the landlord, a reciprocal lifting of my heart.

You should smile more often, Mr Bell.

'The last meal before I become a meal for the tiger?' he says.

I laugh, too loudly and too much. Maniacal mirth to keep the anxiety at bay. There have been no more roars but the forest is still suspiciously quiet. The night hushed, waiting. Wary.

'So was that a yes or a no?' I ask.

'I beg your pardon?'

I think of Vandana Ma'am then – she taught me that very phrase: *I beg your pardon.* I bite my lower lip, hard, to push the ache away, replace it with physical, more immediate pain.

'Would you like something to eat?' I ask, running my tongue over my lower lip, which is starting to swell.

'No, thank you.'

'Please, sit,' I say again, indicating the stool.

And so he sits. I sit on the floor opposite him.

'Why don't you sit on a stool as well?' He looks around.

'There's only one stool,' I say, my voice abrupt. I will not be ashamed of my house and its lack of furniture.

'Oh, right. Then I'll sit on the floor with you.'

'No, please…'

But he ignores me and lowers himself gingerly to the floor beside me.

'How do you sit like this?' he asks. He is uncomfortable on the floor, I can see, as he settles his back against the cool wall, as I am doing.

'I'm used to it.'

He stretches his legs out in front of him. He has long legs and they almost touch the opposite wall. A mosquito buzzes beside me and I clap my hands, catching it.

We lapse into silence. The lamp has burned out. The cottage smells of oil and spilt secrets and anxiety and musk and ginger – his scent, alien in here and yet strangely soothing. He is so close that I can feel his breath on my face: lime and peppermint.

Who would have thought that the sahib himself, the man who stood up to the landlord, would be sitting companionably on the floor of my cottage beside me, shadows surrounding us, danger skulking in the darkness outside?

'Listen,' I say after a bit.

'What?'

I nod towards the door, cock my ear and he understands: the ordinary jungle sounds have started up again. He smiles at me, the relief I feel reflected in his face. His talking to me about Kitty, us facing the danger of the tiger together, has made him drop his severe persona, stripped him to who he really is. On the floor of my small cottage, where he is so very out of place, he somehow looks less imposing, more relaxed than I have ever seen him.

'It's gone,' I say, my voice heady, 'moved on.'

'You spoke in English just now,' he remarks, bemused.

I did not even realise I had switched to English. Perhaps I did so because I am sitting where I used to with Vandana Ma'am when we studied and practised and she insisted I speak only in English.

'So how is it that you can read and speak English fluently?' He asks the question he has obviously wanted to ask before but did not feel comfortable enough to do so.

'I had a very good teacher who taught me to read, to love books. I wanted to become a teacher like her before I came here.' To my astonishment my voice breaks and I feel tears swell and trickle out of my eyes. I try to stop them but they will not heed my call.

Mr Bell goes rigid, looking embarrassed on my behalf. I bet he wishes he was anywhere but here, with a prostitute who cannot control her emotions.

I rub the back of my hand across my face.

'You should go now, I'm sure it's safe,' I sniff.

He leans towards me, his jaw working, a strange expression on his face.

I shuffle back, away from the door, thinking he wants to leave.

But instead he gathers me in his arms and says, softly, into my hair, using the same tone of voice he has used when he said *Kitty*, 'Ah now, don't cry.'

And then he kisses me.

I have been so lonely, Goddess. I have missed simple human connection, kindness and conversation so much. I have been yearning for someone to see *me*.

And although I know deep down that he is not really seeing me but the woman I remind him of, his Kitty, for the first time in my life I respond to a man's attentions instead of stiffly waiting for them to be over.

I kiss him right back.

Afterwards, he stands up, dresses and gathers his machine, which he has set down by the door. He slings it around his neck and turns, looking directly at me. 'I'm sorry, this was a mistake.'

For me it wasn't, I think. It wasn't anything like what I'm used to. He was tender with me, gentle; he was kind.

I admire this man – I have done so ever since he stood up to the landlord, regardless of the consequences. Unlike the landlord, he is kind to his men, he cares about them. I have read the books he has given me conscious of the fact that I was reading words he has read before, touching pages that he has touched.

After the kiss, before he went further, he asked me if it was what I wanted. Never before had I been afforded that courtesy.

I will not regret what happened. For him, it was a mistake, but for me, for the first time in my life, it was *my* choice.

I am struck by the desire to tell him all this, but instead I say, 'I am sorry about Kitty.' I know that once he goes through the door, I will never see him again. Not like this. And I have wanted to say those words to him since he confided in me about Kitty.

He closes his eyes, drags a hand across them. 'She is the mother of three boys now, she is happy.'

He sounds so sad. I want to take him in my arms, kiss his ache away, like he did mine just a while ago. But I don't have the right.

He sighs deeply. Then, looking at me, 'She had wavy dark hair too, like yours and those hazel, catlike eyes. In that light, with your hair just so... May I take a photo of you?'

Caught off guard, I can only nod.

He lifts the camera up to his face. I pat my hair into place and look not at him but at the hearth, trembling with shadows, as he takes my picture. He lowers the camera and his façade is back; that forbidding face. 'I'm sorry. This…' He waves his hand around. 'It… I shouldn't have…'

In the book of his life I am a mistake, secreted away in the margins, destined to be a dusty old memory, shaken out once in a while by a smell or a book, perhaps, and then tucked away, back in the recesses of his mind, to be forgotten in time.

He turns away, his shoulders stiff and purposeful as he opens the door, a draught of cool night air wafting in, bringing the scent of jasmine and intrigue.

Then the door is shut and he is gone, walking out of my life as easily as he walked in.

Chapter 30

Kavya

Five Words Long

Home.

The courtyard with its tamarind and mango, banana, jackfruit and coconut trees and pineapple bushes, the heady scent of a fruity feast mingling with spice; the dog bounding up and licking Kavya's legs in joyous welcome.

The neighbourhood children peek shyly from behind their mothers' skirts at this newcomer while their mothers smile at Kavya. 'Look at you, city girl,' they say, a mixture of awe and pride coating their voices.

Save your awe for someone else. It's misplaced with regards to me, thinks Kavya, an ache in her chest.

They wipe their hands on their pallus and cup her cheeks. 'We knew her when she was a waif of a thing, tinier than you, and look how big she is now,' they say to their children and the youngsters giggle delightedly, dirty hands covering agog mouths, germs going in.

Smoke rises from the bathroom and Kavya's mother comes down the kitchen steps, peering anxiously through the fruit trees, the frown on her forehead relaxing and her face lifting in a smile when she spies Kavya. Her mother's smell of talcum powder, onions and sweat as she strokes Kavya's cheek briefly. 'Come inside, your ajji and Da are waiting.'

Kavya feels a rush of affection for her mother, who is looking older, she notes, more grey in her hair.

Her father is sitting under the chikoo tree, beside the tulsi – holy basil – plant, peering at her from over the top of his glasses, lungi straining over his belly, a wide grin taking over his face. 'Kavya! My favourite daughter.' Joy bubbling over in his voice, gentleness and love.

'Your *only* daughter,' she says, laughing, happiness briefly pushing away the heaviness in her heart as she engages in this much-overused riposte with her da.

Despite the circumstances, it is good to be home, Kavya thinks as she steps inside. The cool cement floors. The smell of incense from the shrine to the gods in the puja room mingling with the spicy sweet aroma of sambar.

Her ajji emerges from the puja room, her whole face lighting up when she sees Kavya.

'Come here, child,' she says, opening her arms wide and folding Kavya in them. Comfort and security, coconut oil and sandalwood.

'How are you, child? You're looking pale. Have you not been eating enough?'

'Ajji, I'm fine.' She brushes Ajji's concern aside.

Ajji says, gently, 'I heard you've come back for good. It's a brave thing to do, Kavya.'

Kavya smiles gratefully at her grandmother. How does she know just what to say to make her feel better? 'You think so, Ajji? I feel like a failure.'

'Nonsense. You're very far from a failure. We all stumble and take wrong turns along the way – it makes finding the right turn even more remarkable and thrilling.'

Kavya smiles properly for what feels like the first time in a long while. She leans forward to give her ajji another hug. 'I've missed you, Ajji.' She surveys her grandmother, eyes twinkling, 'What is this I hear about you being connected to this notorious temple in Doddanahalli? Tell me all.'

'First things first, wash and freshen up and eat. You must be hungry.'

Kavya knows both her mother and her grandmother have been waiting to feed her since her last visit and that they will not rest until she has eaten. And she *is* ravenous. When she comes out of the bathroom, fragrant with woodsmoke and soap, her mother sets a heaped plate in front of her. A feast of idlis and dosas and sambar and chutney, curd rice and bisibelebhath. Kavya eats like she has not eaten in a decade, three pairs of love-filled eyes taking her in.

Afterwards she sits back, empty plate, full stomach, and is rewarded by three beaming faces.

'I bet you didn't eat properly while you were in Mumbai. You don't look after yourself,' her mother remonstrates.

'Laxmi!' Her da and Ajji say her mother's name in unison – a warning – and Kavya smiles.

Warm and sated and soporific, she finds her mother funny, not annoying.

'You haven't touched the sambar powder I sent with you the last time you visited, have you? What have you been living on, bread and jam?'

She leans back on her chair, closes her eyes. 'Mostly, yes, Ma.'

'Well, good job you are here. We need to fatten you up slightly before showing you to prospective grooms. No one likes a scrawny, underfed—'

'Laxmi!' Her da's mild voice rises ever so slightly, at the same time as Kavya cries, her peaceful acceptance of her mother's nagging of a minute ago forgotten, her voice taking on the shrill overtones of her teenage years, 'Ma, how many times do I have to tell you that I'm not getting married yet? I need to know what I am doing with my life first—'

'You can get married and then—'

She stands up, pushing back her chair so abruptly that it falls over. 'I don't want to get married full stop until—'

'You are almost twenty-eight, nobody will want you in a couple of years.'

Her father sighs loudly and Ajji has closed her eyes, both of them having been witness to too many of these altercations and knowing there's no point getting involved when Kavya and her mother are like this.

The rational part of Kavya sees all this through adult eyes, the sensible voice in her head urging her to stop and walk away, but the part of Kavya that has been reduced to a teenager the moment she came home does not want to give up. The teenage part wins, of course – it always does.

'Thirty is no different from twenty-eight.' Her throat is hoarse from yelling.

'There's no talking sense into you,' her mother huffs and that is the last straw.

'This is why I didn't want to come home!' Kavya screams, her voice breaking as she storms off to the veranda and plonks herself down on the swing seat that hangs suspended from the roof.

'Kavya?' Her ajji's soft voice.

'Coming here was a mistake, Ajji,' she says, furiously swinging, her eyes too blurry with hot, angry tears to focus on her grandmother.

'She worries for you.'

'Fine way of showing it, forcing me into marriage.'

'Nobody is forcing you into doing anything, least of all your mother.'

'Ha!'

'She could have forced you to stay here but she allowed you to go to Mumbai and follow your dream.'

'Under duress and only because I didn't give in.'

'She only wants what's best for you.'

'Getting married is not best for me at the moment.'

'You don't know that.'

'Ajji, not you too!' She buries her head in her hands. 'I want some peace of mind while I decide what I want to do next.'

Something is pressed into her hands. She lifts her head, opens her eyes.

'While you're deciding what to do, read these. Hopefully they'll lend some perspective.'

Her ajji is in front of her, looking keenly at her with her bright, intelligent eyes.

Kavya looks down. Her ajji has pressed a thick sheaf of paper into her hands. Pages and pages of Kannada writing penned in a beautiful hand. Not one she recognises.

Letters. They look like letters.

Goddess Yellamma, the first one reads.

Letters to a goddess?

She looks at her ajji, a question in her gaze.

'Read these, then you'll understand. About the temple… The deeds… And they might help you too.' Ajji sighs deeply. 'Sometimes, when I've felt overwhelmed by life, I've read them and then my problems haven't seemed so insurmountable any more.'

'But they're private.'

'They belong to me,' Ajji says softly.

'You wrote them? But this handwriting…'

Ajji shakes her head. 'I didn't write them, but they're mine now.'

'How? And who wrote them?'

'Once you read them, you'll understand. We've all read them,' her mother says, turning up suddenly beside Ajji, in a placid tone of voice.

She is offering a truce but Kavya's emotions are too churned up, so she ignores her mother, addressing her ajji instead.

'So, Ajji, you really *are* the owner of that controversial temple?'

'Not me…'

'But you have the deeds?'

Ajji nods.

But it is all too confusing and Kavya is tired. She cannot see how reading someone's private letters will help her. She opens her mouth to say so, but her ajji interrupts.

'Read these, then we'll talk.'

From his chair underneath the chikoo tree, her father coughs. The dog is sitting at his feet and both man and dog look serene, her da reading the newspaper and the dog watching the world go by.

Wish I knew where my life was headed, Kavya thinks for the umpteenth time. But until then, she might as well take her ajji's advice.

Kavya sits on the swing in the veranda of her parents' house, letters written to the Goddess Yellamma and belonging to her ajji in her hand, a zesty breeze stroking her cheeks, bringing sounds of a dispute in the neighbour's house, crows cackling, a child crying.

Her ajji sits beside her, patting her hand.

Kavya picks up the first letter. It is five words long:

Goddess Yellamma, it reads.

Why?

Why me?

The words oozing angst, upset.

Why write to the goddess? What happened to this person? Who is it? And why, how, does Ajji have these letters?

She looks at her ajji. Ajji looks down at the letters, her eyes brimming.

Kavya picks up the next letter and starts to read it.

Chapter 31

Lucy

A Fleeting Connection

The journey to the plantation passes in a weary blur. Lucy watches as the city falls away and long stretches of countryside take its place. Fruit trees burdened with exotic offering, vendors of food and flowers and garish coloured water and lurid orange tea and wilting vegetables assembled along the sides of the road, shouting their wares, semi-naked children clothed in dust, huge hopeful eyes and cupped hands, begging for alms; a woman, eyes closed, praying to what looks like an anthill adorned with flower garlands, farmers ploughing fields, the bulls looking weary-eyed as they dig furrows through the dark brown, powdery soil; women carrying pails of water on their hips, children clinging to their legs, multi-hued saris a wash of colour in the sunlight, monkeys leering from trees, brazenly trying to steal food from the vendors, a boy chasing them away with twigs.

In the small towns that they pass Lucy sees women like her – uprooted from home and transplanted here, yet still clinging to home in their habits and attitudes and in their hearts – decked out in stately clothes, hats and parasols to combat the heat, some in carriages, others gingerly walking past, taking care not to step on the rotting tomatoes, the banana skins, the dirt and rubbish casually flung by the side of the road, and looking out for those ants, she supposes. They are followed by two or three servants who carry their shopping. As they pass they lock eyes with Lucy, empathy in their gaze, a fleeting connection.

That night they stay at a hotel not so opulent as the one the previous night, but comfortable all the same. Lucy lies down on the bed, her pleasure at resting her body, aching from the drive, warring with the upset she feels at James having retired to his room with a curt goodnight, just as he would with a stranger.

She is about to close her eyes when there is a movement at the periphery of her vision. Something above her – on the ceiling. She looks up and, through the mosquito net sees a brown scaly lizard darting nimbly across the cream plaster, which is cracked in places and bubbly. She lets out a small yelp and, jumping out of bed and pulling on a robe, opens her door and peeps outside. Nobody about. She dashes across and knocks on James's door.

'Come in,' he calls.

He is sitting in an armchair reading, and stands up when she enters. 'Lucy, what's the matter?'

He follows her into her room and smiles when she points to the reptile, which has in the space of a few seconds been joined by a friend – bulbous eyes, flicking tails, darting tongues.

'Don't worry about them, they're looking for flies.' His voice soft, not abrupt like before.

'But… but what if they lose their grip and fall on me?'

'They're harmless. Honestly.'

She shudders.

James reaches up to the lizards.

She shuts her eyes tight, startling when she hears a loud clap.

'You can open your eyes now.' A smile in his voice.

Tentatively she peers upward. The lizards have scattered, chased away by James's clapping. She can still see them hugging the corners of the ceiling, but they are no longer directly above her bed.

'Thank you.' She manages a small smile.

'Goodnight,' he says. 'You must be exhausted from the journey, I certainly am. Sleep well.'

He leaves her room, closing the door gently behind him.

Although desperately tired, she cannot sleep. She lies awake, wishing the lizards away while keeping a bleary eye on them. Her eyes ache with unshed tears.

How is she to repair her marriage, which seems to be disintegrating even before it has properly started because of her mistakes? What is she to make of this country, with its menagerie of animals that seem to be everywhere, at the harbour, on the roads, even *inside* houses and hotels?

Somehow, sometime during the night, she does fall asleep for she wakes to sunlight washing the room in yellow light and no lizards anywhere in sight.

They set off again after breakfast. The countryside is more beautiful now, hilly and bejewelled by lush vegetation, punctuated by sparkling rivers dotted with boatmen and swimming children, women washing clothes and utensils. Small, quaint villages with humble dwellings. Huts topped with straw, barely big enough to hold Lucy, let alone a whole family. No door, just a yawning gap of an opening, covered by a holey cloth. Some houses are made of cloth rigged together in the shape of a tent by tree trunks.

'No use at all during the rains,' James observes.

Children cluster outside these abodes, women cook on open fires and men sit around in their rainbow-patterned loincloths. Lucy watches the children skipping in the mud, playing a strange game that involves hitting a pebble at a pile of stones and dislodging it. One of them manages to do it. He screams in joyous surprise. The others laugh and cheer.

'And yet they are so happy,' she says.

James nods. 'Yes.'

Lucy thinks of her life until a few months ago, cossetted and pampered, everything handed to her on a platter. Until recently she had not known unhappiness, angst. She had claimed to be bored with her life, selfish spoilt girl that she was, but she understands now that she has been so lucky. And although she did something terrible, something she has to live with all her life, even after everything that's happened, she has landed on her feet.

She thinks of how, just the previous day, she was anxious about managing a posse of servants, hosting a party, and reproaches herself. Compared to these people, how little they have, she is so fortunate. And yet she worries, while they live in the moment.

They are happy. Why isn't she?

Eventually, she falls asleep as the car meanders through winding, bumpy roads.

She is jarred awake when the car swerves wildly and careens to a halt. Lucy opens her eyes, finds her head resting on a warm shoulder, the scent of woodsmoke and spiced apples. Her husband.

She sits up, looks out and gasps with shocked awe. Plants sway gently in the breeze, stretching around and beside them, an undulating velvet emerald, flanked by tall trees with vines climbing up them. The sky dense cream with hints of pink and peach. Through the open window, Lucy inhales the fertile green smell of new growth, tinged with something piquant and tantalisingly chocolatey.

'It's beautiful,' she murmurs.

James smiles. 'Our coffee plants,' he tells her, his voice thick with pride.

'Wow!' Lucy looks around again, taking it all in – the rows and rows of neatly planted shrubs: burgeoning, healthy, blushing green. Trees at the periphery, standing sentinel. The peppery taste of fresh life. Vines hugging the trees, sprouting small berries. Green vegetation and red mud. She feels something unfurl in her heart: hope.

It is all going to be okay.

'Why have we stopped?'

James's smile disappears, his mouth tightening in a grim line as he looks at something. Lucy follows his gaze to a fancy car making its way towards them, along the narrow road.

It is almost upon them, and now she understands why their chauffeur pulled into the ditch on the side – there's not enough space for two cars.

'The landlord of the village,' says James. His voice is level, but something in his tone makes Lucy turn to look at him. 'He is related to the Maharaja – the King – and makes sure everyone knows it. We have to tiptoe around him... all of us.'

The sound of his voice, as if he has been made to swallow a tumbler of bad coffee, indicates that there is more to this than just the landlord throwing his weight around. From what Lucy has gleaned about hierarchies on board the ship coming here, she understands that everyone kowtows to them, the English landowners – even landlords. She can see why it grates on James to have to give way, literally as they are doing now, and figuratively, to the landlord. But there's more here than just that.

From the impression Lucy has of James so far, how he is with the staff, his caring disguised within his brisk manner – he calls the chauffeur by name instead of the generic 'Boy' and treats him with respect, making sure he has eaten, rested – he is not one to take umbrage at having to give way to another car; in fact they have stopped for trolleys and carriages, even bullock carts, along the way.

The car rumbles to a halt beside them.

A bald head pokes out of the window – huge moustache, bug eyes. The man smiles at James, the smile not quite reaching his eyes. No love lost between these men, Lucy notes.

Then the landlord looks at her. His gaze is assessing, lecherous and mocking all at the same time. It is as if, in that one look, he has taken a measure of Lucy, knows who she is, what she has done. It makes her feel exposed, dirty.

'Who is the pretty lady?' he calls out of the window, his voice as slimy as his face.

Lucy has averted her gaze but she can still feel his eyes violating every inch of her.

'My wife… She's just arrived.'

'Well, well, well, you kept that quiet,' the landlord sneers. 'Aren't you going to introduce us?'

'Lucy, this is Mr Jayaram Wodeyar, the landlord of this village.' James's voice is clipped, tight.

Lucy forces herself to look up, pulling her lips into the semblance of a smile, as his gaze rapes her. 'How do you do?'

A movement then: the jangle of bracelets, the shadow cast by a veil. There is someone beside him.

Lucy peers past the landlord's repulsive face into the car.

A girl. Very young. She looks up, and at Lucy. Huge eyes radiating sadness. A face, although hidden by a veil, unable to mask its beauty. She is stunning. How is she related to this man?

'We should be introduced properly. Come to us for supper… hmmm… let's see – the second Sunday in July,' the landlord says, his voice magnanimous as if bestowing a huge favour.

Lucy can't think of anything worse than spending time in the company of this man. Just a few moments in his presence have been enough to put her off him for ever.

'We have—' James begins.

The landlord cuts him short. 'I'm sure you can spare a few hours to show your wife around, introduce her to the community.' His tone implies that he *is* the community, all there is to know and see. 'As it is you work too hard,' a smirk in James's direction before he once again turns his unwelcome attention to Lucy. 'You don't want your pretty wife to be bored now, do you?'

'Thank you, but no. We are busy.' James's voice is wintry.

'If that's how you want to play it…' The landlord's voice is mild but the words definitely contain a threat, Lucy discerns. He smiles languidly at her and pulls his head inside again. The car moves away.

Lucy exhales.

'Who was that girl?' she asks as soon as they have started moving.

But James doesn't seem to have heard her. The encounter with the landlord has unnerved him.

'James?'

'Hmmm?' His eyes when he looks at Lucy are raw, troubled.

He seems not at all interested in the girl but she is all Lucy can think of, trapped beside that bull of a man. So beautiful and yet, even in that one small glimpse, exuding such sorrow. 'James, was that woman in the car with him his daughter? Or even… Not his wife? Too young, surely?'

'No,' James says shortly. 'No one of any consequence.'

'What do you mea—'

'Ah! Here we are,' James says and his voice is deliberately light, determinedly cheerful. 'Mrs Bell, welcome to your new home.'

And as the car sweeps past an ornate gate and up a tree-lined drive, landscaped gardens and tennis court giving way to a huge courtyard, fruit trees and lush lawns leading to the sprawling mansion that is to be Lucy's new home, all thoughts of the girl disappear.

The car rolls to a stop beside a fountain shaped like a mermaid from whose mouth greenish-yellow water spills out. The house, vast and palatial, is spread out in front of them. Creepers climb up the pillars of the veranda (which is what Lucy has been instructed by the women on the ship that balconies level with the house are called here): roses, small white flowers and a profusion of pink and yellow and orange cascading blooms. The scent of blossom and heat and dust and excitement and trepidation.

On the long veranda are collected a vast group of people, all of them peering anxiously at Lucy as the chauffeur opens the door and James helps her out of the car. As she climbs up the steps to the veranda on James's arm, the collective gaze of the staff follows her, and when she comes to a stop in front of them, they smile as one and say, 'Welcome to your home, Memsahib,' their vowels drawn out as they stumble on the unfamiliar English words.

James whispers, his breath warm and sweet in her ear, 'They've been practising, as you can see.'

'Thank you.' Lucy smiles. A cool breeze fans her face, smelling of adventure and new beginnings. She watches the car being driven away to be parked for the night in one of the outbuildings beside the main house, which she presumes is the garage. Land stretches out from around the house, green and fertile. Lawns and tennis courts adjourn the courtyard; there is an arbour and even a small bandstand. Trees – palm and others she cannot name, a profusion of flowers in all colours. White pillars bolster the veranda, ringed by ornate railings. The smell of beeswax and polish, spice and something sugary wafting on the evening breeze. Elaborately framed paintings and animal skins decorate the walls, a couple with heads still attached; beady eyes, long, woody horns. Armchairs are arranged around a small table. Lucy can see herself sitting out here, writing to Ann and her parents. In the distance the outbuildings, and beyond that the coffee plants interspersed with tall trees, vines clinging to them like tired children.

It is nothing at all like home and for the first time this is a freeing thought. She can reinvent herself, push aside everything that has happened to her, all that has gone before.

I could be happy here.

And for once, her conscience is quiet, not yelling accusations at her, apportioning blame.

'Let me introduce you to the staff,' James says.

Lucy turns to the assembled group and smiles at each one in turn, beginning her first evening as memsahib of her new home.

Chapter 32

Gowri

A Small Smile

Goddess,

Every day since my sojourn with Mr Bell, I anticipate the landlord's rage, his punishment. I wait for yours, Goddess. But there is nothing. I seem to have got away with what happened.

And yet, I do not relax. Perhaps the landlord is biding his time. Perhaps you are. I have learned the hard way not to take the landlord or you for granted, Goddess.

A fortnight after Mr Bell's visit, the market is jubilant, the relief among the villagers palpable.

I head over to the vegetable vendor couple to find out what everyone is celebrating.

'The tiger is not headed here any longer,' the wife says. 'It's moving further away from us, to the villages in the north.'

'Ah.' I smile but inside I feel a bit bereft. I have grown to quite like the tiger now; it delivered some magic into my monotone life. A secret all of my own.

I imagine telling the vegetable vendor couple, picture their open-mouthed expressions of amazement.

I grin widely. 'That's a relief,' I say.

* * *

A month after Mr Bell's visit, the boy arrives, dog in tow.

I squat down and bury my face in the dog's dirty fur. 'I missed you,' I say and the dog yaps in delight.

'Here, the sahib asked me to give this to you.' The boy holds out an envelope, my name written across the front in English.

I wipe my hands on my pallu and take it, my heart dancing, and tuck it into the pocket of my sari skirt beside my current letter to you, Goddess.

After the boy and dog are gone, I sit on the washing stone and carefully open the envelope.

A photograph. I am lying on the mattress, my hair fanned out around me, my eyes dreamy, a small smile playing on my face. I look beautiful.

I tuck this reminder of a charmed night back into the envelope and place it in one of the books Mr Bell gave me.

When the landlord visits, he's in a jolly mood.

'Come, we're going out.'

I stare at him. 'But you've never taken me out before.'

'There's always a first time. A music performance, I find them tedious. You might at least alleviate the boredom by giving people cause to talk about something other than the merits of tablas over sitars. I want everyone to know that you are mine.'

His suspicious mind at work again. As time has passed, the landlord has become more possessive and mistrustful, not less.

'Wear that turmeric sari I gave you last week,' he adds, pulling me to him, breathing sourly down my neck.

We are on our way back from the concert when the car jerks to a stop. It is evening, the sky a panorama of saffron and vermilion and marigold. I have been dozing in the back of the car when it shudders to a halt.

I keep my eyes closed, loath to find out why we have stopped. The landlord's voice, smarmy. 'Well, hello!'

Then I hear a voice that makes my heart still, then jump, rapidly, for the last time I heard it was just after I had been in his arms. I continue pretending to doze. To open my eyes now would be to give myself away.

'Who's the pretty lady?' the landlord says in his oily voice.

I can't stop myself. I open my eyes and peer surreptitiously beyond the landlord.

Mr Bell is as impassive as ever, his back straight, shoulders rigid. He betrays no knowledge of having noticed me. An image of that magical night we shared rises before my eyes and resolutely, I push it away. And then my gaze is arrested by the woman beside him. Golden curls cascading from a fashionable hat. Blue dress to match eyes the undulating turquoise of the lake reflecting the sky in its depths. Skin the rose-tinted cream of dawn. Even the circles under her eyes, from the journey no doubt, do nothing to mar her beauty – in fact they enhance it. She is striking, breathtaking.

'Oh, ho! He does know how to choose well, I must say!' the landlord says as the car starts up. 'Looks as well as money, a potent combination.' He nudges me with his arm. 'Let's see how long that English rose lasts in this unforgiving climate with the owner of a struggling plantation, especially when all the money she is bringing into this marriage goes down the drain with nothing to show for it.' He cackles as if he has cracked the world's biggest joke.

I wonder what havoc he has planned next for Mr Bell. Does the landlord know what happened between the plantation owner and me? Is he biding his time to spring his revenge?

I close my eyes, my whole being weary, feeling thoroughly, completely wretched.

Chapter 33

Sue

So Many Fires

Sue types 'Elephant rampage in India' into Google and it returns with pages and pages of information. She clicks on the first of the search results, a video of a news clip, and is quickly drawn into the story of the mad elephant who uncovered a slumbering temple ensconced in a jungle and adjoined by a coffee plantation and paddy fields. 'The temple and land is believed to be cursed,' the newsreader announces. 'It is rumoured crimes were committed there – the bones of a human baby were found. Was this child sacrificed to the temple? What really happened there?'

For the first time since she heard about her husband's death, Sue is absolutely riveted by a story; by the discovery of this temple that has stoked so many fires.

The camera pans to the temple, a smallish structure beset by vines and workers in hard hats assiduously clearing the vegetation. The land surrounding it is beautiful, rain-washed emerald, and overrun with people: trinket vendors, food hawkers, devotees and protestors alike trampling on plants. She can almost smell the crushed, bitter scent of ruined berries – the people's chatter an indistinct rumble in the background of the video.

narrator's voice grows louder and more excited as he breath-
unts the facts, and Sue inches closer to the screen, the

better to take it all in. 'There are many claims to this temple that has lain unnoticed and hidden for so long. It is being disputed in court as to whether it is public or private. A man claiming to own it has come forward but there are also unsubstantiated rumours that it belonged to a devadasi, a woman dedicated to the service of the goddess Yellamma, the temple deity. This is believed to be her cottage.' The camera pans on a tiny abode, overgrown with vegetation, to one side of the temple. It looks enchanted, like a child's drawing. A witch's hut. Hansel and Gretel's gingerbread house. There's also what looks like a well next to the cottage, and a granite stone – seat? – beside it.

Hang on, Sue thinks. *I've seen this before. The temple and the cottage – but where?*

She replays the clip, pausing when it shows the temple and the cottage again, trying to recall where she has seen them before. A news article, a magazine? But how when the temple and cottage have only just been discovered?

The temple, the elephant, the protestors, the cottage seem millions of miles from what she is experiencing and suddenly she wants to run away from her own life and into that green, lush, exciting one, where anything can happen, where elephants run wild and rouse sleeping temples and storms of controversy.

I want to go there.

Although it is a fantastic wish, something she might say if she was watching a travel programme with her husband, it is also the first positive thought she has had since she heard about Tony, the first that looks ahead into a future without him.

All this time she has had a long list of things she hasn't wanted to do: eating, sleeping, smiling, talking… And the baby? She wants the baby but she also wants Tony to be here, raising it with her. But he isn't, and she doesn't know what to do.

And now, it is liberating to finally feel the urge to *do* something, even though it is completely impractical. At least she has felt something other than stunned anguish – it's a start.

Sue devotes the rest of the afternoon to learning everything she can about the temple in India. It gives her something to focus on other than her grief, what is missing from her life.

It is late afternoon and she is almost coming to the end of the Google search results for the temple when it finally dawns on her where she has seen it before. All this time she has been racking her brain to think of a connection, to recall why the temple and cottage seem so familiar.

I have never even been to India, so why does it feel like I know this temple and cottage from somewhere? Why does this story resonate with me so? Why am I drawn to it?

This is the only story that has managed to hold her concentration for longer than a few minutes since Tony died. The only one that has aroused the journalist in her. Why?

And then it comes to her: *she* hasn't been to India but her great-grandparents lived there… And that is when she recalls where she has seen the temple and cottage before: in a photograph among her grandmother's belongings.

Chapter 34

Lucy

Moments of Beauty and Ugliness

The sun sets on the first evening in Lucy's new home. The lamps are lit, doors and windows shut to keep out mosquitoes and bugs.

Lucy is propped up in bed, sipping the cup of cocoa her maid has just brought her. Her bedroom is easily twice the size of the one she had at home in Fairoak (she must remember that Fairoak is no longer home, *this* is), and even more grand. A huge bed takes centre stage, encased in the obligatory mosquito net. There are wardrobes along the length of one wall, the wood panels on them all ornately carved. There is a dressing table, armchairs, a bookshelf, a writing desk facing the window – again, elaborately engraved. The upholstery on the armchairs is a gorgeously patterned velvety silk – exquisitely comfortable. Curtains open on to a balcony from where Lucy can see all of their property: a wide stretch of lawn and beyond that coffee plants adjoining the forest, stretching as far as the eye can see.

A knock on the door. Lucy sets the cup down on the side table, pulls the sheet up to her neck as she is wearing just her petticoat, having abandoned her long-sleeved nightgown in favour of it due to the pressing heat, and calls, 'Come in.'

'Does it meet with your approval?' James asks, standing just inside the door.

She is not sure whether he means the house or her room – perhaps both. 'Yes,' she murmurs.

'No lizards?' He smiles at her.

She looks up, scanning the ceiling again – already she has checked twice. 'None that I can see.'

Thank goodness.

James had left for the plantation soon after they arrived. 'Just to check things have been fine in my absence,' he explained.

She did not hear him return – perhaps he came back when she was having a wash. He looks tired now, lines pinching the corners of his eyes. She feels a pang for him, this hardworking, quiet enigma of a man who is her husband. She wants to ask him to stay, but how? And what if he does stay and she is not able to respond to his affections? What if, when he is intimate with her, he realises the truth?

Nevertheless, she has made up her mind to make the best of the circumstances, the best of her marriage, despite its unpromising start, and so she opens her mouth.

'I...'

'Yes?'

'I...' The words flap in a nervous fluster on her tongue. 'Goodnight, James,' she manages.

'Goodnight.' He leaves, closing the door behind him.

She dreams of home, of a man with muscular arms and a wide smile kissing her in the rose arbour on a summer's evening, birdsong, the fragrance of freshly mown grass and the taste of illicit love.

'I will not let you go,' he whispers, folding her to him, and she believes him.

* * *

She wakes and for one brief and glorious moment, she is back home in England and fiercely in love. Before everything happened, everything changed.

She pushes her melancholy away as she pushes the sheet aside and gets to her feet. When she opens the door to her bedroom, her maid is outside. She has been sitting on the floor by the door, waiting for her mistress to wake, Lucy surmises. When the maid sees her, she scrambles to her feet, tucks her sari in and smiles.

'I bring tea.'

The tea is milky and sweet and spiced with something strong. It drowns the lingering taste of regret and nostalgia in her mouth.

From her balcony, she can see past the lawns to the land beyond, washed with dawn, glowing honeyed emerald. It is going to be a lovely day.

James is on the veranda, sipping coffee and reading.

'Sleep well?' he asks, looking up, when she arrives.

'Yes.' The mermaid in the fountain smiles at Lucy, gushing glittering water from her mouth.

'I'm afraid I have to leave for the plantation directly after breakfast,' he says, 'but I'll be back for lunch.'

'Yes.'

'Shall we eat?'

She has fruit and more of the sweet, spiced tea; James has eggs and coffee, after which he leaves for work. She waves him goodbye and begins her first full day as mistress of a house on a plantation in a corner of the world far removed from home.

* * *

The house is huge, bigger even than it looks from the outside, and stuffed full of wonders, each room so opulent, brimming with tapestries and ornaments.

'I inherited the house, along with the plantation, from my uncle,' James had informed her when he showed her round the previous evening. 'He was into antiques.'

That morning – her first full day at the house – Lucy wanders from room to room, bemused and awed by the splendour: the high ceilings, the beautifully preserved artefacts, the Indian treasure chests and paintings sporting jewelled frames, the animal skins and exotic draperies. And photographs – numerous mounted photographs in every room. Mostly of nature: cows and bullocks and snakes, an elephant like the one she saw at the port, even a leopard, sleek and poised; a majestic bird with its tail plumage open like a fan; native women, their hands chopping vegetables, their mouths busy chewing, captured mid-conversation, looking so companionable together; women bent double in the rain, their backs sheathed in what look like wooden buckets, walking barefoot, between fields overflowing with muddy water, the shoots almost submerged; farmers ploughing fields; a little native girl jumping in a stream, the water splashing higher than her, on her face an expression of pure delight.

A group of children gathered around an old woman who squats in the dirt, taking something out from the folds of her sari and distributing it around. Bread, it looks like, a flat version of bread. She is breaking it into bite-sized pieces and handing it out to the posse of youngsters, all of them bare-bodied except for underclothes, dust-sheathed, dirty faces, matted hair, their eager eyes gleaming at the sight of food.

A native man smoking a rolled-up version of a cigarette, his eyes seeming to glare right back at Lucy, suspicious and angry; his naked torso gleaming with sweat, his body, folded into itself, all sinew and bone with ribs poking out, the tip of his cigarette punctuating the darkness, orange and spitting like his eyes – Lucy imagines; her mind's eye is supplying colour as the photo is in black and white. The sky behind him dusky grey with shades of brightness, sunlight giving in to dusk, inevitable as death following life.

A young boy grins as he stands among reeds taller than him, the shock of white teeth in a brown face – Lucy can make this out even though the picture is, again, in black and white. He is holding up a stick that has a slithery body wrapped around it. A snake! She recoils. It seems to be jumping out of the photograph and into her arms.

These photographs, so real. They speak to Lucy, making her experience the emotions of the people they depict. The person who took these photos cares so much – it comes through in the images. Is he an Englishman? He has such empathy.

For these people.

For life in all its glory.

A shout from somewhere within the house. A bark, followed by frenzied yelps.

Lucy stumbles from room to room, arriving finally in the vast kitchen. The fragrance of spices, brewing tea, something sweet…

Cook looks up from where he is stirring a pot. A short, squat, balding man, he wipes the sweat beading his upper lip with his apron. 'Memsahib, what you want?' he enquires.

The cook's assistants, one topping and tailing beans, another chopping onions with streaming eyes, pause to look up at Lucy. A young man sits on the floor beside them, balanced on what appears to be a scythe, scaling fish by running them across the blade of the scythe, scales gleaming as they fall onto the sheet of paper he has spread underneath, shimmering silvery blue.

'I heard a noise,' Lucy explains.

They look at each other, then out of the doorway. A boy stands there with a bedraggled dog, stroking its mangy fur and grinning at Lucy.

'Market Boy saw scorpion in storeroom in rice sack. Caught it, dog ate it…'

Lucy shudders. 'There are scorpions?'

Cook nods gravely. 'But no worry, dog catch them. Dog good, stray but good.'

The dog barks as if it has understood the conversation. Gaunt, its fur missing in patches, it regards Lucy with intelligent eyes.

'What is the dog's name?' Lucy asks.

Puzzled, Cook screws up his face at Lucy's question while the others regard her silently. 'Dog name? Is Dog,' he says. 'Market Boy give him bones so he come to kitchen and catch scorpion and cockroach and spider. Help us.'

Lucy shivers despite the heat. 'There are spiders and cockroaches in the house?'

'Sometime. But no worry, dog catch them.'

Lucy has heard enough; she turns to leave.

'Memsahib, we bringing tea and snack at eleven.'

'Thank you.' Smiling at all of them, she returns to her exploration, resolving not to pay heed to any more noises coming from the kitchen. She'd rather not know about any other creepy-crawlies residing in the house and being feasted on by that poor scruffy excuse for a dog. But nevertheless, as she investigates the house, Lucy takes care to tread carefully, looking out for insects, lizards, spiders, scorpions, cockroaches; shuddering at the mere thought of coming across one.

Her survey takes her into James's room. It is huge, like every room in the house, and distinctly masculine but not nearly as opulent as some of the other rooms. A bed, armchairs, a wardrobe and a writing desk similar to the one in Lucy's room. A dresser, and arranged on top of it, silver-framed photographs. She picks them up, trying to get closer to this reserved man whom she has married to escape her past, this man she has fooled and inadvertently spurned, trying to understand him, learning to love him.

A photo of James with his parents and his brother; a smiling little boy, his mother's arms around him. Then, older, more grim-faced, with his similarly grim uncle. That one must have been taken when he came to India after university – an orphan, having lost his brother in the war and his parents to consumption – to live with his uncle, from whom he inherited the coffee plantation. His eyes were distant when he told Lucy about that after he had asked her to marry him, his voice curt to the point of coldness when she pressed for details. She understands now that he was protecting himself from a deep sadness, hiding it from the eyes of the woman with whom he hoped to spend the rest of his life.

For the first time Lucy imagines how it must have been for him, this smiling child bolstered by his mother's arms, to lose his family and travel to another continent to live with an uncle he had hardly met and barely remembered. The smiling little boy, no longer smiling in subsequent photographs.

She opens the wardrobe with some trepidation, owing both to snooping in James's private space and to the scorpions and spiders she does not wish to find, breathing in her husband's scent of lemon and woodsmoke and spice, which nestles among his neatly arranged suits, ties and shirts. Another presence, the ghost, the essence of him.

In the bureau she discovers the identity of the photographer whose work adorns the rooms of the house, the person who has so carefully captured all those faces: moments of joy and sorrow, anger and suspicion, of beauty and ugliness.

Three boxes, each containing machines, the biggest of which Lucy recognises. She stares at it, transported to two Christmases ago, before what she had done had rocked their world, when they were a happy family unit: Mother, Father and Lucy.

Father had invited a photographer to Fairoak.

'A photograph,' he'd said, rubbing his hands in glee – Father loved and embraced everything modern, from cars to telephones, 'to replace the family portrait.' He had always commissioned a painting annually.

'Pose,' the photographer had commanded, peering at them through the machine, an identical one to which Lucy has now found in her husband's wardrobe. 'Smile.'

Mother and Lucy had perched on the chaise longue, Father standing behind them, all of them sporting self-conscious smiles. Blinking at the flash.

She thinks of that photograph, blown up and hanging above the mantelpiece.

By the next Christmas, her last with her parents, everything has imploded. Her parents were disillusioned, she was a married woman preparing to travel here, to India, to join her husband, and there was no family photograph.

Do they miss her, or are they glad she is far away, hoping she does not cause more mischief, fresh scandal? Their letter – for she has received one; it was waiting for her here when she arrived the previous day – gives nothing away. She brought it to her nose and imagined she could smell the lavender scent that is her mother's trademark, and it had ignited both a longing to see her parents and an intense bout of homesickness. She had pictured Mother sitting at the writing desk in the library overlooking the garden, Father in his armchair by the window, and she had wanted to be there with them, watching the birds alight on the rose bushes. She opened the letter with trembling fingers, thrilled to have this missive from home. *Hope you are keeping well. We are fine here. It is unseasonably warm.* She wanted more, so much more; she wanted to know *everything*. Whether they had hired a new scullery maid, whether Mother's roses were in bloom, whether Father's gout was better, whether Mother had been to her Tuesday evening card party and what the latest gossip was that she had gleaned from Mrs Denbigh.

She blinks to shake away the recollections of home and cradles James's cameras.

Her quiet husband. Orphan. Plantation owner. Photographer.

It suddenly dawns on her why James is so taciturn: he has had hardly any womanly influence in his life. When he talks about his uncle, Lucy has discerned respect there, as well as affection. His uncle must have cared for him, but judging from his photograph, he does not look the kind to express emotion. And James must have surely modelled himself on his uncle, talking only when necessary, and only about practical things like the running of the plantation. And yet James has a softer, kind side. She has glimpsed it in the way he is with his servants – he treats them with respect, and they obviously care deeply for him.

And now, seeing the photographs dotted around the house, she understands that he shows his caring, his love, everything he feels, through the medium of pictures as he struggles to do so in words. She feels a surge of empathy for this man she has married, the boy he once was and the person he has become.

I will make an effort to get to know James, to draw him out. I will try to rectify the wrong I have done him by lying to him, by being unresponsive to his attentions.

As Lucy sets the cameras down carefully and finds, tucked beside them, a sheaf of photographs, she realises that she knows just how to do this.

She leafs through the photographs.

A cow standing serenely in the middle of the road, a trolley half in the ditch as it tries to overtake. Two ladies sitting in a carriage while beside them two sari-clad women walk, hoisting what look like heavy conical pans on their heads. An old woman, her ageing, wrinkled body wrapped in tattered cloth, lined face, downturned mouth, hands spread out, begging for coins, eyes exuding sorrow. Lucy thinks of that girl then, sitting beside the landlord, overshadowed by him, her eyes radiating pain. And as if she has conjured her up, she spies a photo of her, alongside some other girls. She inhales sharply, looking closely at the photograph. It *is* her, among a group of girls, all bejewelled and bedecked in saris, posing in front of what looks like a statue ornamented with flowers and gold. She stands out from all the other girls. She is stunning, but as before her eyes ooze grief. How is she here, in this photograph, in James's wardrobe?

Who is she?

'No one of any consequence,' James had said, his voice tight.

If so, then why is she here, among James's things, sharing space in his house, *her* house?

'So, how was your first morning?' James asks, a shadow of a beard on his face as he tucks into the lunch that has been set out for them on a table on the veranda.

Exotic birds, lime green with bright red beaks, sit on the fountain, pecking from the water.

'Good,' Lucy says, brightly. 'I acquainted myself with the house.'

Roses and other multi-hued flowers she cannot name sing from the bower. The smell of fresh air and dust and fruit mingles with the aroma of spices emanating from the food spread out before them: rice and green beans and fish in a creamy sauce.

Lucy toys with the fish, seeing the scales that were glinting from the floor when she went to the kitchen. The rice reminds her of the scorpion. Her head is full of the girl whose photograph she found among James's things. Somehow she is drawn to her, the aura of melancholy that emanates from her evident even in a photograph. Lucy wants to bring her into the conversation, to ask James about her – but how, without giving away the fact that she has been looking through his personal possessions?

'Not hungry?' he asks as Lucy pushes her food around. 'The heat does sap one's appetite. Tell Cook to prepare something lighter for you – sandwiches, perhaps?'

Lucy nods, smiling at him.

'I have no such problem, I can eat whatever the weather.' He smiles. 'Did you find the household accounts? They are in the bureau in the study.'

'I haven't had time to go over them yet.'

'Take your time. The servants know what to do. They are trustworthy and run the household smoothly, they just need directions every week, instructing on the menu and provisions. Wednesday is market day at the village. Most of the groceries are delivered here and Market Boy gets the rest—'

'I saw him. There are scorpions. The dog ate one… It doesn't have a name.'

James laughs. It's a carefree sound, at odds with his habitual reserve. 'That boy, he's adopted the stray dog that used to hang around the house. They are an item, the dog and him.'

'Shouldn't he be at school?'

James sighs, his eyes clouding over, any trace of laughter gone, and Lucy feels a pang for causing this change. 'My uncle started a small school for the children of the workers. I have persuaded the boy to go there many times. I have bribed him and once I forcibly took him there. But he runs away, every time, and comes back here. I even arranged for a tutor to work with him here.'

He sighs again and Lucy is struck by how animated James becomes when talking about his staff, how much empathy this man, her husband, has for the people who work for him. Surely the other landowners are not half as kind? She thinks back to the way some of them behaved towards the natives on the ship and she knows that James is an exception.

'He is very practical and hands-on, but no good at learning, so the tutor told me. Like all the staff, he has picked up a smidgen of English, but that's as far as it goes. Books are not for him.' James pauses, rubs a hand across his eyes. 'He's an orphan. Nobody knows who his parents are, or where he is from. He just turned up here one day, malnourished and feral almost. He must have been living in the forest for a while. I dread to think what he endured.'

She has never heard her husband talk for so long and so earnestly before.

'Anyway, the staff adopted him,' he continues, 'and he has adopted the dog and now, I cannot imagine the household without him. He does anything he's asked, so cheerfully.' Suddenly James smiles, the twinkle chasing away the shadows in his eyes. 'Did Cook tell you about the time during the monsoons when the house was overtaken by frogs? The boy was a godsend then, I must say—'

'Frogs, in the house?' Lucy gasps in shock, laying down her cutlery and giving up all pretence of eating as she imagines the floor beneath her feet overrun with frogs, the slimy feel of them, their bulging eyes regarding her peaceably.

'They come inside seeking shelter during the rains. Little things, afraid of rat snakes, you see. Anyway, the boy caught them all, every last one.'

Lucy shudders – it is becoming a habit, the more she learns about the creatures inhabiting this house alongside her.

'They are quite adorable as creatures go,' says James, his eyes sparkling.

A mischievous side to her husband! Another first!

In that moment, looking at him, his face lit up from the inside, Lucy can see herself growing old with James. His face sagging, becoming jowly, yet those eyes twinkling with joy and brightness, reminiscent of youth. She shakes her head to clear her thoughts. What is the matter with her? It is the photographs she has seen, what has been captured by the lens. All those raw feelings, trapped in black and white.

'The photographs around the house, they are beautiful,' she says. 'Did you take them?'

He smiles. 'Yes, it is a hobby of mine.'

'It's quite a talent, telling stories through pictures.'

James flushes. 'An expensive hobby. I have to send home for the pictures to be developed and for film and camera parts.'

'Will you teach me?' Lucy asks, putting into action the plan that occurred to her as she was snooping in her husband's room, the plan to connect with him, to get to know him.

He looks up and it is as if he is seeing her properly for the first time.

'There is so much beauty here. I would like to capture it too, like you do,' she says.

He smiles again and she realises she hasn't ever seen him smile this much.

The plan is working already.

'We'll start this evening when I come home for supper so we can make use of the light,' he tells her. 'You see, in photography, light is everything.'

Lucy has a nap in the afternoon and on waking, she washes, gets changed and waits for James.

'Ready for your lesson?' he asks when he comes home.

He hasn't forgotten.

'Yes.'

He goes to his room to fetch the camera.

When he opens the box containing the camera, the pictures Lucy discovered in his wardrobe are inside – she placed them there when he left for the plantation after lunch, hoping he would choose this camera, the newest and most modern of the three, so she could ask him about the girl without him knowing that she had been prying among his things.

'Oh,' he says. 'I didn't know I had kept these in here.'

You didn't, it was me. 'More photos,' Lucy says, fiddling with the skirt of her dress to avoid catching his eye.

'I haven't managed to get these framed yet.'

Lucy flicks through them, as if seeing them for the first time.

'I recognise this girl. Wasn't she the one with the landlord?'

His face stiffens, closes down, as he nods.

'Who are these girls?'

'I took this photo at a puja – festivities at the temple for the celebration of one of the landlord's daughters' nuptials. At the time I didn't know… I thought they were dancers, you see. I realised later that they are given to the temple, these young girls, by families who cannot afford to keep them.'

'What do you mean?'

'They're called devadasis. They're servants of the goddess, supposedly, but in actual fact they have to please the men who want them.'

'I don't understand.'

Lucy thinks of the girl with the landlord, her bruised gaze.

He sighs heavily. 'They cannot marry, they have to live out their lives in the service of the goddess and the men who worship the goddess.'

'But that is…'

'Cruel, yes. The families are very poor and the parents cannot afford to get their daughters married, so they dedicate them to the goddess. Whatever money these girls earn they send to the families. So the families benefit from it, but the girls…'

'Their lives are ruined,' Lucy whispers. 'And this girl,' she points to the girl she saw in the car, 'the landlord has claimed her?'

'Yes.'

'He is married?'

James nods.

'And yet he flaunts her publicly.'

'He's a law unto himself.'

'But…'

'The landlord, he's a dangerous man, a formidable enemy. My uncle warned me of him, he has caused trouble in the past.'

Lucy recalls the tension between James and the landlord when they met on their way to the house. 'The trouble at the plantation… You had to leave early. Was the landlord responsible?'

James nods, his face grim. 'He had his minions set fire to the plantation last year.'

'Oh!'

'I tried finding the thugs who did it, but the landlord had spirited them away. Nevertheless, I confronted him, but I couldn't prove anything… He claimed it was nothing to do with him, that it was negligence on the part of my workers. All lies, of course, but without evidence, there was nothing I could do.' James rubs a weary hand across his brow. 'Thankfully, we were able to contain the fire before it reached the plants but many of my workers were injured – it razed their houses and some storage sheds – and some of them lost the use of their limbs.'

'Oh no!'

'I am going later, after work, to check up on them – they are still in my employ although they cannot work.'

There's so much more to her husband than meets the eye, Lucy is learning. He cares deeply about the people who work for him, both on the plantation and here, at the house.

And then, as what he just said sinks in, she says, 'You're going back to the plantation this evening?'

'I'm sorry, Lucy. I have to. It's…' He wipes his face again tiredly. 'It's been tough keeping the plantation going after the fire and the drought—'

'The drought?'

'We had a drought last year. The monsoons—'

'Monsoons?' Lucy can't help interrupting James. She recalls him mentioning monsoons before, when talking about the frogs, and she had wondered then what the word meant but was too overwhelmed to ask.

'The rainy season, it's called monsoon here. The rains come in June but they were delayed last year. And then the fire… it set us back. And since many of my workers were injured and some are still indisposed, the rest of us are working all hours,' he explains.

'But surely you can hire more—' Lucy begins, but stops abruptly when she sees the look on James's face. 'I'm sorry, I'm not qualified to tell you what to…'

'No, it's fine,' he says shortly, but she knows it is not.

He cannot hire more people because he cannot afford to, perhaps, having poured all his money into keeping the plantation afloat. That is why he married her and where her dowry has gone… Towards the plantation and its people, which her husband is passionate about, as he is about his photography.

She understands this, but what she doesn't understand is… 'But why? Why did the landlord set fire to the plantation?' she persists.

James's eyes are hard, his voice flinty, as he says, 'He wants everyone to do as he says, what he wants. I refuse to…'

He has already made an enemy of the landlord.

Lucy thinks of the man they met, his intrusive, reptilian gaze, that beautiful girl beside him with her aura of sadness.

'Anyway,' James adds, his voice determinedly bright, 'shall we get started, while the light is still cooperating with us? Here, you hold the camera like this.'

Lucy shivers, despite the air caressing her body being warm as an embrace, and concentrates on learning how to take pictures of the loveliness around her, while at the same time getting to know her husband, all the while trying to put the girl, her haunted eyes in that stunning face, firmly out of her mind.

Chapter 35

Gowri

The Warmth of Human Touch

Goddess,

The monsoons have arrived on time this year and everyone is happy. The market is slick with gossip again. Rumours buzz and swell, as overhead thunder dances and lightning cruises between clouds thick and heavy with rain. The ground is slippery as the gossip that is exchanged, the mud spongy and moist, oozing between my toes as I try to make my way among the crowds, hiding behind my soaking pallu as I eavesdrop.

'Have you seen the memsahib? Isn't she beautiful?' I hear.

'The sahib is just as grumpy as ever, despite his wife being here.'

'He will be, he doesn't get much time with her, does he? He's at the plantation at all hours, trying to inspire the men, keep them together, get the place running smoothly again – the fire was quite a setback.'

'And the landlord is up to his old tricks again, no doubt.'

'Wonder what he's planning this time?'

'The memsahib will be bored, what with the sahib occupied at the plantation…'

'Best thing for the memsahib is if she gets pregnant, starts a family.'

'But how, when the sahib is always at the plantation and never home…?'

Much nudging and giggling.

I slip between the nattering women, unseen, my eyes stinging with tears, grateful for the rain disguising them. Lately, I have been so emotional, and insanely tired. I miss Vandana Ma'am with all my heart. I am so *lonely*, Goddess. I cannot face going back to my empty, bleak cottage. I want to stay here, among these people and the illusion of company, although none of them, except the vegetable vendor couple, will speak to me.

I make my way towards them, these people I count as my only friends, fighting the impulse to slump down on to the churning sludge and sob.

What is the matter with me?

'Are you okay?' the vegetable vendor woman asks me. 'You look shockingly pale.'

'I am…' I begin, and then I am slipping, falling, lost.

'Gowri?' I hear as if from afar. 'Gowri?'

The smell of rain and churned earth, greens and sweat. The warmth of human touch. My mother?

'Ma…?' My voice tentative, hopeful.

'Here, child, drink this.'

Cool metal against my lips. The silvery gush, the velvet silkiness of water in my mouth. I swallow, open my eyes.

Fleshy arms enveloping me. Droplets of perspiration and rain dotting a kind face, anxious eyes.

I am in the vegetable vendor lady's arms, under their holey awning from where they hawk their vegetables. I am surrounded by plump aubergines and potatoes crusted with mud, green beans and chillies, marrows and mangoes. A fruity, rich, organic scent.

Behind the awning a crowd has gathered, watching and pointing.

I am aware of whispers elbowing through the crowd.

Now, *I* am the subject of gossip.

I sit up, ashamed, embarrassed. My heart sinks, knowing this will surely make its way to the landlord and that he will not be happy.

'Sorry,' I say.

'Don't apologise,' the woman says kindly. 'You shouldn't be exerting yourself in your condition. Plenty of rest and regular food. I have packed extra fruit and vegetables for you, here,' she murmurs in my ear, mindful of the crowd, not wanting them to hear, her breath hot and smelling of guava, juicy pink.

My condition…

I look up at her.

'You didn't know? Oh, child! If you need anything, I am here, every Wednesday.'

She squeezes my hand gently and I blink back tears as the gravity of what she is telling me settles in my mind, and my heart swells with the beginnings of great joy.

'Hear you've been creating quite a spectacle of yourself at the market…' The landlord grinds his jaw as he paces the room.

'I'm sorry, I was tired.'

'I will not have you make a show of yourself for the villagers.'

Isn't that what I do every time I dance for the goddess? I want to ask. I bite back my words and nod meekly. 'It's because I am expecting. I didn't know.'

He pauses for a moment, watching me, his gaze speculative. Then, 'Oh? And it is mine?'

I look up at him, for once showing the anger I feel. 'Whose else can it be? You haven't bartered me off to any of your friends lately.'

He laughs. 'Feisty today, aren't we?'

I let out the breath I have been holding. Hopefully, I have convinced him that he is the father of this child.

'Pregnant or not, no more making a scene in public.'

'Yes,' I say humbly.

'It better be a boy. I am tired of siring only girls.'

I bite back my rage and I nod, docilely, and rise to do his bidding, knowing I will be punished for fainting at the market, but hoping he will take my pregnancy into consideration and not go all out to make me pay.

Chapter 36

Lucy

Magical Outcrop

Lucy wakes, knowing exactly where she is, for the first time since she came to India. She blinks at the chequerboard world swimming gradually into view through the mosquito net and realises, also for the first time since she fell in love with Robert, she has not dreamt of him.

She opens the curtains, stepping out on to the balcony and savouring the dew-flavoured, rain-sprinkled morning air. The sky is the pink of promise, the hills undulating in the distance, velvet green. Below her the lawns are spread out in a lush emerald wash, edged by flowers and beyond that, as far as the eye can see, coffee plants, bordered by tall trees – betel – threaded through with vines – pepper. James has explained what they are: 'Sniff the air, you can detect the spicy hint of pepper – those are the vines. The bitter fragrant bite of coffee and the sharp limestone taste of betel nut – that's from the betel trees.'

James… Every evening he teaches her to take photographs, with diligence and patience. The previous evening, he had complimented her: 'You have a photographer's eye.' It had made her inordinately pleased.

James is gradually becoming less taciturn and more relaxed around her and she herself is more comfortable in his presence, more at ease in his company. Him teaching her the art of taking photographs has helped bring this about, as she had hoped it would.

And yet, every evening after their lesson, James leaves, once again, for the plantation. She waited up for him the first few times, sitting on the veranda and braving the mosquitoes, watching the sun set amidst a glorious rainbow of colour, but when he didn't return at nightfall, she went up to bed.

Now, she doesn't wait up for him. She cannot bear to see the servants' faces, the pity they must surely be hiding behind their polite subservience, for the new wife whose husband doesn't come home and who doesn't grace her bed. For surely they must know?

'What time did you get home last night?' she had asked James one morning at breakfast.

'Oh, quite late. I knocked – wanted to say goodnight, but you must have been fast asleep – there was no reply.'

So the next night she had stayed sitting up in bed. *Give me a chance, James. This time I will not rebuff you, I promise.* She waited and waited, but there was no knock and in the end she fell asleep, still sitting up.

You deserve it for what you did, her conscience had whispered as she waited, her eyes weighted down with tiredness.

She sighs, pushing aside her melancholy, concentrating instead on the beauty spread out in front of her. The morning is seasoned with rain, a moist, churned mud scent.

In the garden below the dog comes into view, followed closely by the boy – Lucy still hasn't discovered his name; she keeps forgetting to ask James. They gambol past, dog panting, boy laughing, and Lucy smiles, the air cool on her face, carrying no hint of the heat of the day to come. She takes a deep breath and leaves the room, surprising her maid, who is squatting patiently outside the door, waiting for her mistress to wake up so she can bring her morning cup of tea.

* * *

The previous evening, James and Lucy were sitting on the veranda after Lucy's photography lesson and supper, James taking a break before going back to the plantation, when Lucy noticed an expectant stillness in the air. Then a most awful racket, like an orchestra gone wrong. Despite being bombarded by new experiences every day since she set foot in this country, she was shocked. What was *this*?

James laughed at her expression. He was nursing a tumbler of brandy the exact colour of the setting sun. 'Frogs,' he explained.

'Frogs are making that noise?'

'They are heralding the monsoon.'

'Oh.' Then, remembering what he had told her, 'Is this a prelude to them taking up residence in our living room?'

He threw back his head and laughed then, eyes crinkling. And Lucy laughed along with him, although she hadn't exactly been joking, until there was another, louder noise. Crackling and sputtering in the sky. A growl and a rant. The sky breaking open in a zag of light. They ran inside, clutching their glasses.

Rain. Dramatic. Lashing at the windows with a ferocity that shocked Lucy. Trees swaying like people in a trance, the coffee plants just visible through the swelling, pitching screen of water. How different from the civilised, polite showers of England! This rain was angry, temperamental – an adult having a tantrum.

This morning, everything sparkles in the aftermath, glowing fresh and washed.

'Have you dropped something?' James asks as Lucy ducks under the table before she sits down to breakfast opposite him.

'I'm checking for frogs.'

He laughs. 'They only come in during torrential downpours.'

'What, there's worse to come? Last night's rain sounded like a torrential downpour to me.'

James laughs some more. He has a very carefree laugh, rumbly and hearty. Lucy loves it – it offers a glimpse into the boy he is inside the proper, zipped-up man.

'What are you planning to do today?' he asks when he has finished laughing.

'I was thinking I'd go for a walk, explore the surroundings,' Lucy says.

'Keep to the paths, it's quite wild out there. Make sure to take one of the servants with you.'

The boy offers to accompany Lucy, and he brings the dog along, of course.

'What's your name?' Lucy asks him as they set off.

The boy walks slightly ahead, the dog frolicking at their feet.

He turns to look at Lucy, scrunching up his nose. 'Huh?'

'What do I call you?'

He smiles, understanding dawning on his grubby face. Lucy is possessed by an urge to take a cloth to it, wipe it clean.

'Market Boy,' he says.

'That's your name?'

He nods vigorously.

His parents must have called him something different, surely? But then Lucy recalls James telling her how he had arrived at the house seemingly from nowhere. Did he know his parents?

Lucy glances at him, his smiling face, innocence radiating from him. *What happened to you?* She thinks of that girl sitting beside the landlord, sold by her own parents into prostitution in the name of religion. She wraps her arms around herself, suddenly cold.

'Market Boy.' He slaps his chest and grins proudly, displaying yellow, broken teeth, with a few missing.

He can only be thirteen at most. How did he lose his teeth? Lucy wants to draw a bath for him and give him a good scrubbing. She wants to stand over him and make sure he brushes his remaining teeth until they shine. This boy arouses maternal instincts in her, instincts she did not even know she harboured. And on the heels of those feelings comes an intense sadness, hurt so deep and yawning that she doubles over, clutching her stomach.

'Memsahib.' The boy is close, his clear brown eyes, shiny and guileless in his dirty face, boring into Lucy's. 'What matter?' The dog barks in distress, running in circles around them, whipping up mud.

Lucy stands up, with effort. Smiles at him. 'I'm okay, shall we go?'

He returns her smile and walks ahead, the dog skipping beside him, turning around now and again to make sure Lucy is okay and following right behind.

The mali (which is what the gardener is called here, she has learned) sees them and nods at Lucy, grinning widely at the boy. The boy seems to incite affection in everyone. The mali says something to the boy in Kannada, the native language.

He replies in the same language, pointing to Lucy and grinning, the dog barking so as not to be left out of the conversation.

The mali laughs, shakes his head and goes back to digging holes in an area of the garden he has sectioned off, the ground wet from the previous night's rain and gleaming moist red.

The boy walks down the path, gesturing for Lucy to follow, his chest puffed out in self-importance, as, Lucy understands, smiling to herself, he has the important task of escorting his memsahib out of the grounds and into the wild.

Once they are out of the gate, the boy turns to Lucy.

'Where you want go?'

'To the village?'

He nods again, the dog panting beside him. 'I know shortcut. Come.'

They walk for a few minutes along the road and then he suddenly veers off the path and into the foliage.

'Are you sure?' Lucy asks.

'Come,' he says, charging into the field of coffee plants, and Lucy has no choice but to follow. The air smacks of budding shoots, fecundity and fertility. The plants and branches slapping her face taste moist and bitter, of sap and rain and adventure. Lucy's feet sink into the mud, which is slippery from the previous night's rain and clumpy, sticking to her shoes.

A few paces of this and then suddenly there is a path, a strip of raised land between coffee fields. They walk along the path, single file as there is not enough space for two people walking side by side, and after a bit, Lucy relaxes, getting into the rhythm of it, not worrying that she will slip and fall into the mud – after all, the worst that can happen is that she'll be covered in soggy grime. It is cool among the plants, green and peppery with the bitter aroma of coffee. Dew and remnants of the previous night's shower glint on the leaves.

Lucy hears a crunch and looks down. She is standing on something curled up – a miniature snake? She lets out a small yelp of fear and the dog echoes it, picking up on her anguish.

The boy turns and bends down, picking up the squiggly crushed thing with his bare hand. It has millions of legs, which are all waving in distress. He hurls it far into the fields. Lucy shudders.

'No hurt you,' he says. 'Is okay.'

After that, Lucy pays a bit more attention to where she is stepping, which is a good thing as she manages to avoid plenty of those big orange ants.

'Look,' the boy says, pointing to more of the curly things. Some of them are not curly at all but long, the span of a finger, their light green shells striped with horizontal brown lines, and sporting many pairs of feet. The boy touches one lightly and it curls up into a tight ball.

'Ah, that explains why some of them are curled up!' Lucy exclaims and he smiles.

A few paces on, he points out a thinner, smaller relative – this one red with black stripes, also with myriad legs – which also curls when touched. He points out beetles and grasshoppers, frogs and flies, bees and bugs and snails and different kinds of ants and lizards to Lucy until she no longer cringes at the sight of them.

Presently, they come to a fence – wooden poles at intervals with barbed wire running through. There's a section along the fence where two of the wires are bent out of shape, so there's just enough room for a small body to wriggle through. The dog passes through first, then the boy. They both stand on the other side of the fence and look at Lucy, questioningly. Two pairs of huge eyes. Waiting.

'You don't expect me to go through that, surely?'

The boy nods earnestly. 'Is shortcut.'

The dog barks once, urgently, as if encouraging Lucy.

Lucy sighs. *What have I got myself into?*

She looks back the way they came. The path stretching away between the fields. She is curious to know what's beyond the fence.

I am here now, I might as well see what there is to see.

Making up her mind, Lucy lifts up her skirts, bunches them, bends her body and manoeuvres it through the gap. The boy claps and does a little dance when she makes it across. The dog jumps and barks, bounding up to Lucy and licking her palms.

'Good job I'm small, eh?' Lucy says and the boy nods even though she's certain he hasn't quite understood what she means.

* * *

On the other side of the fence it is dark and wild. No fields here, and no path from the looks of it, just forest. Huge trees, the scent of ripening fruit and rotting mulch and danger. The sound of leaves shifting, air whistling through the trees. The trees form a canopy above them through which golden light filters, streaking the forest floor in muddy greens and golds. Lucy picks her way gingerly through the peat.

'No walk in leaves. Snakes hiding,' the boy says and Lucy jumps backwards, stifling a terrified squeal.

He beckons to her and points to what looks like a pile of mud, which is, Lucy realises on closer inspection, actually a rough path hewn out by feet. He disappears into the shadows, saying something to the dog, which cocks its ears and sticks close to Lucy. She hears him hacking at something and after a bit, he returns with two sticks.

He gives the thicker one to Lucy, keeping hold of the thinner one. And then he walks ahead, slashing at the branches around him that dare to whip his face, and Lucy follows, doing the same, and they laugh and it occurs to her, the dog barking and jumping around them and snapping at flies and growling at ants, that in this moment she is completely happy.

But not for long.

The dog growls, long and low, a warning, coming to an abrupt stop.

There is a swishing and a scrabbling and the next minute, the boy is hoisting something on his stick, flinging it aside. Lucy gets the impression of a long coiled body before it slithers away into the undergrowth.

She screams. The dog barks.

'Is fine,' the boy says. 'Is gone now.'

Lucy shudders, staring in the direction it disappeared.

'This not scary,' the boy explains. 'Big animals is.' He nods vigorously.

'What do you mean?' Lucy stops walking to stare at him.

'Eat dog and me and you, Memsahib.' He stretches his arms wide, makes his hands into paws, bares his teeth, mimicking roaring sounds.

'You mean tigers, here?' Lucy's voice a shocked whisper.

The nodding increases in tempo, his eyes huge and wide. 'And…' He waves his arm up and down in front of his nose, fashioning a trunk.

'Tigers *and* elephants?'

He is joking, surely? 'Have you seen any?'

He shakes his head.

Whew!

'Eating cows from village next river.' The boy flings his hand westward to show Lucy.

That's far enough away, isn't it? Can tigers cross the river? Can elephants? 'Anybody died?' Even as she asks the question, she wonders if she really needs to know.

He nods, holds up four fingers on one hand, tears a leaf off the tree with the other and waves it in front of Lucy's face. The tart tang of vegetation and fear.

'Flat like this by ele… ele…'

'Elephants,' Lucy finishes for him.

She looks around the jungle, the sound of crickets and the song of birds high above them, the wind swishing through the trees and plants. The small insects and ants scurrying beside her feet. She stops and listens. What is hiding in there?

'Yes.' The boy nods earnestly. 'Other village. Bite many man, eat hand and leg. Tiger. Three kill,' he says in his broken English.

Lucy shivers, cold despite the heat. The sounds of the jungle ominous all of a sudden.

'No today, I can tell,' he adds.

'How?' Lucy asks. 'How can you tell?'

He sniffs the air. Points to a squirrel disappearing up a tree, the sound of small animals scuttling in the undergrowth. 'No scared, small animals. No tiger or ele… Come.'

Lucy follows him, eager to get out of this place now, the patter of creatures in the bushes, the darkness cast by the arching tops of trees, the drip, drip of water falling from leaves, courtesy of the shower from the previous night.

They walk for what feels like for ever, the gloomy awning above Lucy foreboding, light permeating here and there, golden glow dabbling the vegetation. Her skirts are muddy, the bodice of her dress ripped in a couple of places where she yanked it none too gently when it caught in the branches. If Mother saw her now, she would call her a disgrace. Oh, but Lucy is already in disgrace, a disgrace far bigger than one caused by mere torn dresses. Mother's letters to her are polite and distant and she can't seem to pierce the barrier she put up when she fell in love with Robert, a mere gardener, and—

No, she can't think about it all.

Up ahead, the trees thin and there is a sudden, yawning cave of light. The path widens and is intersected by another, wider mud path. And across from it, fields, wide open and lush. Planted with long thin ears of green, which nod in the fragrant breeze. The moist red mud rich and bright in vivid contrast to the raindrop-stippled emerald.

Right beside the fields is a clearing profuse with flowers and a few trees. Chickens cluck in the garden, pecking at the mud. And in the middle of this lovely cornucopia of flowers and fruit trees sits a cottage. A hut, really. Small, like a witch's lair, and beautiful, almost doll-like. A tiny entrance. No windows. A magical outcrop in the midst of fields, facing a jungle. There's a well in the clearing, next to a huge tree. The well sports a wheel with a rope. A cat suns itself on its rim and there is a pail beside the cat, half full of water that glints in the sun. By the well, a washing stone, marbled blue granite, a small brown bird perched atop of it, blinking curiously at Lucy and her companions.

A few paces from the enchanted little house is a bigger building. This one is more ornate and looks official, important somehow. It is flanked by trees, tall sentinels guarding it. Steps lead up to a red-pillared, open veranda and there is a bell swaying from one of the pillars, shiny gold. An open doorway hints at something flowery and gilded inside – Lucy can detect glimmers and flashes of gold. A strong smell emanates from it, rose and votive.

'Is temple,' the boy says, running nimbly up the steps and ringing the bell. He kneels in front of the doorway, hands folded, eyes closed, head bowed. The dog, as if understanding, stands at the bottom of the steps, panting, waiting for the boy.

The chimes of the bell peal, sweet and beautiful in the sunshine. And as if by magic, from the charmed little house, a woman appears, tucking in her sari.

With a start, Lucy recognises her: she is the woman who was beside the landlord in the car. No veil this time. The silver anklets on her feet chime a melody as she walks, as do the gold and maroon bangles on her hands as they smooth her hair. It is pulled back from her face into a long plait, gleaming ebony blue in the sun. Her eyes meet Lucy's, those eyes with their haunting depths, singing of deep despair; then she looks swiftly away, to the boy and then the dog.

The dog bounds up to her, running rings around the skirts of her sari, and she squats down right there in the mud and gathers the dirty dog to her.

Close up, she is even more beautiful than Lucy realised in the car. She completely ignores Lucy, laying her head on top of the dog's, so that it emits a low sound of satisfaction. The boy opens his eyes, leaps down the steps and smiles at her in his open, beaming way.

She talks away to him, their language musical and incomprehensible, the dog looking from one to the other.

Why does this woman intrigue Lucy so? Is it her beauty? Who she is? But Lucy was drawn to her even before James told her the truth about who she is. Is it the pain radiating from her eyes? For Lucy has tasted pain too. Not like this woman, of course, nowhere near. But she has…

Do Lucy's eyes emit her inner pain like this woman's?

'Memsahib,' the boy says, pointing at Lucy.

Lucy is suddenly aware of how she must look. Hair dishevelled and poking out of her hat, which is adorned with twigs and leaves. Her dress torn and muddy.

The woman in contrast looks like a goddess in her simple blue sari sequinned with silver stars.

'Hello,' Lucy says, smiling at her.

She nods, but does not smile, looking quickly away, down at the mud. Chickens peck at her feet. She is wary, and there is something else clouding her eyes now, besides pain. Shame? Embarrassment?

Lucy can understand why. She feels unworthy. Because of who she is.

The sun dips behind a cloud then. Shadows stain the mud at their feet, the black of disrepute.

The woman and the boy talk again, in rapid-fire Kannada. The dog chases the chickens and they scatter, squawking. The cat mewls plaintively from its post on the rim of the well.

'We go home now, village next time,' the boy says, coming up to Lucy, the dog following, looking pleased with itself for scaring the chickens. 'Is rain.'

'Goodbye.' Lucy turns to wave to the woman but she is gone already, disappearing inside the house as smoothly and fluidly as she appeared.

All the way back to the house Lucy thinks of her – the circumstances that have led her here, this woman, a girl really. She thinks of other girls like her, sold to the goddess into a life of prostitution so they can support their families. How is it that she and James have to sit back and do nothing? Why can't they try harder to change things?

Lucy resolves to speak to James, as she, the boy and the dog dash across the jungle path, duck and slither under the barbed-wire fence, run up the path between the fields and through the gate just as the heavens open and they are drenched. They laugh as the fierce rain tasting of mud douses them, so they are soaked in an instant, and skip all the way up to the house, even as the servants run up to Lucy with a parasol and shout admonishments at the boy.

Lucy holds the boy's hand and laughs, the dog skidding on the wet earth beside them, their feet sliding in the dust, which has turned to muddy slush, her dress and hat irrevocably ruined.

James, who is home for lunch, watches from the veranda, cradling a drink and laughing along with them, saying, 'Come on out of the rain, you misbehaving twosome! Do you want to catch a cold?'

And Lucy slips out from beneath the parasol, opens her mouth to the skies and tastes happiness, slick and slippery as warm drops seasoned with earth.

Chapter 37

Gowri

Spilling Water

Goddess,

I am pregnant.

And I don't know if it is the child of the man I look up to and admire or the man who owns me.

Is this part of your twisted plan for me, Goddess?

A child, a miracle blooming in my arid world… I love it already. And, as you know, this renders me defenceless, vulnerable.

What if Mr Bell is the father? I shudder to think what the landlord would do were he to find out…

This child is more trapped than ever. This child, with two fathers to lay claim to and yet, it will be without a father. One is married and heartless. The other has too much heart, which he hides behind a stern demeanour, and he never belonged to me in the first place.

It is completely the wrong time to have the baby. Not that there is ever a right time for women like me.

I am sick much of the time and after I have fed the priest and done my chores, I lie down, stroking my stomach, talking to the little marvel that grows in there.

I am ecstatic and I am terrified. I want this child, whom I already love more than life itself, despite the dilemma of its parentage, to be a boy. For if it is a girl, she is destined for the same fate as me, that of a devadasi – and I will die before she lives my life.

She cannot.

Goddess, I want to run away with this budding child, thus finally honouring my promise to Vandana Ma'am.

My sister is married now, to a teacher – a kind and modern man, she writes, who is happy for her to continue with her education so that she can also become a teacher. She wanted me to come to the wedding, but I knew I was not welcome and that I would cast a pall upon her big day, which is why my parents did not invite me. I understand. But it hurts nevertheless.

I do not have to worry about the landlord's threat regarding my sister any more. She is taken and he will not touch her now; he cannot.

But...

Even if I ran away into a new life (just the thought makes me come alive), how would I explain to everyone why I am with child, and whose child it is? How will I bring it up alone, without a father to offer protection, without an education with which to gain a job? I can speak English fluently, but I do not have a degree or a certificate to back me up. I have Vandana Ma'am's money, which I have not touched, keeping it for just this eventuality, but with a new baby it will run out very quickly.

If I did run away, I would not want to do what I am doing now, selling myself, my self-respect, my very being in exchange for a roof over my head. So, what work would I do?

If I went to my parents, even if they took me in, which I very much doubt, the landlord would come. He would punish me by taking my child. More than anything, I don't want his slimy hands laying claim to this precious being, this miracle growing inside of me. So very loved already. I don't want him trivialising my child, treating him or her with the casual disdain he currently reserves for me. Possessing him or her like he possesses me.

This child is a precious gift. I will protect him or her the best I can. With my life, if necessary.

And yes, I accept that I cannot run away quite yet. But I *will* keep my promise to Vandana Ma'am, Goddess, just you wait.

Mr Bell's wife has been to see me.

The boy brought her. He and the dog turned up unannounced one day, as is their wont. But this time they brought the memsahib.

The boy introduced her to me.

I felt betrayed; like he had switched allegiance from me to her.

You are becoming fanciful in your loneliness, I chided myself. *Inventing friendships and loyalties where there are none. And anyway, this is not a competition. You are not in the running where affection stakes are concerned. Don't forget your place, devadasi.*

Her dress was torn, her boots scratched. She was wearing a ludicrous hat, wielding a stick and trying to appear at home in the surroundings. But she looked so very out of place, like a delicate flower uprooted and wilting in the mud, her skin shiny with sweat and red with exertion.

I yelled at the boy, in Kannada, which I am sure that, unlike her husband, she does not know. 'Why did you bring her here? You know the landlord doesn't like me having visitors.'

The boy smiled innocently at me. 'She wanted to go to the village and this is the shortcut.'

'Well, take the long route from—' I began, but he interrupted with, 'She wanted to go to the village. But I wanted to come and see *you* on the way there.'

My anger evaporated like water in a pot left outside in the sun, and I smiled at him. He grinned, that innocent, devil-may-care smile.

'I wonder what you're hiding behind that cheeky smirk,' I said and he laughed.

The memsahib, this wife of the man whose child I might be carrying, smiled winsomely at me. 'Hello,' she said, in a voice like spilling water, like birds twittering from trees and plants sighing after the first shower of the season.

I did not smile back.

Chapter 38

Lucy

A Good Impression

When Lucy asked James to teach her photography, all she wanted was to have something in common with this man she had married but didn't really know. What she didn't realise was just how much she would enjoy taking photographs, how good she would become.

'You are a natural,' James declared, giving Lucy one of his older cameras to practise with during the day, and she is absolutely thrilled.

Lucy takes the camera everywhere with her, hoping to capture the essence of this place – which is gradually beginning to feel like home – in her photographs. She takes photographs of Cook and his posse slaving away: the kitchen maid wiping tears as she peels onions, the spices being ground and pounded into paste by one of Cook's minions, curry sizzling in the pot, rice bubbling on the hearth, ghostly fingers of frothy, glutinous water escaping the sides of the vessel.

She snaps photographs of Market Boy (Lucy has taken to calling him so, for he loves and is proud of this name and will not accept any other, despite her best attempts and James's before her), teaching the dog tricks, throwing a stick high in the air – Lucy has managed to capture him mid-dance as he celebrates the dog jumping in the air to triumphantly catch the stick in his mouth.

She has taken a photograph of the lime green birds with bright red beaks that come to drink from the fountain and chatter away among themselves after, and one of the famously grumpy mali as he talks lovingly to the plants in a way he doesn't with humans – the only exception being Market Boy. There's one of the sweeper, her sari tucked in at her waist, a cloud of dust rising in the wake of her broom. And one of the dhobi balancing the load of washing on his head, his hands swinging freely by his sides.

In the somnolent afternoons, when the sun is at its fiery worst, or when the monsoons are at their dramatic best, she sits at the desk in her room and writes letters home.

My dear Ann,

I received your letter yesterday and I had to write back immediately! Reading it was like talking to you, my friend.

In her letter, Mother informed me that you are expecting. I understand why you haven't told me yourself. You are so kind, Ann, so selfless. I wish you all the best with your confinement, my dear. With you and Edward for parents, your child is blessed.

I wish I could be there for you, helping you through your confinement as you were there for me in my time of need. It's true that with you in Brighton, we would not be able to meet as often as we wished, but anything would be an improvement to me being here and you there, letters only arriving once every few weeks, if that. I wish I could watch you bloom with child. I wish…

Writing these letters to you is so cathartic. They are my connection to another life that seems so very far away now.

You tell me how eagerly you await my letters, even more so than Miss Heyer's and Miss Sayers's novels. Thank you, my friend. I feel the same way about yours. They connect me to a home that often feels so distant, as I wade through days sticky with heat and taut with experiences I never thought I would have. It is very different here, Ann, but as James promised me, the place, the people, are growing on me. Although of course there is still a lot to learn…

'Memsahib, if we serving beef, we get different cook. He cook in outhouse,' Cook says as he and Lucy plan the menu for Saturday's luncheon that James and Lucy are hosting for the neighbouring plantation owners.

'Why?' Lucy asks, puzzled.

'I is Hindu, I no eat beef.'

'But—'

'No, no!' Cook shakes his head from side to side. 'No eat, no touch. Holy cow.'

Lucy buries her head in her hands. It has been more than a month since her arrival and she is still navigating the ways of the household, the quirks and beliefs of the staff. Nevertheless, despite the language barrier and taking into account all the food items the staff won't or can't cook, after a couple of hours of intense discussion, the cook and Lucy manage to put together a decent menu for the party. Lucy is, she has to admit, quite nervous. This is her first time as hostess; the first time she will be meeting the other planters in the area and their wives. She is determined to make a good impression.

On the day of the luncheon, Lucy opens the curtains of her room to a miracle. A posse of exotic birds parade under her balcony, their plumage open in a wondrous fan of winking eyes shimmering turquoise and sapphire and gold. She gasps in wonder and her maid, who has come in with her tea, says, 'Peacocks.'

Peacocks. So very beautiful. And right under her nose! It is as if they are performing just for her. An auspicious beginning to the day of the party. Coffee plants and lawn shining wetly in the early-morning soft gold light. The monsoon is in full force, the rain heavier during the evenings, when storm clouds gather navy blue against the setting sun. Every night Lucy falls asleep to the drumbeat of rain as it lashes violently against the windows.

James leaves for the plantation – he is there every day, not even making an exception at the weekend. 'Just until we manage to get the plantation back on track,' he promised Lucy.

'I will be back at noon, in good time for the party,' he adds as he sets off that morning.

James is a wonderful teacher, explaining patiently the workings of the camera. He is just as happy as Lucy is when he looks through the viewfinder and informs her that she has taken a good shot, his voice pleated with pride.

The more she warms to this quiet, kind man, the more she feels guilty and torn about what she is keeping from him, the deceit she has indulged in. The knowledge that he deserves someone better than her sits like a weight on her chest.

And as she lies awake every night wondering if this is the night he will come to her room, share her bed, as she falls asleep alone and awakes alone, she wonders why he is not consummating their marriage, and when and if he will do so. Is she wrong about him? Is his kindness to the servants, his caring and empathy that shines through in his photographs, the gentleness he hides behind a stiff demeanour, an act? Does he hold grudges? Is he still punishing her for her reluctance on their wedding night and the morning after she first arrived here?

She is sure now that he married her for her money, in order to save his beloved plantation. But even so, doesn't he want her? She is beautiful, she knows. Doesn't he desire her, at least a little?

As she lies awake, she goes over and over those times he tried to kiss her, tried to love her – and in her re-enactments she behaves differently. She responds to his attentions, she kisses him back. There is James and James only – no Robert intruding.

Lucy has now been going whole days without pining for Robert. She no longer misses him. What she does miss, though, is what she had with Robert, that heart-stopping, world-glowing feeling of everything being possible because they were in love. Like walking on a carpet of clouds. Like tasting the first day of spring: crisp and green, pink buds and yellow daffodils, cherry blossom and the promise of summer.

But James, the man in her life now, is as distant as ever. A great teacher. A good man. But husband?

James, you care for your workers and your servants. You are so patient and kind to them. Why not me?

You deserve this, her conscience jeers. *All your life, men have feted you, attended to you, fallen for your charms. You have mocked their passion for you, the way they behave around you. You have claimed to be bored by it. You used and discarded Robert. Well, now it's your turn to learn how it feels to be spurned.*

Lucy shrugs off her gloomy musings and makes her way to the kitchen to check that preparations for the luncheon are proceeding smoothly, stopping on the veranda to watch the birds drink from the fountain.

Since getting soaked in the monsoon shower that day when she went for a walk with Market Boy and the dog and saw the woman in her magical cottage, Lucy has thought of the woman every day, wanting to help her, to rescue her from her fate. She has even walked to the house a few times, when the rain has stayed away long enough for the sun to shine through the storm clouds, taking the boy and dog and her camera with her, meaning to talk to the woman, to convince her to accept her offer of help.

When they approach the cottage, Lucy asks Market Boy to go on ahead into the village, and she pauses, dawdling. She sees the woman come outside, feed the chickens, take tea and a covered plate of food into the temple – for the priest, Lucy assumes. On her way back from the temple, the woman chases away the chattering monkeys who try to make a grab for the unattended food, the sweets left behind by devotees, the shiny plate of milk offered to the goddess.

Often Lucy sees her standing by the peepal tree, lost in thought for ages at a time. Sometimes, she pulls papers out of a pouch in her sari skirt and writes in them.

Compelled to capture the woman's haunting beauty, her fluid grace, on film, Lucy takes photos of her as she draws water from the well, as she washes her clothes by the stone under the tree, hens clucking about her, their feet covered in sudsy water. If the woman is aware of Lucy's presence, she never lets on. She pegs the clothes up and Lucy aches with the loneliness evident in that lone sari, fluttering a cheery blue and gold in the dust-laden breeze. Solitude is etched into the sag of the woman's shoulders, in the pain in her eyes, in her every considered movement, in her measured steps, as if by taking her time she can keep isolation at bay.

As she had resolved to do when she first saw the woman, Lucy asked James if there was anything they could do for her, and girls like her.

'We can't barge in and try to entice the girls away from the goddess. The landlord would read it as interference, unwarranted meddling in native customs and affairs,' James had warned, his voice hard.

'But—'

'The landlord is a potent enemy to have, Lucy.' His voice was softer. 'And not only that, the girls themselves are afraid to go against the goddess. Their beliefs, their religion, is a very powerful bind.'

Lucy understands that James's hands are tied, but surely there is something *she* can do? She wants to help all of these women, these devadasis, and she will start, she has decided, with the woman she has met. She will talk to her, persuade her to leave, to come and work at the plantation or even at the house, to be part of the staff.

'You have a choice,' she will say.

But the woman never smiles, and beyond acknowledging Lucy with an unfriendly nod that very first time, she ignores her, pretends she isn't there. It fazes Lucy and she doesn't know how to initiate the conversation she wants to have.

Music wafts from the temple, mournful, an elegy. The cries of the birds carry on the wind from within the jungle, high-pitched and plaintive.

The woman Lucy is spying on and taking pictures of looks up then, startling her from her ruminations. When her beautiful eyes, made all the more so by their depths of sorrow, their liquid rims of ache, meet Lucy's, her face goes still. She walks up to her, hips swaying elegantly, and Lucy is so shocked that she almost drops the camera. She has never approached her or initiated conversation before.

'My job is to look after and serve the goddess. It is not my job to pose for you, Memsahib. I'm not a show run for your benefit,' she says, pointing at Lucy's camera.

Shame scalds Lucy's face, hotter than the sun's rays. 'No, it isn't like that…'

It never occurred to Lucy to ask permission. Both she and James take photos of the staff all the time, and the staff are used to this and don't bat an eyelid. Some of them, especially the young men who make up Cook's posse, pose for photos even when Lucy is aiming for a simple, candid shot. She had assumed that this woman too would not mind.

You are too used to getting your own way, to everyone around you always doing your bidding. You assumed this woman would be thrilled to have her photo taken, her likeness captured on film by the memsahib no less. You think you have changed, learned from what happened to you, what you did. But have you really? Aren't you just the same spoilt, indulged girl, taking everyone too much for granted?

The woman's voice shakes as she says, 'I know that you know that it is my job to please the goddess and the landlord. But in my house, when the landlord is not around, and after my duties to the goddess are done, I want only to please myself. Not you, nor anybody else.'

Lucy nods, mortified. 'I… I'm sorry.'

The woman turns, so Lucy's apology is given to her retreating back, and then she is gone, her anklets singing a musical chime at odds with her anger.

It is only later, when walking back with Market Boy and Dog, that she realises that the woman spoke to her in fluent English far better than she has heard from any of the natives so far. From that thought comes another, before Lucy can stop it: *Of all people, I wasn't expecting her to speak such good English.* She realises, cheeks flushing, that perhaps there was something to the woman's accusation, that perhaps, deep down, she is guilty of thinking her a spectacle worthy of prying and voyeurism.

She is so different from you. Is that why she is fascinating? Will she be your 'adventure', like Robert was? her conscience pipes up.

No, I keep visiting her because I want to help her. I meant to talk to her, to ask her to come and work at the plantation or at the house instead of being a slave to the landlord, but with what happened, I was too shocked. I am not a ghoul or a busybody, I took photos of her because I find her intriguing – that strange mix of beauty and loneliness and fire and pain.

The morning of the party progresses busily. The house is dusted thoroughly by the servants. There is much chatter and discussion as they take the carpets out on to the grass and beat them with sticks to rid them of dust, as they clean the fountain, as the mali cuts flowers and the maid arranges them in vases throughout the house, humming all the while, as the dining table is polished and laid with the best china and cutlery.

Lucy watches the servants as she sips the sweet ginger-infused tea (unbelievably refreshing and she is quite the convert) and munches on deep-fried plantain fritters, Cook's speciality, that she has grown to love, from the balcony of her room, their banter as they work, the way they shout and rib each other, the dog following their every move, and she feels inexplicably lonely.

'You look lovely,' James says when he sees Lucy in the cream chiffon dress she has changed into for the luncheon.

'You don't look too shabby yourself,' she replies, grinning, thrilled by James's unexpected compliment.

He is wearing the frock coat he wore to their wedding and Lucy is overcome suddenly by an intense pang of homesickness, a longing for her parents and Ann. Since she watched the servants at work and was overcome by loneliness she has been feeling unsettled. She has been thinking of the girl going about her chores at the cottage, and understands that she has no right to feel this way, she with her husband and her big house and servants to attend to her every need.

And yet she *does*…

'Are you okay?' James asks and Lucy swallows, looking at her handsome husband, overcome by an impulse to ask him why he has not been coming to her room, the words, salt and ache, on her tongue, when there is the loud toot of a horn from outside and the first of their guests arrive.

The luncheon passes in a haze of polite conversation. The men compliment Lucy and the women admire her dress and ask for news from England; for the fashions and the gossip making the rounds.

Cook has surpassed himself and the food is exquisite.

'James, heard about the trouble you've been having. It's a tough time for plantations in general. And your hiring a native for foreman doesn't help. What was wrong with Peter, who we suggested at the last planters' meeting?' one of the men – Mr Halliday – asks, as the soup bowls are collected and the next course is served.

'Ganesh is good, the best there is,' James replies. 'I don't see why I should employ someone who does not know my estate and my plants the way he does, just because he's English.'

Lucy misses the next bit of the men's conversation as Mrs Brown, seated on her left, turns to her. 'How are you settling in, my dear?' she asks as she tucks into the stewed quail.

'Very well, thank you.' Lucy smiles.

'It does seem a bit overwhelming initially, there's ever such a lot to do, what with managing the household and keeping an eye on the servants. You have to be firm with them, keep them in their place.'

Lucy pictures the servants gathering every night in the kitchen for their meal, talking and laughing and sharing their day in their sing-song language. She recalls the time the kitchen maid came in soaking wet and she watched as one of the other women gently wiped her hair. It had made her ache for home, for affection such as this; for female companionship, for Ann, her childhood friend. She thinks of Market Boy, whom all the staff tease, affectionately, but whom they also care for and love, and the dog they have adopted and feed scraps to. How they make sure that every grasshopper and cricket that enters the house is gently caught and freed into the garden. How one day when the maid who did the washing up fainted from the heat, they all covered for her.

Growing up, Lucy never paid any attention to the staff. They were just there, silent and unassuming, fading into the background when not attending to her. That changed with Robert, of course. And it has changed even more with Market Boy. And being here...

Just like James, Lucy is beginning to care for these people who care for her, catering to her every whim and making sure she is comfortable at all times. She wonders at their lives – something she would have never given a moment's thought to before when she was a spoilt, bored socialite – so apart from hers and yet, she realises, underneath it all they are not so very different from her.

'The dhobi must never be allowed to keep clothes overnight – and always make sure to check the clothes he brings back. Don't be too trusting with the natives. If it is possible to cheat you, they will do so,' Mrs Brown is saying.

Lucy notices the servants bringing in the next course – mango tart with custard – stiffen at her words.

She thinks of the girl at the cottage, with her sad eyes, the pain that she hides as she goes through her day, the loneliness she carries like a weight, visible in her careful movements, the grace in her every move. She pictures her face, her expression when she said, 'I'm not a show run for your benefit.'

She thinks of Robert, whom she seduced and then betrayed, lying to save her own skin, getting him in trouble so she could get out of it. And she says to Mrs Brown, smiling sweetly, 'They are just people. They love and they hurt, like us.'

'You are getting too accustomed to them,' Mrs Brown sniffs.

'So be it,' Lucy replies, turning away from her and taking a sip of wine.

James catches Lucy's eye and smiles, very slightly raising his glass to her. And that is when Lucy understands that she is beginning to love him.

Chapter 39

Kavya

A Hint of Denouement

'Oh, my!' Kavya laments. 'Oh, Gowri!'

She wants to tear something, break something. She wants to hurt the parents of this girl, she wants to kill the landlord. She wants to go up to the temple, to all the people protesting in front of it, and tell them what really happened there, how it was created at the expense of a sweet young girl, her body, her dreams, her future.

'Building this temple required the sacrifice of a young girl's innocence, the shattering of her life as she knew it, the rape of her body, the murder of her hopes!' she wants to yell. 'Stop protesting, go home. This temple is wretched. It is built on the tears, the hopelessness of a vulnerable young girl, the plundering of her future.'

Fighting her anger, her upset, she sets the letter down, very gently, on the floor beside her, wishing it was Gowri she was handling.

Slowly, she comes back into the present, away from the angst-ridden words, the hurting mind of the young Gowri.

Her father has fallen asleep, his glasses askew, the dog's head on his lap.

Her ajji is looking up at her, her eyes wide and wise behind her glasses.

Her mother is clanging pots in the kitchen. The aroma of frying onions, roasting spices. The hot, woody scent of water being boiled in the bathroom.

She pictures swirls of smoke tinting the pink evening dusky blue.

The sun is setting, the sky a mishmash of colours, an artist's messy palette after the masterpiece is executed.

The air smacks of tragedy, an ending. Soft, dusty and carrying a hint of denouement. The taste of flowers and fruit and earth.

Her ajji picks up the letter Kavya has set down and, very carefully, she smooths it out as if caressing the soul Gowri has poured out into the letter, as if the gesture will put her back together.

'Ajji, who…' Kavya begins, her query stalled by the huge droplets that fall from her ajji's rheumy, cataract-riddled eyes, making them look even bigger and more defenceless.

Her ajji opens her arms and Kavya settles into them.

'How is she connected to you, Ajji?'

But her ajji just holds her, in the quiet punctured by the shouts of children playing in the fields, the last game of cricket before dinner and bed, her father's gentle snores, the birds twittering as they fly to their nests, her mother humming tunelessly, a dog's bark, a woman's laughter.

Ajji reaches up and wipes Kavya's eyes with her sari pallu smelling of talcum powder and turmeric and coconut oil and it is only then that Kavya realises she is crying too – for Gowri and what she went through, for Ajji's obvious upset. And Kavya is also crying for herself – for the baby she loved with all her heart and lost, for the man she loved and who she had assumed had loved her in return, for the wrong turns her life has taken, her fears for her future. But at least Kavya has had choices. She chose her career. She chose to love Nagesh. She chose to keep her baby. Now she has chosen to come home. And soon, she will choose what she wants to do next, where to go from here.

This girl from the letters, Gowri, was forced into a situation where she had absolutely no say and Kavya is raging on her behalf, livid that she cannot do anything about it, that these despicable things go on.

'This happened a long time ago. It's all in the past now,' Ajji says softly.

She knows me so well, thinks Kavya.

'But it happened, Ajji.'

Ajji sighs. A weary exhalation from within her very depths that diminishes her somehow, reduces her to an even tinier version of herself.

'Yes, sadly, it did.'

Ajji picks up the next letter and hands it to her and Kavya, still ensconced in her ajji's arms, starts to read.

Chapter 40

Lucy

A Rainbow Winking

'How dare you bring disgrace upon this family's distinguished name?' Lucy recoils from the venom, the unaccustomed rage that has transformed Father's mild voice into a thunderous roar. 'I am ashamed to call you my daughter.'

Father strides across the room, picking up the gun that he uses for hunting.

He points it right at Lucy, takes aim.

An almighty flash and then several earth-shattering bangs.

No. No, no, no—

Lucy sits up, her whole body shaking. Her face is wet with tears and sobs escape her mouth in remembered terror.

Slowly, she comes back into herself.

Just a dream.

There's a bright flash like that from a giant camera and her room is illuminated in silvery light. A furious storm batters the windows, snarling and growling like a rabid beast. Thunder crashes and booms, reverberating in her chest. She is frightened, remnants of her dream inciting fresh sobs. She needs her husband; she wants James.

She stands and, hiccupping from the dregs of her crying, makes her way across the hallway and knocks on James's door. It's only been a half hour since she fell asleep before the storm woke her and she doubts he's back from the plantation. But she's scared to be alone – it's enough to make her overcome her reticence and push open the door to his room.

Another flash of lightning. More thunder.

She stumbles her way to his bed and lies down, pulling the sheets, smelling of him, around her. The storm rages and howls, lightning dances and thunder performs. Lucy, sheltered in the snug embrace of her husband's scent, woodsmoke and lime and ginger (the spice she couldn't identify when she first arrived, but recognises now), soothed by it, falls asleep.

She wakes to a weight beside her. Warmth. The sensation of strength, safety, of being anchored in a solid embrace. The smell of rain and outdoors, and ginger and smoke and musk.

'Lucy.'

Her eyes flutter open.

He is looking down at her, his face tired, his eyes soft, an expression in them she has never seen before.

Her face flushes with colour as hot blood rushes to it.

'I… I am… I was scared. The storm.'

She blushes some more, her voice tailing off. The room is quiet. Dark. No rain. No storm. Just breathing. His – steady. And hers – flustered.

His finger traces the contours of her face. 'I'm sorry I wasn't here…'

'I was comforted by being here.' Her breath catches as his finger caresses her lips.

'May I kiss you?'

'Yes.'

It is peacocks dancing, a rainbow winking in the moist, sun-kissed sky. It is forgiveness, acceptance. It is moving on and it is absolution.

Afterwards, he talks. 'I'm sorry I haven't been home, but the plantation... Every evening I don't want to leave you but every evening I must – I cannot have the men do it all on their own, it is not my way. And there is always an emergency.' He takes a deep breath. 'When I come back, you are in bed.'

'I tried to stay up a couple of times, but...' She takes a breath. 'I wouldn't have minded if you woke me.'

'I didn't want to foist myself on you. I wanted to give you all the time you needed to adjust both to this country and to life with me.'

She wants to tell him then. Lay bare the truth that has been choking her ever since he asked her to marry him. But then she hears Mother's voice: 'Every marriage has its secrets. Telling the truth will destroy yours.'

And so, she keeps her mouth shut.

Chapter 41

Gowri

Precious Possessions

Goddess,

Writing to you has become a habit, a compulsion.

We are bound by so many unseen ties.

And bound by these letters too. I have become used to setting down my thoughts, my worries, my dreams in these letters to you.

And now, I am also detailing my plans for escape from you. You see it all, know it all anyway, don't you, Goddess? So why shouldn't I write it down like I have everything that has happened to me since I was dedicated to you?

I suppose, in a way, I am daring you to take note.

I suppose, in a secret corner of my ever-optimistic heart, I still hope, like in my first trusting, pleading letter, that you will intervene, that you will prove me wrong by doing what is right.

As my pregnancy progresses, so does my worry, my fear.

I am tired much of the time, drained, my mind woolly, my body bent upon regurgitating the food I supply it with. And yet, thankfully, my baby grows. It tumbles about in my stomach and I stroke it and talk to it, my stupendous marvel.

This child who relies on me and whom I love more than life itself... What if it is Mr Bell's and looks like him? What will I do then?

I need time to make a plan and time is one thing I do not have.

If I can get away with passing off the baby as the landlord's child, then I can continue as I am doing for a while longer.

You see, Goddess, when it comes right down to it, I am scared, terrified of running away to a new life and making a hash of things, ending up worse than I am now. For I don't have only myself to worry about but my beloved baby as well, who is completely dependent on me. And bad as it is here, at least I *know* this hell. I can endure it. I have people I call friends – Mr Bell's boy, the vegetable vendor couple at the market, even, at a stretch, the priest.

Also, if I stay here then I don't have to worry about you, Goddess, exacting revenge on me for daring to leave by harming the people I love.

If I cannot get away with passing off the baby as the landlord's, if it looks like Mr Bell then I have no choice but to run away. I don't have to worry about the landlord taking my sister or destroying my family in revenge. My sister is married. My brother is in Bombay, working as an apprentice for a white sahib who is involved in the electrification of the railways.

But I do know that you won't let me go without exacting a harsh punishment, Goddess.

I don't care if you smite me, Goddess. But please, smite *me*, spare my baby. Please.

If I have to leave here, I realise that the money Vandana Ma'am gave me before she died, and which I have safely stowed away, with the books she also gifted me, is not nearly enough for a new life far away for myself and my child. I need more money than this to survive.

I wonder what to do and then, one day when the priest is stumbling down the temple steps in his blind misdirection, stubbing his toe on the stone that guards the hatch to the basement, the answer comes to me: the vault. Where the landlord stores much of his wealth, all his gifts to you, his money in lieu of favours you have granted him, his bribes for answered prayers.

There is only one key to the vault, which the landlord wears around his neck. How to get it from him?

Then it comes to me. The landlord always sleeps for an hour or two after he has had his way with me. Nothing wakes him then, not a storm lashing at the cottage, nor thunder, nor the wind moaning among the trees. Risky though it is, I'll need to take the key then.

Once I have made up my mind, I don't dither. First, during that drowsy time of afternoon when the sun is at its peak, right after lunch, when the priest is asleep and nobody ventures to the temple, I try to move the huge stone covering the trapdoor that leads down to the vault. It takes a few tries, but living alone has made me strong, both mentally and physically. Once I have moved the stone, I pull open the trapdoor and go down the steps. They are slippery, and I practise going up and down them with my eyes closed, for when I do come in here, it will be dark, and the sliver of sunlight that now inches in and lights the way will not be there. Once I am confident of navigating the stairs without falling, I cover the trapdoor with some grass and pebbles so it is not too obvious that the stone that is its disguise has been moved.

When the landlord visits, I do as he asks, trying not to show my anxiety, as I wait for him to fall asleep.

Once he is fast asleep and snoring, I reach for his neck. He twitches and I recoil. I wait a beat, then two, and, very gently, ease the key off the ring, my hand shaking so much that it takes longer than it should. But at last, I have it. Clutching the key, I slip out of the cottage, all set to steal from you, Goddess.

This is my reasoning, Goddess. I know you are going to punish me. I know you might stop me from running away, like you did last time by taking Vandana Ma'am from me.

There's only one difference. This time, I am prepared. This time, I know what is coming. This time, I know you.

I will steal from you. I will prepare to run away in case my child is Mr Bell's and takes after him. And I will pay the cost you extract from me.

But please, Goddess. Punish me, please don't hurt my child. That is all I ask.

As I sneak from the cottage to the temple, sticking to the shadows, I check on the landlord's chauffeur. He is fast asleep in the car as he waits, unaware of the world around him, although he will snap to attention when the landlord comes out of the cottage, wiping the bleary drowsiness from his eyes and obsequiously holding the door open for his employer.

The hatch squeaks as I pull it open, the sound loud in the quiet stillness of night. I wait a couple of minutes and when there is no movement from the direction of either the car, the temple, where the priest sleeps or the cottage, I scurry down the steps to the vault. The key takes a few tries to slot into the lock.

Please, I think, *please*.

Then it turns with a click and the vault is open and even in the darkness I can see the glint and slither and shine of gold.

I grab some gold, and some money, realising with a sinking heart that I have nowhere to put it. My sari skirt pocket is not big enough and I need my hands free to lock the vault and close the trapdoor. I dig around in the vault, thinking, *Please*.

My hand touches some folders away in the back. I take a couple of folders and stuff some necklaces and chains and as many paper notes as I can into them.

Before closing and locking the vault, I check that there's enough gold and money left behind so the landlord will not be suspicious when he visits here next. What I have taken has hardly made a dent in the pile. I heave a sigh of relief.

Locking the vault is much easier than opening it. I sprint up the steps, hugging the folders to me. Before coming out of the hatch, I listen. Just the usual night sounds. The smell of adrenalin and trepidation overlaid with the secretive ink and conspiracy perfume of night.

I close the hatch, cover it with mud and grass – I will pull the stone over it tomorrow, when it is light and I am alone.

Then, under cover of the shadows, I run to the cottage, pausing outside the door.

The landlord's snores resound through the thick, sour air of the cottage.

I slip inside, hiding the folders among my saris, beside all my precious possessions – Vandana Ma'am's money, her books, the books from Mr Bell and the photograph he took of me that magical night – grateful that the landlord has never once thought to look in here, supremely confident in the knowledge that everything I own he has given me.

Then I prepare myself for the last part – gliding the key back into the ring that hangs from the landlord's neck.

He wakes as I am slotting it in place.

'What are you doing?' he asks, just as I pull my hand away.

'There was a fly there. I swatted at it,' I say.

My heart is beating so loudly, I think he can hear it.

He stares at me.

Then a fly buzzes, right by his ear.

He blinks, flaps at it.

And I release the breath I have been holding.

After he's gone, I pull out the folders.

There's enough wealth there for a fresh start for me and my child, to keep us going until I find my feet. And I also find something else: deeds to the cottage and the land surrounding it. Deeds signed over to me.

The folders into which I stuffed my stolen spoils – they contained the deeds. I had packed the folders willy-nilly without thinking to empty them of their contents first.

I stare at the deeds to make sure. Yes, they are in my name.

My mind recalls that fateful day when the course of my life changed for ever – my da and the priest and the landlord negotiating a price to sell me to the landlord, although I didn't quite comprehend it then.

'I will build a cottage for her on the land beside the temple,' the landlord had said.

'Will you make it in her name?' my father had asked.

He knew exactly what he was doing when he sacrificed me, my da, I realise now. He was bargaining for my security, for something for me for when I was no longer beautiful, discarded by the landlord for someone prettier, younger.

'I will. You and the priest can be witnesses,' the landlord had said. 'I will build a vault beneath the temple and keep the deeds there. She is dedicated to the goddess, so keeping the deeds to her land there is only fitting.'

My father had nodded, looking hopeless.

At the time, I had not understood what was going on, shocked as I was, reeling from my fate.

Now, though, I get it.

The landlord had had the last word after all. He would have the key to the vault. Although the deeds were in my name, he had the key so he would eventually own them, just as he owned me.

But now.

Now *I* have the last word.

I had only meant to take some money and gold to see me and my child through our first months in a new life, but with it, I have inadvertently stolen the deeds – which belonged to me in the first place.

I fold up the deeds and gold and money into one of my saris and put it all away.

Now that I have the means, I want to run away immediately, into a new life. But there is the fear of your retribution, Goddess. And also, this pregnancy has taken it out of me – I am so tired. Sick much of the time. I don't have the strength to run away just now. I don't have it in me to stand up to and counter the vengeance you and the landlord might bring upon me.

I will bide my time until the baby is born and I know one way or the other whose child it is. And then, I will act.

Chapter 42

Lucy

Sudden Stillness

The monsoon season ends and the days are dry and warm again.

In September, James leaves his foreman in charge of the plantation for a couple of days and whisks Lucy off to the planters' ball in the city. They stay overnight at an opulent hotel, dancing into the early hours of the morning.

James continues to work long hours, but now, when he gets home at night, he shares Lucy's bed. Lucy is torn between coming clean with him and keeping her secret from him so they can continue the way they are. She is beginning to care for him and finds herself wanting to protect him, to keep him from hurt. And yet, she knows that when he finds out about her – for he will find out one day, and isn't it better she tell him than wait for him to discover it for himself? – he *will* be hurt.

Lucy maps her husband's every feature while he sleeps, the way his eyelashes curl over stubbly cheeks, the play of shadows on his face, which looks defenceless and vulnerable in repose, thinking, *Are you keeping secrets from me, James, like I am from you? Would you still patiently teach me to look at the world through a camera lens, would you care for me, share my bed, if you knew the truth about me?*

When she married him, she was in part succumbing to parental pressure and in part running away from the mess she had made of her life. James was a means of escape and she did not really think of his feelings – she was mired in her own.

But now…

Now that she is taking James's feelings into account, she can see clearly what a horrible thing she has done. She has deceived him and she cannot see how he will ever forgive her for it, no matter how much he cares for her.

James hasn't told Lucy that he loves her, not properly, not once. Sometimes, she wonders if he *does* know who she is, what she has done, which is why he is caring but still maintains that aura of reserve that she cannot quite penetrate. Has he seen inside her to what she is keeping from him, what she is not? Has he sensed her dishonesty?

Some weeks after the planters' ball, Lucy goes to visit the woman who fascinates her, boy and dog in tow. After the woman asked Lucy not to take photos of her, she resolved to keep away. And she has for almost four months. But now that the humiliation of that encounter has worn off, Lucy feels once again the urge to visit the woman in the pretty little cottage that belies what takes place within it.

The woman's palpable loneliness ignites an ache in Lucy. She admires her spirit, the way she confronted her, eyes blazing, unbroken despite what has been done to her. And yet, there is a vulnerability to her too, evident when Lucy has watched her. A weariness, an intense wretchedness, in the way she pushes the hair out of her eyes, when she closes them and turns her face to the sun as if asking for divine intervention.

Lucy wants to convince her to come and work at the house. At least at the house she'd have company, the easy camaraderie of the servants.

This time I will talk to her. I won't give up easily. I understand that after all that has happened to her, she is prickly and wary. But I will assure her of my motives. I will not allow her antagonism to put me off.

As Lucy has done every time they come out of the jungle, she sends the boy off to the village on an errand, the dog ambling after him, both of them looking back at her every so often until they turn the corner and disappear in a cloud of dust. During the course of their walk, Lucy tried, once again, to make him interested in some name other than Market Boy, but he would not budge.

'Is my name,' he said, pointing proudly at himself and grinning at Lucy. 'Market Boy.'

Lucy hides behind one of the trees at the edge of the jungle and watches the woman's cottage. She is being surreptitious and acting suspiciously, she knows. But she balks at walking up to the cottage and knocking on the door, somehow knowing the woman wouldn't appreciate it, her words, 'But in my house, when the landlord is not around, and after my duties to the goddess are done, I want only to please myself. Not you, nor anybody else,' echoing in Lucy's ears.

Despite gleaning that the woman is fiercely private, Lucy *wants* to see her and to help her. She doesn't believe in destiny or such nonsense – Ann does and Lucy has pooh-poohed her countless times over the years. But with this girl, it is as if she and Lucy were destined to meet. Lucy is drawn to this woman despite not knowing her at all. She feels for her. Not pity, not scorn, just empathy, although she cannot even begin to imagine what she has gone through.

After a bit the woman comes outside. Her movements are slow, unhurried.

I will wait for a suitable moment and then approach her, Lucy thinks. And yet, she dallies. *You are a coward, afraid that she will snub you.*

The woman takes tea and a covered plate up to the priest, scatters grain for the chickens, feeds the cat. Then she sits on the washing stone by the mossy brick wall of the well, under the stately tree, leaning against its trunk. She takes a pen and some papers out of the pocket in her sari skirt and starts to write.

Lucy spies on the woman from her hiding spot and memories of how she and Ann used to fancy themselves intrepid scouts as they hid in the scullery, waiting for Cook to leave the kitchen so they could steal some of the jam tarts she was making for Mother's card party, ambush her. As she breathes in the woody bark and resin scent of the forest, she realises that now, she can look back on those memories with fondness and without that longing for home accompanying them. *This* is now becoming home.

Lucy turns her attention back to the woman. *Am I fascinated by her because she is so different from me? Because I cannot begin to imagine her life? Is there a truth in what she accused me of? Am I feeding off her pain?* Her cheeks blaze, as she defends herself in her head. *No, I just want to help.*

Then why aren't you talking to her? Why are you standing here and furtively spying on her? The strident voice of her conscience declares.

But the woman is lost in concentration and Lucy decides she will not disturb her just yet.

You fancy yourself a do-gooder and yet you're afraid.

She quiets her irritable conscience, content, for the time being, to stand here and watch the woman, feeling very much at home in the forest now, the ants and other creepy-crawlies not bothering her as much as they used to.

The woman tucks the sheets of paper into her sari skirt and stretches. And that is when Lucy sees the bump. There is a curve to her perfect body, an arc to her stomach. She is pregnant, Lucy realises. She must be expecting the landlord's child, the poor girl.

Lucy recalls the smirking man ogling her from the car. She shudders to think of this woman carrying his offspring.

The woman turns then, and peruses the forest, her gaze wistful. Lucy tries to shrink even more behind the tree, but somehow their eyes meet.

Lucy blushes furiously, realising how this must look to the woman. This was not her intention at all. She had meant to walk casually up to her, not to be caught hiding behind trees, spying on her.

The woman crosses the road, face aflame, and comes into the forest, anklets tinkling. She stops right in front of Lucy. She smells of coconut oil and washing soap.

'Why are you doing this?' Her voice musical even in its ferocity.

Lucy is struck again by how good her English is. Somehow the speech that she had prepared to persuade the woman of her good intentions flees her mind and she stammers, feeling out of her depth in the face of this woman's anger, 'I—'

An almighty crashing in the undergrowth and a roar, startling them both, cutting Lucy off. The roar is loud and majestic and ominous, unlike anything Lucy has ever heard, vibrating in the sudden stillness of the forest, sending shivers down her spine.

Birds fly off the trees in a wide soundless arc and, across the road, the chickens scatter with a scared squawk and flutter. The cat wakes from where it is sunning itself on the rim of the well and runs off into the cottage.

The woman looks up at Lucy then, the fear and shock in her eyes reflecting her own. Seeing this woman scared makes Lucy's alarm shoot up a few notches.

Another, louder roar. Something rustling and pushing through the undergrowth.

'Come.' She grasps Lucy's hand.

And then they are running. Not towards her cottage but deeper into the jungle.

'B... but...' Lucy protests.

'Shhh,' she says, panting, running fast for a pregnant woman, her anklets making a noise as loud as Lucy's petrified heart. 'This is closer and safer. Quick, it's nearby.'

'What is *it*?' The roaring is louder now. Whatever it is, it is headed right at them, hurtling through the vegetation.

Lucy wants to know; she doesn't want to know.

She is terrified, her legs like jelly. But she follows the woman as fast as she can, adrenalin driving her forward.

'Tiger,' the woman whispers, panting.

She stops under a tall, thick tree and scrabbles around in its bark. Somehow, from a hole in its trunk, she pulls out a rope, which, Lucy notes with amazement, is a ladder that has been camouflaged by the woody bark and the end of which has been expertly hidden out of sight inside the tree. 'Up,' she says. 'Go on.'

And the woman pushes Lucy up the ladder.

Lucy climbs, her trembling legs somehow following her frightened brain's command. She peers down and sees the woman following. Is it even okay for her to climb up in her condition?

Better than being eaten.

Despite Lucy's fear, she admires the way the woman deftly climbs, elegantly manoeuvring the voluminous folds of her sari, the end of which she has tucked in at her waist. She is barefoot. Lucy feels clumsy in comparison, her clunky walking shoes groping to find a grip on the rope ladder, and her skirts flying all around her. She worries about what the woman can see as she climbs up behind Lucy and her conscience kicks in, chiding her. *You are desperate. There's a tiger down there somewhere and you are worrying about how your corset looks to her? This girl-woman who has been sold by her parents into prostitution in the name of a goddess? You can be certain she has seen much worse.* A terrified giggle, born of fear, tasting of salt and panic, escapes Lucy's mouth.

She climbs higher and higher, the branches scratching her face getting thicker and more dense, until she sees it: a treehouse. Small, snug. Planks of wood laid across branches and nailed to them. Branches tied together overhead to form a sheltered canopy.

With a relieved sigh, Lucy heaves herself on to it. The woman follows, breathing heavily. There's just enough space for two. Lucy can smell her fear and sweat and washing soap and something sharp, lemony. Once she sits beside Lucy, lifting up her sari skirts and settling them around her, Lucy looks down.

And gasps in awe. The forest is spread out before them, visible through the green foliage, dappled light filtering through gaps in the branches and making the leaves glow velvet emerald and gold.

And prowling down there, somewhere, a tiger...

Lucy spies the path, dark auburn, snaking through the mulch, where Market Boy and Dog and—

'Market Boy and Dog,' she cries, terrified.

'They'll be fine. He is smart – he lived in the forest before he came to your house,' the woman says.

Lucy nods, gulping back her terror.

'Thank you for bringing me here, to safety,' she whispers.

The woman shrugs, waving her thanks away. She looks beyond Lucy, covers her mouth with one hand and grabs Lucy's hand with the other, silently pointing downward.

Then Lucy sees it. Sinewy body. Lined and long and beautiful. Shimmering orange-gold and black-striped fur. Tawny eyes flashing, cream whiskers alert. So very beautiful – and so intimidating.

Lucy sits there with the girl and they watch, spellbound, as it sniffs and paces under their tree, her hand in the girl's slick with perspiration and fear. After an endless moment during which Lucy forgets to breathe, it bounds off into the jungle, its every leap and movement graceful and menacing, danger radiating from its sleek flank.

It is a stunning, frightening and profound moment and they sit there, the two of them, tied by dread, bonded by having experienced this together.

Above them, as if echoing their sigh of relief, parrots – the exquisite birds that come to drink from the fountain – fly off the branches in a green wave, silhouetted emerald against the turquoise sky.

Slowly, the sounds of the forest return to normal. Everything has been suspended, it seems, even the breeze afraid to sough through the branches, the monkeys staying still and silent for once. Now they once more start to chatter away, and one of them, a mother with her little babe clinging to her tummy, nimbly jumps across branches – and stops short when she comes upon Lucy and the young woman. She looks at them for a long while, unsure what to do. Then she moves to another branch, sitting there and beckoning to her sisters, who come one by one, all of them staring at Lucy and the young woman and scratching their stomachs as if not knowing what to make of them, looking for all the world like a posse of gossiping women undone by the subject of their gossip suddenly appearing in their midst.

'It didn't go to the cottage. The chickens and cat are safe,' Lucy's companion says, and her voice is soft with the awe Lucy feels.

She rummages around in her skirts and digs something out: a ripe mango.

'Hungry?' she asks.

'Scared,' Lucy says.

She throws back her head and laughs, startling the birds perched on nearby branches. And it is the most beautiful sound, sweet with the heady relief of having courted danger and escaped. It is temple bells and velvet moss and silvery anklets. It is the taste of summer in Lucy's mouth and joyous respite in her heart, of finding refuge in the strangest of places, a haven among the treetops with a girl who fascinates her and the mesmerising forest floor, with its undercurrent of peril, spread out below them.

'What is your name?' Lucy asks.

'Gowri,' she says.

It sounds pure, like bells and worship.

'Mine's Lucy.'

The young woman nods. Then she wipes the mango on her skirt and squeezes it all over. She takes a small bite from the curved apex and spits the skin out, making a hole and sucking the juice of the mango through it. The monkeys watch keenly, but they don't make a move towards them.

She passes the mango over to Lucy, and Lucy copies her actions and sucks on the sweet juice. They sit there, among the treetops, sharing the mango until the juice runs dry, until they see Dog and Market Boy arrive, Market Boy's sweet voice calling, 'Memsahib?'

It is then, as they smile at each other in relief, that Lucy realises Gowri was waiting for this, for Market Boy and Dog to come back here; she was looking out for them from this vantage point.

What if they hadn't come back?

Lucy shudders as the thought goes through her head, and Gowri squeezes her hand.

'I knew they'd be safe,' she whispers, smiling at Lucy, as if she has read her mind.

It is like when Lucy was with Ann, and she would know what Lucy was thinking before she said it. How Lucy has missed this, the simple, uncomplicated joy of female camaraderie.

Lucy squeezes Gowri's hand back and she pulls it away, embarrassed, as if realising only then that she is still holding Lucy's. But they climb down the ladder and walk contentedly together, side by side, the forest that just moments ago, before the tiger scare, had seemed familiar to Lucy now feeling different altogether, thrumming once again with that thrill of danger: *Never take me for granted.*

They walk towards Market Boy and the dog, Gowri's anklets giving them away, so Market Boy turns, sees them and laughs happily. 'You safe, you be friend. Good.'

They go back, Market Boy and Dog and Lucy (the long way, through the village, not risking the shortcut through the forest), discussing the near miss with the tiger. They communicate very well now, Market Boy and Lucy; the dog joins in every once in a while with a considered bark or two.

Villagers collect in clumps, talking and gesticulating.

'They talking about tiger,' Market Boy says, grinning at Lucy, displaying his yellow teeth. She has bought him a toothbrush and supervises his brushing every morning and evening and yet his teeth – the unbroken few remaining in his mouth – are as yellow as ever.

They walk along the mud road through the village, flanked by huts on either side. Pots boiling on twig fires. Women neglecting them; the smell of burning rending the sky as they chinwag about the tiger.

A car comes up the road, raising dust and sending Lucy into fits of sneezing.

As it gets closer, she realises with some embarrassment that it is their car.

The driver stops beside them, his face lighting up in a smile.

'Memsahib, we worry for you.'

They climb in, Market Boy, the dog and Lucy.

'They walk,' the driver says, pointing to Market Boy and the dog.

'No, they'll come with me.'

The driver, who takes great pride in the car, washing it twice a day, looks them up and down, his nose scrunched up as he takes in Market Boy's dust-coated body, the mongrel's scratched and patchy fur.

He sighs, closing the door with a curt nod at Lucy, almost certainly wishing that he had never come to collect her.

'I wash car when we home,' he grumbles.

At the house, the servants are agog.

'Landlord two cattle taken, blood everywhere,' they say. 'Tiger so big, like giant. Good you safe, Memsahib, and no see.'

Lucy thinks of that lithe animal, exuding danger from its lissom haunches, the colour of a stormy sunset streaked with dusk. And she smiles as it dawns on her afresh that she actually encountered a tiger, a real live tiger, and survived.

When Lucy wanders out on to the veranda, having washed and changed, James is there, pacing.

'Oh, thank goodness you're safe,' he exclaims, coming up to her, taking her face in his palms and kissing her deeply – an unprecedented show of public affection that touches her. 'I've just heard.'

They sit on the veranda and sip tea and eat vadais – deep-fried dough balls, which Lucy loves (she knows this is why Cook has made them). They are perfect eaten together with the chutney he's made from mint and coriander.

Lucy insists that Market Boy sit with her and James. He does not sit at the table, however, but at their feet, on the veranda steps, throwing scraps to the dog.

James picks at his food, which is very unlike him, his gaze never leaving Lucy's face. 'To think of what could have happened...'

And although thrilled by his concern, she makes light of it. 'Oh, for goodness sake, James, it was nothing.'

Market Boy looks up at him, speaking in rapid-fire Kannada.

James goes pale. Lucy looks from one to the other, wishing she understood the language. The only word she recognises is Gowri.

James wipes his brow. 'Market Boy tells me of your acquaintance with that girl. I just…' He sighs. 'She's not good news, Lucy.'

Lucy bristles. 'I will decide who is good news and who is not, thank you very much. She's just a girl, possibly younger than me, living in horrible circumstances that she cannot control. And she just saved my life!'

'I know, and I'm very grateful she was there. It's just – she lives close to the jungle. And what with her association with the landlord…'

'He must visit her at night. I've not seen him there when I've been around.'

'Perhaps,' James says shortly. 'Just…' He brushes his hair away from his face, greasy with sweat. 'Market Boy tells me you take the shortcut through the jungle. Please stay away from the jungle from now on if you can help it.'

He looks so worried; he *cares*.

Lucy smiles, her heart singing, surprised at how much his regard matters to her.

Chapter 43

Sue

The Story Behind the Headlines

Sue goes to the study and lugs the box of her grandmother's belongings into the living room. It contains the few personal things she found, gathering dust in the attic, when her grandmother's house was being sold. She had eagerly gone through them, looking for clues as to the enigma that was her grandmother, hoping to fill in all the many blanks in her own past. But all she found was photographs, old and yellowing, dating back several decades and generations. Interesting though they were, she was left none the wiser as to all the questions she had about where she came from.

Now she sifts through the box with trembling fingers, knowing that she will be catapulted back through the years and wondering if it is wise to do this now: invoke more emotion on top of everything else. But she is curious, and she wants to know if she is right, if this is where she remembers having seen the temple and cottage.

The first few photos are of Sue's mother during various stages of childhood, including all of her school photographs. In them her mother is a bright-faced, eager-looking child. Sue feels a pang for this girl who had yearned for a token of affection from her mother and had instead only received love from a man whom she wanted y to have been her father but who most likely wasn't.

Her attention is arrested by a photograph of her mother with Elizabeth, her grandmother; her mother smiling shyly, Elizabeth looking preoccupied. They look so very different: Elizabeth fair and blue-eyed, her daughter dark-skinned and dark-eyed. No photographs of her mother as an adult. She had cut off all ties with Elizabeth by then.

There is album after album of photos of Sue's grandmother, Elizabeth, at every stage of her life up until the age of twenty-two – when Elizabeth's mother passed away – when they abruptly stop. There are also clippings of Elizabeth's successes at school and university, an indication of the direction her life would take, carefully preserved among the albums. The albums of photos and the clippings speak of the love and pride Elizabeth's mother felt for her daughter – she was clearly treasured and cherished. So why did Elizabeth feel as if something was missing from her life, as she had told Sue in her email?

Sue pushes the question aside to follow up later and digs through the box. The rest of the photographs are all in black and white.

The first of these: the wedding photograph of Elizabeth's parents, Sue's great-grandparents. Lucy, beautiful and virginal in her bridal attire, smiling shyly and a bit apprehensively at the camera. James beside her, rigid and stern. On the back of the photograph, the words 'James and Lucy Bell on their wedding day' are written in a dainty hand in purple ink, which is now faded to a pale violet and smells very faintly of lavender, carrying a hint of damp and the distant past.

This is the only photograph Sue possesses of her great-grandparents.

The rest are all of various unidentified people taken in and around what appears to be James and Lucy's house in India and its coffee plantation.

The coffee plantation… The elephant had trampled through a coffee plantation… Was it, by any chance, the one her great-grandfather had owned?

Sue identifies the prickle tightening her spine as excitement. She randomly picks up a couple of photographs from the jumble that's left in the box, scrutinises them.

Both are in black and white, worn with age. The first is of a striking girl with sad eyes, hands on her hips, chin jutting out as if in defiance of the photographer. She stands in front of a small cottage beside a temple, and although both are faded, they are quite unmistakably the ones Sue saw on the video clip. The prickle of excitement intensifies, becoming a pulse.

Since she heard about this temple, Sue has been spellbound, transported into a different country, her grief, her indecision regarding the baby, her personal heartbreak, which is always there, bitter at the back of her throat, if not forgotten then suspended briefly.

The next photo is of a priest ringing the bell of the temple, his back to the camera. The girl from the previous picture stands at the bottom of the temple steps, staring into the distance, her expression pensive. Who is she? Sue is drawn to her. And once again, she is ambushed by the particular thrill – the tingling at the base of her neck, goosebumps – that she feels when she is about to start work on an article, trying to unearth the story behind the headlines.

Chapter 44

Lucy

Public Property

A few weeks after she survives the tiger, when the scare has died down along with the worries that it will reappear, Lucy, armed with Cook's marble cake, pays Gowri a visit. She wants to thank her properly for saving her life.

She goes the long way, through the village. She tells herself it is a concession to James and his worry for her safety – she does not want to admit that she is secretly terrified of encountering the tiger in the jungle, with no treehouses or Gowri in sight, just a stick and a boy and a dog.

Once in the village, Market Boy stops to buy groceries for Cook and Lucy walks onwards to the cottage.

Gowri is in her garden, washing dishes in a bucket beside the well, sudsy blue water pooling in the mud and wetting the chickens pecking about her feet. Lucy holds out the cake to her: 'A thank you for helping me escape the tiger.'

Gowri wipes her hands on her sari skirt and sets them on her hips. 'Despite who I am, what you might think, I don't take charity.'

Goodness, this woman is prickly! 'It's not charity, it's a token of gratitude for saving my life.'

Gowri laughs shortly, a severe joyless bark. 'You make it sound so grand! I wanted to rescue myself, you were in the way. I couldn't leave you there, could I?'

'Whatever way you put it, I could have died. I didn't, thanks to you. Here, please, take it.' Lucy holds out the cake again.

Gowri looks at Lucy then, her gaze assessing as if to make sure she is not pitying her, toying with her.

Lucy meets Gowri's gaze, keeping hers level and earnest.

When she is satisfied, Gowri takes the plate from her. 'Thank you.'

There is a pause. Gowri looks towards the house, debating, Lucy supposes, on whether to invite her in.

'Come,' Gowri says, finally, having arrived at a decision. 'We'll go to the treehouse and share this.'

Lucy understands that Gowri is still reluctant to accept the cake – perhaps she feels that it will come at a price.

What has been done to you?

If Gowri is only comfortable accepting the cake if it means sharing it with Lucy, then so be it. At least this gives Lucy a chance to put her plan to help Gowri into action.

'Are you sure about the treehouse?' Lucy nods at Gowri's burgeoning belly. It seems to have doubled in size in the few weeks since Lucy saw her last.

Gowri looks down, blushing furiously. Then she looks up at Lucy again, eyes flashing, as if to say it is none of her business. She opens her mouth, closes it.

Lucy suppresses a smile. The woman has decided not to have a go at her; that must count for something.

'Let's go,' Gowri says at last, firmly. 'I'll climb up while I still can.'

* * *

The monkeys have taken over the treehouse and they chitter furiously when Gowri unceremoniously shoos them away.

'Don't show fear,' she says, when one of them, a huge hairy one with an incredibly long tail that swings down from among the branches, stares challengingly at Lucy. She claps loudly and calls 'Go, shoo,' and the huge creature finally turns and leaps away.

The monkeys don't go far, just to the next tree, swinging nimbly from the branches and keenly watching Gowri and Lucy. Waiting for them to capitulate, give them back their domain – and the cake with it.

'Do you know,' Gowri begins, wiping her face with the dangly end of her sari, 'the legend of this treehouse?'

'Tell me,' Lucy says.

'It seems there was once a sage who was tired of the world and wanted to escape. So he found the tallest tree he could and built a treehouse – this one. He used to meditate here every day. It was close to the heavens and he felt at one with God.'

'*I* don't.'

'That's because you're not a sage, far from it!' Gowri laughs.

'Speak for yourself.' Lucy feigns anger, even as she revels in the music of Gowri's laughter. When she laughs, she sounds like the girl she would have been, had she not been given to the goddess, all innocence and light.

'So anyway, the sage climbed up here and he did not come back down ever again. It seems he became a saint.'

'He died here?' Lucy looks around the treehouse – it feels claustrophobic suddenly. 'Is that death I smell? No, only monkeys…'

Gowri laughs even harder. 'Legend has it he ascended into heaven. There was no body. One day he was gone, only his robes and staff left behind. His followers saw the heavens opening and then a shock of light.'

He must have run away, Lucy thinks, but does not say it out loud in case she offends Gowri.

'I know what you're thinking.' Gowri nudges Lucy with her elbow, eyes twinkling. 'I presume he ran away too.' She smiles then, a sudden, beautiful smile that brings to mind birdsong, and which disappears almost as soon as it appears.

Lucy smiles back, thinking, *what a shame.* Gowri should be happy, smiling like this, her eyes twinkling with joy – not sad and pensive as she is much of the time. But even now, when she is grinning, there is the echo of sadness behind her eyes, the shadow of everything that has happened to her lurking.

Once again, Gowri surprises Lucy by following her train of thought.

'You know who I am, what I am,' she says.

Lucy looks at Gowri's brooding face as she stares at the horizon as if it has all the answers. Now is her chance to help.

'You don't have to be ashamed,' she begins. 'What happened to you, who you are, is not your fault.'

Gowri's eyes blaze. 'I'm not ashamed, not of that.' Then, 'It is not *I* who should be ashamed.'

Lucy flushes, embarrassed. 'I – I didn't mean…'

'Why are you here? Is it to mine me for information?'

'No!' Lucy bristles, unable to keep the shock from her voice even as her chiding conscience asks, *Is it? Is that why you are here?*

'Then why? Why have you been spying on me, taking photos?'

'Look, I'm sorry I took the photos without permission—'

'You thought that I would be grateful because you, the memsahib, turned your precious attention on me, deigned to choose me as a subject for your photographs. Or perhaps you thought that since I am a devadasi, I am public property.' Her gaze spitting fire.

'*No*, I—'

'Available to anyone to do anything they want.' Her voice brittle.

'Can you get off your high horse for a bit—'

'Me, on a high horse, Memsahib?' Her voice harsh. The 'memsahib' loaded with scorn.

'I came to offer help.' Lucy feels close to tears, her voice breaking. Hating herself for showing weakness. Hating this woman for making her second-guess her actions. Hating her for her bitterness and anger although of course she is more than entitled to it. 'I wanted to ask you if you would come to work at the house.'

'Ha!' Gowri laughs, a harsh sound very different from the festive, wholehearted music of a few minutes ago. The monkeys, who are watching them carefully, too afraid of Gowri to come closer but eyeing the cake all the same, ready to pounce if necessary, mimic the sound with startling accuracy. 'You want to help me so you can feel good about yourself.'

Is it? Do I? 'No, I want to help you because I am fascinated by you.'

'Because I am so very different from you. Because you cannot even begin to imagine what I have been through, what I have done.' Her hand placed protectively over her protuberant belly.

She has struck a chord. Lucy is quiet, near to tears. How can this woman read her mind so precisely?

'Because it thrills you to know a woman like me. Because you can feel better about yourself when you have extended your charity towards me, the least fortunate of women—'

'No, it's not like that!' Lucy protests, although in her mind her conscience chimes, *isn't it?*

'Did you think to ask your staff how they would feel if I joined them? Did you stop to consider how they would react? You can't just come along and play with people's lives without knowing the first thing about them, and expect them to be grateful.' She stands, her hair skimming the branches that make up the treehouse roof. 'I don't like being patronised, I get enough of it from the landlord. Keep your cake, Memsahib, and don't bother coming back.'

How dare she? Lucy rages, all the way home, having left the cake behind for the monkeys.

'What matter, Memsahib?' Market Boy asks when he joins her in the village, reading the anger on her face.

'Nothing.' She tries on a smile. But it doesn't fool Market Boy – she can see from the way he looks at her, his face alternating between worry and upset.

I only wanted to help.

Dog sticks close to her, licking her palm every so often, sensing her distress.

That's it, she thinks. *I'm done. I understand now what James was trying to tell me when he warned me off her; he was only looking out for me. I should have listened to him.*

Chapter 45

Kavya

Haunted Thoughts

Kavya sets down the letter, her heart aching for Gowri.

Dusk has fallen, the sky the colour of ripe grapes, birds flitting across it like haunted thoughts. Her mouth tastes of yearning, salty black, for this girl to be rescued, to have the life that has been denied her, the education she longs for.

I am so lucky, she thinks. *I have known love. I have also known sorrow, and I haul the ache of loss, yes. But… I have choices. I am not trapped.*

Her father is in his chair in the courtyard, the dog at his feet, his glasses askew.

Her ajji has fallen asleep beside her, her mouth open, soft sighs escaping it, and Kavya is overcome by tenderness towards her. Warm dusk presses upon them, the occasional breeze tasting of the past, stale and sour.

Kavya stands up very gently so as not to disturb her grandmother and goes in search of her mother. She is in the kitchen, crying copious amounts of tears as she chops onions. Every so often she uses her elbow to push away from her leaking eyes the hair that has escaped her bun and is crowding her face, but it falls back into her eyes anyway.

Kavya goes up to her mother and tucks the loose tendrils of hair back into her bun for her.

'I have yet to meet an onion that didn't make me cry,' her mother says, sniffing.

'I'm sorry, Ma, for earlier,' Kavya says, all in a rush.

Her mother stops chopping and looks up at Kavya. Her nose is running, her eyes red. She opens her mouth, then closes it. Nods once.

She sets her knife down, washes her hands, wipes them on her sari pallu and takes a head of garlic, hands it to Kavya. 'Here, peel these for me.'

'All of them?'

'Three cloves.'

'What are you making?'

'Khichdi. And kheer for afters.'

Both Kavya's favourites, her mother's way of apologising.

Kavya peels the garlic and then chops ginger, while her mother heats up oil in a pan, adds cumin and mustard seeds, and, when they are sputtering, the onions she has chopped.

'I ran away from home,' Kavya's mother says, as she gathers the chopped ginger and garlic and adds it to the pan.

Kavya stops pounding cardamom seeds in the mortar and pestle to stare at her. '*What!*'

'When I was younger. I was just as headstrong as you – you get it from me.'

'Ha!' Kavya manages a short bark of a laugh, her mind still unable to come to terms with what her mother is saying.

'I wanted to be a dancer and my mother, your ajji, wouldn't let me…'

'What?' she blurts, unable to come up with anything else. 'Ajji?'

'She was very strict, you know. Even stricter than I've been with you.'

Mild-mannered, kind, forgiving Ajji? Strict? 'Not possible.'

'I was,' Ajji says, coming into the kitchen. Her eyes are bleary and sleep-thickened. In the harsh yellow light of the kitchen, she looks impossibly lined and old. 'I've learned from my mistakes, mellowed with age.'

'I stole money from your ajji and ran away to Bangalore.' Her mother shuts her eyes tight and yet tears spill out of them. Real tears, not ones induced by onions. 'The worst few months of my life. I stayed in a hostel with twenty other girls, tried and failed to get into the dancing troupe. When my money ran out, I went home and meekly accepted every punishment my parents meted out.'

'I can't see you meekly accepting anything, Ma,' Kavya says and her mother manages a weak smile.

'It was terrifying, living away from home. I was propositioned almost daily by random men who took me for a different kind of woman. The girls I lived with weren't nice and the landlady was a money-grabber. When I came back home, my reputation was shot – I had been the talk of the town and we had to move. I didn't want you to suffer like I had. That's why I put up such a fight when you wanted to go into acting. I knew more than anyone how difficult it is to break into the industry.'

Kavya recalls her ajji telling Kavya's mother when she went on her fast to stop her daughter from leaving: 'Everyone needs to find their way, Laxmi. You know that.'

Her mother was looking out for her, in her own way.

'Oh, Ma, why didn't you tell me?' Kavya puts an arm around her mother's slumped shoulders.

'I suppose, with hindsight, I should have. But I still find it difficult to talk about that time. Some of the things that happened...' She shudders. 'Anyway, when my marriage was arranged, I told your da everything and he was so kind and understanding. He even said I could try and give the dancing another go, but this time he would be by my side. That is why I keep pushing you to get married. Everything is so much easier when you have someone beside you, supporting you, sharing with you. You don't feel so alone, so lost…'

'Your mother only wants what's best for you,' her ajji had said just that afternoon when she pressed Gowri's letters to the goddess into Kavya's hands.

She hides her heart behind a nagging voice and a strident demeanour. Kavya has always known this and yet it is hard to remember when her mother is in full flow. She looks at her mother and her ajji, two women with their own stories and experiences – not as terrible as Gowri's, perhaps, but they have also endured and survived, as women through the generations have done. She will never know everything they have been through, but they are here now, having emerged from it.

I will too.

We are not the weaker sex, we are the stronger one, she realises, surveying her mother and her grandmother, their worn faces illuminated by the strength radiating from inside.

She knows, then, that she will tell them.

'Ma, I… I've made some bad decisions.'

Her mother wipes her hands on her sari pallu. 'Kavya, we all do. This is how we learn.'

'I—'

'Is something burning?' her da asks, coming into the kitchen, and Kavya and her mother and Ajji all jump, flustered, and turn towards the hob, where the onions and ginger and garlic have burned to a crisp in the sputtering oil.

Chapter 46
Lucy

Different Kinds of Love

The evening after Gowri spurns Lucy's offer of help, Lucy takes to her bed, feeling unusually tired and miserable. She is hot during the night, beset by nightmares.

Father and Mother appear in her dreams, their beloved faces distorted with anger, voices screaming, 'How *could* you? With the gardener of all people! You have to get rid of it.'

'He's been discharged without a reference, you've destroyed his life,' Robert's mother cries, her face ruined by tears.

'You must get rid of it.' Mother's voice.

The woman in that poky room, those sharp instruments reaching inside Lucy, tearing, destroying.

It hurts; everything hurts. Her stomach. Her baby.

It is gone... Gone.

The woman, her hands bloody, eyes soft and wet, saying, 'I am sorry.'

No, no, no.

Ann squeezing Lucy's hand. Holding her while she sobs.

Ann came, dropping everything, leaving her husband behind. Lucy sent a telegram and she came.

What have I done, Ann? What have I done?

'Shhhh, it's all right, Lucy. It's all right.'

A male voice – Robert.

But Robert's gone. Lost his job, no references. All because of her. And she…

Oh, it hurts. Her stomach. Her whole body. Her mind. It hurts…

'It's all right, Lucy. Everything's all right.'

But nothing is; nothing.

A cool hand on her forehead.

'Robert?'

A throat being cleared.

Lucy opens her eyes, squinting at the face fading in and out of sight.

And it comes to her, where she is: the mosquito net, the thick press of heat.

'James?'

He is leaning forward, eyes tired and worried.

She tells him then. Her secret. Illness has wiped away her defences and she opens her mouth, pushes away Mother's hectoring voice and tells him. She bares herself to him, no more deceit.

There is silence after she speaks. A stunned, dazed hush. His face shorn of colour, his eyes glittering like frost on a frozen lake.

'I am so sorry, James,' she whispers.

He stands up.

'James?'

The door shuts behind him, and Lucy closes her eyes. She feels hollow, bereft, undone. She is a tree shaved of bark, weeping resinous, translucent golden tears. In her head, her mother's voice: 'Every marriage has its secrets, that is the key to its success. If you tell him the truth, you will lose him.'

I don't want to lose you, James.

Come back to me. I am sorry, so very sorry.

* * *

He does not come back. Lucy thrashes and agonises in the throes of her fever, and her heartache. A succession of servants tend to her.

'Master asking after you,' they say.

Then why isn't he here?

'Please eat, Memsahib. You eat, you better.'

But she does not want to eat, she wants James.

She loves him.

It has taken her a while to come to this realisation but now – too late – Lucy understands that she loves James. Completely. With her everything. And it's the shattering, all-consuming love that her naïve younger self had envisaged, longed for. Only that innocent, impetuous Lucy could never have fathomed that it would hurt this much.

Market Boy visits. He tries and fails to make her laugh – she thinks she will never laugh again.

She thinks of Ann, what she said while sitting under the rose arbour that day when she told Lucy she was engaged, that fateful day when Lucy first saw Robert. 'I looked at Edward and I knew then that he was the one for me.'

I have come to understand that there are different kinds of love, Ann.

I loved Robert with that heart-stopping, crazy love that did not listen to sense. And then James came along. He grew on me. He is kind and gentle and he looks after me. He is patient and quiet and calming. He makes me laugh.

Robert was my impulsive, good-time lover.

James brings out the best in me. With him, I see the world and everything around me in a softer, more beautiful light.

I need him, Ann. I love him with all my heart. I cannot live without him.

Have I lost him?

Chapter 47

Gowri

Cooling Earth

Goddess,

A couple of nights after I rebuff the memsahib's offer of cake and help, there is a knock on the door of my cottage and it is Mr Bell.

He is panting, like he was the last time he came to my door, as if once again he has tried to outrun a tiger. A muscle in his cheek twitches, and his eyes are tortured as he says, 'I – Can I…?' And then whatever he was going to say is interrupted, abruptly, as his gaze snags on my stomach.

'Mr Bell?'

He stands in the doorway, his jaw working but no words coming out, the night sky silhouetted behind him, stars twinkling, nocturnal creatures calling, leaves crackling, clouds drifting, wind soughing through the trees in the jungle, the smell of darkness and cooling earth and conspiracy.

'I – Oh… I didn't know.' His voice is barely a whisper. 'Is it…?' He clears his throat, starts again. 'Is it mine?'

'Please, come in. It's safest we talk with the door closed in case the landlord…'

He looks agonised; he cannot tear his gaze away from my stomach.

He takes a few steps inside and I close the door.

His smell of ginger and musk floods the cottage.

'Tell me, please.' Such angst in his voice, like when he had talked about Kitty.

'I don't know if it's yours or the landlord's.'

His jaw works furiously again. When he speaks, his voice is soft with ache. 'After I lost my family and Kitty, I hoped…' He sniffs, clears his throat. 'I wanted a family, a wife who loved me, children to complete us. But my wife… Today, just now, she…' He drags a hand across his face. 'And now this… I did not expect this.'

Tears swell in my eyes. I hold them back, look right at him, one hand caressing my stomach where *my* baby grows. 'This child – if it is yours – need not have anything at all to do with you. I was not going to tell you, I don't know why you're here.'

'I'm sorry, I've made such a mess of things,' he says.

'This child,' I bite out, enunciating every word, 'is *not* a "mess". It is loved very much, it is wanted and adored. Leave, Mr Bell. I don't know why you are here.'

'My wife… She can't have children.' He takes a deep, shuddering breath. 'I just found out.'

'What?' I wonder if I have heard him properly.

'I've always wanted children. And she… And you…' Nodding at my stomach.

'Your wife, she cannot have children?' I repeat, still unable to take it in.

The memsahib, who is everything I am not. Sweet and kind and naïve, exuding a wide-eyed innocence and a child's delight – and fright – in the wild nature that surrounds us. She hasn't had cause to learn that no creature, however fierce, can be as brutal or as destructive or as violent as a fellow human being.

Wanting to befriend me. Bringing cake and conversation.

It stands to reason that the only person other than Vandana Ma'am and the vendor couple and the boy to reach out to me, to try to see *me*, is this woman who has never had to question her position in life, her status or her privilege. Generous in her thoughtless, entitled way. Carelessly assured that the world will bend to her every whim as it has done all her life.

Whatever she wants, she gets, or so she assumed. Including rapport with a devadasi.

How to explain to her that our worlds were too different? That having escaped a tiger together did not make us comrades. That we weren't, and would never be friends or even acquaintances. That she couldn't fix my problems just because she had decided she wanted to.

I am ashamed of what I did, lashing out at her when all she was trying to do was help.

It wasn't fair, or right.

But I did not want charity. I did not want cake. I did not want, above all else, empathy and the offer of help from the wife of the man whose child I might be carrying. How to tell her all this? So instead I scorned her. I felt terrible afterwards – it was like smacking a child, hurting an innocent.

Now, after this revelation, I feel for her – this woman who has everything I don't except for the one thing I do. How devastating for a woman not to be able to bear children…

'You just found out?'

He nods.

I understand then why Mr Bell is here: he was upset, hurting, undone, and he came to me.

I don't know whether to be pleased or insulted. Did he come because I mean something to him, or because he thought he could use me to drown his sorrows at his wife's deception, the dashing of his hopes for a family?

I suppose I will never know; I tell myself that it doesn't matter either way.

He looks up at me, that dazzling blue gaze. 'Um… Do you need anything? Any money?'

I stand up straight and stare him down. 'Thank you, but I am fine. Goodbye, Mr Bell.'

After he is gone I rest my head against the door and caress my stomach, emotionally and physically spent.

'Gowri…?' I hear. The priest's voice, sounding tremulous, lost. *Oh no!*

Did he hear James? Is that why he is up?

I open the door once more, with shaking hands, and walk up the steps of the temple. The air smells of jasmine, tastes of trepidation.

The priest is on the veranda, floundering in the darkness, his hands spread out in front of him, blindly scrabbling for support. I take his hand, guide him inside the temple.

'Is that you, Gowri?' he bleats, sounding like a small, scared child.

'Why are you up?' I chide gently. 'It's late at night.'

'I thought I heard a man's voice.'

'A man, here?'

'Sounded like the Englishman, that plantation owner.' His voice shrewd suddenly.

My heart seizes.

'The sahib?' I laugh, injecting surprise into my voice. 'Why would he be here at this time of night? You must have been dreaming.' I sit the priest down on his cot. 'I'm going now. Goodnight.'

Please, I plead with the priest in my head, as I walk wearily down the temple steps, the soft night air soothing my flustered face. *Whatever you do, don't tell the landlord what you thought you heard.*

Chapter 48

Sue

Everyday Lives

Now that she has identified the temple on the news as the same one as in her great-grandparents' photographs, Sue's mind is awash with questions.

That girl, who is she? Did she live in the cottage? Why did her great-grandmother have her photograph? Did she know her?

Her great-grandparents were in India in the 1920s, she knows. People worshipped at the temple then, judging from the presence of a priest in one of the photographs. So when did the temple and cottage slip from communal memory, become overrun by vegetation and forgotten, lost? Why?

And what of the girl who must have lived at the cottage, whose photograph is here, with Sue? What happened to her?

Sue goes carefully through the remaining photographs, trying to find more instances of the temple and the cottage. They are wonderful – the affection of the photographer for the subjects shining through, capturing moments from their everyday lives, conjuring a time and place that evokes nostalgia and yearning in Sue. A woman carrying a basket on her head. A gardener on a lawn with a spade, smiling up at the camera. A ing a scythe, about to bring it down on a round woody onut, she realises, on closer scrutiny. She is ambushed by a sudden memory: watching *A Place in the Sun* with Tony and daydreaming. 'We'll bring our babies up there, eh?' Tony had whispered in her ear. Bali, it was, coconut trees and rows of iridescent fields and glistening hills and snaking rivers.

She shakes her head to clear it.

Many of the photos are of a scrawny boy and a mangy-looking dog, in various poses. There are quite a few of the stunning girl who fascinates Sue, most taken beside the temple or in front of the cottage. She squints as she hangs saris on a washing line. She is captured feeding the chickens, grains falling from her hands, chickens clustered at her feet, beaks open, waiting. And the one with the priest in the background, the girl staring pensively into the distance.

Why is she so sad? What is her connection to the photographer? Was the photographer one of her great-grandparents? How are her great-grandparents connected to this temple?

So many questions nudging aside the grief that has taken over Sue's heart, her life.

Chapter 49

Gowri

A Storm in Progress

Goddess,

When the landlord calls for me during the day – unexpected in itself – a week after Mr Bell's night-time visit, his face a storm in progress, I know I am doomed.

I am drawing water from the well for the wash I plan to have before going to the market when he comes.

I have fed the priest his breakfast: upma with onions and peas and coconut shavings. I've also had mine, sharing it with the cat, who edged up to me while I ate, looking at me with tawny, pleading eyes.

The branches of the trees in the jungle sigh in the warm caress of the humid air spiced with the honeyed yellow of ripening jackfruit.

I lower the pail into the well, and am waiting for the squelch, the slippery plink of the pail hitting water, when the landlord's car pulls up. I gasp and the cat, which has been snoozing on the mossy rim of the well, opens one eye to squint at me.

'Gowri,' the landlord thunders, and his chauffeur winces, his gaze full of sympathy and pity as it meets mine.

I pull the pail up with both hands and all of my strength, as the landlord strides up to me and grabs my hair. Water spills from the pail in a silvery cascade as I cry out and this time, the cat opens both of its eyes and bounds down from its perch, rubbing itself against my feet and snarling at the landlord.

He drags me by the hair up the temple steps.

With both hands I hold my stomach, close my eyes and pray.

I do not honestly know, Goddess, whom I am praying to.

Please, please, spare my child, I pray to whoever will listen. There are so many gods and goddesses. Surely some of them, *one* of them, will be merciful?

When we reach your shrine, the landlord lets go of me and I fall in front of you. I am prostrated before you, in abject supplication. Is this what you wanted?

'The goddess saved your brother's life and picked you to serve *me*. Who else have you been serving, eh, Gowri? Tell the goddess, go on.'

The priest comes running out, his blind eyes wild with distress. 'What is happening?'

'Ah, just the man! Whose voice did you hear that night?'

'I – I told you. It – it must have been a dream,' the priest stammers.

'Don't lie, old man,' the landlord screams. 'Did you hear something or not?'

'I...'

'You whore!' The landlord kicks me. Thankfully my stomach is turned away from him and it is my back his foot makes contact with.

I bite my tongue hard to stop myself from crying out. Over the years I have learned that when he is like this, it is best to stay quiet and let him get it over with. If I yelp or plead, it just inflames him.

'No. She's... The child...' the priest entreats.

'I gave you to that man and he refused. And then he dares to come here and take you from me?'

I taste iron and salt and rage on my lips. I'm angry with the priest, but deep down, I know that it is not his fault: the priest is terrified of the landlord, like the rest of us. The landlord periodically grills him about the goings-on at the cottage and in his fright, the priest must have blurted out what he heard.

'Tell me, Gowri, whose baby are you carrying?' The landlord bends close, his sour breath in my ear. He has been drinking. 'Mine? Or the sahib's? How many men besides me have you been entertaining in the cottage *I* built for you?'

He kicks me again and I roll away, towards the stairs leading down from the veranda. My body feels like it will break any minute. *My baby...*

'I set fire to the sheds at his plantation but spared his plants. I should have burned it all down then.'

'Gowri does not—' the priest begins.

'Shut up, old man. I told you to keep an eye on her.'

'I was dreaming, that's all. She has never—'

'I said shut up,' the landlord yells and he kicks me once more, viciously, and then I am falling, my hands clasped tightly around my stomach.

I am falling down the steps.

I am falling...

Oh, please, no. My baby...

Chapter 50

Kavya

A Survivor

Kavya sits on the swing, her mother on one side of her and her ajji on the other, looking out into the darkness, punctured by pinpricks of light: fireflies, flickering candles in neighbourhood houses. There has been a power cut. The world is mellow, tasting of sundown and endurance, of the suffering of women through the generations. Her ajji and mother chew on paan.

'Here, eat some jalebi. You are too thin, you need fattening up,' her mother says. And then, leaning forward and cupping Kavya's cheek, saying in an uncharacteristically gentle voice, 'What happened to you, Kukki?'

The tears come then. The grief that will shadow her for the rest of her life, that she tries to keep at bay by sheer force of will, the sorrow for the loss of the miracle that briefly bloomed in her womb. And sitting there in the soughing, fragrant dark, she tells her mother and her grandmother everything. She bares her heart.

Afterwards, her mother opens her arms and Kavya goes into them. 'Oh, Kukki!' Her mother gently massages her hair like she used to do when she was a child. Beside her, Kavya's ajji takes her hand, offering comfort. They swing, quietly, back and forth as Kavya's sobs diminish to hiccups. This is perhaps the first time she can recall her mother being silent, as opposed to swamping silence with mindless chatter.

'The worst part is,' Kavya says, finally confessing the guilt that has almost undone her, 'when Nagesh asked me to choose between him and the baby. There was a moment, very brief, but there *was*, when I considered getting rid of the child.'

'Kukki—' her mother begins, but Ajji cuts in. 'Kavya, you are only human. We all have thoughts such as these. I have felt like throttling your mother a thousand times over the years and I am sure she has felt the same with you. You loved your child. Just because for one brief moment you felt it would be easier not to have it doesn't mean it was your fault it…'

'Kukki,' her mother interjects. 'If we blamed ourselves for our every base impulse, we wouldn't be able to live for guilt. Your baby was not meant for this world, it's not your fault.'

Kavya sniffs, tasting salt and remorse and also, at the same time, experiencing the first small wash of redemption. She has spent so long blaming herself, carrying this cargo of guilt, that she feels lighter just for sharing it. Although, she thinks with wonder, she never in a million years expected to be doing so with her mother.

Her mother is not angry. She knows the truth now, the whole truth about Kavya – something Kavya never expected to confess to anyone, even though it was eating away at her – and she is not disgusted or outraged or any of the things Kavya expected. Instead, she understands, she is forgiving. *I have grossly underestimated my mother. I have got her so wrong.*

'I still pine for Nagesh. Even after everything he did, even after I found out what sort of person he is…' Kavya takes a breath. 'And I – I am just as bad. I didn't give a thought to his wife when I found out he was married. I was in love and I believed him when he said their marriage was over, although perhaps at the back of my mind I knew it was a convenient lie… Even if he hadn't, I would have come up with some excuse to convince myself and loved him anyway, continued to be with him. I – I thought I didn't deserve my baby. Or a successful career.'

'Oh, Kukki,' her mother says softly. 'Nothing justifies what happened.'

Kavya nods. 'I see that now. But at the time, I was feeling so down, especially after losing the baby…' She takes a breath. 'I have always fancied myself as someone who will stand up for myself and others, but I didn't do so when my career fell to shambles around me. I docilely accepted what happened as my due. I let myself down badly. I see now that although I got my first break via Nagesh, everything else came because of my talent and hard work. I shouldn't have meekly accepted the industry closing ranks, shutting me out.'

'You were hurting. We can't be strong all the time, Kukki,' her mother says tenderly. 'Even you.'

Kavya smiles.

'And that Nagesh is a cad.' Her mother's voice rising in disdain and contempt. 'I would like more than anything else to give him a piece of my mind. After I have strangled him for hurting my girl.' Then, 'I wish I had been there for you when you lost the baby. I can't bear to think of you going through that alone.'

'You are here for me now, Ma.'

'It must all be so raw. No wonder you can't stand my forcing marriage on you.'

'Aren't you angry at me? I have done exactly what you were worried about when I told you I would go into acting.'

'Don't push your luck,' her mother says and Kavya manages another weak smile. Then, 'Oh, Kukki, how can I be angry at you when you are hurting so? When you have been punished enough? As soon as I saw you, looking so wan and tired, sadness etched into your eyes, yet trying to hide it behind your usual bluster, I knew there was more to this homecoming than you were letting on.' Her mother continues, 'Kukki, your conception itself was a miracle. The doctors had told us my womb was hostile and yet still you managed to grow in there, fighting for your life from the moment you were conceived. You were born at thirty-four weeks, such a tiny fragile little thing – there were complications, there was a high chance you wouldn't make it. And yet, here you are. You will be okay. You will get through this, like you have everything life has thrown at you. You are a survivor, my girl.'

Kavya feels fresh tears springing at hearing the pride coating her mother's voice, her heart aglow.

Then, 'The world has moved on, men are becoming more broad-minded. I will cross out the more traditional men from my list of eligible bachelors for you. I'll concentrate on the ones who have lived in the West, they'll be more open-minded.'

Kavya can't help it; she laughs, a wet briny splutter. 'You are incorrigible, Ma.'

Chapter 51

Lucy

A Leaf Shaped Like a Fan

'Memsahib, I go village. You come?' Market Boy asks.

It's been a week since Lucy told James the truth about herself and she has not seen him since. She is better physically, having healed from her fever, but a wreck emotionally. James is avoiding her, spending all his time at the plantation, even taking his meals there, leaving before she wakes and coming home after she has gone to bed. She lies awake listening out for him and her heart leaps when she hears his tread on the stairs. His footsteps pause outside her room and she waits, hoping, wishing, praying, and then they move on, across the hallway, and she hears his door opening softly and closing again.

Several times, she stands up, gathering the courage to cross the hallway, knock on his door, throw herself into his arms, at his mercy; plead with him to forgive her. She takes one step, two, and then her courage fails her and she climbs into bed again, spent, crying herself to sleep.

Why did I tell him? I should have listened to Mother.

I should never have kept it from him. But if I had told him, he wouldn't have married me.

I have cheated him of a family. How is that right?

Our relationship will never be the same again. I love him and I think, at the moment, he hates me. Will it change?

Market Boy is looking eagerly at her – he has been trying so hard to cheer her up. All the servants know, of course, that she and James have fallen out – how could they not?

'I'd love to,' Lucy says, needing a break from the thoughts going round and round in her head.

Market Boy beams.

They go the long way, as they have since the tiger incident, eschewing the shortcut through the forest. When they reach the village, Lucy decides to walk on while Market Boy is at the market, wanting to be on her own for a bit.

'I'll walk onwards to the temple. Come and find me when you're done with your errands,' she tells Market Boy.

He grins happily. 'You see you friend.'

Lucy nods, not bothering to correct him. *She is not my friend. I am not going to see her, I just need to be alone.*

As she walks, Lucy pushes her thoughts away from lingering on James – it chokes her up and she doesn't want to be the subject of gossip in the village, 'the tearful memsahib' – and focuses instead on Gowri, this woman who hides her loneliness and her sadness behind a fierce independence and a touchy fieriness. It is a welcome change to fume at how Gowri treated her, instead of dwelling on James's silence, to rail about how Gowri took Lucy's simple offer of help the wrong way, embellishing it with sinister motives. Gowri's words hurt more, Lucy admits secretly to herself, because they were, at least in part, true. *Try to put yourself in Gowri's shoes,* her conscience urges. *Gowri has a right to be suspicious of people's motives, given how she has been treated.*

As Lucy nears the temple and the cottage, she spies a car coming down the road. Her heart jumps. *James?*

She squints at it and discerns, disappointment acrid in her mouth, that it is in fact the landlord's car, churning up an avalanche of dust. She slips into the forest and hides behind a tree, not wanting to encounter his smarmy gaze.

Is he returning home from seeing Gowri? What's the occasion? All the times Lucy has been here, she has not known the landlord to visit during the day.

The cottage is just as it has always been – a picturesque oasis, something from another world. A lone sari flaps on the washing line. But the peaceful calm that usually envelops it is not in evidence; it is marred by an almighty howling coming from the temple. The old priest sits facing the shrine and wailing like a child having a tantrum.

Lucy feels the first stirrings of alarm.

And then she sees what she thinks, at first, is a sari, lying crumpled at the bottom of the temple steps. She approaches it with growing trepidation, which balloons into a full-blown panic when she realises that it is Gowri, lying in a spreading pool of red.

'Gowri?' Lucy's voice is wobbly as she squats down beside her, afraid to get closer in case... *No, please.*

Gowri's eyes flutter open.

Thank God.

The spreading pool is mostly water, Lucy notes with relief. It is reddish water, but it is still water, not blood. On the mud, it looked red. *Thank God.*

Gowri's mouth opens. She is trying to say something.

Lucy bends close to the girl. She smells of washing soap and raw fear. 'The baby…' she whispers. 'It is coming.'

This is why I felt the urge to come here today. To help Gowri.

Destiny, fate, there is something to it after all.

I am not qualified to do this.

Her mind harks back to a poky room, sharp instruments inside her, tearing, destroying. She pushes the image away and looks around for someone who can help. The priest is no use. He is blind, she knows, Market Boy having mentioned it a couple of times. And he is wailing, an agitated, unstopping lament. Lost to the world. Lucy is certain he hasn't noticed her. He is consumed by his own private grief, his back turned away from her and Gowri. It occurs to Lucy suddenly that perhaps he thinks Gowri is dead. Well, she cannot worry about that now, Gowri needs her.

Please, God, help me.

And as if in answer to her prayers, Market Boy comes.

He looks as shocked and anxious and frightened as Lucy is to see Gowri in a broken heap at the bottom of the temple steps.

'Help me,' Lucy says.

Market Boy, for all his scrawniness, is strong and together, he and Lucy manage to lift Gowri up – Gowri whimpering in pain so Lucy almost drops her, afraid to hurt her more, but heeding Market Boy's frenzied command to hold on – and heft her into the cottage, laying her down as gently as they can on the floor.

The priest is oblivious to Gowri's soft moans, to Market Boy and Lucy's urgent communication, to the dog's barks, sobbing away, his back turned to them.

Gowri's cottage is just as charming on the inside as it looks from the outside. Small, windowless, with just two rooms and an adjoining shack that is presumably where she washes, but clean and tidy. The main room also doubles up as a kitchen, judging from the hearth, mud pots and chimney in one corner. A few choice treasures are neatly arranged on the one small stool that seems to be the only piece of furniture: a feather, a leaf shaped like a fan, a tumbler of wild flowers, a basket of fruits.

Gowri's moans intensify and then she starts to keen.

Lucy bites her lower lip to stem the panic she feels on Gowri's behalf, to not cry out along with her, to close off the horrific memories of the worst time of her life that are assaulting her.

I am not the best person to be here with you.

She looks around for something with which to mop Gowri's sweaty forehead. There's nothing immediately to hand. She gently removes her arm from around Gowri, preparing to stand up.

'Please,' Gowri gasps, holding on to Lucy's hand as if it is her lifeline. 'Stay with me.'

'I'm just going to find some towels, be back in a minute,' Lucy assures her. 'Market Boy will be here with you.'

Market Boy nods vigorously, eyes wide but determined.

Rooting among Gowri's saris in the flimsy cardboard box that masquerades as a wardrobe, Lucy finds books hidden behind the saris. So many books.

She is hiding them from the landlord.

That man, controlling every aspect of her life. Lucy is overcome by rage.

Unable to restrain her curiosity, this glimpse into this private woman's secret life, Lucy leafs through the books. Old, crumbly, but treasured, Lucy can see. They are in Kannada, but judging from the illustrations, she thinks, they are textbooks. There are also novels – these in English. A Kannada to English dictionary among them. All of them much-thumbed, as if Gowri has read them over and over. Lucy feels like a voyeur, holding this girl's dreams in her hands.

Oh, Gowri! This girl loves knowledge, loves to learn; it is apparent from how worn the books are. But she cannot even be open about this simple thing, having to hide the books away, tied to the landlord, more so than ever now by his baby. Lucy is overcome with sadness for her.

You might think we are worlds apart, Gowri. You might think I have everything. But I too know what it is like to yearn for something I cannot have. I want more than anything to be able to give James my love, a child. But I never will.

And because of this I think I have lost him, my James.

Lucy shakes her head to push away her ruminations. She can't worry about James now, Gowri needs her. She carefully places the books back and an envelope falls out of one of them. Gowri's name is written on the front in a hand that is very familiar.

Oh!

Lucy knows what she is seeing but she doesn't want to know. Her hands shaking, she flips open the envelope nonetheless. A photograph. Gowri lying in bed, eyes shining, her waterfall of hair fanning naked shoulders.

The person who has taken this photo knows her intimately. Intimately.

'When you're taking someone's photograph, try to capture the story behind their eyes,' James has advised Lucy.

But Lucy does not want to read the story this photo is telling her. And yet it all makes sense. James's distance, his reserve. All the late nights when he was supposedly at the plantation. His absence this past week…

And Lucy, like a lovelorn fool, pining for him when all the while…

'*There are secrets in every marriage…*' Mother's voice in her head.

And now, she is discovering James's.

But all those times he was thoughtful, caring. His gentleness towards Lucy. His patience.

He felt guilty so he was kind. He could afford to be – he was cuckolding you.

Surely not? What about his concern when the tiger came? How he warned Lucy—

Oh, oh, oh…

He was warning her off Gowri so his deception would not be discovered. That might also be why Gowri was so harsh with her: it was nothing to do with Lucy at all but to do with what was going on between Gowri and James.

James – the patient teacher, the kind husband. James, whose laughter is exuberant and explosive, like that of a child who hasn't yet experienced the artifice and disillusionment that comes with being an adult. James, who's taught Lucy to recognise the beauty in the most insignificant of things: an ant hefting a crumb, dew clinging to the underside of a leaf, the world glowing like new in the aftermath of a storm. James, who's showed Lucy how to see through the lens of a camera to the inner part of a person's life: the wistfulness evident in a curl dropping over an abashed eye; the hopeful regard of a new lover; the hardened gaze of an old man who realises that life is just disappointment heaped upon disappointment, that this is as good as it gets. James, who has taught Lucy to look for the best in people and who brings out the best in her. James, who is kind to servants and workers, kind to animals.

James, who has betrayed Lucy, cheated on her.

He must have come to England to look for a wife, in order to set up a front of respectability from behind which to carry on his affair with a prostitute. Now Lucy understands his hatred of the landlord. James, mild-mannered, forgiving. Not someone to hold a grudge. Unless it is against the man whose mistress is his lover.

The betrayal hits Lucy then and she holds her stomach and doubles over.

She can't stay here; she doesn't want to for another minute.

She places the photograph back in the envelope, her whole body trembling. She leaves it where she found it, tucked among Gowri's books. She walks back out, everything different; her world tilted but her head held high, the hurt tucked fiercely inside despite tears pushing against her eyelids, hot and persistent.

'Memsahib,' Market Boy says, 'I get help, you stay.'

Gowri wails from the mat. The hot, bitter-sweet scent of blood and pain and panic.

Lucy wants to ignore her. She wants to walk away from this cottage, and keep on walking until she has rid herself of the torment that has beset her heart. But she thinks of herself that fateful day when that woman tore her baby from her, destroying with it her opportunity to have more children; thinks of how terrified she was, how alone.

She thinks of how she failed Robert, betrayed him. If she walks away now, when this woman needs her, regardless of what she has done, she will never forgive herself. So she squats down beside Gowri and holds the hand of the woman who she has just discovered is her husband's lover, soothing her as she groans while Market Boy goes to get help.

When Lucy hears noises outside, hurried footsteps, Market Boy's voice, she jumps up and walks to the door, calling, 'Market Boy, come in and sit with Gowri a minute. I need some fresh air.'

She is nauseous; she wants to eject the knowledge of what she has found out from her mind, her heart, her being. She ducks out of the door of the cottage, walking right into James's arms.

'Lucy.'

She recoils as if slapped, jerking out of his embrace, although a part of her wants to stay in his arms for ever, breathing in his smell of woodsmoke and ginger, which has been synonymous to her, these last few months, with comfort, safety, happiness, love.

The priest has stopped wailing. He is not at the shrine – he must have gone inside the temple.

From within the cottage Gowri's moans increase in intensity and Market Boy says, 'I go,' and sprints inside.

Chickens cluck at Lucy's feet and the air that strokes her stunned face smells of sugared fruit and baked earth. The cat mewls from the well rim and eyes Dog, who is rubbing his body against Lucy's legs, spraying dust all over the skirt of her dress. From inside the house she hears Market Boy murmuring gently to a panting, groaning Gowri.

'Lucy…' Her traitorous husband says her name again and there is an ocean of pain in his voice.

'How could you?' Lucy's voice wobbles.

A muscle twitches in his jaw. His eyes are wide and raw with hurt and surprise.

'That's what I would like to ask you. How could you keep the fact that you cannot have children from me?'

'You—' Her voice breaks. 'You married me for my money when all the while you were carrying on with the woman inside—'

'What? What are you saying, Lucy?' He sounds genuinely surprised. Has she made a mistake? But that handwriting…

'I saw the photograph.'

'Oh.'

That one word, dashing her heart, breaking it all over again.

'It was the one time,' James says, softly.

As she closes her eyes, sways on her feet, she feels bruised, devastated, undone.

'You must believe me.' His voice hoarse with emotion.

'Why? Why must I believe anything you say?'

'Because it is true,' he says simply.

'If she didn't mean anything to you, if it was just the once, why the photograph?'

'It was an impulse. She reminded me of a girl I had once loved.'

A girl he once loved. What else is she to find out?

'Kitty and I… we were childhood sweethearts. I loved her and wanted to marry her, but nothing happened between us bar a few kisses.'

'You don't love Gowri?'

'No. It was only the once, a mistake.' He takes a breath. Then, 'But what you did, it was no mistake. You married me knowing you couldn't have children. I… After I lost my brother, my parents, Kitty, I yearned for someone to love me. I wanted children, a family. When I married you, I thought… You have deceived me.' His voice naked, pulsing with hurt.

A bird swoops low, screeching, and Lucy flinches.

Lucy's actions, her past, reverberating into her present. Marking and maiming her future.

'I am sorry, James. So sorry.' The tears she has tried so hard to hold back spill from her eyes.

'Lucy…' He takes a step forward. 'I have tried to stay away, I have tried to hate you, but I can't.'

She stares at him, not daring to hope even as her battered heart whoops.

'I am angry with you. I feel cheated, betrayed. But…'

Please, she thinks.

'I love you, Lucy. I want to spend the rest of my life with you, children or not.'

She has ached to hear those words from him. Yearned for them.

'Oh, James!'

He opens his arms and she goes into them. He kisses her and for one brief moment, everything is all right. All that has gone before and all that is to come is wiped away. There is only now, the two of them, in this moment.

Then Market Boy at the door, 'Quick! Baby come…'

The baby… Lucy pulls away, swaying on her feet. 'When? When was this one time with Gowri?'

In James's eyes, she sees the answer.

I can't take any more.

She is having the baby I cannot. She is having my husband's child. Oh, oh, oh…

'It could just as likely be the landlord's,' James says softly.

He comes to her, arms outstretched. She balks. His arms fall down by his sides.

The air that caresses her face carries the ashes-and-smoke scent of burning. *My love, our relationship burning at the pyre of our mistakes.*

And then she sees the smoke, swirling above the forest.

'Oh no,' James says, following her gaze, his face tight. 'I have to go.'

'The plantation?' she asks. And, remembering, 'I saw the landlord drive off as I was coming here.'

It seems like a lifetime ago.

James rubs a hand across his face, the action interminably weary. 'He must have found out, somehow.' He takes a step closer to her. 'I have to go. I love you, Lucy, only you.'

He reaches a hand out to her, cups her face, and she leans into his hand.

They have both made mistakes, but he loves her. And she does him.

'I love you too,' she tells him.

He kisses her and then he is gone. Her husband who has cheated on her with the woman inside and whom she, Lucy, has cheated out of a family – the family he so desires.

'Baby coming. Help!' Market Boy shouts again from the doorway before running back inside.

Lucy pushes her head back, squares her shoulders and walks into the cottage to help Gowri deliver the child that might just be her husband's, the child she, Lucy, will never be able to give him.

Chapter 52

Sue

A Gift

Sue gently sets down the photographs from her great-grandparents' time in India and looks up, taking a minute to come back into the present.

Sunlight slants in, relentlessly cheery through the sagging, stained yellow net curtains, now that the heavy blue drapes have been pushed aside. It shows up her house, the messiness, the thick layer of collected dust that she has ignored in her stultifying grief. She thinks of her great-grandmother Lucy, marrying a coffee planter in India and bravely embarking on a new life in a new country, hoping for the best.

I need to do that, she thinks. *I cannot wallow – I don't have that luxury, especially not now.* Rubbing her stomach as if caressing the baby growing within. *I need to face the future, make a future for myself and my child.*

Nausea threatens, and she rushes to the bathroom. There is nothing in her stomach; all she disgorges is some saliva. She really should go shopping, remember to eat; look after herself and her child.

She comes back into the living room and is struck once again by the dirt and clutter that has accumulated. She used to give it a thorough cleaning as soon as she heard from Tony about when he was due back. She doubles over, holding her stomach; she will never again clean in anticipation of Tony's arrival. Grief crashes down, crushing her beneath its heavy weight.

There's a faint scent of lavender in the air, just discernible behind the syrupy scent of rotting flowers from the funerary bouquets that she still hasn't got round to throwing away. She can't decide if the lingering aroma of lavender is from the photographs or from the woman who was here. Margaret, bringing her flowers and memories of Tony as a child, and also, unintentionally, drawing Sue's attention to the temple in India. A gift. A way to lose herself and the decisions awaiting her – the future she must face without Tony, the child growing trustingly in her belly and relying upon her, she who cannot even remember to eat – if only for a brief while.

She brings the photos to her nose, sniffs. The damp, pungent aroma of the past. The filmy swirl of memories preserved in snapshots, communicating with Sue across the span of a century.

Once again, in the light of what she has unearthed, she watches all the videos the Google search unearthed about the temple and reads everything she can find on it. Despite the personal connection, she feels like those rubbernecking people crowding the newly rediscovered temple.

From what she can see, the temple seems to have raised more questions than answers. Nobody knows for certain to whom it belonged, what happened for it to have disappeared from people's memory and remain hidden for so long. Could she, Sue, have some answers and not even know it? If nothing else, at the very least she has some indication as to who lived at the cottage – she is pretty sure the girl from the photographs lived there once; something the people in India doing the digging don't seem to know as yet.

She feels a stab of excitement as she flicks through the photos and, once again, scrutinises the girl.

Who are you? Why are you here, thousands of miles away, among my grandmother's personal things? Why, when I look at you, do I feel that tingle that tells me there is a story to be uncovered?

Chapter 53

Lucy

Womanly Right

Lucy squats beside Gowri, her eyes snagging on the other woman's distended belly.

Gowri is wild-eyed with pain as she holds Lucy's hand in a pincer grip and moans.

'I keep watch outside,' Market Boy says.

Gowri groans, loud and long, and pushes. And then… A mess of dark hair, a scrunched-up face, a slick, eel-like body. A small, plaintive wail.

A boy. A beautiful little boy.

The baby is covered in blood and slime, but she can see that he is dark-skinned. Like Gowri. And the landlord.

Gowri reaches for her child and then her eyes meet Lucy's, anguished.

'I think—' she begins and then she screams. And screams. And then there is another scream. A baby's thin wail. Two babies' thin wails.

Another baby. A little girl. This one with wispy gold hair. Winking blue eyes. Creamy skin sheathed in slime and blood.

This little girl is, without doubt, James's.

Gowri lies back, spent.

'Market Boy!' Lucy calls.

Market Boy's expression is one of wonder as he leans forward and gathers one of the babies, the little boy, in his arms.

And so Lucy picks up the second twin. The infant girl stops crying and nuzzles into Lucy, her startling eyes – James's eyes – closing as her little rosebud mouth roots for milk. She is warm and perfect and alive. She is James's. And Gowri's.

Not Lucy's.

Lucy thinks then of the baby she could have had. And the grieving part of her, the hurt hiding inside of her in that empty space where her womb should be, the ache she recognised and responded to in Gowri, overflows the boundaries she keeps it rigidly encased within, escaping as tears with which she baptises this baby, this newborn who sits so snugly in her embrace.

With the child in her arms, Lucy is able to revisit the most harrowing time of her life, recalling the exact moment she became an adult, discarding the selfish girl she once was. Not when she slept with Robert, but when her babe was wrenched out of her, along with the chance to have more children. The agony of it. And the irony. She became a woman when she could no longer perform the womanly right of procreation.

Lucy will never experience this, the bloodied fierce pain and the equally fierce joy of giving birth. She will never hold her baby in her arms; she has forfeited that right.

But now, *this* child in her arms feels so right. Her body accommodates her of its own accord. Her whole being melts from the inside as a rush of love for her, the love she was harbouring for her own babe and never got to use, surges into her.

'The landlord will kill her. And me,' Gowri whispers, her voice, awe and ache, gazing with longing at the child Lucy holds in her arms.

You should have thought of that earlier, before you slept with my husband.

Gowri holds her hands out for her child.

Lucy does not want to give the child to her.

She wants to take her and run. But she is not Lucy's to take.

Lucy's arms ache with emptiness when the babe nestles in Gowri's embrace, when she sucks from her breast with a soft sigh. She looks so alien on Gowri's body.

Gowri takes her firstborn from Market Boy and settles him on to her other breast. Her babies are so startlingly different, one white, one brown.

'I can't keep her.' Gowri's voice thick with torment as she stares at the little girl as if committing her every feature to memory.

And before Lucy can think about what she is doing, she says, 'I'll have her, give her to me.'

Gowri stares at her, a question in her beautiful, exhausted, haunted eyes. 'Memsahib?'

'I will take her,' Lucy repeats.

She has never meant anything more, has never wanted anything more.

Please, please, say yes.

'You can't stay here. If the landlord finds out…' Gowri says.

Lucy lets out the breath she has been holding.

'I will leave, go back to England.' She doesn't even need to think about it.

'Are you sure?'

'Completely.'

'And your husband?'

James, the father of this little girl. 'I will convince him.' *He will have to give up his plantation, but he will have the family he's always wanted.*

Market Boy looks from Lucy to Gowri, his mouth open.

Gowri nods at Lucy, tears swelling in her eyes and travelling down her face. She kisses her baby girl, holds her close for a moment, and then, taking a deep, shuddering breath, hands her to Lucy.

'I know you will love her,' she says. It is a challenge, a request and a plea.

'I will,' Lucy assures her, holding the babe close. 'I do already.'

This much Lucy does for Gowri.

Then she turns away from the woman who has cheated on her with her husband and walks out of Gowri's life, taking with her Gowri's child, James's child, this child whom she helped bring into the world and who she has fallen in love with the moment she arrived in it; this child whom she already loves more than life itself.

Chapter 54
Gowri

In the Shape of a Deity

Goddess,

Screams tearing out of me, the walls closing in on me as I push and push, the pain owning me, claiming me, devouring me. The cat howling, terrified, mirroring my cries.

And after a lifetime and a half, the scent of blood and sweat, the taste of agony and terror, a slithering, slippery ease, a liquid gush, and then…

A cry.

A kittenish mewling perfection of a cry.

Followed by another.

Twin blessings.

Goddess, when I held my babies in my arms, that brief moment when they were both sucking from my breasts, despite my bruised ribs, my aching, torn body, I felt a peace I had not experienced since I was dedicated to you.

When I give my daughter away and keep my son, that is when I realise the bind my parents were in. I guess I never quite forgave my father and mother for doing what they did, bargaining their daughter's life for their son's.

But now…

I suppose they thought they were doing the right thing, that in exchange for their son's life they were offering their daughter to you, not losing her completely, although that is what happened.

I couldn't bear to look them in the eye, the knowledge of what they had done sitting between us, an unsurmountable obstacle in the shape of a deity. If I were to meet them now, I would look right at them and tell them I understand. Finally, I understand.

You shouldn't have to choose between your children but sometimes, you have no choice. To save them both, you have to let one of them go.

I am thrilled that my boy, my firstborn son, takes after me and looks nothing like his father. At least this way I get to keep him.

Ten tiny perfect fingers that curl around one of mine. Ten dainty miniature toes. A small, perfect body with a squashed, unformed face.

He is perfection.

He is mine.

And with the joy comes longing, and sorrow, even as I celebrate the fact that she is safe. My little girl, so precious and delicate and beautiful. Not mine any more but not yours either, Goddess. Not destined to be a devadasi. Following a different path – fated to live out the fantasies I hadn't dared to imagine for myself, being part of a family, loved and cared for, I hope. I talk to her in my head, nursing the wish that by articulating my desires and dreams for her, they will come true: *You will not have the life I have endured. You will live a happy, contented life: a life you choose. You will be free to make your own mistakes. Free of shackles binding you to goddesses and men who take and possess and plunder and control and take some more and grind you down, wear you away, wipe away who you are, try to own the very essence of you. But this won't happen to you, you will be free.*

It makes me happy even as it makes me cry with the ache of missing her.

For weeks after my twins' birth, I cannot stand straight, or even sit up properly. I hobble about, my back bruised and bent, the pain excruciating. I know I broke something during my fall and – although I know it cannot be fixed by this – I shuffle outdoors, gather medicinal herbs, make the potion and apply it anyway, reaching round with my hand, as far up and down my spine as it can go. I am most comfortable when lying on the floor on my side, my son beside me. I feed him, soothe him, cuddle my boy to me and drink in his flawlessness, his exquisite purity.

On the third day after he kicked me down the temple steps, kick-starting my labour, the landlord visits.

I don't get up. I don't make food for him, don't dance attention on him like he expects, like I usually do.

I lie on the floor, my son beside me, my back, which the landlord has broken, to him.

I am terrified but I will not show it. Does the landlord know about the memsahib and the deal we struck? Has he got word that Mr Bell was here during my labour? Has he found out about my little girl?

Please, no.

'Ah,' the landlord says. 'A son, at last.' Pride in his voice. He has three daughters from his wife and two daughters from other devadasis whom he has claimed for himself.

I thought you didn't accept this child as yours, I think. *If the memsahib hadn't arrived when she did, my children might be dead.*

I keep my face impassive, turned away from him.

'He looks just like me,' the landlord says.

Now, I look at him.

He smiles at me, a genuine smile. 'I saw the old priest just now and he thought I was his brother, who has been dead twenty years! He is quite mad. He must have been dreaming that night or hearing voices from his past.'

An apology of sorts.

I breathe a sigh of relief. I have been worried that the priest will, when questioned, tell the landlord about the memsahib helping me with my labour (after which it wouldn't take much for the landlord to find out about my little girl), although the memsahib was certain that the priest was wailing with his back turned and lost to everything but his grief, that he did not notice her or Market Boy arriving or carrying me into the cottage. And even if he did, and told the landlord, now the landlord will not believe anything the priest says.

'You are truly the goddess's chosen one – the one meant for me. It makes perfect sense that my only son is sired by you,' the landlord is saying.

He is not worthy of your anger, your hatred, I tell myself. *He is beneath scorn.*

'Don't get up. You are tired, I can see. Childbirth takes it out of women – my wife stayed in bed for two months after each delivery. I expect, being much younger, you'll be up and about in a week.' A warning – he will not tolerate me lounging about when he comes next. 'I will see myself out.'

I hold my son to me and close my eyes, shutting out the landlord and the world, revelling in the little miracle I have created, desperately missing the twin miracle I had to give away.

Chapter 55

Kavya

Gentle as the Night

'How could Gowri's mother sacrifice her to the goddess, knowing what it entailed?' Kavya asks, thinking of her baby. How, as her stomach cramped, she had hugged her stomach and prayed to the gods to please let her keep the child. How she is even now angry for not having been able to shield her child, to save it. Angry with her body, with herself, questioning her every action: perhaps if she had looked after herself more, eaten more healthily, would her child still be here?

Her baby was with her for just over three months and yet Kavya had been fiercely protective of it, had loved it with all her heart. How could Gowri's mother give her daughter to the goddess, knowing her fate?

'She had an impossible choice to make.' Kavya's mother's eyes gleam in the darkness.

Inside her father sleeps. He can sleep anywhere, for any number of hours, as if making up for the years when he woke at five every morning and trudged to work in the velvety grey, dew-kissed embrace of dawn.

'The devadasi tradition dates back centuries and back then, the devadasis were respected and revered,' Kavya's mother says softly. 'They were considered auspicious and their presence was required at all important ceremonies. They were musical and artistic. The Bharatanatyam dance form evolved from the devadasis. Gowri was not a devadasi in the traditional sense of the word, a woman well-versed and educated in dance and the arts, coming from a family of dancers and artistes. She was a girl trapped into becoming a devadasi because of the discovery of the statue of the goddess and the subsequent misinterpretation and manipulation of an age-old system. She suffered the additional misfortune of being claimed by a controlling and despicable man. It still happens you know, even now. This practice of giving women to the goddess, people misusing religion and tradition to meet their own ends, even though it has been made illegal.'

Kavya shudders, her skin coming out in goosebumps. 'It can't happen, it just cannot.'

'But it does, child.' Her mother's voice is as gentle as the night and as pressing.

And that is when it comes to Kavya what she must do. The rejection and heartache she has experienced in her career and her personal life have prepared her. Built her up for this.

She knows now with absolute clarity what everything has been leading towards. Just as unsure as she was a day ago, even an hour ago, now she knows, with complete conviction, what she will do with her life.

Chapter 56

Lucy

Smouldering Darkness

Lucy takes Gowri's babe, *her* babe now, wrapped in Gowri's sari and pressed close to her heart, home to the house she has promised to leave in exchange for the child, using the shortcut through the jungle so that none of the villagers see her with the child, praying no tigers choose that day to make an appearance. Market Boy follows with Dog, the scorching odour of fire and the charred taste of smoke trailing them.

She summons all the servants and when they are gathered, she tells them about the baby.

'Please, word of this must not reach the landlord or anyone else. It stays here.'

They nod, promising to be discreet.

She knows they will be – they are loyal to the last and they have, over the months, come to care for her as she has for them.

Lucy rocks the baby to sleep. Her maid helps her transform one of the drawers of the sideboard into a makeshift bed and she tucks the babe into it. Then she waits for her husband, as afternoon gives way to evening and shadows steal the light from the room.

The hours crawl by, each longer than the last, rife with blistering anxiety, tortured foreboding, the singed flavour of fear.

The baby sleeps, but Lucy doesn't, her heart flaming, seared in panic as she peers into the smouldering darkness.

Where is my husband?

Midnight. Still no sign of James.

The servants stay up with her, bringing her cocoa that she cannot drink.

She thinks of his kiss, his impassioned declaration of love: '*I love you, Lucy. I want to spend the rest of my life with you, children or not.*'

I have your daughter, James. We can be a family. Please. Come home.

At 1 a.m., a knock on the door.

It is Ganesh, the foreman.

Where is my husband? The words smoke on her tongue.

He smells of ash and ruin, trailing fire into the house she shares with James.

He is in tears.

No.

'I am sorry, Memsahib.'

Please.

'He managed to save much of the plantation and most of the workers trapped in the fire…'

James, I love you. We have a daughter, the family you wanted.

'But, despite us warning him not to, trying to hold him back, he went into the warehouse to rescue the men stuck in there and the roof collapsed.'

I love you, James. I cannot live without you.

'He died, Memsahib.'

James's newborn daughter wakes and starts to wail, mimicking the cries that have welled in Lucy's devastated heart.

'*I love you, Lucy. I want to spend the rest of my life with you, children or not.*'

You gave up your life for your first love, James – the plantation.

'Memsahib?' she hears as if from far away.

Her conscience has the last word, before despairing oblivion takes its place. *Justice is served. You denied Robert his love. He wanted you but you betrayed him. It is only fair that you are now deprived of your love.*

Why should you have your happy ending when Robert didn't have his?

Chapter 57

Gowri

In Lieu of Legitimacy

Goddess,

The landlord arranges for a grand puja to thank you for his only son, to which he summons the whole village.

'Please invite my parents,' I say. 'I would like them to see their grandson.'

I write to my sister and ask her not to come even if my parents do. Although she is now married and relatively safe, I do not want her anywhere near the landlord. Our brother cannot come as he is in Bombay with his job.

My sister writes back to say my parents will not be coming – 'Da is ill. Nothing serious, just a cold. Ma will not travel on her own.'

I swallow down the disappointment, bitter at the back of my throat, a taste I am used to, as it is lodged there almost permanently.

The landlord calls my boy Jayaram, after himself, giving him his name and a gold bracelet in lieu of legitimacy.

I hate the bracelet. A shackle, binding my son to my oppressor. But it is fixed on his little arm by the landlord and I cannot remove it.

Secretly, I eschew the landlord's name and call my boy Ravi, meaning 'Sun'. For he is my son, my sun. The star around which my life revolves now, the centre of my universe.

Every day I scrutinise my son's face, his changing, growing features, for traces of his father. I see none and I am relieved as this means my son is safe. For now.

One day soon I will go away, with my boy, but I want to stay here until I know my daughter is safely in England. Mrs Bell – I still think of her as the memsahib – has arranged for one of the servants up at the plantation house to discreetly send word to me, here at the cottage, about when that will happen. Once my baby girl is on that ship sailing towards England, all contact with her will be lost but until then, I will stay here, eagerly awaiting any news of Mrs Bell and my girl reaching me via the servants.

My boy grows and loneliness is a thing of the past, a distant wispy memory. He gives meaning to my days, lights them up in kaleidoscope of colour. I don't know how I endured the vacant days before him, all those solitary dragging hours. He has changed me, transformed me.

I live for him.

But of course, always, twinned with the happiness Ravi brings me, there is also the dogged throbbing ache of yearning for my little girl.

Ravi is a happy child, delighted at everything. And yet some days he cries and will not stop, no matter how much I soothe him.

I know then that he is crying for his sister. That he misses her, although he cannot articulate it.

I imagine my little girl is the same. I know the memsahib will be gentle with her, patient. I saw the love in the memsahib's eyes for my daughter – *her* daughter now. That love, maternal and tender, cannot be faked. I have only ever seen it in Vandana Ma'am's eyes, and in my mother's before you came between us, Goddess, and she couldn't meet my eye any more.

And, despite the emptiness inside me that only my daughter could fill, I am grateful that she is safe, that she is loved.

The persistent ache of missing my daughter is made bearable by my son's delighted laughter, his chubby legs wobbling towards me, arms outstretched for a hug, his sweet voice saying, over and over, 'Ma,' before collapsing into giggles in my arms.

'Ma,' he says and even as my heart is overcome with love and gratitude, I think of my daughter who does not know of my existence and will never call me 'Ma'.

Ravi is a mischievous little soul, pulling the cat's tail so the cat looks at me with wounded eyes. He runs on unsteady legs among the chickens, and they disperse in a fluster of chaotic flapping. He hums constantly, tunes he has made up: *Ma, ma, ma. La, la, la.* I watch him and wonder about my daughter, whether she still looks like James, whether she shares Ravi's cheekiness, whether she too is curious and inquisitive and happy.

Ravi is always covered in dust and I bathe him by the peepal tree, drawing pails of water from the well and upturning them on his head. He draws his breath in at the first cold mouthful and then chortles in absolute delight as silvery water cascades down his head and over his compact, rounded little body. The cat observes from the rim of the well, an indulgent look on its face.

Parrots sing among branches in the jungle across the road and somewhere within the huddle of trees a peacock shows off for its mate, its cry loud and crowing, its rainbow plumage, I imagine, spread out in all its glory, winking sapphire gold.

'Ma,' Ravi calls, his voice alight with wonder, his hands full of suds and mud.

'I just washed you, you imp!'

He gasps as another chute of water rains on him, his laughter ringing out, masking the mating cries of the peacock, the chattering of the parrots.

Even the old priest, eyes dulled now by cataracts, is charmed by him. He heaves Ravi up on his shoulders so he can ring the bell of the temple and teaches him to adorn you with the flowers I have picked from the garden, Goddess.

Ravi grins at the sound of the bell and when the priest sets him down, he tugs the old man's hand until the priest has no choice but to lift him up again, to help his small fingers hold the rope and pull so the booming gong echoes into the jungle.

Ravi fingers the holy thread laced around the priest's torso and surprises a chuckle out of him. He pulls the priest's glasses off his nose and the priest, who cannot see much, even with the glasses on, smiles kindly and puts his hand out to ask for them back.

I sit on the washing stone, inhale the mango-flavoured breeze and watch my son, Goddess, and I am happy, despite missing my other child.

I should have been suspicious, Goddess, wary, but for once I live in the moment, setting aside my cynical, guarded self.

It is a mistake.

Something makes me look up, away from my laughing son, happy in the priest's arms, and the smile stills on my face. For the landlord is there, waiting, his gaze fixed upon the boy he thinks of as his son, assessing. Shrewd.

A shadow, dousing the sun – my Ravi – and my mirth with it.

I did not see him arrive. I did not hear the car, lost as I was in my son's antics. I did not notice the lengthening shadows creeping up the temple walls, the charmed saffron evening giving way to cerise twilight.

I watch him watching my son, fear taking my heart captive. I have never seen this expression in his eyes before. He has been a lukewarm, indifferent father. Smug and basking in his ability to sire a son; Ravi only useful in that he is proof of the landlord's fertility.

But now…

That speculative look. What is he thinking? Does he know the truth about Ravi's parentage? Has he guessed? Has the priest said something?

No. Please…

Ravi looks up, sees him, smiles. 'Da,' he says, spreading his arms out, and my heart sinks.

'Come here,' I say to Ravi, more sharply than I intended, and both he and the landlord look at me.

The landlord's eyes meet mine, his lips widening in a smirk that smacks of victory and punishment.

I have been unguarded in my happiness. I have allowed my unconditional love for my son, the pride I take in him, to show. I should know better than anybody that like you, the landlord uses every chink in the armour of people he owns to his advantage. He knows how to stab just where it hurts the most.

The sun sets, grey dusk wiping away the last traces of the soft pink twilight. I gather my son in my arms and lead the priest inside the temple to his quarters, settling him for the night. As I walk back past your shrine to the cottage, and the waiting landlord, I look at you, Goddess, your smiling face, and wonder what it is you have in store for me now.

Chapter 58

Lucy

A Plan

James is gone, but the baby is here and so Lucy cannot stop. She is in shock, she wants nothing more than to hide in a corner and bawl, but she can't afford to, she won't. She needs to protect this child, this living legacy of James, a part of him, this precious gift in lieu of her love, with her everything.

The landlord has taken James from her – he will not have James's child. *Her* child.

'I can't stay here,' she tells an anguished Ganesh.

They talk through the night and come up with a plan.

Lucy signs the plantation – what's left of it – over to Ganesh and she travels to Madras, renting a house in the city, equipping it with the requisite staff. Market Boy comes with them; he begs Lucy to take him along and besides, Lucy is unable to part with him. But they have to leave Dog behind. Cook and his posse promise to look after him for Market Boy.

The servants line up on the veranda to bid goodbye, as they did in welcome when Lucy arrived, just a few months ago, although it now feels like a thousand lifespans. They are all in tears. They have promised not to breathe a word about her whereabouts, her plans or the baby to anybody, as there is the danger of it leaking to the landlord. They are united in their anger and hatred towards the landlord, who has taken their beloved master from them.

Madras is humid, sweltering, busy. It is nothing at all like the green, open land Lucy has come to love. She knows Market Boy misses it too. Their walks, the village, the market, the house, the servants' affection, James and Dog. But he is relentlessly cheerful and seems to know just when Lucy flags, feeling that she cannot go on any more. He tries to perk her up then, make her smile. He and the baby, whom she has named Elizabeth after James's mother, are the bright spots in her world, the only reason she is able to go on.

Market Boy has a new love: the baby. He never leaves her side unless absolutely necessary. For her part, Elizabeth seems mesmerised by him, her startling blue gaze following him, her tears forgotten.

'You better ayah than ayah,' the new staff in this new household say – there is a language barrier as they speak Tamil and Market Boy speaks Kannada, so they communicate in broken English, Market Boy having effortlessly charmed them as he does everything and everyone.

Market Boy grins and Elizabeth waves her small, fisted hands in the air as if in agreement.

James is gone but the sun rises regardless. Each endless day, Lucy keeps going by sheer force of will. It is in the long hours of night that she comes undone. Her household, her little girl, Market Boy, are asleep, and this is when she grieves for James, mourns him. He was the flash of a camera, bringing light into her world, and now he is gone. It is hard to believe, harder to accept.

She pictures him standing in the courtyard of Gowri's house, saying, 'I love you.' She replays that moment again and again, and this time, she stops him going to the plantation. 'Let it burn,' she says. 'You stay with me. Please.'

When she does fall asleep, she dreams that he is with her, holding her, loving her. And then she wakes to emptiness where his arms should be. Ache. Sorrow. Longing.

Lucy writes to her parents and to Ann, informing them of the tragedy. She tells them she is coming home. She informs them that she and James had adopted an orphan child of good lineage just before James's death, and that she will be bringing Elizabeth and her ayah – a young boy, unorthodox but there it is, he is the only one who can soothe Elizabeth – home. She asks them to please never reveal to anyone, including Elizabeth, that she is adopted. Lucy has decided that she will belatedly take her mother's advice and keep her daughter's parentage secret from everyone, even from Elizabeth herself.

Lucy takes Market Boy aside and asks him the same question that she has been asking every day since he declared, as she was leaving for Madras, that he would never leave her side. 'Market Boy, England is very different from here, very cold. Are you sure you will be okay there?'

He nods enthusiastically. 'I is coming.'

'You will be away from everything you know, all that is familiar.'

'Is okay.'

'You will miss home.'

'You is home.'

She bites her lower lip, but the tears come anyway. He squeezes her hand. 'Memsahib, no cry.'

She sniffs, blows her nose and manages a watery smile. 'I need a favour from you, Market Boy.'

He nods some more, eyes earnest. Waiting.

'You know how I've asked you not to tell anyone about Elizabeth and Gowri?'

'Memsahib, I no tell.'

'Not now, not ever, Market Boy, okay? Not in England, not even to Elizabeth. Promise?'

'I is promise. I never tell, never ever.'

'Thank you, Market Boy.'

He beams. 'Thank you, Memsahib.'

Ganesh visits every month with updates and accounts and news. He is settling all of James's affairs and it is a slow process. Once it is all done, Lucy can leave for England.

'Take your time,' she tells him.

She is in limbo here in Madras but loath to leave, to start over in England, a life James will never be party to, creating memories he will never be part of. This is, after all, the country where James will be, always. The place that will feature in her reminiscences of him. The country where Lucy arrived to escape her past and where she found love and received the precious treasure that is her daughter and which she has, despite everything that has happened, come to love.

Lucy pines for the plantation and the life she experienced there briefly, so different from her cosseted childhood and yet so idyllic. She had friendship and love in James and despite being miserable about not being able to bear children and keeping it secret from her husband, it was, nevertheless, one of the happiest times of her life.

Late at night, when her babe cries, Lucy tries to settle her back to sleep – she herself cannot sleep; it is in the dark that she feels James's absence most keenly, so she tells the ayah to rest and soothes the babe herself. As she paces by the window, she looks beyond the street, beyond the houses to the horizon, and, silhouetted against it, she can just about make out the waving fronds of coconut trees. Lucy closes her eyes then and imagines she is among coffee plants garlanded by rain, James beside her, vine-festooned trees standing sentinel, the coffee-flavoured, betel-spiced, peppery breeze cool on their faces.

When she opens her eyes, her daughter is fast asleep in her arms, her living warmth anchoring Lucy, so she can endure the ache of losing James.

Elizabeth is her home now.

Chapter 59

Kavya

In Different Circumstances

Kavya sets down the letters and wipes her eyes.

'Oh, Ajji, I want to walk into the past, into that cottage and bring Gowri with me here, give her all the books she wants to read, all the love and caring she has been denied.' She sniffs. 'You know, I read somewhere about domestic abuse. The victims – some highly intelligent and educated women – can leave at any time, but are not able to. They feel tied to the abuser. They're too afraid and conditioned to accepting the abuse to escape. Their minds aren't thinking straight, assigning too much power to the abuser. In Gowri's case, it was the landlord *and* the goddess whom she felt bound to; she thought she couldn't escape either of them.'

'Yes,' Ajji says softly beside her, rubbing her face with her pallu.

'Who is she, Ajji? How is she connected to you, to us?'

'Read on and you will find out.'

'Gowri is so brave. She takes everything that happens to her in her stride. An amazing woman.'

'Yes.'

'In different circumstances, she could have been such a force to reckon with. She would have been a brilliant teacher, like her Vandana Ma'am.'

'There are so many women like her, even in this day and age, who want small things, simple things that we take for granted. Education. The right to live out their childhood without being forced into marriage. The right to choose their future. But it is denied them. They are forced to comply with decisions made for them in the name of duty, religion,' her mother says gently.

It is dark, the world still. The dog snoozes on the doorstep, oblivious to the flies circling its fur. The night air is heady with jasmine and secrets, punctuated by Kavya's father's snores. The sky pinpricked by stars, shining like hope.

Kavya picks up Gowri's next letter to the goddess, thinking of the decision she has made since coming here, since encountering Gowri's letters, reading about her life.

You thought you couldn't fight the landlord and the goddess, Gowri. You were overwhelmed by the bind you found yourself in. So was I. I fancied myself strong, but I too was cowed by my situation and instead of standing up to Nagesh, fighting for the roles that I had won because of my talent – despite Nagesh's recommendation, I wouldn't have bagged any of them if I hadn't showed flair and put in the hard work to back it – I gave in and came home, thinking I had no choice.

I will fight for women like you, Gowri, make sure they are not helpless and alone, trapped in situations not of their own making, victims of the prejudices and beliefs of an ill-informed society. I will also fight for women like myself, naïve, young, ambitious, desperate, who are manipulated to feel they have no choice when they have plenty, who are made to feel defeated and helpless when they are not.

Chapter 60
Gowri

Without Preamble

Goddess,
   You are far more powerful than even I have given you credit for.
Happy now?

A letter arrives for me, via the servants up at the plantation house.

As I open it, I thank Vandana Ma'am in my head for teaching me to read and write and understand English.

Ravi, who has been running around the courtyard after his wash, although I expressly told him not to, and is sheathed in dust, comes and hides in the folds of my skirt.

'Your daughter – *our* daughter – is happy and growing up nicely. Speaking now. She bosses everyone around,' the memsahib writes.

I smile as I try to picture my daughter, a cheeky, golden-haired, blue-eyed version of my son.

From behind my skirt, Ravi giggles.

'Hmmm… I wonder who that is?' I say, reaching around to tickle him.

Ravi tumbles to the ground and rolls about with laughter.

I read the rest of the letter. 'She's an absolute delight, bringing joy into my world, lifting me from my melancholy.'

I feel a pang. If Mr Bell had never associated with me, he would still be alive… But then, if he had never been with me, these children, my children wouldn't *be*. I tell myself this and yet some nights I am assaulted by guilt at the destruction of that good man's life. For Mr Bell was noble, kind; a gentleman. Then I tell myself, as my son breathes softly beside me, innocence and perfection, that if not me, the landlord would have found some other excuse to get at Mr Bell. The landlord wanted to be the only important man in the village and now he has achieved that – with Ganesh struggling to keep the plantation afloat, he is being suitably servile to the landlord – he is happy.

I turn my attention back to the letter.

'She is loved so very much,' Memsahib writes. 'I've named her Elizabeth, after James's mother.'

I roll the name around in my mouth. My daughter Elizabeth. A beautiful name for my beautiful girl. A name that will give her access to a society that I would never have been allowed into. Happiness takes up residence alongside the longing for my daughter in my heart. *You be happy, my beloved girl, my Elizabeth.*

Ravi climbs on to my lap.

I pull him close, laying my chin on his dirty hair tinged orange with mud, and imagine I am holding my Elizabeth.

'I want the boy,' the landlord says to me, without preamble, as soon as he comes into the courtyard of the cottage, some weeks after I caught him assessing my boy while Ravi was playing with the priest.

I am feeding Ravi, carefully sifting the flesh off the bony fish that was the only one available at the market for the likes of me. Despite knowing that I have favour with the landlord, everyone at the village, with the exception of the vegetable vendor couple at the Wednesday market, still does me these small injustices: stones in the rice, watered-down milk, bony fish about to go off – things I cannot really complain about as they are easily explained away. I didn't mind before but I do now that my boy is here. I want to give him the best, but I can't, despite my best efforts.

It won't be for long, I tell myself. *Just a few more weeks until Memsahib and my baby girl leave for England. And then Ravi and I will leave too.*

I have been staying here for the letters that arrive from the memsahib, the news of my daughter that makes its way via Ganesh the foreman, who visits the memsahib in Madras, to the servants at the plantation house and through them to me.

But perhaps I have waited too long.

I tuck the fish into a ball of rice – Ravi does not like the taste of fish and I need to disguise it to feed it to him.

He runs around the courtyard with me giving chase, giggling with delight as I follow with the plate in one hand and the rice ball in the other, chickens scattering at his feet, cat running beside him, dust everywhere.

'Come on, you need to eat this, son,' I am saying when the landlord drops his bombshell.

I look up at him, breathless with the running around and the sudden fear catching in my throat.

'What do you mean?'

But I know deep down even before he opens his mouth to explain. I take huge gulps of jasmine-scented, mango-tipped evening air to calm my racing heart.

Ravi stops running and comes up to me, hiding in my skirts, smiling shyly up at the landlord. I wish he wouldn't smile at the man. I wish he wasn't so welcoming, so open, so friendly with everybody.

I set the plate down on the mossy rim of the well and put a protective arm around my son.

'My wife cannot have any more children. I want to bring him up at my home, as my legitimate son.'

I look down at my son. *My* son. His downy mop of hair. His trusting, innocent face.

He is not yours.

I cannot tell the landlord this – how can I?

As if aware of my scrutiny, Ravi looks up at me and smiles his guileless, wholehearted smile, the one that involves his whole face. I swallow down the panic that takes my body hostage, keeping me rooted to the ground. I want to lie down on the mud and wail. I want to take my son and run as far away as I can.

Ravi tugs at my other hand. 'Rice,' he says, pointing.

He is hungry. I squat down and concentrate on feeding him, dumbing down my terror, willing it away so I can think rationally.

'Did you hear what I just said? I want him.'

My stomach flips over, but I continue feeding my boy, ignoring the landlord.

The landlord whips his hand out and tucks it under my chin, dragging it upward. He looks into my eyes and says, enunciating each word clearly, his voice hard and dangerous, 'You don't ignore me, you understand? Or I will take him now.'

I gather my boy to me and stand up, slowly. I look the landlord in the eye. 'Please, please don't do this.'

The landlord smiles, a slow grin that starts at the corners of his lips and spreads outwards. It is a smile as cunning and shrewd as my son's is guileless. He is enjoying this, my subjugation, my defeat.

'I will do anything you want,' I whisper.

He throws back his head and laughs, the mean, mirthless laughter echoing in the gathering dusk.

My son looks at him and puckers his mouth as if unsure whether to cry. He turns to me, his eyes uncertain. 'Ma?'

And I decide at that moment that it is time to run away.

I have waited long enough, I will not lose my son too.

How can I give up the one person who makes my life bearable? And to this man who didn't give a thought to the lives I was harbouring in my womb when he kicked me down the temple steps, who almost killed Ravi, but now that he is here, wants him?

I will not; I cannot.

Once he has decided, the landlord moves quickly.

'We will have a celebratory puja on Friday,' he says. 'You will dance, along with the other devadasis. And at the end of the evening, I will take my son home.'

Although that doesn't give me much time, I plan our escape very carefully. I pack my son's meagre belongings and mine, along with the money and the jewels and the deeds to the cottage, into one of my saris. I debate whether I should take the books. I want to, but in the end I decide not to – they will just weigh us down.

I decide to leave on the Wednesday, market day in the village. I will hitch a ride in the bullock cart of the vegetable vendor couple. Although there is not enough time to arrange this with them, I know they will not refuse to take Ravi and me into town, and I believe they will be discreet.

From the town, I will buy a ticket for a bus leaving for the city. I don't have to worry about money, initially at least. Once in the city, I will figure out what to do. Part of me wants to find my parents – I have their address from my sister's letters. I want to throw myself at their mercy, beg them to protect my son. But they haven't met Ravi or shown any inclination to do so. They might turn me in to the landlord, deciding that Ravi being given the gift of legitimacy by him is best for my son.

* * *

Tuesday morning, I am packed and ready. In case the landlord takes it upon himself to visit, the sari containing our belongings that I am taking with us is tucked in the hiding place among my undergarments, beside the precious books Vandana Ma'am and Mr Bell gave me. I cannot rest, cannot eat for nerves.

Ravi refuses to eat anything either. I decide that it must be because my nerves have rubbed off on him.

As the day progresses, Ravi is listless, his cheeks flushed. He is quick to cry and clings to me, hardly looking at the priest when we take him his supper. That night, he cries and cries. He is hot to the touch, feverish.

The nearest doctor is in the town I was planning to escape to with the vegetable sellers from the market. I debate whether to go to the landlord, pound on his door, beg him to take me into town. But how to carry Ravi to the landlord's house, which is nearly a mile away, when he is in this condition? The landlord's house where I am not welcome but Ravi will be soon. What if they snatch him away from me now?

Nevertheless, I gather Ravi up, intending to beg the landlord to take him to the doctor in his car. I have never hated my isolation, the fact that I live on the outskirts of the village, more. I could turn to the priest, but he is old and almost completely blind, his body riddled with aches and pains – he won't be much help.

If the memsahib was here, I would go to her. But she is in Madras, preparing to sail to England with my baby girl.

Ravi moans as I wrap him in my arms, before flopping in them, restless. I open the door to the cottage and wade into the darkness. He shivers, bundling closer to me, letting out a pained, weak whimper.

I cannot do this to him, cannot carry him for the better part of a mile in the darkness; already the cool air is making him shiver and come out in goosebumps, even though his body is throbbing with heat. I cannot risk it. I will take him in the morning, if he is not better by then. But he will be, won't he? All he needs is a good night's rest, isn't it? *Please.*

I take him back inside and sit vigil by his bedside.

As the night wears on, I try to bring his temperature down with cold compresses to his forehead, the memory of another closed room, another ill little boy pressing upon me, insistent as my son's arduous, heated breaths.

I think of you then, Goddess. I think of the bargain my parents struck with you: my brother's life for mine.

I am bound to you. And I mean to break that promise, take my son and run away.

I think of Vandana Ma'am, whom you took two weeks before the exams that were to be my means of escape from you.

Please, I entreat.

But you are silent.

Don't do this, I beg as I hold my hot, fretful son to me and pace the small cottage, my haven, which now seems claustrophobic, too small. *Please. You are a mother, too. Please, Goddess.*

I will not run away, I implore, *if it means you spare him.*

I will trade my life for his. Please.

But it is too late.

Too late.

As dawn stains the horizon the rosy pink of a newborn, my son stills in my arms.

I thought I had time to take him to the doctor in the morning but that was the one thing I didn't have with him – time.

'That boy was cursed! To die of a fever in just a few hours, to be laughing the day before and dead by morning… Cursed!' everyone in the village exclaims, as the news spreads and they collect at the temple to mourn my son, whom they had ignored while alive. 'Wonder what sins he committed in his previous life?'

'It isn't anything *he* did,' I want to shout. 'He is – he was – *was* cursed, I agree. Cursed because of his mother.'

Goddess, you want me to love you and you alone. You want my soul and you will not share.

When I was dedicated to you, when the landlord possessed me, I told myself I would not be broken.

When Vandana Ma'am died, I told myself I would not be broken.

When I had to give up my daughter, I told myself I would not be broken.

But now, Goddess.

Now I am.

Ravi lies under the peepal tree by the washing stone, next to the well where I used to bathe him, tipping buckets of water on to his head. He would squeal with joy, chickens flapping at his feet, parrots calling from the trees; the whole world, it seemed, sharing his joy.

The landlord wanted to cremate him but I thwarted him in that. He would not have my child, not in life and not in death. My son would not be burned to dust, I could not bear it.

When the landlord was away arranging the details of the cremation, I took my boy's small, perfect body and laid it down gently under the peepal tree, in the hole I had dug with a scythe, sifting the mud with my hands. I could not take the bracelet off, that gold bracelet binding him to the landlord, so I buried him with it. I wrapped him in my green sari with yellow flowers – his favourite.

I wore it first so he could smell me and it would comfort him. He had the habit of holding the pallu of my sari, stuffing it into his mouth. I made sure he was comfortable. Then I buried him.

I chose the spot where he rests carefully. He gets water there, you see, Goddess, from the washing stone and the well – the ground there is always moist, even in the unbearable heat of midsummer. The chickens that he loved to chase and play with peck by him. The cat sits on the rim of the well beside him. The peepal tree offers shade. I sit there and talk to him. He will never be lonely.

When the landlord came, there was no child. He was angry; he raged. But his rage doesn't affect me any more. Nothing does.

In the end the landlord left in a huff. 'Being with you is like trying to rouse a dead body,' he said, deliberately trying to get a rise out of me. I ignored him, his goading voice just noise to me now.

Ravi, my sunshine, is gone. My daughter, Elizabeth, is sailing towards a new life in England.

It is dark all the time, darker than when Vandana Ma'am passed. So very dark.

If this is what you wanted, Goddess, me, all to yourself, well, you can have me – you and the landlord.

I don't really care what happens to me any more.

My son visits me in my dreams and I do not want to wake from them.

I hear his laughter and I see him sometimes, in the heat haze conjured by the sun, in the swirling mud, in the thick mist enveloping the jungle at dawn.

And I live for that.

Chapter 61

Lucy

Safe

It takes almost eighteen months for Ganesh to settle James's affairs in India. During this time, Lucy learns to live with James's absence, the perpetual wound of missing him. She learns to smile and laugh while hurting and longing. She can now sleep for a few hours each night.

There are times in those months when Lucy is beset by doubts, wondering if what she is doing, bringing this little girl up as her own, on her own, is right. But then Elizabeth calls 'Mama,' slipping her tiny arms around Lucy's neck and burying her face in her shoulder, and all her doubts vanish.

Lucy takes photos of her daughter – too many. She's lost so much and she worries she will lose her too, this precious, precious girl. Every time she holds the camera, she thinks of James teaching her how to handle it. His gentle voice. His patience. Wishing he was here with her, watching his beautiful daughter grow, recording her every milestone, her budding teeth, her delighted smile, her wholesome, beautiful self.

Although Elizabeth cried at the flash the first few times, now she grins wholeheartedly, for she knows Lucy is behind the camera. She waits for her to play peekaboo, which Lucy will do after the flash, and then she throws back her head, golden curls a whirl of honey like the sun appearing on a rainswept day, a flash of caramel among the wet clouds, and she laughs, a tinkle like musical anklets, which brings back memories of slender feet dancing in mud as they go about their chores, willowy legs that shepherded Lucy up a tree away from the danger of a tiger slinking below, and the monkeys stared at them – humans who had dared enter their territory.

Lucy wonders if, when she develops the photos, she will see an echo of Gowri, the pout behind which she hid her shyness, the sadness she lugged. Will she see Gowri in the arch of Elizabeth's chin, the curve of her smile? For now, her daughter resembles her father in every way, her likeness to James delighting Lucy while at the same time igniting in her an ache for him.

She wonders how Gowri is faring with her firstborn son, whether the landlord believes the fiction that he is his. Lucy wants to know and then she doesn't; she doesn't want to know.

Lucy looks at her daughter and wonders about her twin brother. Does he look like Elizabeth? Does Elizabeth unconsciously echo her brother's features, her brother's actions, although she doesn't know and never will know that she has a twin? As she grows, will she look more like her mother, a slender, dark beauty, and less like her father? Lucy prays then that Elizabeth will stay as she is, all golden curls and blue eyes. A happy, lovely delight.

That said, some days Elizabeth cries and cries and will not be appeased, not with food or changing, not with a story with silly voices and all the actions, like she loves, not with tickles, or a walk outside in the dusty, crowded streets, where she charms vendors and pedestrians alike. Not even Market Boy can calm her wails. Those times, Lucy holds her close and allows her to vent. She is grieving, Lucy knows, for something she cannot understand but feels keenly – the lack by her side. The absence of the presence that accompanied her in the womb: her twin.

* * *

Elizabeth's blue eyes darken to a startling aquamarine and with every day she becomes more beautiful, more her own person. Lucy is glad they are moving to England, wanting to be far away from Gowri and from the landlord. She wants to be away from Gowri in case she changes her mind, manages, somehow, to get rid of the landlord or stand up to him, and asks for her child back. Lucy cannot countenance that option but she is still reluctant to leave India. After all, it is her husband's resting place, her daughter's birthplace. It is all Elizabeth knows.

And yet Elizabeth is young, she will adapt. Also, as Elizabeth grows, if she begins to look more Indian, Lucy doesn't want to be here when questions are raised and word gets back to the landlord. She cannot bear the thought of her daughter being in any danger. She would much rather bring her up in England. Cold, colourless and yet… safe.

As Elizabeth grows, she reveals herself to be, in temperament at least, her mother's daughter. Smart and fiery, she wants to learn everything at once, is hungry for knowledge. Gowri was too – this was evident from the books she accumulated. Lucy wonders what Gowri could have achieved if given the chance to learn.

I am looking after her and loving her, Gowri, she tells the other mother of her daughter in her head. Gowri is missing all of this – she must be pining for her child, her lack an unceasing ache.

In the end it is Elizabeth who names Market Boy.

They are making final preparations to go to England when Elizabeth, with her fierce intellect, her wanting to do everything as fast as she possibly can, begins to speak a few words.

'Mama,' she says, and 'Mark.'

'Mark,' she says, pointing at Market Boy, toddling towards him, holding out her hands imperiously, which is Market Boy's cue to lift her up and swing her around.

'Memsahib, I is Mark now, not Market Boy,' he says, grinning.

'Now, why didn't I think of that? Mark it is!' Lucy smiles. *Hear that, James? Isn't your daughter a character?*

'Mark, Mark!' Elizabeth says, clapping.

'Yes, Miss Lizzie, I is Mark, I English name for England. Mark.'

And Elizabeth throws back her head and laughs, golden ringlets bouncing.

Chapter 62

Sue

Out of Love

Sue goes to the kitchen, makes herself a cup of tea and empties the last of a box of cornflakes into a bowl. There is no milk.

I really must go shopping, I can't survive like this.

She carries the bowl of dry cornflakes and her cup of black tea back into the living room, settling down on the sofa.

Outside the sun is setting, mellow rays teasing the curtains, making the dust glow like an angel's halo. Men walk past on the road outside, suits flapping, ties loose, going home to their wives and children, a hot dinner awaiting them.

She spoons cornflakes into her mouth.

I should get a cat, she thinks, *to keep me company until the baby comes.*

The baby...

She and Tony had daydreamed about having a dog, cat, chickens, a menagerie of animals; and at least five children. Of managing a big farm and a big family in a warm country.

Oh, Tony, how I miss you.

She blinks away the melancholy and picks up the photos again, these snapshots of lives from nearly a century ago, giving her a brief respite from her own life. And it is as she is looking at the girl that something resonates in her mind, something clicks and falls into place.

Devadasis. Sue has heard the word mentioned in the news clips she has watched over and over, and she Googles it now. When she has finished reading, her face is wet with tears. She is shocked and fascinated by this country she is exploring, thanks to the discovery of the temple on the news and the photographs her grandmother preserved, a land of breathtaking beauty, prejudices and controversy, rich history and fascinating customs. Most of the reports she has watched speculate that the cottage discovered alongside the temple belonged to a devadasi.

She picks up the photographs of the girl, leafs through them.

Are you one of the devadasis? Is this why your eyes are so troubled? My, what you must have gone through!

And here I am wallowing when there are so many people far worse off than me. At least I had a man who loved me, valued me, if only for a brief while. I have been blessed with a child conceived out of love. Something precious, of Tony's – a gift from beyond.

Chapter 63

Gowri

Empty Air

Goddess,

I am still here, still writing to you.

Some things never change.

'Found a groom for my youngest daughter. Once she's married, my duty as a father is done. The celebratory puja is on Friday, Gowri. You will wear the silver and sapphire sari I gave you when our son was born.'

My son, I think, even as the grief hits afresh. My sunshine. Without him, my life is shrouded in darkness.

I school my face to show no emotion – the landlord keeps bringing Ravi into every conversation, knowing that is the only way he can get at me – or, more accurately, at the shell I have become since Ravi's death.

'You will dance, along with the other devadasis. You will make me proud.'

I don't want to dance, I don't want to dress up, but I know I must.

After the landlord leaves, I dig in the wardrobe for the sari he is talking about. I find it at the back of the flimsy cupboard, beside my books – untouched now for a long while. I have lost interest in books, along with everything else, since Ravi passed and my daughter embarked on a whole other life with the woman she knows as her mother.

As I pull the sari out of the cupboard, I hear him – my boy.

'Ma, my clothes.'

I turn to look at him as his clothes spill out of the sari, packed and ready, waiting for our great escape. But he is not there. Just empty air and my foolish imagination supplying his voice.

He would be speaking now, in full sentences, like I heard just now. Would he still be the smiling, happy boy he was? Had I not persisted in my stupid plan of keeping him, running away with him, he would now have been at the landlord's house. He would be present at the puja. I would have to watch him sitting on the lap of another woman, putting his arms around her, calling her 'Ma', but at least I would have had the pleasure of seeing him grow.

'Too small, those clothes,' Ravi says, clearly, and despite myself, I whip around again to try and find him.

Silly, fanciful woman.

The house echoes with his absence, the ghost of his laughter. It smells of nostalgia and heartache, smacks of happier times overshadowed by loss.

I go and sit under the peepal tree, on the stone where I wash clothes. I would moan at the amount of clothes he got dirty, how quickly he muddied them. What I wouldn't give for that now.

I hold his clothes to me, bring them to my nose, trying to bring back his scent: dust and sweetness and purity and joy. All I can smell is mould and damp and staleness.

'Ma.'

Once again, my heart jumps at the familiar, much-beloved voice calling me by the sobriquet that no longer applies to me.

I keep my eyes closed and he looms behind them, materialising from behind a rainbow of colour. 'Boo!'

It makes perfect sense – he was after all the one who lent colour to my life. Without him, I have been living a life of subdued and sombre shadows, inky swathes of dark navy and black. The varying shades of night.

Small and compact, bare legs muddy, black curls sporting a red sheen of sandy dust, his eyes twinkling with mirth, mouth open mid-laugh, arms outstretched for me to pick him up.

I swoop down to gather him in my arms.

They are empty, of course. Always, inevitably, empty.

I get up wearily, walk into the cottage, keeper of memories that taunt and mock, and shut the door. I sit on the floor in the grey, windowless gloom and pull up my knees, resting my head on them. Then I close my eyes and I dream. I dream that he is alive and with me and all is well. In my dreams, there is sunshine and laughter. When I open my eyes, it is perpetual night, stained with Ravi's loss.

Sometimes, late at night, I hear Ravi calling for me and I swear it is coming from the tree where he is buried. I run to it and there is nothing, Goddess. I stand there, rocking on my haunches, until I come to my senses, until the urge to get down on my knees and dig and dig until I have unearthed my son, rescued him from his muddy resting place, leaves me.

Chapter 64

Sue

A Sign

Sue sets the photographs down and rubs her eyes.

It has gone dark without her realising, lost as she has been in her great-grandparents' world, conjured up by the photographs. She stands, pulls the curtains closed, switches on the light and surveys the room.

Empty. Soulless.

There is nothing for me here. Not any more.

She is on bereavement leave from work at the publication she writes for. And the freelance work she was doing to supplement her income she can do from anywhere.

A thought that has been hovering since she saw the temple, discovered her connection to it, crystallises in her head.

I want to go to India, see the plantation and the temple, find out how this girl from the photos and my great-grandparents are connected to it all.

After all, what is left here to stay for?

The most precious thing she owns is growing in her belly. She hugs her stomach, whispering to her womb her tentative plans for a future without the light of her life to guide her forward.

I need to see a doctor, check if it is safe to travel with you, but I am sure it is, my love. It is early days yet. You will be fine. I will use some of the money I received as compensation for your dad's... his accident. He would have wanted this, I am sure. We were going to travel together, one day, see the world.

'We'll bring our kids up in a tropical country where they'll run barefoot in the sun. Instead of landscape gardening, I'll be a farmer, a man of the land, keeping chickens, growing veggies,' Tony used to say, his eyes sparkling, when they were fantasising about what they would do when he retired from the army and they started a family.

You'll be coming along too, Tony, with me, in my heart.

Somehow, in a few hours, her depression, the fug of grief consuming her, her indecision and worry as to whether she will be a good mother to her child, has lifted slightly. Now, Sue is able to look ahead. Get a glimpse into the future – a future that will be dulled by loss, but, as much as it hurts, a moving-on nonetheless.

Perhaps all she needed was this hug from the past, this connection to where she came from. It seems like a sign.

Chapter 65

Gowri

Blessed

Goddess,

I am ill, dying. I feel it in the ache in my bones, in the pain that is a constant presence shadowing me, owning me. In the fever that riddles my body.

I feel it in the way people look at me, pity instead of their usual scorn when I make my weary way to the market. Even the landlord stays away. Only Ravi still comes to me, talks to me. Only Ravi is there. A constant. Like his namesake, the sun. Like the wind whipping the trees in the jungle to a frenzy.

Like you.

He looks like he had just before he got ill and died. Small and round and dust-sheathed. Happy.

He looks happy.

In the nights, when I am dizzy with pain, haunted by the memory of what I had, what I have lost, the empty air within my arms, beside and around me sighing with loneliness, soft with yearning, thick with loss, I go and sit by Ravi's grave and talk to him. It is dark, the middle of the night, but curiously, it is only by his grave that I feel completely at peace.

Across the road something stirs in the darkness. The wind stroking my face, smelling of lime and incense, tasting of ache and reveries, whispers comforting assurances. But I am listening for my son, not for confidences imparted by the night.

As I wait, I look at the jungle, the sounds emanating from it: rustle and scurry, screech and squeak, slither and creak. I recall how scared I used to be when I first came to this cottage as a young girl. How I would lie terrified inside, door shut tight against the night, sounds from the jungle drifting in regardless.

Those sounds soothe me now, the reminder that life of all kinds goes on. That the ruthlessness of the jungle – the tiger eating the cow although the cow is not at fault – is just the way of the world. Plants might be destroyed by drought and floods, and smaller beings killed by bigger ones, but new vegetation will sprout, new animals will be born. There will be new life.

In the surging, murmuring, living darkness, I talk to Ravi. *I am ill, Ravi. Dying. I will never see your sister. But I hope to be reunited with you, Ravi. I pray I will get the time with you in the afterlife that I was denied here on earth with you. I hope I might even get to see Vandana Ma'am.*

If I had given you away, like I did my girl, my Elizabeth, if I had given you to the landlord, like he wanted me to, you would be alive too, wouldn't you?

'Let it be,' the breeze hums as it lulls my aching face, my drained, illness-racked body, and it croons in my son's voice. 'It's all in the past now, it cannot be changed.'

Sitting there in peaceful communion with the night, talking to my son who has been dead so many years, I wonder about my daughter, growing up in a country I cannot picture, leading a life I cannot imagine.

I hope she is happy.

I think of the memsahib, the love in her eyes as she held my daughter, my little girl who looked more at home in the memsahib's arms than mine, who looked like she belonged there. I know the memsahib will love my daughter like her own, I know this in my heart.

My daughter. Safe. Not destined to be a devadasi, no longer destined to live my life.

If for that I have had to pay the price of living without her, so be it.

She is protected, cared for, loved. She will grow up, go to school, learn to be independent. She will have choices. Her life will not be decided for her.

And that is enough for me.

This is my last letter to you, Goddess.

My life is here in these missives to you. I will send these letters to my sister, along with the money and the gold and the deeds — for what use are they to me now? — via the vendor couple at the market. They will do this for me, make sure that this cargo reaches my sister and no one else.

I do not want the landlord to find the letters, you see, and discover my secrets, go after my daughter. He is old now, and quite frail, and yet I can't quite shake my fear of him.

I am afraid of you too, Goddess. But we are even now, aren't we?

You took my future. You took Vandana Ma'am and my son from me. I stole my daughter and some of your wealth from you, and as punishment, you are claiming me via my illness.

I will die and this will end.

Finally, it will end.

* * *

When I look back at my life, I have much to be grateful for.

I have always had a roof over my head, I have never gone hungry.

I have experienced so much more than I thought I would, Goddess.

At fourteen, I thought my life was over when I was given to you. And in a way it was.

But…

I found friendship, respect and love with Vandana Ma'am. She was my teacher and my surrogate mother. She loved me and was proud of me. She believed in me and she taught me to believe in myself.

So many women yearn for children and I had two. Twin blessings. Ravi, my smiling sun. My beautiful Elizabeth, who I hope is growing up well. Loved, cherished. She will not live a life dedicated to you, a life not of her choosing.

Goddess, I have been blessed.

Chapter 66
Kavya

Breaking Tradition

Kavya looks up from the sheet of paper and blinks, disorientated. It feels like a lifetime has passed between when she started reading these letters and now. It is as if something inside her has changed, fundamentally. Something has broken and shifted and realigned, so she is seeing the world from a different, clearer, less self-absorbed, more empathetic perspective.

'Ajji,' she whispers, wiping her eyes as she looks at her beloved, staid grandmother in a new light. 'You are Gowri's sister's daughter, aren't you?'

Ajji nods, her eyes shimmering. 'My mother… when she was dying, she gave me the letters and an old sari with gold jewellery and the deeds tucked inside.'

'The deeds… Which rightly belonged to Gowri but which the landlord had hidden in the vault.'

'Yes. The landlord made over the deeds to the cottage and the land surrounding it to Gowri, knowing of course that she would never get them as he kept them in the vault. That's why he could afford to be magnanimous, or careless, as the case may be, for the land surrounding the cottage also includes the temple. I've checked.'

'So Gowri owned both the cottage and the temple?'

'Yes. She owned the stretch of land on which both cottage and temple stand,' Ajji says softly. 'By the time I read the letters, Gowri had been dead many years. I did some digging around. The landlord was also dead. His legitimate daughters – and he had only daughters with his wife – had married and moved away. The devadasis had moved to the red-light areas of Mumbai and Bangalore with their children. Gowri's land lay unclaimed and overgrown. The priest's descendants were trustees of the temple, but gradually they died out or moved away and the temple fell into disrepair. My parents were dead. I just... I wanted to leave well alone. It was all too much.'

A thought occurs to Kavya. 'Ajji, is this why we always stay at that plantation resort on the way to Da's ancestral home?'

Her ajji nods, looking sheepish.

'And is this also why you ask me to take you for a walk to "stretch your legs" and we end up near the jungle and that overgrown land on the other side of the road that I always tell you is haunted?'

'That's where they are – the temple and the cottage.'

'You knew! You knew all along, even before the elephant forced them into the public eye?'

'Yes. I... I was tempted to look inside Gowri's cottage, once or twice. But she endured so much there. And now, finally, she is at peace. Over the years, I read and reread her letters, but I did nothing more. I couldn't... My mother, Gowri's sister, must have felt the same, although she preserved her sister's legacy, passed it on to me. I didn't know what to do with the knowledge I had, so I did nothing. But then the gold bangle and child's bones were discovered by that rampaging elephant and the temple lost its anonymity.'

'The bones. The bangle. Ravi...'

'Yes, there is no doubt that those bones belong to Ravi.' Ajji's voice trembles. 'When the discovery of the temple came on the news, I was shocked. And then I accepted that it was inevitable that the truth would finally out. But I never expected the circus that would follow, with everyone wanting part of it.'

'And you've not wanted it?'

'It's not my place, I am just the keeper of Gowri's legacy. That cottage… She was a prisoner there, wasn't she? A slave to the goddess…' Ajji's eyes shine, droplets swelling over her eyelashes and falling down her lined cheeks.

'Oh, Ajji.' Kavya squeezes her grandmother's frail hand.

'But Ravi deserves a proper burial. He needs to rest under the peepal tree again – it was what Gowri wanted.' She takes a breath. 'Once I saw the news, I knew there was no keeping it quiet any longer. So, I gave your mother and father the letters to read. And then of course, you came, at the most opportune time as if it was all meant to be…'

'I would never have suspected our family of harbouring such a colourful past,' Kavya says, gently wiping her grandmother's face, her overflowing eyes. 'Devadasis and sacrifice. Stolen treasure and breaking tradition.'

'You know, I see some of Gowri in you. Her strong will, the way she managed not to break despite everything that happened to her. Gowri would have liked you, I think, Kavya,' her ajji says, smiling tenderly.

At this Kavya bursts into tears, the emotions churned up by reading the letters mingling with her own upset.

'Kavya,' Ajji says gently. 'All Gowri wanted for her daughter, her sister, for all of us, her descendants, was to be free to live our lives the way we wanted to. You needed to get away from the protective love of your parents to find yourself. And you have, child. It all counts towards experience – yes, even the mistakes.'

Kavya thinks of Nagesh. He was a mistake. But the baby… the baby was a brief, beautiful miracle.

'And I think, Kavya, that you are ready now to face the rest of your life. I think you know just what you want to do, don't you?'

'Yes.'

'Well then. I can't speak for Gowri but *I* am proud of you.'

Kavya goes into her ajji's arms, settling inside her fragile, crêpe-paper hug as if she were a much younger child. Ajji smooths Kavya's hair away from her eyes as she used to do when Kavya was little. She smells of love and comfort.

'We should visit the temple,' Kavya says.

'Yes. It's about time, isn't it?'

'Have you thought of trying to find Gowri's daughter?'

'I have. Every day since I read the letters. But trying to find Elizabeth... it was too huge a task, something I was afraid to contemplate. And even if I did find her, was it fair to barge into her life, turn it upside down?' Ajji takes a breath. 'As it was, I myself was finding it difficult to take everything in. I alternated between anger on Gowri's behalf and upset. I – I imagined finding Elizabeth, going up to her, telling her the truth. But I couldn't even picture her. Would she be blonde and blue-eyed? And how would she feel if I told her that her mother was actually a devadasi and not a genteel plantation owner's wife? That she had had a twin who died? *I* was suffering from what I had discovered and Gowri was my aunt. How would a daughter feel? I decided that the best thing, the least selfish, would be to spare Elizabeth the truth – if I even managed to find her, that is. But now Ravi needs to be put to rest again, and perhaps Elizabeth should have the option of whether she wants to be present.'

Kavya touches her grandmother's hand, runs her palm over her brittle skin, puckered by age. 'Would you like me to try and find her?'

Her grandmother smiles through her tears. 'Yes, please. But first... First we will go to the temple, show the authorities the deeds. They are in Gowri's name and that should put an end to the hullaballoo about who owns the temple once and for all. Then we can set about trying to find Elizabeth.'

Chapter 67

Sue

Chillies and Dust

India – sweat and sun and stickiness and spices and dirt and beggars and hawkers and noise and crowds and blaring horns and rickshaws and shacks and mansions and twinkling gold and shimmering saris and holey rags and colour and busyness and beauty and green fields and brown earth and winking rivers and chattering monkeys and potholes and cows and chickens and scrawny dogs and skeletal children with concave stomachs and sudden smiles like a rainbow sparkling through clouds.

I wish you were here, Tony, experiencing this with me.

The village: a row of small huts flanking a road almost too narrow to accommodate the juddering taxi that she has taken from the airport. People pressing on all sides, careless of the smothering heat. Sweat trickles down Sue's back in wet trails, her clothes sticking to her body, her hair plastered to her scalp. The air tastes gritty, of humidity and chillies and dust.

Vendors line the street, peddling wares: ornaments and toys, piles of rice, stainless steel vessels of simmering tea into which they dip small cups and dispense them to customers, huge boiling vats of oil on which they cook deep-fried snacks. Women sit on newspapers spread out on the ground beside the road, teetering piles of spices on plates set in front of them: orange and bright red and green and yellow mounds, smelling potent. A man on a cart sells vegetables: heaps of tomatoes, wilting spinach, green beans and other vegetables Sue does not recognise. A woman hefts a basket of flower garlands on her head, the red and blue glass bangles on her arms chiming a merry tune. Begging children run beside Sue's window, thrusting bowls out at her, huge eyes pleading.

'Take me to the temple,' she says to the taxi driver. She had chosen the one who spoke the best English and seemed to understand her from the crowd of drivers who had surrounded her when she came out of the airport, blindsided by the bright yellow alien sun.

He laughs, shaking his head. 'Everybody want go temple. He famous.'

A turn in the winding road and she sees coffee plants to her left, red and green berries clinging to sun-brushed, mud-splattered green leaves, the thick, bitter scent of coffee mingling with spice. This gives way to trees, tall and thick, pressing against the road on one side, fields on the other. A cow wanders on to the road and the driver brakes, honking and swearing. The cow ambles leisurely past, not caring. Sue is thrust forward and holds the seat with one hand, hugging her stomach with the other. *Hang in there, little one.*

She loves this child so very much already, which is why she was so uncertain as to whether it deserved her – flawed and scared as she is without Tony beside her. *What am I doing*, she had thought as the aeroplane was taking off, her stomach dipping in anticipation and fear, *I who am afraid to take chances? What am I doing here?*

But once the plane was in the air she had calmed down. *I will look after you*, she whispered to her baby. *I love you, I will not let you down.*

Her biggest fear is that she will be like her mother. But despite all her mother's faults, all the times Sue felt like she was the parent and her mother the child, she always knew her mother loved her. During her good times, they would cuddle on the sofa, her mother with a drink and Sue with a Coke, eating popcorn, watching movies.

She knew her mother loved her. And that her grandmother did too, in her own way. She recalls her grandmother's email: 'I am proud of you, Sue.'

I have been loved. And I will love you. We will make memories together, the two of us, so you can revisit them when you need to. I worry that you will be growing up alone, without a father. But I did, and I am okay. You will be too.

'Ma'am?' the driver says and Sue blinks as the car shudders to a stop. 'Can't go. Stop here.'

There are people everywhere. People blocking the path. People with placards, people shouting and people sitting right there in the mud, people watching people asking questions. There are vendors here too, selling peanuts and what looks like yellow flecks of rice mixed with vegetables in paper cones. Another vendor circulates the crowd, selling tea and coffee, the smell of sugar and stewed milk rising from it.

It could be a street party if not for all the protestors and the yelling.

Reporters stand in front of the road, squinting in the sun and talking into microphones. Questions are being fired at a small man, sweat all over his balding head and dripping down his face, who says, over and over again, 'It belonged to my ancestors.'

The air is perfumed with coffee and excitement, laced with spices.

On one side of the road some men in robes stand holding boards that declare: 'Give us back the body of our elder who rests in this land.'

The other side of the road is blocked by a crowd of women chanting, sing-song, 'No more devadasis. Women's Rights for all.'

Sue's gaze is drawn to the group of women standing beside them but slightly apart, clad in saris, made-up faces, wounded eyes. Devadasis.

Possibly like the girl in the photograph.

She shivers. And then all thoughts fly from her head as she sees the temple. Men are hard at work cutting vines and clearing the path, but it is, without question, the temple from the photographs. And next to it a small cottage, falling to ruin, almost completely hidden by vegetation. Beside it, a well, and a washing stone under a huge tree; these too covered by foliage. She almost expects a girl with sad eyes to be standing there, hanging clothes out to dry.

She wants to see the cottage close up and so she starts walking towards it, tripping over a root and righting herself, only for her path to be blocked by an official-looking man.

'Sorry, ma'am, you can't go in there.'

'But—'

'Please, ma'am.'

She goes back to the taxi, thinking she'll return later, wangle her way in somehow. She wants to look inside the cottage – she's wanted to do so since she saw the cottage on television and in the photos.

The driver is leaning against the bonnet and smoking a roll-up. As she approaches, he snuffs it out and opens the door for her.

'Where to, ma'am?'

'Is there a hotel nearby?'

She will freshen up, put on something more suitable for this gummy heat and then explore the area. She wants to find her great-grandparents' residence. She also wants to find out who is officially in charge of discovering the history of the temple and show them the photographs.

The taxi driver grins, displaying a thick, scaly tongue, yellow teeth rampant with gaps. 'Only one. I take you, ma'am.'

Then, after an about-turn that makes the tyres screech and produces a mini-avalanche of dust and much honking and swearing from the driver, they are driving along winding roads, once again clogged with vehicles and animals, even a bullock cart topped to bursting with hay, the bulls looking placid and calm, the man perched atop, wearing nothing but a loincloth, matching their expression.

And then they are entering a gate, a spread of lawn, a fountain in front of steps leading up to a grand mansion in colonial style, the veranda in front, teeming with people.

It can't be, can it?

The hotel her taxi driver has brought her to, she thinks as she gets out of the car and gazes up at the building in wonder, is Lucy and James's house, the house Lucy came to as a young bride all those years ago. Sue has the photographs to prove it.

Chapter 68
Kavya

In Search of a Good Story

The village is busier than they have ever seen it. People everywhere, overflowing from the tiny huts that pass for shops. Photographers wielding cameras. Reporters. Vans. The mud in the village churned into a frenzy, nowhere for all the vehicles to park or move; the road is tiny, just a gap between residences.

Their car grinds to a halt and Kavya stares out of the window. A shop selling groceries: gunny bags of rice, vats of oil; the tangy aroma of mustard seeds and tamarind. A small hut doing a brisk business selling tea and idlis, rice and curry.

'We should have called ahead and booked a room, perhaps,' Kavya says, looking at the crowd of people. 'All these journalists will be staying at the plantation resort. It's the only hotel for miles around.'

They have decided that they will go to the hotel first, have a rest, for Ajji is tired out from the journey, and then make their way to the temple.

Vendors have sprouted as if overnight, selling bangles and wares, bondas, potato chips, peanut brittle. A child comes up to the window as their driver honks loudly, trying to get past an auto rickshaw that is stuck behind a bus. Bedraggled hair, bright eyes, hands full of dolls, cloth versions of the goddess with her grinning face.

Kavya winces, looks away towards her grandmother, small and diminished beside her, radiating nerves.

'All these hawkers must have come from town as soon as the scandal erupted,' her mother notes.

Her father is snoring in the front seat beside the driver and Kavya is squashed in the middle of the back seat between her grandmother and her mother, breathing in the odour of sweat and talc and crushed jasmine bought from the little girls selling it in baskets by the bridge across the river a mile or so back, which her mother has wrapped around her hair.

Kavya gently rubs her grandmother's hand, feeling as if she is the grown-up and her grandmother the child, as if she has matured years since she read the letters bearing testament to what her great-grand-aunt, Gowri, went through when she was but a child, enduring more in her brief life than Kavya will ever know.

I am so lucky, she thinks, as she has countless times since encountering Gowri's story, *so loved*.

The car jolts over a pothole, the driver swears, her da opens his eyes, blinks, mumbles something, then closes his eyes again. Her mother jumps in her seat and is pressed against Kavya. Kavya breathes in her mother's smell of sandalwood and perspiration and is overcome by a rush of affection for her. All they want, both her parents, is for her to be happy, to find love and companionship as they themselves have done.

She smiles at her mother.

'I've been thinking…' she says.

'Yes?'

'Gowri's story – what she went through – having no choice in her fur're, being made to believe she had to endure all the abuse on her, thinking she was trapped, worrying that if she in, her sister would be subjected to the same fate…' She ·h. 'And I've been thinking about myself too. Although I fancy myself strong and independent, I meekly accepted everything Nagesh dished out to me – what happened, the industry shutting me out on Nagesh's say-so, was wrong. Much as I don't want to accept it is so, I was naïve, out of my depth.' Kavya's grandmother squeezes her hand as she goes on: 'I would like to train to be a lawyer, fight for women everywhere. I think I would be good at it – you've always said I argue exceptionally well, Ma.'

'I stand by it. You would make an outstanding lawyer.' Her mother laughs and the worry lines that Kavya has noticed have appeared around her eyes since the last time she visited dissipate, and she looks like the mother who used to pick Kavya up when she was little, protecting her from the world. 'But Kavya, you don't have to rush into anything. Take your time.'

Kavya stares at her mother. 'Really, Ma? I thought you of all people...'

Her mother cups her cheek. 'Kukki, I know I don't tell you this often. In fact, come to think of it, I suppose I haven't told you at all...'

'Told me what?'

'I am so proud of you.' Her mother's eyes shine. 'We both are, your da and I. Although I was upset at the time, I was also impressed by how you stood your ground when you wanted to make a go of acting. I was secretly proud that you had the conviction to follow your heart. And all you went through recently, alone... You are such a strong person, Kukki. I, your da and I, we feel incredibly privileged to be your parents.'

Kavya's eyes overflow, her heart blooming. Her mother is so much more open and understanding than she has given her credit for. All these years Kavya has been upset about what she thought of as her mother's disapproval of her, her narrow-mindedness. She was adamant about not courting her mother's favour while secretly longing for it. And now...

'Ma, I…' She swallows, tucking her mother's unexpected words in a corner of her mind to mull over and cherish later. 'I am absolutely sure, I want to be a lawyer.'

'You know, all that acting experience will come in useful in the courtroom.' Kavya's mother laughs again, the delighted, carefree tinkle of a younger woman. She leans forward and shakes her husband awake. 'Did you hear? Your daughter would like to be a lawyer. Isn't that something?' Her voice bubbles with pride.

Her father grunts, shakes his wife's hand off and drifts back to sleep in the soporific sunshine, ignoring the crowds outside, the noise, the chaos, the horns from the gridlocked traffic caused by too many vehicles in a small village that would normally have had a bus service twice or three times a day at most and the odd rickshaw. Cows and dogs cower in the ditches by the side of the road, unsure what to do, where to put themselves.

'Now all that remains is to find you a good man to marry.'

'One thing at a time, Ma. One thing at a time.' Kavya laughs, along with her ajji, who manages a small guffaw despite her nervousness.

'It's going to be okay, Ajji,' Kavya says, softly, putting an arm around her grandmother. 'It will all be okay.'

For the first time since Kavya started coming here as a child, the courtyard of the hotel is crowded with vehicles, Jeeps and Ambassador cars vying with flashier models, all jostling around the fountain that takes pride of place at the base of the steps that lead on to the majestic veranda, as they disgorge their passengers before going around the back to park.

'I really should have called ahead and booked,' Kavya says, as she steps out of the car and stretches, her mother leaning forward to shake her husband awake, then patting her sari down vigorously to shake it free of the crumbs of the chakulis and laddoos devoured on the journey there.

Kavya guides Ajji around the fountain, spewing multicoloured water, twinkling rainbows in the sunshine, and up the steps. The veranda is crowded too, all the tables occupied by chattering people partaking of tea and snacks. A yeasty aroma of idlis, the curry leaf and mustard seed tang of sambar, makes Kavya's stomach growl.

The woman at reception looks harassed and put-upon. 'Do you have a booking?'

Kavya's mother stands up to her full height, which isn't much – she is, in fact, smaller than the woman behind the counter. 'Excuse me! We've been coming to this hotel for years. Surely you can find a room for us loyal customers as opposed to all these voyeurs and vultures who have just come in search of a good story?' Her loud voice reverberates through the room, and Kavya sees more than a few people turn their heads to look at her.

'Come, Ajji, sit, while Ma either sorts this out or starts a brawl,' Kavya says, leading her ajji to one of the sofas scattered around the room.

'No,' Ajji says, 'I'm tired of sitting. Shall we look at the photographs?'

Even though Kavya has been coming to this hotel all her life, this is the first time she has looked properly at the photographs that grace the walls of the lobby. And now, knowing the story behind them, she scans them eagerly, searching for anything she can find that has been mentioned in Gowri's letters.

Black and white photographs capture moments from daily lives. A young boy laughing as he jumps in the stream, bare-legged, long-limbed; a scrawny dog beside him. His mouth open, face caught in an expression of delight, water droplets arcing out of the photo.

'Do you think Mr Bell took them?'

Ajji's eyes are raw as she nods.

'This must be the boy who used to accompany him and his wife?'

'Probably.'

A maid skinning fish, scales glinting, captured on film as she uses the back of her arm to rub off the sweat that has collected on her upper lip. Her eyes, just visible above her elbow, show surprise and a hint of laughter. The fish entrails gaping and messy, her hands shimmering with scales, sari ruched up.

A man lifting a scythe to bring it down on a coconut.

And then—

And then a woman. One hand holding her bonnet in place. The other holding up her dress as she lowers her bare leg gingerly into the waters of the fountain. The boy and dog beside her, the dog gnawing at her discarded shoes. She is looking right at the camera and smiling widely. Innocence mingling with openness. Mrs Bell... 'She's beautiful, isn't she?'

An accented voice. Sweet. Lilting.

Kavya whirls round. The woman who has just spoken is standing to her left, also looking at the photograph, a wistful expression on her face. Brown-gold hair. Brown eyes with flickering, saddened depths.

'I wonder what she would think to see it now, like this.' The woman waves her arm about, indicating the vast room, thick with people, some sitting on sofas and sipping tea, others munching on bondas and vadais and jalebis, yellow tubes filled with syrup.

Across the lobby, Kavya's mother's voice, strident as she argues with the hapless woman manning the reception desk.

The woman next to Kavya turns to look at her, dragging her eyes away from the photograph. 'She owned this place, the plantation, in the 1920s. Well, her husband did – his photo is over there.' She tips her chin towards the reception area, where the woman has called a colleague over to bolster herself against Kavya's mother's attack, but they both stand looking wretched as Kavya's mother rants on, her tirade in full flow.

'He died in a fire while saving some of his workers here at the plantation, in 1929, becoming, to all accounts, something of a local hero and legend. The plantation then passed on to his foreman, who preserved this house as a shrine to James Bell and his wife – he kept everything just as they had left it, all the original photos and paintings and artefacts. This hotel chain acquired it from the foreman's children. They have maintained it well though, haven't they?'

'Umm… yes,' Kavya says.

The woman shakes her head and flashes a rueful smile. 'Sorry to bore you. I'm not normally so forward but I've only just learned all of this and I wanted to tell someone. I've been following the manager around, asking questions. The poor man is sick of me, especially as they are so busy, but I have a vested interest, you see.'

Kavya looks up at her sharply. *What does this woman mean?*

'Sorry, I haven't even introduced myself – I'm Sue.' She extends her hand, dainty fingers, chipped fingernails as if she has bitten them to the quick. 'History is fascinating, isn't it? I can't believe I'm standing here, where she must have walked and stood almost a century ago…' Nodding at the woman in the photograph. 'She was my great-grandmother, you see: Lucy Bell.'

Kavya stares, unable to speak as she processes what she is hearing.

Beside her, her grandmother goes very still. Then she slowly lifts one arm up and wipes her eyes.

'Sorry, what's the matter? I… Sorry, have I upset you?' the woman – Sue – who Kavya is beginning to understand is related to her, says, anxiety colouring her voice.

'We – we were going to look for you after we had…' Kavya whispers.

'Look for *me*? But…' The woman's forehead scrunches up in befuddlement.

Kavya opens her mouth to answer but is interrupted by her mother, who has crossed the room and is beside her, saying, 'Kavya, Amma, come, we've got our rooms. Amma, why on earth are you crying? What's happened?' Panic spikes her voice.

Ajji lifts up a quivering hand and cups Sue's cheek, saying, in a tremulous voice threaded with wonder, 'Child, we have something to tell you.'

Chapter 69

Sue

Karma

When the woman says 'Child' and cups her cheek, Sue feels something inside her settle.

'We were going to look for you, after…' the younger woman, who looks feisty and somehow familiar, her arm wrapped protectively around the older, tearful woman, says again.

'*Me?*'

'Come,' the older woman says. 'Sit.'

She takes Sue's hand and directs her to one of the sofas and it is a relief to be led, after all these months of indecision and worry, to be called 'child' with such affection and warmth.

'I can't believe it,' the younger woman is saying, shaking her head. 'The odds…'

And then it comes to Sue. This woman, who she looks like…

'It's funny, but you look a lot like my mother.'

The girl nods. 'That's actually perfectly understandable.'

'Really, how?'

'That's what we wanted to tell you…'

Oh my, Sue thinks after she has heard what they have to say. *Oh my!*

Now she knows why she was so drawn to the temple and the beautiful, sad-eyed girl who lived in a fairy-tale cottage in the temple grounds.

She stands up and begins to pace, unable to sit still as she tries to make sense of what she has learned. She caresses her stomach where her baby – the child she made with Tony, the child he will never know, the child who will not know its father – grows. The child whose great-great-grandmother was a devadasi, who gave up her daughter so she wouldn't have the same life as her. 'My grandmother, Elizabeth, she became a world-renowned archaeologist. Gowri would have been so proud.'

'Yes,' the older woman, Gowri's niece and keeper of her legacy, says, eyes shimmering.

'She… She said she became an archaeologist because she had felt as if there was something missing all her life. She said she had always felt incomplete.'

'She was missing her twin, Ravi, without even knowing she had a twin,' the younger woman, Kavya, says.

Lucy, my great-grandmother, was in much the same situation as me. James died before he could be acquainted with his children. Lucy lost her love but she had to be strong for Elizabeth's sake.

'Elizabeth was telling the truth,' Sue muses. 'Sean really was my mother's dad. Elizabeth was pale, light-skinned, and so was Sean. It was only in Elizabeth's daughter, my mother, that the truth Lucy took to her grave revealed itself, the story of Elizabeth's parentage written in the colour of her daughter's skin. But by then, Lucy was not around…'

How the implications of one act can reverberate through the generations!

And then a thought occurs to Sue. 'Hang on a minute, Uncle Mark…'

All three women, grandmother, daughter and granddaughter, look at Sue as one.

'When Lucy travelled back to England, she brought a boy with her – Uncle Mark. He was only around thirteen years older than Elizabeth, I think, perhaps less. Could he have been the boy who orchestrated the meeting between James and Gowri and later, between Lucy and Gowri?'

The women nod slowly. Their way of tilting their heads as they consider a question is so alike, a mannerism passed down the generations, from mother to daughter to granddaughter.

What have you passed down to me, Gowri?

'He would have known the truth. And yet, he kept it secret.'

'He must have been asked not to tell.'

'And he kept his promise.'

Sue closes her eyes, images of a temple, a cottage, a white girl and a brown one sitting side by side in a treehouse in a jungle rising in front of her mind's eye. An unlikely connection, begun with a scare from a marauding tiger, sealed with a shared mango in front of an audience of monkeys, ending in a baby exchanging hands.

'Child,' the grandmother, Gowri's niece, says, 'we were going to look for your grandmother and we are so very glad we've found you. But how come you are here now? What made you come?'

Somehow, hearing this gentle woman ask her so tenderly why she is here, something opens and flowers in Sue. She is able to tell them everything that has happened in recent months that has led to her coming here. 'I was wallowing in depression, directionless after Tony. I'd just found out about the baby. Then I saw the news clip about the temple and realised I had seen it somewhere before.'

It is the first time she has spoken to anyone about her grief, about the baby. And she is surprised she has done so with these women she barely knows. She has always found friendships, even simple interactions with other people, difficult. After what happened to her mother, she kept herself to herself. But the reason *she* is alive at all is because of a chance meeting, a shared connection. Between Gowri and James, and Gowri and her great-grandmother, Lucy. No, the other way round: between her great-grandmother Gowri and Lucy.

'It was karma, destiny. It was meant to be,' Kavya, says. 'Gowri and Ravi orchestrating all this. Ravi's bones being discovered by the elephant – this way, he and Gowri organised for us to meet.'

Sue marvels at how Kavya, an educated, intelligent woman, believes as a matter of course that dead people can bring about reunions. How she seems to trust that the beloved dead are here, watching over you, although you can't see them. It is strangely comforting.

Tony, Sue thinks. *Are you here somewhere looking out for me? Did you too orchestrate this?*

She caresses her womb, the thought of Tony beside her, watching over her, an enormous comfort.

Her grandmother never knew her roots. Neither did Sue's mother. But Sue has had the chance, the opportunity to connect with this other branch of her grandmother's family, living on the opposite corner of the world.

Fate, she thinks. *Karma.*

Thank you, God, destiny, ancestors, Tony.

'Child,' the grandmother says, rummaging in the bag by her side. 'Here, these are rightfully yours.'

Documents. Ancient and crumbly with mildewed edges. The odour of damp and stale ink. Written in a script she cannot read. The regional language, she supposes.

'What are these?'

'The deeds to the temple and the cottage.'

Sue stares at the documents in her hand. So innocuous, and yet hiding so much heartache and pain, barter and sacrifice within their depths.

'But why...?'

'They belong to you, child.'

'I – I don't...' She is overwhelmed.

'I'll tell you what we'll do.' It is Kavya's mother who speaks, in a decisive voice. 'We'll contact a lawyer and once we have them on board, we'll inform the authorities that we have the deeds and that they are in Gowri's name, and go from there.'

'Thank you.' Sue nods, still unable to fully process everything that has happened in the last hour.

'And now, let's go up to our rooms and freshen up. Sue, please join us – we can order up some tea and snacks and continue our chat.'

'That sounds lovely, thank you.'

And notwithstanding her lack of social skills, her fear of small talk, she means it. For with these people whom she has only just met, she feels, oddly enough, quite comfortable. Relaxed. At home.

Chapter 70

Kavya

For Change

Kavya sits with Sue and Ajji on the balcony of the hotel room, looking at the grounds below, where guests mill and overflow, and in one corner of which Kavya's mother is giving an interview to a babble of reporters.

So much loss and hurt and tragedy, Kavya thinks, *because of ownership, possessiveness, blind faith. I will use my voice, honed from all the years of acting, and I will shout out loud against injustice, for change. I will channel everyone into my fight. And we will bring about change. We will.*

Beyond the lawns are the coffee plants, verdant green, rose and pink berries budding from them in bursts of colour. It is peaceful here, gusts of fragranced air caressing their faces, whispering secrets of the past.

'Lucy might have sat here once,' says Sue wistfully, 'and shared the same view.'

'Not the reporters trampling over her lawn,' Kavya observes drily.

'No. More likely the boy – Uncle Mark as he was then – and his dog.'

'Your mother is having the time of her life, I see,' Ajji says, nodding towards where Kavya's mother is gesticulating at the reporters.

'Yes, instead of just telling me what to do, she can now tell the world,' Kavya laughs.

The newspapers and media have been going berserk since Ajji and Sue came forward with the deeds. At Sue's request, Kavya's mother deals with the reporters, answering all their many questions, mildly at first and then not, snapping at them if they ask her the same thing twice, and launching into a diatribe that makes even the most seasoned reporter look duly chastised.

Kavya has been very impressed by the lawyer, a man not much older than her, quietly confident and very competent.

'I'm Dev,' the lawyer told Sue when he arrived. 'I'll do everything I can to make sure the land that is rightfully yours reverts to you.'

'Well, not exactly mine…'

'It belonged to Gowri and you are her great-granddaughter – her letters prove it. So it is yours,' he said, smiling at Sue.

'What about that man who claims he is the landlord's descendant?' Kavya asked.

'Sue here owns the deeds. He has no claim whatsoever.' Then, rubbing his chin, 'Now the temple… I think that will be made public by the court, judging from the precedents in these cases. And the treasure… Since it belongs to the temple, the court will decide what to do with the rumoured treasure in the vault.'

'That's fine,' Sue had said, looking to Ajji and Kavya and Kavya's mother for confirmation that she was doing the right thing.

'Absolutely,' Kavya's mother said and Sue smiled.

'I would like Ravi's remains to be buried again, under the peepal tree by the washing stone, like his mother, my great-grandmother wanted,' Sue added.

'We will make that happen,' Dev smiled, nodding at them all before leaving the room.

'He is single, you know,' her mother said after the door closed behind Dev, popping a laddoo into her mouth, not looking at Kavya, trying too hard to be casual.

Kavya ignored her, sitting beside Ajji and Sue, who was now practically living in their room, which was just the way they wanted it. It was amazing how quickly they had bonded, how easily and seamlessly Sue had slotted in with them, how comfortable it felt. Kavya was reading the documents Dev had left with them, underlining salient points. If she was going to study law, she might as well start now.

'Did you hear me, Kavya?' her mother asked, raising her voice ever so slightly.

'I don't know who you are talking about – it could be the porter who brought our luggage in, the reporter who was hounding you or even the man at the reception desk.'

'Don't be cheeky,' her mother said, munching on the laddoo, her mouth full of yellow crumbs. 'The lawyer, Dev. He is thirty-one and single, looking for a bride. He was establishing his career, which is why he isn't married yet. He is ready now.'

'When did you have time to find out all these details? You talked to him for all of five minutes!' Kavya protested, injecting annoyance into her voice, although she couldn't explain why her heart executed a small leap when her mother tapped her nose and said, 'I have my ways. Anyway, I'm pretty sure he likes you – he couldn't take his eyes off you.'

Ajji and Sue tried and failed to hide their grins behind a yawn and a scowl respectively while her da snored from his easy chair by the window.

Now, Ajji asks Sue, 'Do you have any thoughts on what you'll do with Gowri's cottage and land once it reverts to you?'

'I've given it some thought,' Sue says. 'I feel something good should come out of it, to negate all the bad connotations.'

'What were you thinking of?'

'What about a women's refuge?' Sue says, her voice hesitant at first but sounding more enthusiastic as her idea gains wings. 'Somewhere all these women, the devadasis and others like them, women who feel trapped and think they have no escape, can come to for help and advice, where they can stay until they find their feet.'

Kavya stares at her in amazement, this woman she is related to. 'What a great idea! Why didn't I think of that?'

Ajji beams, cupping Sue's face with both her palms. 'Child, you have come up with a plan that will make your great-grandmother dance with joy. Gowri must be so proud of you from where she is watching over us.'

And Sue's eyes spill over, gleaming droplets sequinning her cheeks.

Chapter 71
Sue
Family

'Call me Ajji,' Sue's grand-aunt says. 'It means Grandmother in Kannada.'

Sue bursts into tears and Ajji hugs her, stroking her back, murmuring, 'There, there.'

'Thank you, A… Ajji. I… I feel comfortable here. Like I belong.'

Tony, I wish you were here, with me. I wish you could have met kind, maternal Ajji, feisty Kavya, Kavya's formidable mother and her peaceable father.

'Of course you do. We're family.'

Family. Sue's eyes fill as they have been doing often lately. She doesn't know whether from hormones or from all she is experiencing; perhaps both.

'Sue, I believe in destiny, that some things are meant to be. The elephant stampede, you coming across that news snippet about the temple and recalling the photograph you had seen among your grandmother's things, it was all leading to this. Your coming to India and meeting the family you didn't know you had…'

'Yes,' Sue whispers. She remembers the butterfly outside the bathroom window when she found out she was pregnant, how it had appeared like a sign. 'My beautiful butterfly,' Tony used to call her. 'I… There's nothing left for me in England any more. I have some money from Tony's – his… um… accident – to tide me over. Also, I spoke to my boss at work before leaving and he was happy for me to work from here as long as I send in my articles on time.' She doesn't know why she's telling Ajji all this, but she wants to.

'You'll stay with us until the court case regarding the temple is resolved,' Ajji says in a no-nonsense voice and Kavya and her parents nod assent.

'Thank you,' Sue whispers.

Ajji waves her words away. 'And since it is a high-profile case,' she says, 'it will be resolved quickly. Some of these court cases here can go on for years, you know. Once the land reverts to you, you can put into action your plan to renovate and extend the cottage, make it a refuge for battered women and for devadasis.'

'You'll help?'

'We'll be with you every step of the way,' Kavya's mum says firmly.

'Your two great-grandmothers would have been proud of you,' Ajji adds softly.

Sue closes her eyes, breathing in the fragranced air. She is standing on the balcony of the hotel room, the breeze fanning her face.

When she opens her eyes, her family – *her family!* – all smile at her.

'Yes,' she says, grinning back at them. 'I hope so.'

Epilogue

Kavya

Rescue and Deliverance

The opening night of her play, performed by the women of the refuge, is magical, one Kavya will remember for the rest of her life.

It is Dev who comes up with the idea. Dev the lawyer, who has become her mentor as she navigates her law degree, and, much to her mother's delight, more than that too.

'I've always written plays, it's my secret solace,' she told Dev early on in their relationship, when he asked her about her hobbies, what she liked doing.

'Can I read one?' he asked.

No one had read her scribbles before, but she shared them with him.

Afterwards, he said, 'Wow! This is powerful stuff, Kavya.' Then, 'Why don't you talk to Sue? She was saying the women at the refuge need something to challenge them, to take their mind off things. Perhaps they could perform one of your plays?'

The play is performed in the grounds of the temple, beside the cottage where it all began in the form of letters to the goddess – pleas from a desperate girl for rescue and deliverance, beside the tree where she buried her son and talked to him, where she wrote her letters and where her son once again rests.

Marquees have been set up in the temple courtyard, lights strung all round, and Kavya thinks that this is how it must have been during the puja when Gowri first set eyes on Mr Bell – James. The forest beyond broods forbiddingly; perhaps the nocturnal animals are prowling among the trees, watching humans at play.

Vendors have set up shop on the road, which is no longer a dirt track as it was in Gowri's time, but tarmacked now. They sell peanuts in newspaper cones, and tea and coffee, sweet and milky, from stainless steel kettles; bhelpuri and vadais. The tang of red onions, the zing of spices and excitement, the whine of mosquitoes, the whirr of the generator, the rumble of the crowd as they wait for the women to take to the makeshift stage, colours the air.

Ajji sits right at the front, along with Dev, Kavya's proud parents and Sue. Beside Sue is Manish, whom Sue, Kavya's mother and Ajji appointed as bursar of the refuge when it became more popular than any of them had imagined, requiring them to build an extension to the extension already added to the cottage to accommodate all the women wanting sanctuary. Sue used the wealth that her great-grandmother Gowri had stolen from the vault, the wealth that Gowri's sister gave, along with Gowri's letters, to Ajji, to renovate the cottage and build the extensions. There were also plenty of donations pouring in, the temple having made international news; and thus it was decided that they needed a bursar. Manish was chosen from among the numerous candidates who applied and has more than lived up to his stellar credentials.

Manish's eyes soften whenever he looks at Sue, which is often, Kavya notes. Sue is not immune, and has recently been inserting Manish's name into every conversation, her face alight when she speaks of him. They sit side by side, just touching, and look quite at ease together; Kavya suspects there will be an announcement soon.

Sue's daughter, Toni – cherub-red cheeks, brown-gold curls, laughing brown eyes – is passed from lap to lap: Ajji's lap, Sue's lap, Manish's lap, even Dev's lap – he handles her awkwardly, afraid to drop her, but gently, and Kavya is overcome by tenderness for this man she loves. He is rescued by the women from the refuge, who have come to watch and cheer on their sisters, and Toni claps with joy as she is entertained by their children. One of the older girls plucks Toni from her mother's arms and hides with her behind one of the chairs. The child giggles, her dimples flashing, and the girl says 'Shhh,' bringing a finger to her mouth. Toni copies her, and then falls about laughing, sounding like waterfalls and wind chimes.

'I worried about bringing her into a world where it would be just the two of us, but now she is growing up with a whole extended family,' Sue told Kavya, eyes shining, a few months ago. 'The women have all adopted her, as have their children. I feel at home here. So does my daughter. I have found my place in the world, my purpose,' she added, smiling as she watched her daughter being gently rocked to sleep by one of the women, as another hummed a haunting lullaby.

Kavya can see Sue's contentment written on her face. The drawn, worried look is gone. Now, she glows. With joy. Fulfilment. Love. She has written a book about their family, with Ajji's blessing. 'Yes, Gowri's story must be told,' Ajji had said when Sue tentatively suggested it. It has had publishers from all over the world interested and bidding for it. She is now writing a book about the women of the refuge, compiling their stories, recording their struggles, their daily heroic acts. How they fight against their circumstances in small ways, the only ways they can.

The play that Kavya has spent all her free time writing and directing begins. The women of the refuge do a sterling job –

nobody forgets their lines and the audience watches, spellbound. There are tears, thundering applause and calls for an encore.

'That was fabulous, Kavya!' Her mother wipes away tears, exchanging proud glances with her husband and with Dev, the suitable groom she is convinced *she* has chosen for her talented daughter.

Dev gives Kavya a thumbs-up, his eyes shining. Her da is grinning and Ajji is crying, her hand gripped tightly in Sue's. Sue smiles proudly at Kavya and scans the crowd for her daughter, her eyes following the trail of her laughter.

Fireflies dance. Lamps cast the night in a magical glow.

Kavya looks at Ajji and sees the same thought reflected on her face: *Gowri would be proud.*

The Temple
A Miracle

The temple was peaceful in its anonymity, happy to have been claimed back by the jungle. But then the gold bangle and the child's bones are discovered by a rogue elephant and the temple explodes into prominence.

Suddenly, everyone wants a piece of it. Everyone lays claim to it.

There are rumours of clandestine treasure and buried secrets. Tales abound that there is a hatch that leads to the vault somewhere on the temple grounds, but it is not discovered, not even when the foliage that has ensnared the temple is razed.

A young woman comes forward and says that the temple belonged to her great-grandmother, a devadasi; that she had had twins, one white, one brown. The bones are of the brown twin, a boy, and she is the granddaughter of the white twin.

A white twin? What sort of nonsense is this? Or is it a miracle?

The descendant of the white twin relinquishes her claim to the temple. Nobody asks her if she knows where the vault is and she does not volunteer any information.

The High Court rules that the temple be made public and the wealth – if any – remain in the temple as it has for almost a century: 'If there is a vault underneath the temple, then the wealth therein was given to the goddess and hence should remain with the goddess.'

Most of the devotees hail this pronouncement. A dissenting few are upset and feel cheated. The landlord's descendants are not pleased and say they will appeal the decision at the Supreme Court.

And so, this dilapidated, long-forgotten temple, falling to ruin, is put into practice again, the sandalwood and rose scent of incense and the silk and satin taste of supplication, a long line of worshippers bringing gifts of milk and flowers, a sadhu anointed and attracting disciples, the cobwebs wiped away from the bell, which now shines as bright as the gold rumoured to be languishing underneath the believers' feet.

The Muslims slink away, their clamour to have their holy elder's body dug up ignored, his bones – if he truly rests there, that is, and there is no solid proof – percolating into soil wet with Hindu chants and milk offerings and stained with incense and prasadam.

The monkeys are back, trailing the devotees and getting bolder by the day, stealing the chappals that worshippers arrange at the base of the temple before they walk up the holy steps, and prasadam straight from children's hands, the youngsters squealing with delight and terror in equal parts, bhajans and playful hollering and the monkeys' frantic chatter, and women's laughter from the refuge next door rending the prayer-infused air.

Author's Note

This is wholly a work of fiction.

Devadasis have been called by different names in various parts of India but for the purpose of this novel, I have decided to stick to the term 'devadasi'. There are a lot of controversies regarding devadasis. They were held in very high regard in the nineteenth century and earlier – they were considered auspicious and were proficient in the arts – but their status in society declined during the twentieth century. Some were, by all accounts, happy with their lot and had patrons who were good to them. Others, like Gowri, were/are not.

I have attempted to tell a story from the point of view of a bright girl forced through circumstance into a life she did not choose. Gowri is not a devadasi in the traditional sense of the word, descending from a family of dancers well-versed and educated in the arts; she was forced to become one because of the discovery of the statue. This is her story alone, fiction imagined from the point of view of a woman with no say in her own destiny.

I have invented a fictional village and given it characteristics of different villages from different parts of India; and the area I have set them in may not necessarily have a village like the one I have described.

I made up the drought of 1928.

I apologise for any oversights or mistakes and hope they do not detract from your enjoyment of this book.

Letter from Renita

First of all, I want to say a huge thank you for choosing *A Daughter's Courage*. I hope you enjoyed reading it just as much as I loved writing it.

What I adore most about being a writer is hearing from readers, finding out what they thought of my stories. So please do let me know, either via a review, through my website or my Facebook and Twitter pages.

Also, if you'd like to keep up to date with all my latest releases, just sign up here: www.renitadsilva.com/e-mail-sign-up

Finally, if you liked *A Daughter's Courage*, you might also like my other novels, *Monsoon Memories, The Forgotten Daughter, The Stolen Girl, A Sister's Promise* and *A Mother's Secret*.

Thank you so much for your support – it means the world to me.

Until next time,
Renita.

🐦 @RenitaDSilva

RenitaDSilvaBooks

www.renitadsilva.com

Acknowledgments

I would like to thank everyone at Bookouture, especially Abi Fenton, Lauren Finger and Kim Nash.

A huge thanks to Natasha Hodgson – for advice and support during the early stages of this book and for your warm, wonderful emails.

A million thanks to the best editor in the world, Jenny Hutton, without whom this book would not be. Jenny, you are amazing and I am so very grateful for your clairvoyant eagle eye, which can see through the mess of my initial drafts to what the book can become.

Huge thanks to Lorella Belli of Lorella Belli Literary Agency for all your brilliant efforts in making my books go places. You are the best, Lorella, and I am honoured and humbled to have you championing my books.

Thank you to Jacqui Lewis for your discerning eye with the copyedit and to Jane Donovan for the proofread.

Thank you to all my lovely fellow Bookouture authors, especially Angie Marsons, Sue Watson, Sharon Maas, Debbie Rix and Rebecca Stonehill, whose friendship I am grateful and lucky to have.

Thank you to all the fabulous book bloggers who give so freely of their time, reading and reviewing and sharing and shouting about our books. I am also grateful to my Twitter/FB friends for their enthusiastic and overwhelming support.

An especial thanks to Jules Mortimer and Joseph Calleja, book bloggers extraordinaire, who I am privileged to call my friends and who are the best cheerleaders one could wish for.

I am immensely grateful to my long-suffering family for willingly sharing me with characters who live only in my head. Love always.

And last, but not least, thank you, reader, for choosing this book. Hope you enjoy.